Praise for *The Catalyst*

'*The Catalyst* is a complicated, rich world of magic and danger. While it seems simple at first, nothing is black and white, and nothing is what it seems. Both fantastical and startlingly relevant and contemporary, it's tense, exciting, engaging and has at its heart a central character whose incredibly personal story becomes caught up in huge battles and some even bigger ideas.'
Claire North, author of *The First Fifteen Lives of Harry August*

'Helena Coggan is only 15, and yet her debut novel has all the assurance of a writer in mid-stride. If young writers can overcome the stare of the blank page – and take care with characterisation – they can stand as an inspiration to all.'
Guardian

'At the heart of this hugely ambitious story, by a 15-year-old newcomer, is a great big universal truth – we all think we're different. *The Catalyst* takes this idea and runs with it. This is a stunning debut, exploding with life, ideas and passion.'
Daily Mail

'[*The Catalyst* is] very appealing and completely lively throughout. This was an absolutely impressive debut novel from a young voice who is fast going to attract a huge following. *Hunger Games* eat your heart out. Loved it. Highly Recommended.'
Liz Loves Books

'*The Catalyst* was a gripping read. It is action-packed and not once are you left feeling bored or waiting for something to happen. What Helena brilliantly manages to create is suspense. . . a truly brilliant, gripping and suspenseful read.'
Laura's Little Book Blog

Helena Coggan wrote the first draft of *The Catalyst* when she was thirteen. Her ambitions up to this point had been somewhat linear – she had wanted to write stories since she was six, and before that, she wanted to live in one.

She lives with her family in London and divides her time between writing and procrastinating, which her parents insist on calling 'school'.

This is her first novel.

More praise for *The Catalyst*:

'It had me hooked from the initial chapter, and I enjoyed every second of it. Overall, I am completely in awe of Helena Coggan's ability to create such an enjoyable work at such a young age, and would recommend *The Catalyst* to fans of *The Hunger Games*, the Divergent trilogy, and also the Mortal Instruments, since it slightly retains that 'fantasy in modern society' element. This book explored something deeper, too: how divides within society can be so influential and life-changing, and how it is impossible to categorise something or somebody because, well, we're all different.'   *Guardian*

'Coggan is a terrifically talented author...This is a thrilling and addictive read, that was certainly darker than I expected it to be; the ending was also perfect. I am very excited for Coggan's future works.'   Once Upon a Moonlight

'A unique storyline set in the heart of London [*The Catalyst* is] filled with exciting characters and a plot that keeps on thickening throughout. This first book in the series holds a lot of promise for the next book to be even more thrilling and action packed.'   Emma's Bookery

THE
CATALYST

Helena Coggan

HODDER

First published in Great Britain in 2015 by Hodder & Stoughton
An Hachette UK company

First published in paperback in 2015

1

Copyright © Helena Coggan 2015

The right of Helena Coggan to be identified as the Author
of the Work has been asserted by her in accordance with the
Copyright, Designs and Patents Act 1988.

A CIP catalogue record for this title is available from the British Library

ISBN 978 1 444 79465 6

Typeset by Palimpsest Book Production Ltd, Falkirk, Stirlingshire

Printed and bound by Clays Ltd, St Ives plc

Hodder & Stoughton policy is to use papers that are natural,
renewable and recyclable products and made from wood grown in
sustainable forests. The logging and manufacturing processes are expected
to conform to the environmental regulations of the country of origin.

Hodder & Stoughton Ltd
Carmelite House
50 Victoria Embankment
London EC4Y 0DZ

www.hodder.co.uk

This book is for Catherine.

Catherine, you are far braver, far kinder and far cleverer than me, and as such you will most likely end up doing something wonderful with your life. So consider this dedication a down-payment. When you're curing cancer or implementing world peace and people start asking you, wide-eyed, what your secret is, I would like you to smile ruefully, and tell them it was really down to your annoying older sister all along. In some unspecified but extremely crucial way.

You're welcome.

PROLOGUE
The Veilbreak

The first they knew of it was the crack in the sky.

It stretched across the sun, cutting swathes of light from the city streets – a great, black, jagged mouth, from the eastern horizon to the westernmost clouds. Through it came darkness, spilling shadows into the streetlights. It was only just twilight on the Meridian. In more easterly parts of the world, darker and deeper into night, it was as if a thousand stars had suddenly gone out.

In London, drowsily turning from the early touches of nightfall, a few seconds passed before it was felt. Streams of traffic slowed, clogging the arteries of the city. People got out of their cars; they were astonished, frightened, confused. The crack in the sky loomed above them, captured in a million grainy phone-shoots. London sparkled with camera flashes.

That was when the storm began.

Paul Folbright, assistant electrician in the Ichor labs, was one of the first on the balcony in their godforsaken corner of North London. He had been one of the opportunists: he'd managed to prise a promotion off Richard Ichor before the old man retired from the project, leaving it to his son. Andrew Ichor was a genius, certainly, and arrogant enough with it, especially for someone who didn't even have a driving licence yet. A lot of people who worked with him, including Folbright, found him deeply creepy. He was always one step ahead of you in your own thought processes, and, partly because of this, he always got what he wanted – apart from, recently, project funding: the powers that be had been disappointed with the lack of results from the Veilbreak initiative. And disappointment wasn't a money-spinner.

Andrew Ichor, however, had something big planned.

The whole department had been waiting for this day for four years. In those four years, there had been exactly seventeen failed launches. Of those launches, fourteen had taken place under Richard Ichor. Andrew was more careful, slower. That was what scared most of his colleagues. Andrew was dedicated to – you could even say obsessed with – the Veilbreak project. And when someone that clever was that focused on anything, as one of Folbright's retired colleagues used to say, you were only biding your time until a lot of you-know-what hit the fan.

That evening, many of the staff in the Ichor labs had taken the day off. Among those who'd stayed, Folbright and his superior Davina Anthony were two of the few who could consider themselves high up in the food chain. This, they knew, was their last chance. If this launch went wrong, then they could kiss their careers goodbye. Folbright hadn't slept in days.

It went wrong, all right, but not in the way anyone expected.

Andrew Ichor rushed onto the balcony, pushing people out of the way to get to the very edge. He leaned over, staring up at the sky, and then leaned back in shock, his eyes wide. Then he turned to his astonished and scared staff, and started to jump up and down like a child, punching the air.

'I told you!' he screamed; he was ecstatic, triumphant. 'I *told* them I could do it!'

Behind him, out of nowhere, a hundred thousand lightning bolts suddenly stood, bright white, blind-white, against the soft purple of the thickening night. London reeled from the shock of it as buildings and trees exploded into flame, buses and cars were hit where they stood, and black scorch marks were etched into the landscape as if an angry five-year-old had slashed a pencil mark across a drawing. Almost immediately came the thunder – a hard, deafening wall of sound that rolled across the city, smashing windows and glasses, drowning out the screaming. Folbright was on his knees with his hands over his ears. Andrew Ichor had his hands pressed to his face, staring through his fingers at the sky and laughing with joy.

The noise receded. Invisible to the naked eye, but still very much there, a huge wave of energy had seeped through the dimensional break, disrupting the climate enough to create a cloudless storm.

And then.

Although no one in the Ichor labs knew it at the time, the energy generated by the break manifested as electricity. Every single electronic device around the world was immediately shorted out. Smartphones died in an explosion of sparks in people's hands. The electrified rails on city metros were suddenly dead, sending transportation grinding to a messy halt. London, New York, Shanghai were plunged into sudden darkness. In it, the explosions of the Ichor labs' computers were a blinding fireworks display.

Folbright stared, aghast, as four years of his life went up in flames.

Andrew Ichor wasn't looking at the computers. He was staring down at London, darkened and dead but for the small patches of fire glittering here and there among the buildings. He was paler now; the laughter had slid off his face. He had one hand on the railing of the balcony to hold himself steady. His knuckles were white and the hand was shaking.

'What the—' he whispered.

There was silence, but for the sound of distant screaming.

Then it came.

It was as if the sky rippled, like a heat mirage, or the air over a fire. The still evening air twisted into a strong breeze, pulling papers off desks and sending them sweeping over the floor. People stood up shakily, looking around to see what was happening.

Then, with a shock like a gunshot, someone on the balcony started to scream.

Folbright whirled. Davina was on her knees with her hands over her ears, shrieking as if in agony. Everyone looked around for the threat, but there was nothing.

'Get it off!' she screamed. 'Get it off me, get it out of my head!'

A couple of people took out their phones and tried to dial 999 on useless bits of plastic before remembering that was what they were, and that even if they had worked, the emergency services would be in little better shape than them.

'Help me!' Davina shrieked. 'Help me, help—'

Her voice choked off and she doubled over. Behind her, someone else fell to their knees, coughing hard. People began to drop. A few screamed, like Davina had done.

Folbright looked desperately to Andrew, but he was merely standing, frozen in panic, watching as his department fell.

Then, suddenly, Davina opened her mouth.

She said nothing, but from her mouth shone a beam of bright light, as if she'd swallowed a torch. The light came from under her skin, her eyelids, from her nostrils, under her fingernails. It grew brighter and brighter, until she was a huddle of light, too bright to look at. One by one, each person who'd dropped began to shine as if they were burning from the inside. Folbright stumbled back, cringing, staring through his fingers, not daring to blink.

There was a pause where the survivors still stood, stunned and terrified, and then six people dropped at once. Visible, almost tangible blackness reached from them, swallowed them; they became hulks of shadow.

And then suddenly, everything stopped. The lights went out; the shadows receded. Folbright sighed shakily, not sure whether or not to be relieved. He knelt beside Davina.

'Come on, Davina. It's okay now, you're fine. You can . . . can get . . .'

His voice, faint as it had been, trailed off. Davina gave one, last, trembling sigh, rolled over, and did not move again. Folbright stared at her.

'No,' he said. 'No.'

People began to get to their feet around him. Some, however, remained lying on the floor like Davina, quite clearly dead. Those on their feet seemed unsteady, unsure of their motor functions. Their jaws hung open in confusion. Their eyes were an unnaturally bright, cold green, varying in strength and depth from person to person, and that was terrifying enough, but not what he was really afraid of. The few that had dropped with the darkness, standing now, had irises stained black. They seemed even less steady on their feet than the green-eyed ones; they stared blankly around, stumbling blindly, grasping at empty air. Everything about them seemed *wrong*, and, from the looks on their slack faces, they knew it.

Folbright took a step back.

One green-eyed woman, whom Folbright had worked with on the funding portfolio, stuck out her hand towards a stack of papers on her own desk. They exploded into the air as if they had been hit with a child's toy vacuum gun.

'What the hell?' Andrew Ichor whispered.

All around the room, objects were exploding into flame, flying, moving, without anyone going anywhere near them. Folbright stared at them.

But this isn't real, he thought dimly. *I mean, this can't seriously be—*

It hit him from behind, grabbing his mind and locking

his thoughts into place. For a second he forgot his own name and who he was and the world he lived in and reality dissolved into confusion and the image of a cold desert wasteland and the thought of the crack in a deep red, starless sky, and being sucked towards it and the enveloping, crushing darkness and a wind rushing him towards a tiny, shattering city and this man, shining with life . . .

But the Angels, he thought, and the thoughts were both alien and completely his own. *The Angels. Where are they? Where am I? I have to fight—*

But he was trapped inside a strange body in a world that was not his own and he was kneeling on the floor with his body burning and confused, flickering thoughts of a war inside his head. The memories mixed, jarred together, fixed into a single person with a single soul in a single body and he stood up.

He was Paul Taylor Folbright. He had an ex-wife and a girlfriend and a five-year-old son. He had a steady job and a midlife crisis. He was also a . . . a *something* from the world that Andrew Ichor had just opened up. He had a vague image of a battlefield, but nothing else any more.

Except the knowledge that he must fight.

Fight? He wasn't a fighter. Who was he supposed to fight?

The memories were draining away from him.

Someone touched him on the shoulder. He tried to throw them off without moving, to move them back with his new black eyes, but nothing happened and their grip intensified and he moved with sudden strength and his fist made contact with something hard and someone cried out and the grip was gone.

He turned to Andrew Ichor. He could see them now. Tiny shreds of light and darkness plunged through the sky like meteorites, targeting people with unerring accuracy. Where they hit, the people were consumed with blinding light or shivering, curling darkness as the two souls fused. When all of the people were taken, the few otherworldly souls remaining hung in the air, frustrated.

Then, as one, they turned to Andrew, standing cold and terrified against the wall.

Behind him, London burned.

There is no scale on which one can measure the First War of Angels.

It allows for no true comparison, because against it all previous wars are reduced to scuffles and street-fights. No casualty figures can truly encompass the level of devastation it caused. The human mind cannot comprehend numbers so unnaturally, astronomically, obscenely large.

Statistics, then, are useless, but then so too are case studies – because however bad any one person had it, you can be fairly sure that someone, somewhere, had it worse.

The only scale by which it can really be understood is when one puts it beside the Second War of Angels; but even that is flawed. The outbreak of the Second War was more devastating than the First if only because, for twelve long years before it, the world had enjoyed what seemed like unbroken and unbreakable peace.

No one quite knows why, late in the Eighteenth Year of Angels, that peace was shattered so spectacularly. The origins of that conflict may forever remain hidden in the mists of time.

Well, not entirely. There is one person still living who knows the whole story of how the Second War began – but, unfortunately, she isn't talking.

Not to your correspondent, anyway.

FROM THE INTRODUCTION TO *A History of the Angelic Wars*, BY AMY TERRIAN (PUBLISHED IN THE FIFTY-FIRST YEAR OF ANGELS)

The Eighteenth Year of Angels

CHAPTER I

It was a chilly evening in February, and a girl was walking alone beside the river.

She did not appear, in and of herself, to be a particularly remarkable girl. She was a few weeks past her fifteenth birthday, and the usual trappings of twenty-first-century adolescence seemed to have passed her by. She had no piercings or highlights or designer clothing. She wore jeans and a T-shirt that showed the scar in the crook of her elbow where she had once been shot, and her dark hair was tied up into a ponytail that brushed the small of her back. She had a narrow face and a long, sharp nose, which, when compounded by her gangly height and slim frame, gave the impression of extreme thinness; her skin seemed almost unnaturally pale, and her olive-green eyes darted from one crowded city shop to another as if scanning for danger.

If you were really looking, and no one was, you might have noticed that her back was oddly straight and her steps strangely clipped: she had the gait and the posture of a soldier, although she was far too young to have served in the last War. Apart from that, though, there were only two remotely unusual things about this girl. One was her name, Rosalyn Elmsworth, although the significance of that had yet to become common knowledge on the streets. And the other was where she was going.

Her destination, like her, looked deceptively innocent. Rain-streaked and shiny, it huddled in a side street off the newly completed high road by Westminster station. Dwarfed by the skyline, its windows were tinted and the only person visible to the average passer-by was a bored-looking receptionist with a computer that looked like it dated back to the reconstruction of the Internet. The only thing that might have distinguished it as out of the ordinary was the black seal of Government, standing out bleakly on the whitewashed wall.

On a normal day, this being Westminster, the building would not have attracted any undue attention.

The picketers were the first sign Rose got that this was not going to be a normal day.

There were only about fifty of them. Had they been troublesome or violent, the Department would have been able to take them down with ease and without any casualties. As it stood, though, mere bigotry was not adequate excuse for arrest, so the Department remained stubbornly silent behind its tinted windows. Stubborn silence, however, was not the method the protesters had chosen to voice their grievances. Rose stopped just round the corner, out of sight, to listen. A high, reedy male voice rose above the roar of the crowd. They had started up an elementary call-and-response chant.

'What do we want?' cried the reedy voice.

'Ashkind out of our schools!'

'When do we want it?'

'Now!'

And round again. Rose sighed and leaned her head against the wall. She knew who these people were. This was not going to be a fun ten minutes.

She took a deep breath, and stepped out from round the corner into the street.

For a second, she almost thought they hadn't noticed her, and that she might just get away with it. They carried on chanting, oblivious to the solitary, dark-haired girl watching them from the corner, waving their signs. Many of them bore the winged-door logo of the Gospel campaign group, and the rather unimaginative slogan *Stop corrupting our children*. Like Rose, they all had green eyes, some ringed with an unhealthy, bleached-looking white – the unmistakable sign of Test failures, the Leeched, whose Gifts had been forcibly removed. Minimal danger, then. Rose took a tentative step towards them.

The reedy-voiced man, who was standing on a make-shift podium, yelling his chant, turned to the part of the crowd that he had not been facing and saw her. His voice trailed off. Everyone else followed his eyes. Within ten seconds, Rose had the attention of what she was quite prepared to believe was the entirety of the Gospel.

She sighed.

'Hello, Mr Greenlow,' she said. 'Would you at all mind letting me through?'

Stephen Greenlow jumped off his podium and started walking towards her, hands outstretched. Rose stood her ground.

'Rosalyn, Rosalyn!' he said, in what sounded for all the

world like a friendly tone of voice. 'How are you? How's your schoolwork going?'

'I have a few days off before my Test, sir.'

'Oh, call me Stephen, please,' he said warmly. He reached out to shake her hand, but she snatched hers back quickly. His eyes narrowed.

'Let me through, please, sir,' she said quietly.

He ignored her and turned to the crowd. 'This, my friends, is no less than David Elmsworth's daughter!'

The crowd, unsure what was expected of them, made a hesitant sort of noise; not quite a cheer, but not a heckle either. Even in these circles, the name of David Elmsworth was well known, and not for good reasons.

'Tell me, Rosalyn,' he said, 'what do you think about the practice of contaminating spaces for pure Gifted children with Ashkind presence?'

'I think it sounds a lot like integration, sir, and as such is laudable.'

'Only to those who want to hear that.'

'Mr Greenlow, if the only people who hear your messages are those who want to, you are going to have a very small congregation.'

This one was definitely a boo. Stephen Greenlow's smile remained fixed, but a little of the warmth had vanished from it now.

'Join us, Rosalyn.'

'No.'

'You're Gifted, you would have fought the Ashkind during the War.'

'And that would have been a good thing, yes? Me,

fighting non-magicals? One-on-one? That would have been fair?'

His face darkened. 'It would have been a necessary evil.'

'But evil nonetheless. And then, in this hypothesis, I would presumably have accepted the Great Truce when it came, as your bunch of ragtag extremists has never done.'

His eyes narrowed. 'You would have your future children attend school with Ashkind?'

'Indeed, as you did yours. I've met your eldest, and he doesn't seem to have been damaged from it. Now let me through.'

Something not entirely friendly crossed his face when she mentioned Aaron. Seeing it, she tried to move forward, but at his signal the rest of the Gospel moved to block her.

'Let her through, Stephen.'

They turned as one to see the man standing in the doorway of the Department. Rose sighed in relief. He was wearing plainclothes, but his regulation shotgun was in his belt. The Gospel eyed it nervously.

'I said let her through,' Rose's father said. 'I won't warn you again.'

Stephen Greenlow glared at David. 'This is a peaceful protest. You have no jurisdiction over our activities.'

'Of course not, but should you attempt to impede my daughter's entrance to this building by forcible means, it would cease to be a peaceful protest and I would have to react accordingly.'

They stared at each other for a few seconds until Stephen Greenlow clicked his fingers and the Gospel campaigners parted to let Rose through.

David nodded with mocking amusement.

'You have them well trained.'

'Don't push it, Elmsworth.'

'I wouldn't dream of it. Come on, Rose.'

She walked through the razor-sharp gazes of the campaigners towards him. Only when she had stepped through the doorway and the doors had closed behind them did she breathe properly.

She opened her mouth to speak, but he held up a finger to stop her, listening. A few seconds passed before Greenlow's shout of 'What do we want?' rang out again. David closed his eyes and leaned against the door.

'Thanks,' she told him.

'No problem. Sorry I took so long. We were so hell-bent on ignoring them that we didn't realise you were here.'

'We?'

'James is up there.'

She nodded. 'You emailed?'

'Yes. There's been a murder.'

'An interesting one?'

'Very.'

'Don't-discuss-in-the-lobby very?'

'Exactly.' He nodded to the lifts. 'Shall we?'

'I'd be honoured.'

They moved towards the security entrances, but a sharp female voice stopped them.

'Uh-uh. Security procedures, remember?'

Rose turned to the receptionist exasperatedly.

'Emily, you know perfectly well who I am.'

'Rules are rules.'

Rose sighed and moved towards the desk.

'State your identity and purpose,' Emily said brightly.

'Rosalyn Daniela Elmsworth. Here on duty. Well, not duty, but . . . you know. Whatever you call what I'm doing. Volunteering?'

David laughed from behind her. 'Your altruism is unparalleled.'

The receptionist entered her name into the computer and clicked twice. Rose looked up into the camera in the wall and touched two fingers to her forehead in a gentle salute. She knew who would be watching.

'No,' Emily said, 'I'm afraid you only have second-degree security clearance. This department is responding to an emergency, and so is closed to all but those with first-degree security clearance. Your identity will need to be confirmed by one such person before you may enter.'

Rose looked at the receptionist incredulously.

'Come on, Emily. You know who I am. I'm allowed to be here.'

'What *I* know doesn't matter. Your identity—'

'Oh, wave her through, Emily,' David said tiredly.

'Major Elmsworth, correct protocol—'

'—is not high on my list of priorities at the moment. Someone is dead, and I really don't have time for this. Wave her through.'

She looked him up and down, paused, and pressed the

19

button to open the barriers. 'Just this once,' she called after them weakly. They ignored her.

Rose contained herself for the minute it took for the lift to arrive and the doors to close, and then she started to speak, tried to voice the half-a-dozen questions rocketing around inside her head. Her father, however, turned to her quickly, cutting her short.

'Questioning has been delegated to the nearest available operative to the suspect. Did you or did you not contribute in any way to the circumstances that led to the unlawful death of Private Thomas Argent of the Third Royal Battalion?'

'Am I a suspect?'

'Everyone's a suspect with murders, Rose. You know how this works.'

Rose was slightly taken aback. She caught sight of her reflection in the mirrors and wiped her face clear of expression.

'I swear before the powers that be that these accusations bear no truth or relation to myself and my thoughts, intentions or actions. If this be untrue let me face the wrath of the Angels.'

Her father nodded approvingly. 'Good. You're learning.'

The lift pinged to a stop and they got out. Rose's father pushed his way out first, absent-minded; she rolled her eyes, and followed him.

His full title was Major David Jonathan Elmsworth of the Department for the Maintenance of Public Order and the Protection of Justice. She had never heard anyone call him that, though, because he hadn't needed to be introduced in about thirteen years. Everyone – *everyone* – knew who he was. It wasn't just his appearance, although that was distinctive enough: unintentionally messy brown hair, the olive-green eyes of a powerful Gifted, and the constant look his dark stubble gave him of having not quite shaved *enough* that morning.

It was his reputation: ever-present, as bright as it was dark, clinging to him like smoke.

David Elmsworth was one of the good guys. Being a good guy meant capturing and imprisoning the bad guys by whatever means necessary, and while this was messy and often brutal, David was very, very skilled at it. He had been made the effective – though not official – Head of the Department at the age of twenty-seven. Now, at thirty-five, the very mention of his name was enough to relocate a gang to another, more lawless, city.

Rose loved him inexpressibly for it.

'So who was Argent?' she asked him, hurrying past the windows and the grey skyline. Raindrops had started to slash themselves across the glass.

'Grunt, essentially.' He took a right turn; Rose followed him. 'Used to be pretty high-rank, then went and ruined it all by getting drunk and picking a fight with a man in his posting who'd dumped his sister. Got thrown out and was starting to work his way back up again. Late twenties. No partner – broke up with his boyfriend a few months back, didn't stay in contact. The way I heard it, the boyfriend probably wouldn't care if he lived or died anyway. The sister might be a bit more of a problem.'

'Circumstances of death?'

'The killer broke into his flat. And I mean *broke* into it. Door off its hinges, half his stuff smashed. Obviously whoever killed him came in with the intention of killing him. Which means . . .' He indicated for her to continue.

'Which means it was planned, which means the killer had a grudge against him, which means the victim probably knew the killer personally. What happened to the bloke he picked a fight with?'

David grimaced. 'Not in any condition to rejoin the army.'

'Makes it more likely. What did Argent work in?'

'The details are still classified. Nothing that would be unanimously carried by an ethics committee.'

'Personal acquaintance, then. What kind of soul was he fused with?'

'High-class Gifted originally, but he was Leeched.'

'Method of death?'

David looked at her, still moving. They turned into a dimly lit corridor lined with metal doors. 'That . . . is sensitive information, Rose.'

'Who just said that correct protocol was not high on their list of priorities at the moment?'

'That was waving someone known to the organisation through security. This is giving secrets to a possibly volatile element.'

She laughed. 'Don't talk to *me* about "possibly volatile elements".'

Her father looked at her.

'Sorry.'

Silence for a few yards. Rose tried again.

22

'Method of death?'

'I can't tell you. I am, for once, following regula~~~
and not telling you. That should be enough informati~~~
in itself.'

Rose looked at him, perplexed. And then it hit her and
she stopped dead. Her father took a few steps before
realising that she wasn't with him any more, stopped and
turned to her, eyebrows raised.

'No.' she told him.

'Apparently, yes.'

'How?' Rose demanded. 'How the *hell* could you know
that?'

'There was no weapon found at the crime scene. Half
of the objects broken were a good six feet away from
either footprints or blood. There's only one explanation
for it: the killer used magic to kill his victim. Which means
. . .' David sighed, and ran a hand through his hair. 'Which
means somewhere in this ridiculously large city is an
unregistered, dangerous and powerful killer armed with
magic.'

Rose's heart, having missed a beat a few seconds ago,
was thundering at double-speed now to make up for it.
Despite herself, she grinned. 'I'm not surprised they called
you in. Who else have they got on this?'

'Everyone. This is big, Rose.'

'Oh, I know.'

David gestured for her to keep walking, and she followed
him round a corner and left, towards the largest door, a
grey bulk of reinforced steel and bulletproof glass. The
Department had applied for the grant for the door after

the father of a man killed in a struggle during an arrest for manslaughter got through the lax security with an AK47. The door had been built in record time. The people in here were precious, but they made a lot of enemies.

David walked up to the door and pressed in his code. A red light opened up above the keypad and scanned him.

'State your identity and purpose,' a male voice said, far more firmly than Emily had done. It wasn't a bluff. Rose knew that anyone whose identification was not affirmed to the satisfaction of the scanner was not long for this world. This was one of the few buildings in the city allowed to use magic in its security arrangements. Her father had never told her the exact fate that would befall an intruder, and Rose had no wish to know.

'Major David Elmsworth,' David said clearly. 'Staff. Here with daughter.'

The red light blinked and turned to Rose, who likewise confirmed her identity.

'Thank you,' the male voice said, and the red light shut off. The door swung open.

'David!' someone yelled. The room was full of computers and the mingling clicks of typing. Old posters lined the back walls. There were no windows; the ceiling was filled with pipes and strip lighting. Being in this office was always slightly disconcerting. As what the Department did was so central to the safety of London, only the magically Gifted, whose loyalties were in no doubt, worked here. This meant that the office was a sea of swirling, blinking green eyes, from the faintest turquoise to deep emerald.

Most of the people were glued to their screens, quiet. In one corner, however, people were rushing about from one computer to another, throwing instructions and obscenities at each other. Rose had learnt most of her swear words in this place.

In this corner was the man who had called her father's name. James Andreas had been discharged from military service and brought here after David noticed how well he coped under pressure, in a case where an agent had gone rogue. James had been the one whose head the rogue had held the gun to. One of the bullets from that gun was now in James's torso, preventing him from working in the army ever again, but now he had a successful career in one of the more exciting departments. He always said, perfectly cheerfully, that it was a price he would pay any day. He was seventeen years old – barely an adult – with a smile as bright as his red hair, and an addiction to adrenaline that meant he was always the first to venture out into the crossfire with a very large gun and no bulletproof vest. Rose had been with her father in this department for as long as she could remember, and she knew every type. People like James never lasted more than three years, and James had worked here for two. Rose hoped he would survive his expiry date. She liked him.

David and Rose hurried over to him. James was bending over a computer screen, scratching the back of his neck and muttering under his breath.

'Did the Gospel hold you up?'

'Tried to recruit me,' said Rose.

'What did they want this time?'

'Educational segregation.' David knelt down and peered under James's desk, looking for a pen. 'I nearly had to pull rank on Stephen Greenlow. Just wait and they'll go away, they always do. What have we got here?'

'Just got the autopsy back on Argent. As expected. Lacerations down the right side of the body, shallow but painful: probably from a broken object. Blow to the back of the head, because he was thrown against the wall – that's where we found him. Killed with a clean hit to the chest.'

'What from?' David asked sharply.

James grimaced. 'That's the problem. There wasn't a bullet, or any blood from that wound. He was killed by a blow that crushed his ribs and his lungs. No damage to the heart or spine, no bullet holes, no stab wounds. So the killer must have used pure magic. If you want to look at his body, though, you'll have to be quick. His cremation's scheduled for tomorrow.'

Rose asked the obvious question.

'Have we got anything on the killer's identity?'

'No. Of course, with the way our luck's going, we never expected to have anything. It's, what, seven o'clock now? Argent was killed about three hours ago. Neighbours heard shouts, crashes. They thought it was an argument. The girl who lived next to him was listening. She'd heard a lot of stuff when he and his boyfriend broke up, and she was scared, 'cause Argent was a violent bloke. But then the noise stopped, and the girl had only heard one person leaving. And, of course, she couldn't hear anyone moving. So she called the police. Took them half an hour to get there, and by the time they did the trail was cold. We've only got Argent's footprints. The killer made sure not to leave any tracks in the blood.'

'What've we got on Argent's missions when he was high up in the army?' David asked, sorting through James's desk for a piece of scrap paper.

James sighed. 'We've applied to get the information, but it has to go through a few thousand layers of management first, which is going to take a while. Argent was pretty good. He was in – are we allowed to call it black ops?'

'This place is CCTVed,' Rose said quietly. 'I'd be careful.'

'Fine. He was in covert operations, then, and he was good enough to get posted a lot, which is only going to make our job easier, because he'll have made a lot of enemies. He passed his Test when he was fifteen, so he had his powers registered and was allowed to keep them. They removed his powers when he was kicked out, and of course that's permanent.'

'But there can't be many people in the general population registered with magic who had an incentive to kill *and* who knew Argent. That's got to be a pretty narrow category.'

David laughed bitterly, still looking through the desk. It always amazed Rose how many pieces of paper people thought it necessary to have at any one time.

'Wide enough. He'll have Gifted friends, family, enemies, exes, colleagues, old classmates, people he beat up in bars, the loved ones of those he killed when he was a soldier. . .' He had found a pen by now and was scribbling while he spoke. 'It's certainly better than the, what, four million registered Gifted in London we were working with before, but it's not enough to go and start making arrests.'

'So what have we got on this guy?' Rose asked. 'Charges, I mean. What would he go down for?'

James sucked in a breath through his teeth. 'Where do we start? Escape from lawful custody, for one thing. Then, obviously, murder, breaking and entering, illegal use of magic—'

'Illegal arena of magic use,' David reminded him, without looking up. 'Let's assume he didn't ask Argent if he could use magic in his home. It would have destroyed his element of surprise somewhat.'

'All right, fine, "illegal arena", and . . . well, that's death, easily.'

Death. Firing squad, lethal injection, electric chair, the snap of a neck in darkness. It was a very short word to mean so much.

'Elmsworth, get over here!'

The shout came from their right. Both David and Rose looked up automatically. Connor Terrian, one of the Department's more manic but unfortunately senior staff – head of the clean-up teams that swooped in after unfortunate incidents, and, irritatingly, two military ranks higher up than David – was staring at the bank of screens that showed the security cameras in the lobby. As they walked over, he swore under his breath.

'You brought your kid, then,' he said shortly. Before

David or Rose could answer, he said, 'Good. Here's a use for her. We've got incoming.'

'Who is it?' David asked, searching the screens.

'Well, good news is, the Gospel have finally decided to give up and go away.'

'And the bad?'

'Argent's sister has found us,' Terrian admitted exasperatedly. 'We cleaned up the flat, but when he didn't answer the phone she called the police. She's that kind of girl, apparently. Your kid can go down there and calm her down. We can put her in for therapy, have her talk to one of the counsellors, who can show her that he died of a heart attack. That's the line you should go with,' he said to Rose, not looking at her. 'If she knows too much and starts getting too loud, you know what to do. Though I hope that doesn't happen. We'd have to do a full mental rewrite. That'd take a lot of manpower, and I don't want this spreading. We don't need a panic.'

'Do we have any data on her?' Rose asked. She, as always, was trying very hard not to get annoyed with Terrian. This rarely worked, but it was good to put in the effort. It wasn't the fact that she'd known him for eight years and he still didn't refer to her by name, but that he treated her father as a rookie rather than the best agent in the department.

James had a new data file on his computer. Rose hurried gratefully over to him. 'Sylvia Argent,' he said. 'Ashkind. Thirty-one years old. Boyfriend died about four months ago – road accident, non-suspicious, nothing we'd have on record. Pregnant, with his kid as far as we know. She worshipped her brother like a god, especially after he beat up her ex a couple of years ago. She's not gonna give up easily on this.'

'Don't worry,' said Rose grimly. 'I've had practice. This is pretty much the only thing I can do here. I haven't exactly got much to get wrong.'

James swivelled round in his chair to look at her. 'Yeah . . .' he said thoughtfully. 'You've got your Test tomorrow, haven't you?'

Rose grimaced in affirmation, pulling on her coat.

'I can't tell you what's coming,' James said gently. 'But I can tell you that you're better at any of this than any pre-Test teenager I've ever met. And after your training – well, when you need a job, I'm definitely an unbiased source who'd be willing to give you a reference.'

Rose stared at him for a few seconds, searching his face for a joke, and then broke into a wide grin. 'Thanks, James.'

'Thank me after I've done something. You've got to defuse this one first.' He nodded towards Sylvia Argent's data file.

'Wish me luck.'

'You don't need it.' Rose gave her father a last glance – he was arguing earnestly with Terrian about something – and then walked out of the door.

She took the stairs down to the staff entrance on the ground floor, on the other side of the building to the lobby. One of the people upstairs had unlocked the door for her. Rose nodded in thanks to the security camera above it and walked through into the room beyond.

She was in the office that belonged to Emily and Pippa, the other secretary, who was on maternity leave. There were two dead-looking computers, several coffee mugs and a glass panel in the door, through which Rose could see a tall, heavily pregnant woman with long auburn hair and grey eyes shouting furiously at Emily, tears running down her cheeks.

Rose bent down to Emily's computer, opened up the messaging account and typed in a short message to the computer in the lobby.

I've been sent down to neutralise her. Just go with it

After a few seconds, she got an affirmation back. Rose straightened up and strode towards the door, slamming it open and genuinely making Emily jump.

'You're off duty now,' Rose told her, straight-faced.

'But—'

'This place is watched, woman, haven't you noticed? We saw how deliberately unhelpful you were being to this poor lady. You are off duty! Probably permanently! Get out!'

Emily jumped up, doing a slightly too convincing impression of fear, and scurried back through the door, closing it behind her. Rose knew she would probably use this as an excuse to take the rest of the day off. At the moment, she really didn't care.

Rose turned to Sylvia, who looked half-astonished, half-frightened.

'I'm so sorry. She's been misbehaving for a long time; this was just one step too far. I'm Rose. How can I help you?'

'I'm Sylvia,' the woman said, tearily. Rose noticed that she held one hand protectively over her bloated stomach. 'Sylvia Argent. Where's my brother?'

'Who's your brother?'

Sylvia, still crying, gave her all the information on Argent that Rose already had. Rose stood there calmly and nodded at the right times, very glad that Sylvia was distraught enough not to wonder why a teenager was on staff at a major government department. When Sylvia appeared to have finished, Rose said gently, 'When did you last see him?'

'Last week.' Sylvia sniffed. 'We met up for lunch . . . and today, when he didn't answer his phone, I went to his flat, and he wasn't there and half his stuff was gone, and . . . and . . .' She burst into tears. Rose gave her a gentle hug, feeling the press of the baby against her ribs. Sylvia was a good two inches shorter than her.

'What happened?' Rose prompted. Sylvia tried to speak, and burst into tears again. Rose grimaced at the camera.

'. . . and there was blood on the carpet!' Sylvia managed.

Rose froze. She closed her eyes and opened them again. So much for Terrian's clean-up operation.

'I'm sorry?' Rose pulled back to look into Sylvia's red, tear-tracked face. She looked entirely serious. Not that she wouldn't be, but the claim had taken Rose aback to such an extent that she had to check for alternatives.

'Blood! Tom's blood, on the carpet!'

'Let me check this.' Rose hurried over to the computer. 'This could be serious.'

Officially, this building was the centre of London's law and order, after Scotland Yard had been destroyed in the War. All deaths would be reported back to it. Therefore they should have Argent on file.

Rose sent James a message.

I hope you're following this. I need a file on Argent that says he died of a stroke, or anything else non-suspicious that would produce blood. Quickly

While waiting for the reply, she pretended to be typing while watching Sylvia covertly. The Ashkind woman was crying quietly in a corner, holding her stomach, trying to sing to her baby. Rose felt sorry for her. She'd lost her brother, and would probably never find out the truth.

She thought of Greenlow. *Necessary evil*.

The slight ping of the computer announced James's message.

Can't do that. Argent's death is under investigation, any files on him can't be created or changed. Sorry, you're on your own

Rose stared at the screen as if stricken – it didn't take much acting – and then looked up apologetically at Sylvia, who had raised her head eagerly at the noise of the computer.

'Yes? What is it? Do you know what's happened to Tom?'

'I'm sorry,' Rose said gently. 'Your brother's in hospital. He was in a fight; he has a severe head injury. The file just came in now.'

'But . . . the girl before you checked in Chelsea and Westminster. He wasn't there. She said.'

Mentally, Rose swore.

'She must have made a mistake,' she said calmly. 'I know Emily. She's not very observant.'

'But she showed me the file! The military personnel in the hospital! He wasn't there!'

'I—'

'You're lying to me!'

It was an accusatory shout, sure of itself, firm and angry. In her three or four years calming down distraught relatives for the Department, Rose had had this shouted at her many times. It was a proportionally small number, for which Rose was proud, but nevertheless, once someone was determined that you were lying to them, it never went well from there.

'Sylvia, please. I know you're distressed, but you don't need to jump to—'

'I knew it!' she shrieked. 'I knew bad things happened here! I warned him! Tom worked here once, and he . . . he said that . . . there were things that happened, things he'd done . . . that no one should ever know about . . . and he went and told someone – and now . . . you've done something to him . . . you killed him, you killed Tom—'

She collapsed into tears. Rose tried to move towards her, but Sylvia backed away, stumbled and fell onto the purple sofa next to the glass wall.

'Stay away from me!' she shouted, sobbing.

She was nearly lying down; that made it easier. Rose stepped up closer to her, one hand stretched out towards Sylvia in a gesture of peace, and in a sudden, smooth movement grabbed the woman's wrist, flipped it over and

34

slid the needle into her vein. The amount of practice she'd had over the years meant that she didn't even have to look. Sylvia screamed, long and loud, and Rose pushed down the plunger with her thumb and let the other woman wrench her hand away. Sylvia cried out, sleep already clouding her eyes.

'What have you done to me? *What have you done to me?*'

'It's just a mild sedative,' Rose told her, wishing it was as easy to inject reassurance into her voice as it was to put sleep into Sylvia's veins. 'It won't harm your baby, don't worry.'

'I—'

Sylvia fell back against the sofa. Easier, much easier. It made Rose anxious when they were standing up. Once, a man had sustained concussion when the sedative had taken effect that way. Rose didn't want any harm to come to Sylvia. This process was all for her own good.

Sylvia's breathing slowed and she was silent. Rose stepped forward tentatively. Her eyes were closed, her face was relaxed and she slept calmly. Rose checked her pulse, which seemed steady enough. Looking up, she saw her father, Terrian, and Laura, a motherly woman in her fifties who headed the Department's memory-altering sessions, hurrying towards her.

'Dammit,' Laura muttered, kneeling by Sylvia and turning her head to examine her. 'This one'll take a lot of convincing.'

Rose was glaring at Terrian, shaking.

'Blood,' she whispered. To her surprise, she felt a tear

on her cheek. She wiped it away furiously. 'Blood on the carpet – how the *hell* could you have missed that?'

Terrian stared at her, outraged.

'Rose,' David said warningly.

'That woman,' Rose said, ignoring him and pointing at Sylvia behind her, 'is going to spend the next few weeks in the memory rewrite wards. You know what the after-effects are. After that much suggestion therapy she won't be able to think for herself for weeks. She'll be apathetic. Emotionless. And she's going to have a baby! What happens to her kid when she's like that? You've just upped her chances of post-natal depression by about fifty per cent – or, if it doesn't work, she'll spend the rest of her life wondering what happened to her brother, and all because you and your incompetent mess of a clean-up team missed a massive bloodstain – a *bloodstain* – on the carpet!'

'How dare you?' Terrian growled. 'I am a colonel of the British Government, and you haven't even taken your Test yet, you are *nobody* – how dare you insult me?'

'It doesn't matter how old *I* am,' Rose snapped angrily, her voice shaking, 'it's *your* competence that's in question here!'

'*Rose,*' David said sharply. 'Connor, she has a point. Rose, so does he. Don't talk to an officer like that.'

Rose shut up. Beside them, Laura was whispering to the unconscious Sylvia. She took a capped syringe of thick, white memory serum from her pocket and slowly injected it into Sylvia's arm. This would be enough to wipe the events of the last few hours from her mind and

36

allow Laura's team to implant suggestions there. They would tell her that her brother had been posted to a peacekeeping mission, somewhere far away. They would tell her not to come back here asking questions. They would tell her everything was going to be fine. And, Rose thought bitterly, they would be lying.

'She should be fine,' Laura said loudly before Terrian could shout anything at Rose. 'We'll do everything we can to minimise the eff—'

Pain expanded to fill Rose's head and it was upon her, and suddenly her wits and her memory deserted her and she was left stranded in a small metal room with no windows, flailing and screaming, and something inside her head was growing and growling and pushing its way through into her mind, forcing her own thoughts down into compliance, and she was falling, falling, and she stumbled back. And then her hand found a wall that shouldn't have been there and she was jerked back to the Department, breathing hard. She looked around. Everyone was staring at her.

She glanced down at her watch. That would be the forty-eight-hour mark.

'Are you okay?' Laura asked her anxiously.

'Yeah,' Rose muttered. 'Headache.'

Her father caught her eye. The sight of him nearly triggered it again, but she bit her lip and focused.

'You need to get home,' David said to her quietly. 'Get some rest. You've got a long day tomorrow.'

She nodded, but she didn't meet his eyes.

CHAPTER 2

The War that followed the Veilbreak was very long, and a lot of people died.

Those were the basic facts of the matter. Everything after that, however, was disputed. When it came to the history of the War, opinion held far greater sway than objective reporting.

Stephen Greenlow and the Gospel thought that the Gifted should have wiped out the non-magical Ashkind completely, instead of merely defeating them and letting them live in relative peace and comfort.

The Ashkind themselves believed that the Great Truce that had finally ended the War should have been fairer to them. They held that they should have been allowed to occupy Government positions, and to work in the public sector.

Still others didn't accept the Great Truce at all. They believed they were still fighting the War, that there were still battles to be won.

The rest of the world tended to laugh at these people.

By most accounts, though, the War had lasted six years – six years of hot, bitter, fiery killing – and, as one might expect from a war in which one side had the advantage of magic over the other, the Gifted had won decisively.

The world that emerged from it was deeply changed. The electricity grids had to be rebuilt from scratch. There were no more elections; the Angels ruled from Parliament. The Internet was reconstructed, with inbuilt surveillance programmes, but mobile phones – which were considered difficult to monitor and thus facilitators of that most dangerous of forces, political dissent – were left to rot. There were Tests for those with magic, Leeching for those who failed them, and the Department to maintain law and order. Those immediate, pressing issues – the ones that concerned actual living people – were so important that people tended to forget about the War now, or try to.

It was not easy.

Rose was not old enough to remember the details of the conflict, but even she knew some of the legends. One particular nightmare had survived so long that, even now, twelve years after the Great Truce had been signed, children still scared each other with tales of it. They were known as Hybrids, and they had been one of the great killers of the War.

You can't see them, the children would say.

You don't know who they are. They could be anyone.

I could be one.

Hybrids were ordinary people, most of the time. They walked and talked like normal people. They smiled and had friends and families and generally blended in well with the rest of society. The legend held that they were always Ashkind, but other, whispered stories spoke of Hybrids with bright, glowing green eyes, with magic on their fingertips and springs in their steps.

But that was only when they were human.

They weren't always human.

One night in every six weeks, they *changed*. They would shriek and scream and snarl and turn into monsters, and those monsters couldn't be held back by wood or steel or stone. They would roam the streets during brilliant, sleepy, starlit nights, and they would destroy everyone and everything in their path.

Actually, when it came to Hybrids, *destroy* was too ambivalent a word. For that matter, so were *kill*, *evil*, *run*, and *terrifying*.

You did not want to die at the clawed hands of a Hybrid. Burning to death was less painful.

And so on.

The legends continued in this vein at great length, though the specifics varied, but there was one thing upon which all the storytellers agreed: if you met a Hybrid in human form, if you knew who they were, then you should kill them. You shouldn't waste time; you shouldn't give them a chance to escape. A bullet to the head was all it required. You wouldn't be arrested for it. Oh, no. For killing a Hybrid, there was probably a medal in store for you.

But that didn't matter. No Hybrids had been caught for years now. They had probably died out, faded back into horror stories where they belonged, and good riddance to them.

Of course, they hadn't really gone.

Rose and her father were living proof of that.

And if anyone found that out – if anyone, Department

or otherwise, ever harboured the slightest trace of a suspicion that they were monsters – then they would not be living at all for very much longer.

As for the rules of magic, they were simple.

You needed a source, an instructor, and a soul. Or, as the textbooks put it: a Source, an Instructor, and a Soul.

The Source was easy enough to come by: it was simply energy. The chemical energy stored in the human muscles was the usual source; the MoD was investigating whether or not it was possible to use a battery, but for the moment, most of the Gifted had to rely on their own bodies.

This meant that how well you had eaten, or slept, or how fit you were, all contributed to how much energy you could use – and therefore how much magic you could do – at any one time. There was no mechanism to stop you using too much, though, so if you were tired and hungry and tried to, say, destroy the foundations of a house, your body would work through excess energy and then start consuming itself. Simply put, if you overexerted yourself, you would spontaneously combust.

As a kid, Rose had always thought that was the coolest way to die. And of course, as a Department kid, she had always known exactly how many ways there were to choose from.

Standing in her garden, Rose stared at the piece of wood on the bench. She came to the conclusion that she would have been a terrible arsonist: no matter how much she tried, it wasn't catching fire. This was because she wasn't concentrating, and she wasn't concentrating because she was nervous, and she really, really *hated* being nervous, so maybe if she got angry enough—

The wood burst into flames with a sound like exploding popcorn. It lay there, flickering, on the grass. She watched it dully.

The second thing you needed was an Instructor: something that could tell the magic what to do. The brain did this, for the most part, although – and this was, again, theoretical – it was possible to use some kind of computer to replace it.

Rose maintained the anger in place of focus, shifting her weight from foot to foot, and the bench toppled over. She threw a bucket of water onto the flames before anything more substantial could be damaged.

The last thing you needed – and this not even the MoD could simulate – was a Gifted soul. In the old days, the days before the Veilbreak, everyone had had only one soul. Now they had two: an otherworldly soul and a human one fused together. Your second soul was either Gifted and coloured your eyes one of a million different shades of green; or it was non-magical, and just hung on you, uselessly, with only your ash-coloured irises to prove it was even there.

Of course, even worse than being born Ashkind was being Leeched. The Leeched were born Gifted, but had failed their Test, and had had their powers taken from them afterwards: strapped to a table, kept down, and forced to breathe Leeching Gas until their magic was gone. If you were Leeched, you would go to a non-magical school, enter into a relatively low-paid profession, and generally be consigned to the lower echelons of society for the rest of your life. Being Leeched did not physically make you Ashkind yourself – it would leave you with your green eyes, albeit with bleached rings around the irises, like many of the Gospel members – but something worse. Being Ashkind was a matter of sheer luck; being Leeched one of personal fault. It meant you were too cowardly or stupid or selfish to keep your powers. You were defective. You did not deserve your second soul.

'Which is why I'm not going to fail, am I?' she muttered to herself through gritted teeth.

The bush beside her burst into flames. She swore and pulled the bucket towards it.

'I'll do it,' came a tired voice from behind her, and the flames dwindled and died. She turned, astonished.

'You never taught me how to do that!'

'No, I didn't,' said David, sitting down on the other bench. 'In retrospect, that should have been lesson one.'

Technically parents weren't supposed to teach Gifted children anything about magic before school except not to kill themselves with it, but David had gone beyond that mandate.

'How's the practice going?'

'As well as can be expected.'

'Did your school tell you it was absolutely imperative to your revision that you destroy my garden?'

'I didn't destroy anything.'

He nodded towards the bush, putting his feet up on the table. 'Those hydrangeas were almost blooming.'

'It's February.'

'They would have done.'

'You wouldn't have cared.'

The final rule of magic was very simple: you couldn't violate the laws of physics. You could manipulate light and heat, even fly if you were clever enough with the air currents and your own weight, but no conjuring matter out of thin air, no teleportation, nothing like that. That was not how the system worked.

Rose disliked the system.

'So how long have we got?'

His voice immediately went cold. 'Don't talk about that in the garden. Anyone can hear us.'

Rose folded her arms. 'You see, it was fine before you said that. *That* made it suspicious.' He did not stop glaring at her. 'Just tell me.'

He did not have to check his watch to know. He always knew. 'Forty-seven hours.'

'I always love when I ask you that and it's six weeks.'

'Well, for every time it's six weeks, there has to be a time when it's forty-seven hours.'

She sighed, and sat down in the doorway. 'Did you file the paperwork for tomorrow?'

'Yep. They asked for your mother's maiden name.'

Rose laughed. Not only was David unmarried, Rose, if you cared about technicalities – and the Government always cared – was not even his daughter: he had found her as a baby in a driveway near his flat when he was nineteen and, for reasons still unfathomable to many of his colleagues, taken her in and raised her. If Rose's mother had had a maiden name, they didn't know it.

'What did you give them?'

He shrugged. 'I was torn between making something up and leaving it blank.'

'Oh, tell me you just left it blank.'

'Of course I did. They would have hunted me down otherwise.'

He grinned. Rose went for the attack.

'Please take off the bomber jacket.'

'No. I like it.'

'God knows I know you like it. The entire *office* knows you like it. But please take it off. For me.'

'No.'

'Dad. Please. It's *green*.'

He grinned wider. 'Are you saying green is a bad colour?'

'On a bomber jacket? Yes. Absolutely.'

He closed his eyes. 'I'm a grown man. I can wear what I like.'

'Naturalistic fallacy.'

'What?'

'The assumption that because something does happen, it should. You can wear what you like; you have *categorically* proved that you shouldn't. And don't pretend you didn't know that. You were just checking that I knew what all the syllables meant.'

He got up. It was starting to rain. 'You know me too well.'

She held up her hands. 'Self-defence.'

They didn't talk after that. They just sat in the dark of the living room. Rose whispered fires into being on her palm and tried to pretend tomorrow wasn't coming.

But it was. And she was nervous. And in a way, it was useful that she was nervous, because it meant that she could plausibly ascribe to overactive anxiety the sudden, prickling feeling that she was being *watched*. It haunted her that evening, pulling at her thoughts and the hairs on the back of her neck like static electricity.

It was paranoia, of course: totally irrational, completely idiotic paranoia.

But she and David, of all people, were allowed to be paranoid.

CHAPTER 3

He led her out from the side street, and together they came to stand in front of the doors.

'This is it,' he said, darkly.

The Test building was unlike anything Rose had ever seen.

It had been a polling booth, back in the days before the Veilbreak, when there were such things as elections. According to her father, only two or three storeys were actually dedicated to the Tests. The rest were occupied by admin teams and generators and technical backup and great, omniscient camera banks. Rose, however, standing in front of it, couldn't help thinking that just connecting it to the mains would have made the building fifty feet less intimidating.

'You'll be fine,' he told her reassuringly. The effect was lessened slightly in that he had to visibly pause before the last word to stop his voice breaking. 'Honestly, it's all right. They don't do this to permanently traumatise you, you know.'

'Easy for you to say,' Rose said darkly. 'Anyway, isn't this the bit where you tell me that I'm so grown up now and that it seems like I was a baby only yesterday?'

'Would you prefer that?'

'No, but it would be soothingly routine.'

David laughed shakily. Rose looked up at him and smiled tiredly.

'You're as nervous about this as I am, aren't you?'

'At least *you'll* be able to see what's going on.'

'True.'

She looked away from him, and for a second he saw the façade slip and her face fall into fear and anxiety. Then she pulled calm back into her expression again, and bit her lip, afraid that he had seen. He took her hands and crouched down in front of her.

'Rosalyn,' he said.

She stared into the distance over his head.

'Rose, look at me.'

She lowered her gaze, waited.

'Rose, I want you to understand, I don't care what happens now.'

'You do, though,' she whispered.

He grasped her hands more tightly. 'I really don't. It doesn't matter to me whether you can do magic or not.'

'It does to me.'

To this he had no answer.

'What happens to us if we fail?'

He knew she wasn't talking about the ordinary procedure used to remove magical powers. It was a sign of how nervous she was that she was daring to mention their secret – even in code, and even in an inconspicuous whisper among the hissing cacophony of anxious muttering around them.

'I honestly don't know,' he told her. It was not the

answer he wanted to give, but it was the truth, and he would always tell her the truth.

'But if I can't do magic, then I can't transform.' New hope was lighting up Rose's features. 'Maybe if I was Leeched, I would be cured, and I could—' she paused, and her face fell as she looked at him. 'You've thought of this, haven't you.'

It was a statement, not a question. He nodded.

'Don't tell me what would happen,' she said. 'Please.'

He smiled sadly.

'Suffice it to say that it wouldn't be beneficial to anyone if you did.'

'I won't fail, then.'

'Good idea.'

She crouched down in front of him. 'So tell me again about the Test.'

'It will probably comprise a test of intelligence, a test of magical ability, and a test of courage. It's different for every child.'

'So I've got to keep calm and think rationally.'

'Exactly.'

David stood up, and she followed him. He grasped her shoulders.

'One more time,' he said.

So important was the Test building that it had its own provision in the law: within a two-hundred-metre radius of it, the no-magic-use-in-public rule did not apply. This was partly so that the candidates could practise, but mostly because the rule could not realistically be enforced here: everyone was so nervous that bricks were dislodging themselves and paving stones cracking around feet left and right. You couldn't arrest teenagers for that kind of thing, not just before their Test. Nevertheless, it went against lifelong instinct to perform magic in public, and he saw Rose look around half-anxiously before she did so.

He had not yet thought to wonder whether or not she could pass this. It wasn't that he didn't care, but he had simply been working from the assumption that yes, of course she could. She was *his*. He had trained her to fight almost since she could walk – what with their secret, and the nature of his work at the Department, their situation was too dangerous to leave her unable to defend herself. So of course, of *course* she could do this.

That was the logical position to take. It was certainly more reasonable than being nervous.

He hated being nervous.

The Test was not designed to find out whether you had magic, or how strong it was – that was clear from the eyes of the children around them, from Rose's dark olive to emerald and grass and cyan and jade and even a bright, unnatural yellow-green in one girl that looked like it would more naturally dye the irises of a hawk.

The purpose of the Test was to find out whether you *deserved* to be Gifted – and if you didn't, well. You wouldn't be Gifted for very much longer.

He tried to imagine Rose with those bleached-white rings round her eyes, and winced involuntarily.

There was one kind of Gifted that wasn't invited to be Tested: the Angels. Angel children were the exceptionally powerfully Gifted, with eyes so deep green they defied colour, and they never had their powers removed, simply because they were so rare the Government couldn't afford to waste them. Being an Angel was not a matter of genetics, or training, or intelligence: it was pure luck, the same factor that determined whether you were Gifted or Ashkind, and as such Angels were highly prized. At a very young age, they were taken and trained and, when they became adults, they were given seats in Parliament.

He shuddered to think what six hundred Angels could do, if they put their mind to it. Move a planet, he suspected. Not that they ever tried. The Parliament of Angels didn't do much, not these days. It was left to the Department to keep the peace in London.

And, with luck, a part of that responsibility would one day rest on his daughter's shoulders.

To see her as an official member of the Department would be wonderful. Of course, it would never happen if she failed her Test, because no one without magic could hold any kind of public office.

But that didn't matter. That wasn't the reason he wanted her to keep her powers.

She needed to have magic because they were monsters.

Their secret was so deep and so dangerous, so frustratingly incurable, that he wanted every advantage for her. She would need it soon enough. It might take ten years, or twenty, or even fifty, but one day they would be discovered and if he was dead she would need to be able to last on her own. To run. To hide. To fight. To protect herself, and carry on living at all costs, because if she died the world was worth nothing any more.

His beautiful abomination of a child.

He was so proud of her. She was white-faced and obviously nervous, but she was holding herself together and she was maintaining some semblance of calm – which, he noticed, was more than some of the others around her were doing. One blond boy with grass-green eyes was pleading with his mother to move the Test – 'Mother, please, surely another few days of preparation wouldn't hurt, Mother, come on' – and a girl with carefully styled plaits was having a loud and unashamed tantrum a few metres to their left, to the obvious embarrassment of her exhausted-looking parents.

'Jennifer, please, it's okay.'

'No, Dad, no!' shrieked the girl, pulling away from her father. 'I don't want to do it! I don't *want* to!'

Rose, too, had let her light go out and was watching them.

'Well, I hope that's not the Testing standard,' she murmured.

'No, I don't think so,' he said. 'If it were, you'd have this in the bag.'

Rose smiled shakily.

'Dad,' she said, and he knew what she was going to ask and tried to stop her, but she carried on, adamant: 'Dad, if they ask, if they find out—'

'They won't.'

'But if they find out about me they'll guess about you and—'

'Rose. It's not going to happen.'

'But if it *does*— what do I do? Do I –' A hesitation. 'Should I kill them, Dad?'

He went very still. Before he could answer, a horn blared across the square in front of the Test building. They whirled, and a grey-haired man in the drab suit lowered his hands. The noise stopped. There was silence.

'Will all Test candidates please enter the building to be Tested,' he called hoarsely. 'Will all Test candidates . . .'

Rose was looking very white again. Amid the sudden noise of murmurings and sobs and hurried good-lucks, she turned to him. 'Dad . . .'

He grasped her shoulders. 'Rose. Rose, good luck. I know you'll be fine. Do you understand me?'

'Yes.' Her voice was barely a whisper.

The steady stream of Gifted children was coalescing around the doors, flooding into the building. Rose was going to be swept away with it. His daughter was going to be taken away from him, and when she came out she would be different. More grown up. Less of a child who needed him.

He realised there were tears in his eyes.

'Rose,' he told her, 'Rose, I love you.'

'I love you, too, Dad,' and then she was gone, lost to sight, and he was left behind with his hand stretched out towards her, and the last stragglers were pushed towards the darkness and the doors closed and there was silence.

He waited for a moment, numb. Then he let his arm drop.

CHAPTER 4

Maria Rodriguez stood inside the Test lobby, staring at her shaking hands. She looked almost surprised when Rose called to her.

'Maria! Are you all right?'

The look on her face was blank. Rose wondered whether you could go into shock *before* a traumatic experience.

Probably not.

'Maria! Do I have to hit you?'

'No,' said Maria immediately. 'No, you don't.'

'Do you want to get a seat?'

The chairs were being filled up quickly by the influx of candidates from outside. They were black and wooden and looked like they might collapse at any moment. Rose guided Maria over to the nearest one, and sat her down. Maria's legs were trembling.

'How are you not nervous?' asked Maria incredulously.

'I am nervous. It's just not stopping me walking and talking at the same time.' Rose looked up at the room around them. 'Classy, isn't it?'

The space looked like a disused hotel lobby. The cement floor was painted to look like marble, and the ceiling was soaring white stone. The Test invigilators sat in glass booths at five-metre intervals around the walls. When they called someone's name, that person would come up, skin going almost as green as their eyes, exchange a few words with the invigilator, and then step into the lift behind the booth. They did not press any buttons, but the metal doors would slide closed anyway. There was no screen above the lift to indicate where it was going.

A few seconds later the doors would open, revealing an empty metal compartment, and the process would begin again.

'And they never come back,' said Rose, mock-ominously.

'Don't *joke* about it.'

'Oh come on. Humour is my only weapon against them.'

Maria glared at her. Rose knew she didn't mean it: Maria was perhaps her best friend in the world, except of course for Nate. She was a few months older than Rose, but they had been in the same class since they were four. Maria, being pretty and blonde, could have abandoned the much less popular Rose for a wider group at any time during the eleven years they had been friends. Against all the odds, though, and frankly against logic, Maria had never shown the slightest sign of wanting to break off their relationship, leaving Rose with a lasting and unshakable loyalty to her. That was probably a bad idea. Loyalty to anyone you had to support, even if it was only with homework, made you a liability.

But that was a Department rule. And this was not her Department life.

'I'm sure you'll be fine,' Rose told her, in her best imitation of reassurance. 'I've seen complete idiots pass their Test.'

'Thanks, Rose.'

'No, really. I mean . . .'

The dressed-up boy Rose had seen outside walked between Rose and Maria's chairs. When Maria's leg accidentally knocked into him, he acknowledged her apology with a disdainful sneer. Rose noticed his eyes seemed rather red.

'Like him,' said Rose, nodding.

Maria smiled, and Rose felt a swoop of relief. The boy had muttered – or more accurately, spat – something as he came past Maria, but, luckily, her friend had not heard. The word he had used was 'Pretender'. It was a derogatory term used to describe those with light eyes and weak Gifts, and while in Maria's case this was an accurate diagnosis, it was exactly the kind of comment she didn't need right now.

'Look!' said Maria suddenly. 'What's that?'

Rose turned and saw what Maria was looking at. A black screen had been set up just over the doorway, and it was currently flashing such gems of advice as

This is not a judgement. This is a measurement.

And

Please stay calm. You have nothing to fear.

And finally, with such false cheeriness that it made Rose want to shatter the screen,

Remember: you are privileged to be able to take this Test!

It was only then that it began, very slowly, to dawn on Rose the kind of system she was up against.

'Elmsworth, Rosalyn Daniela.'

The woman in the glass booth said it so matter-of-factly: presumably she didn't see the way Rose went very still, a frozen computer, and pressed her head to her kneecaps; she didn't hear Maria's gasp, or the way everyone around them stared at Rose as if a bomb had just started ticking on her chest.

She got up.

'Good luck,' Maria whispered. She smiled tremulously. 'I'll pass mine if you pass yours.'

'Deal,' Rose said. She was concentrating on keeping her voice steady. Her legs were shaking and there was a thin sort of ringing in her ears. She smiled at Maria once and then turned away before she said anything stupid like 'goodbye'. This was a Test, not the end. She wasn't going to die.

This was very important to remember: she had been in situations more dangerous than this.

She was absolutely going to survive this.

Oh, pull yourself together.

The other candidates stared wide-eyed at her as she walked through the clusters of people. They drew back their legs as she passed, as though she were carrying some sort of contagious disease. Rose kept her eyes on the invigilator at the desk at the edge of the room who had called her name.

The woman watched her dispassionately.

'Do you have anything to say?'

Rose wanted to tell her that this was not usually how things worked – that usually people left notes – but perhaps her better judgement intervened, because all that came out was, 'I'm ready.'

The woman nodded, and gestured to the lift.

Rose stared at the mirror on the back wall while the doors closed. She could just see Maria, white-faced and empathetic, reflected in the glass, but it didn't occur to her to turn until it was too late.

There was a *ping*.

She started sinking.

CHAPTER 5

The body on the table was white, dark-veined, cold. The silhouette stood frozen over it for a few moments. The theatre was submerged in blackness; it lent the silhouette a momentary peace before the woman came up behind him.

'David?'

She couldn't find the light switch, so she held up her hand and a spark flared in the darkness, blossoming into a flame that hovered an inch above her palm. Blinking, she stepped forward towards where he stood motionless over the corpse.

'David? Who is it?'

He turned towards her: he was very pale in the near-ghostly light, and it was clear from the way it flickered off his glass-green eyes that he was not seeing her, but something else, somewhere else. He walked past her towards the wall, and, with an expression of perfect serenity, kicked it so hard the trolley rattled.

'David!' Laura said, shocked. 'What's wrong? Do we know them?'

He gestured to the table. She peered over; in the gloom it took her a moment to recognise the face, and she gasped.

There was a silence.

'Oh, Jesus,' Laura whispered, emotionless as wind. 'Oh, Jesus Christ.'

She knelt down beside the table, staring at the face. Somewhere inside her a deeper recognition sparked and caught: this woman had been in the care of *her* office, she had been in suggestion therapy, and though the disappearance of one solitary, half-mad Ashkind woman did not a scandal make, Laura knew that this was her own failing.

'Oh, Sylvia,' she whispered, stroking the corpse's face. 'Oh, darling girl. What happened to you?'

'Poison,' said David, still facing the wall. His voice was stronger; these were answers he could give. 'Administered by injection, through the crook of the arm – there are marks.'

'Do you think it's the same person who killed her brother?'

'That was clearly a revenge attack. Violent, brutal. This was professional. Relatively painless.'

'So we have two murderers on the loose.'

David laughed, long, low and hollow. 'Oh, would that *that* were true.'

'Don't be sarcastic with me, David Jonathan.'

'Don't call me that,' he murmured, but moved to stand beside her. He had more control over himself now. He pulled a syringe from the trolley, removed the sheath from the needle, and took a blood sample from the corpse. His manner was quick, clinical. Laura watched him. She rarely saw him like this, over the bodies of civilians. Their remits touched on death, but never so directly: she convinced dazed loved ones that their relatives had died peacefully, while he tracked down murderers, and, more often than not, made quick-burning corpses out of them. Never this. Never serene, cold bodies in the crushing dark.

'You have medical training?'

'No training,' he said, examining the blackened blood in the syringe, 'just War history. I've done a lot of things.'

'So have we all.'

He smiled thinly, let the silence stretch before replying. 'This poison was carefully chosen to display distinct physical symptoms, so it could be noticed and she would be taken to hospital. We'll need a thorough autopsy to show exactly what it was, but we can be fairly sure it was used so the baby could be saved.'

'The baby? Oh, yes, God—'

'Emergency Caesarean before she died; he was unharmed. They told me when they called me over. He's fine.'

'So why—'

'She gets taken into Department custody,' he said, holding the syringe up to the light and stepping away. 'Someone gets wind of the news, decides that she can't be allowed to talk to us under therapeutic drugs. They infiltrate the ward – let's face it, it's not that hard, they're not worried about people breaking *in* – and inject her with slow-acting poison. She dies. Her unborn child is saved. Professional.' He looked back at the corpse. 'Admirably so.'

'That's the scenario?'

'That's the scenario.'

'So what did she know?'

'Ah, well,' he said, eyes still on the body as though daring it to lie, 'that's the question, isn't—?'

Abruptly, he went very, very still.

He was looking at the corpse's clenched fist, and as Laura, bewildered, traced his gaze, she saw him lift a hand to his face. It was shaking.

David Elmsworth's hands were shaking.

He stepped forward, and then, abruptly, his moves were very fast – prising open the corpse's fingers, pulling the scrap of paper roughly from its grasp, spinning away from it as if it were a grenade, staring at the handwriting on the paper. From where she stood, Laura couldn't read it.

She knew she was going to regret it. She asked anyway.

'David,' she said evenly, 'what's—'

He wasn't listening. He was running his fingers over the paper, wide-eyed, white-faced, whispering to himself. He held it up to the light. He went still again, and then he turned to Laura, lightning-quick, slipping the paper into his pocket. He smiled unconvincingly.

'That,' he told her, 'never happened.'

'David. That's a vital piece of evidence, I'm not going to cover—'

'I am not asking you to. I'll file it; I'll run DNA tests. Leave it to me.'

She hesitated.

'Trust me, Laura.'

'David, what is this?'

'Please, just give me—'

'No. Come on. David, how long have we known each other? Fourteen years? Fifteen? I'm not taking this from you. Give me the truth.'

He gave her a searching look. 'It says "Behold the Interregnum",' he said quietly.

She blinked. 'What does that mean?'

Another long silence. She was just about to prompt him angrily again when he spoke. His eyes were flat, and his words seemed to burn him as they left him.

'If this note comes to the attention of the Department, they will go after its writers, yes?'

'Of course.'

'They can't.'

'Why not?'

He glanced at the corpse. 'Because if we try to attack these people – if we do *anything* more than leave them alone and hope they and their intentions just dissolve into nothing – we might very well restart the War.'

'*What*? Why? Who are they?'

He leaned very close to her, glancing around. For a moment she thought he wasn't going to say anything.

'Regency,' he whispered. 'That's what they call themselves. Learn to fear that name, Laura. Let it show up in your nightmares. They are the *last* people we want to provoke.'

'And why is that?'

He said nothing. He put the cap back on the syringe, left lying on the table, and put it into his pocket. He walked down the corridor, and as he passed underneath each argon strip-light, it flickered and exploded in a shower of sparks before dying. Then he stopped, and looked distractedly up at the fading light. He was quiet for a moment, and then he turned towards her.

'Because I used to fight for them,' he said.

CHAPTER 6

The lift doors opened, and she stepped out.

The room was submerged in darkness, lit only by dim floodlights in the corners. It was impossible to judge its size – the shadows stretched into an interminable blackness that Rose's eyes could not penetrate. Two chairs stood maybe ten feet in front of Rose, each in a blinding spotlight. The grey-haired Angel who had announced the Test sat in one of them. He watched Rose gravely with those unfathomably green, unreadable eyes.

'Sit,' he said.

Rose sat. Her nerves were gone now, replaced by a kind of light-headedness that left her mind very clear and sharp, as if her thoughts had been magnified. Something rattled above her head.

'This is the first stage of your Test,' the man said. 'You will need to remain calm.'

Rose raised her head slowly. An oxygen mask, as if from an ancient aeroplane, hung from a string, which stretched up into the impenetrable darkness.

'Place the mask over your mouth and nose,' the man said. Rose noticed that his face was remarkably smooth for a man with so many years in the skin of his hands and eyes. She wanted to be given a second to close her eyes and gather her thoughts, but her pride would not allow her to show weakness, so she reached up with trembling hands and pulled the plastic over her mouth. Claustrophobia gripped her in a sweeping rush of terror. She clenched her wrist with one hand until it went away.

A wheezing rumble, like a faraway ventilator, started up in the distance. Rose stared into the man's dark, expressionless eyes. She noticed that the air she was breathing through the mask seemed suddenly very dense. The fear returned with a vengeance – was this the Leeching Gas? Were they removing her powers? Had she already failed? Was she—

'We need,' said the man slowly, 'to know more about you. And for that we need to eliminate all possibility of deceit. What you are breathing now is a hallucinogen called Insanity Gas. It will make it easier to access your mind and to find the part that stores long-term memory. Do not worry: there will be no pain.'

Rose did not quite have time to panic before the darkness reared and swallowed her vision whole.

The first memory came from the year the War ended. Rose was three years old at the time. She never remembered the bombs falling, but she knew the day when they stopped: the air so clear, so quiet and empty, as if the only thing the sky had ever been for was to hold birds and clouds within its vast embrace. She and her father spent the day simply staring out of the window, holding the silent air between their fingers. The smell of gunpowder was already fading.

The next memory was of the day he decided to tell her. She didn't know what made him speak then, of all times. Perhaps, when peace had been fully established and the Department's effort to keep the streets safe began to actually mean something, his ghosts started to retreat. He must have felt safer, now that the people who wanted to kill him – and they were still many, and growing – were civilian criminals, not soldiers.

He told her straight out, stern-faced.

'You're not my daughter.'

Rose was then almost six. She was not exactly shrewd, not at that age, but she knew enough not to take statements like that at face value. She hesitated, wary, waiting for clarification. When none came, she went for denial.

'Yes I am.'

He sighed, rubbed his face. He was, by then, perhaps twenty-five or twenty-six years old – young, though she had no context then for this, to have so many secrets.

'Not in the way you think. You know how babies are born?'

In a way, the revelations that followed should not have been so much of a surprise. Rose had always been aware, if only vaguely, that she was not her father's daughter – or at least, not in the same way that other people were the children of their parents.

Rose had known this for a variety of reasons. The first and foremost was that other children looked like their parents, and Rose did not. No matter how long or hard she looked in the mirror, she could find nothing of him in her face or features. His hair, though also brown, was lighter than hers; his face narrower; her build tall and lean where he was stocky and strong.

Also – and this should have been her first clue, really – she had no mother.

She had met other people's mothers, and she was old enough to know that only women could bear children. But she took it for granted that their situation was different. How many times had that been proven over the years, after all? She and David were monsters, a secret no one else had; and he was a detective and worked for the Department and saved the world every other day, or so Rose believed, and anyway, they could do magic. He was her father and they were special. The laws of biology did not apply to him.

Nevertheless, with all those clues, it should not really have been a surprise that day when he sat her down and began talking to her in what Rose immediately recognised as his Very Stern Voice. This was roughly the tone he used when telling her not to walk in front of cars.

'Do you know about DNA?'

She had heard the acronym. 'Is that the . . . the little stringy things in your blood?'

'More or less. They determine whether you have pale skin or brown hair or any other trait you happen to be born with.'

'Yes.'

'And parents pass it on to their children.'

'Yes.'

He sighed. 'Rose, you and I don't have the same DNA.'

She stared at him uncomprehendingly. 'But . . . that can't be right.'

'Yes it can,' he told her. 'It's because you're not my daughter.'

This was the story, woven together from a thousand bedtime retellings:

David is a nineteen-year-old soldier. His army have made him do bad things and he's very, very tired of the War.

He's walking home to his flat in the grip of some dark, rainy evening, trying to find a way out. There's a noise in the garage next to him and he thinks it's someone trying to hurt him and he nearly attacks.

But he doesn't. It's a shoebox, covered in cloth. And inside the shoebox is a baby.

He doesn't want a baby. He's never wanted a baby. But he takes the child inside anyway, because it's cold and he doesn't want it to die.

Then he finds out they share a secret. The monster twists the baby's body into its own, one terrible night, and nearly hurts him. He has to change his mind – who else can raise a child like this? He keeps her.

She knows the rest.

She'd known Terrian since she was five years old. This had its downsides – he could remember her as a small child, something she saw almost daily in his condescending gaze – but what it also meant was that she could remember David coming home wearing his sombre expression and, for the first time, realising that it wasn't because of a murder. She had only been seven, but he had told her the truth, as he always did: Terrian's wife Malia had died, of cancer, and Terrian wouldn't be coming in to work for a while.

Rose could remember very distinctly the day he did come back, which wasn't great, as it meant the Tester could see it just as clearly. He had had a boy with him: dark-skinned like his father, about her age, with long dreadlocks hanging down his back and bright turquoise eyes, which meant he was second-level Gifted, like her. The boy skulked behind his father's knee. He had been crying, but the seven-year-old Rose refrained from judging him for that: she had never had a mother, but she supposed that if she had and the mother was dead she would be sad too. David and Terrian called the boy Nathaniel, but they were the only ones who ever did. He had been Nate, as she had been Rose, almost since he was born.

When their respective fathers were out of earshot, Rose and Nate gave it maybe a minute, and then they chased each other round the Department desks. It was the first time Rose heard him laugh: it stuck in her head like a record on replay, echoing through eight years and the speakers of some invisible studio on the floors above her.

This memory was brighter and clearer than the others. She was nearly fourteen, old enough to neutralise aggrieved relatives for the Department. And she knew who this man was. He was a Demon: the darkest-eyed, most dangerous type of Ashkind, historically the most violent and insidious and prone to political dissent, who had to be watched by the Department very carefully lest they rebel against the Government. And this one had done just that. He had broken into the army camp, kidnapped a soldier, dragged him to an unguarded interrogation room and now half the Department were gathered around the one-way mirror, watching the rogue agent as he pulled the gun from the soldier's holster, clicked the safety off and pressed it to the head of his prisoner.

The soldier himself was only a boy: a very young conscript, who had completed his compulsory year of post-Test school and elected to serve in the army for his two years of national service instead of studying for another year. Rose had read his file. His name was James Andreas. He was sixteen years old, he had red-gold hair and eyes the colour of the sea in cloud-light, and right now he was very pale. His mouth was open as if on the verge of screaming, his eyes wide, but he made no sound. Rose's fists were clenched so tight her knuckles had gone white.

'Okay,' someone said from Rose's left. The snap-click sound of typing echoed like gunshots through the silence. 'What are we going for, David? This wall is reinforced, and we've got the ammo capacity to blow this place wide open, if . . .'

The possibility hung in the air for a few seconds.

'We're getting that boy out,' David said firmly. 'Max, stay back here with the comms equipment. Protect Rose.'

'No,' Rose said immediately, looking at her father. 'I'm going in with you.'

'No, you are not.'

'You can't stop me.'

'Yes I can. Max?'

'I'll keep her here, boss.'

Rose glared at Max, who shrugged helplessly.

'Right. Shields up, everyone.'

There was a crackling noise as half a dozen people put up magical shields around themselves. They drew their guns.

'Okay,' said David. 'We've got him outnumbered and outgunned, so we should be all right.'

'We've got the element of surprise, too,' piped up someone from David's right, helpfully. 'Don't forget that.'

Rose never saw the look David gave them, but she could only assume it was up there with the most scathing in his arsenal.

'This man is insane,' he said. 'You never, ever have the element of surprise against a madman. Trust me –' loading his gun – 'how d'you think I've gone fifteen years without losing a fight?'

There was a murmur of uncertain laughter. As if he could hear them, the madman tilted his head. Rose knew madness, but had never seen it in a human being before: it was odd, off.

'All right,' David said. 'Three. Two. One-and-a-half.'

He gave them all his most charming grin. Rose knew that grin. It never boded well.

'One.'

There was a hammering click of gunshots and the mirror exploded into fragments. One of them hit the madman and he fired at the soldier's head, but his hand had slipped and the bullet sprayed red across the boy's chest. He slipped off his chair without a cry.

The soldiers burst through the gap. Rose followed them, ignoring Max's warning, and emptied her gun at the madman. She thought that at least one of her bullets hit, but nowhere vital: he was firing everywhere. Rose ducked, sprinted towards the boy, intending to defend him, but pain exploded in her foot and she collapsed. Her hand lay across the boy's chest, slick with his blood. She heaved herself up and concentrated: magic shot in a white-hot spear towards the madman. It seared his shoulder, and he cried out. There was a flickering, buzzing noise and something else hit him, and then there was a second of utter terror spiralling through Rose's mind – *come on, hit him, come on now* – and a snap-crack of bone shattering. The side of the madman's head seemed to explode and he fell. His eyes were level with Rose's. They were open and staring, and Rose thought she could still see the madness gleaming within them.

She spent weeks in that hospital bed. The boy was next to her: she remembered what they said about him, that the bullet was lodged against his heart, and that to attempt to remove it would be to risk damaging major internal organs. They kept him heavily sedated throughout, which was a shame, as she would have liked to have someone to talk to.

They knocked her out when they took the bullet from her ankle. Even within her sluggish, drug-slowed dreams, she felt the icy metal within her skin and she screamed.

Ah. This memory. She knew this one.

The small metal room. No windows, soundproofed,

and six feet underground. Rose huddled in the corner, shivering. There was something next to her. She was about to turn, to pick it up . . .

No.

What?

The thoughts of the sleeping Rose, the one taking the Test, broke through into the memory of six weeks ago.

No. No. I have to wake up – they can't see this, they can't see this, they can't see the secret—

And something within her responded. Magic surged through her, scouring the sedative from her blood, and she opened her eyes to the green ones of the old man leaning over her. She pulled the mask away from her face and scrambled to her feet, backing away, and found—

Behind him, whiteness. The mask and chair gone. She stumbled, disoriented.

They'd moved.

She stood in front of the Angel in a huge, empty, blindingly lit greenhouse. The sky outside the glass was grey-white. Her eyes wanted to close, adjust. She fought it. Stay alert. They're trying to confuse you. Yes, I know what it looks like, and you're wrong, because you can't have teleported, can you, because *that's not bloody possible*. It's something cleverer than you. Focus. You will be all right. Never mind the laws of physics and all of that; it'll be fine, the world isn't changing.

'That memory,' said the Angel quietly. He tilted his head. His eyes glittered in the shattering light. 'What is it about that memory? Why don't you want me to see it?'

'It's a nightmare,' said Rose. Her voice felt very small

in the wide, white emptiness. She forced it louder. 'Just one of my nightmares.'

'Nightmares weaken you. Why does that memory make you stronger? Why does it help you to fight back?'

A thousand truths and lies bubbled to the surface. She didn't know how well she would be able to lie to his face in this state, wherever she was, whatever was happening, so she settled for an absolute.

'I am afraid,' she said.

The Angel's face darkened, and he raised his hand. Something gathered there, a swirling translucence, like compressed wind. Rose didn't think. She probably couldn't have if she tried.

A well-worn instinct running at the back of her mind leapt to coherence.

This is an Angel, it told her calmly. *He is probably a thousand times stronger than you. You know what he's doing, right? You can see he's going to attack you?*

By Ichor, you are useless under pressure.

What good were all those years of training if you can't do this? Strike first, you idiot. You remember what Dad said about this kind of thing. You know he's going to start this fight, so strike.

STRIKE!

She acted with no skill or technique; she pulled energy roughly from her muscles and twisted the air around the Angel into a tight, hard bubble and pushed her hand forward, sending him sprawling across the floor. Air was much easier to move than people.

Something else her father had taught her.

All right, now run, said her instinct impatiently, *run, now, you don't have much time—*

How serious is this fight, anyway? This is only a Test. It can't be to-the-death, can it?

Have you failed? Is he trying to take your Gifts? Is this it?

Should you just let him?

No, thought Rose numbly. *No.*

She ran, away from the Angel, towards the glass door, maybe a hundred metres away. She could do a hundred metres in fourteen seconds. Ridiculously slow.

See? Useless.

Nine, ten, eleven—

She could feel the Angel behind her, getting up, readying his magic. She threw up a shield behind her, rudimentary, pathetic, it wasn't going to hold—

His blow smashed into her. It was a cold wall of air, more powerful than hers a hundredfold, and it took her off her feet and tumbling through space, and suddenly there was glass against her shoulder. She had only time to hope it would break, but it did not give way, and the rest of her body slammed into it. The pain was dizzying, dazzling: there was something metal against her shoulder, it dug into the skin, something trickling down her forehead and it took her a second to realise it was blood—

But something metal—

Door handle, you idiot!

She fumbled for it. It moved under her grip, and the door opened: she fell gracelessly through, and scrambled to close it again, used magic to find the locks and bar them. Panting, she stared through the glass at the Angel. He stood calmly on the other side, not even bruised from the blow she had given him. He was fast. Very fast. Too damn fast.

She stood, wiping the blood from her face.

They watched each other. Rose wondered why he didn't just break the glass; maybe it wasn't normal, maybe it was reinforced, maybe that was why it had held her weight. Either way, he stayed within the greenhouse, watching her with a mixture of anger and curiosity.

What do you do now?

With difficulty, she turned away from the Angel, aware of his eyes on her back, and saw the world outside the greenhouse. She stood on grass wet with dew; it stretched maybe six feet in front of her, and ended abruptly in a cliff of earth and grey stone. Trails of mist hung from the cloudy sky, above and below her. This was an airborne island.

Her mind stopped working.

'Reinforced plastic,' said a familiar voice behind her. She turned, saw her father kneeling beside the greenhouse, examining the glass. 'I taught you about this, remember? It's used in the structure of the door to our office.' He flicked it gently with a fingertip; it rang like crystal. 'Astonishing material. Developed during the War. Necessity and invention, and all of that.'

He stood up. His eyes met the Angel's. They examined each other, David with apprehension, the Angel with that same half-detached interest.

'That was quite possibly the worst you've ever performed

in a fight,' he told her, without taking his eyes off the Angel.

'This is inside my head,' she said. 'This whole thing.'

'I should hope so.'

The realisation came slowly. 'I'm still sedated. You can't actually be here. I'm imagining you.'

'Don't flatter yourself.'

'Oh my God, I'm talking to myself.' She stared at him. He was very lifelike: David in every detail, up to the half-mischievous grin he gave her. 'No offence, but this is getting weird.'

He laughed, and moved to stand beside her. 'I think that ship sailed a while ago.'

'True. Why are you here?'

He shrugged. 'I don't know any more than you.'

'You can try. Is this happening to everyone? Are they seeing their parents, their friends . . .?'

'We can only presume so. This is designed to see how good you'd be as a soldier, among other things, so the fight is probably a set part of the Test. You're still under sedation, and that does weird things to your brain. Possibly your subconscious is more clearly articulated than most people's, or maybe this is a set part of the programming, and everyone's seeing their subconscious in whatever form it takes.'

'You're my subconscious?'

'I'm the form your subconscious takes to talk to you, yes.'

The Angel behind them tapped on the glass: once, slowly. The crystalline note it held was distinctly more menacing this time. David, or the part of her mind that looked like David, glanced back at him.

'I think we might want to hurry up.'

'Wake up, you mean?'

'Of course.' He looked up at the grey sky, the place where the grass dropped off abruptly into nothingness. 'There's not much we can do here, is there?'

'How?'

'Two possible methods. Firstly—' He turned to her, stared at her intently. 'Wake up,' he intoned. '*Wake up.*'

Nothing. The Angel tapped the glass again.

'You just look stupid,' she told David.

'You're only insulting yourself, you know.'

'I deserve it. What's the other method?'

They looked again at the cliff edge. David bit his lip – that was one of her habits, she knew; the real David would never do that.

The Angel flicked the greenhouse wall so hard it rattled.

'We're running out of time,' said her ghost-father. 'Are you ready?'

She turned to the cliff-edge. It looked very dangerous for something that wouldn't kill her.

'Are you absolutely sure about this?' she asked nervously.

No reply. She turned. The shadow of David had vanished, traceless; not even his footsteps in the grass remained to comfort her. She felt suddenly, irrationally lonely.

The Angel stared at her, and bared his teeth.

Lean back.

He tapped the glass again. They stood facing each other across a wide expanse of grass. If Rose had to guess, she would imagine she was in someone's garden. She wouldn't think there was a cliff behind her. There shouldn't, in any sane world, be a cliff behind her.

Lean back. It'll be easy.

It took, it seemed, more effort to close her eyes than it had done to move the Angel.

Lean. Lean.

A cracking sound – breaking glass. The Angel's muffled voice.

'I'm coming,' he whispered.

Another tap; a high, shimmering ring, and then suddenly, a shattering. A step – a brush of unnatural wind on her skin—

She stepped back, and dropped.

CHAPTER 7

Often she had dreamed of falling.

The wind was bright as ice against her face. She was out of control: twisted and flung, without coordination, through a white world without end.

In her dreams, she would stop before she hit the ground. Wake, gasping, in a cold sweat.

She fell, and the world turned dark.

Slowly, she opened her eyes. The insistent, settled pull of gravity disoriented her for a moment. She was still, sprawled in a chair, breathing clean, clear air through a mask over her nose and mouth.

Her heart was beating very fast.

Tentatively, and painfully aware of the encroaching headache, she pulled off the mask. She blinked against the sudden gloom. The darkened room. The Test room. The sound of the ventilator in the distance slowed, faded and stopped.

The Angel was there, and he was smiling.

The Testing Administrator was a solemn-looking woman in her carly forties with dyed red hair and glossy turquoise eyes. She was sitting in one of two plastic classroom chairs when Rose entered the room. It was bare, with varnished wooden flooring and cracked paint, looking distinctly out of place in the context of an office block or a hotel or whatever the hell this was. Rose felt immediately claustrophobic. Perhaps this was what made her distrust the woman who sat in front of her before she even started speaking.

The Angel pushed her in gently when she hesitated in the doorway.

'Seven-oh-one-six,' he said, addressing the Administrator. 'Just out of her Test.'

'Thank you, Mr Forster,' she said gently. 'Please, sit down, Rosalyn.'

The Angel gave Rose a final smile and wave and closed the door. Rose sat down in the other chair, watching the Administrator. When Forster's footsteps had faded away, the Administrator spoke.

'I'll be straight with you, Rosalyn. I'm here to give you a warning.'

Rose's stomach immediately plunged. Her voice was hoarse. 'Did I pass?'

The Administrator gave her a stern look, and Rose, to her shame, immediately felt stupid. Obviously it wasn't going to be that easy to find out.

'I'm here to warn you about your father's occupation.'

Rose stayed silent.

'You know too much,' said the Administrator bluntly. 'You're clever, Rosalyn, and you're arrogant, so I won't mess about with you. It is very, *very* bad practice to have a civilian, especially an underage civilian, know as much about our operations as your memories show you do. You are dangerous, the both of you, but we need him.'

She let it hang there, and Rose grudgingly finished the sentence for her.

'You don't need me.'

'We want to need you. We want to *welcome* you, when you're old enough. But we need to make sure you stay on the straight and narrow.'

'Is there any indication that I'm not?'

The Administrator sighed, and leaned back.

'You're not the only one. There's a boy taking his Test right now, in Islington, the child of a Department member, who has had much the same upbringing as you. Do you know him?'

'Yes. Nathaniel Terrian.'

'You're friends?'

Rose nodded warily.

'So why am I here? Why am I not over in Islington now, talking to Nathaniel? Why you over him?'

'I don't know.'

'You're very interesting, Rosalyn,' said the Administrator. She smiled; it looked very unnatural. 'You can fight, as you just proved. You're logical. You consistently score highly in IQ tests, and your intelligence was notable even under the Insanity Gas. You're powerfully Gifted, and your subconscious takes the form of a genius. But do you know what makes you most interesting? What sets you apart from your friend Nathaniel? I'll give you a hint. It's one of your faults.'

She was smiling broadly now, but it did not reach anywhere near her eyes.

'I have no doubt they are many and varied,' said Rose, with as much dignity as she could muster.

The Administrator sat forward again, setting her papers down on the floor, and leaned in close. 'One thing we picked up on,' she said. 'One memory. The attack on James Andreas, two years ago – you wanted to fight, am I right?'

'Of course.'

'There was an adrenalin surge in your blood. But when you fired – when that man got near your father – you were thirteen years old, and you shot to kill. You were very young to even *think* of using such deadly force.'

Rose raised her eyebrows.

'Let me get this straight,' she said. 'I was Tested by an Angel, and I'm being interviewed by the Testing Administrator, because I'm David Elmsworth's daughter and you think I *might* be dangerous.'

'"Dangerous" is a strong word. We know you could be a threat if you fell into the wrong hands, so we're keeping you in ours.'

Rose seethed at that – who were they to treat her as a possession to be safeguarded? Another heavy silence. The Administrator got up.

'My name is Serena Mitchell,' she said. 'You're going to be seeing a lot of me over the next few months. I'm sure it will be an . . . enjoyable experience.'

She made no effort to disguise the way her lip curled.

'I assume you know what you were being Tested for?'

'I have a rudimentary idea.'

The smile faded slightly. 'Your memories showed absolute loyalty to the Department and its members. Your hallucinations proved your fighting ability—'

'I *lost* that fight.'

'It's not designed for you to win it. You're supposed to survive, not emerge victorious. Your jump showed bravery, and as for your subconscious – well, it's remarkably coherent, at the very least. You are . . . interesting, Rosalyn.'

That word again.

'You may leave,' Mitchell told Rose. 'You are of course aware of the conditions under which you are allowed to keep your powers. You may only use them in your own home, in the homes of others with their permission, and in specially licensed workplaces. You may not use them to any extent or purpose that would pose a risk of harm to yourself or to others, and of course you may not use them in public at all. To do so is to break Government law and will result in a custodial sentence.'

A silence, a heartbeat-racing silence; Rose let it stretch before daring to tempt fate by speaking. She was drunk on success and the incredible fact that they *still didn't know*. They suspected nothing. Her secret was still safe, thank the Angels.

Finally, she dared to ask the question, because she desperately needed to hear it said aloud.

'I'm keeping my powers, then? I passed?'

A thin, mirthless smile.

'Oh, Rosalyn,' said Mitchell. 'We wouldn't dream of wasting *you*.'

On her way out, she walked past a one-way mirror.

It caught her eye because she had so rarely seen one outside the Department. No one stood watching it, though. Through it a struggling young woman was being strapped to a chair. Gas-masked figures stood over her, holding her down, fastening the straps. Rose stopped, staring in fascination. A Test failure. She must have been screaming, because her mouth was open and her eyes were wide, but the mirror was soundproofed and Rose couldn't hear it.

When the girl was strapped down, the gas-masked figures stepped away. She was green-eyed, light-moss-green Pretender-eyed, and she was wasting the last of her magic. Burns were appearing in the masked figures' clothing; the wheels of the trolley she was being strapped onto burst into flames, and scorch marks dragged themselves across the wall. The girl was not very powerful at all; after ten seconds or so of this she looked thin, weak, pale, cold, and collapsed, exhausted, onto the trolley again.

One of the gas-masked figures raised his hand, and the fire on the wheels went out.

The girl began to cry.

There was a hissing sound that Rose could hear even through the mirror; she jumped away, looking around for any white gas, but she couldn't see any, except that which began to billow into the room on the other side. The girl was screaming again, sobbing, pleading, but even Rose knew it was too late.

She was already breathing it.

The cloud of white gas moved forwards inexorably. The Test failure struggled, trying to move away from it, but the Leeching Gas enveloped her: her feet first, then her legs, her waist, and her torso were inside it, and finally her face, and she was gone.

The gas made the mirror opaque, and Rose watched it, immobile with horror, until the hissing changed pitch to a sucking.

The Leeching Gas began to move back, peeling off the glass. The gas-masked figures stood over the girl. She was not unconscious; she was not even sobbing, but in shock, lying with her chest rising and falling too quickly. She turned to stare at the mirror, and Rose knew she was trying to break the glass, but nothing happened. The laws of physics refused to obey her. She was not Gifted any more. Her irises were ringed with the unclean, bleached white that marked the Leeched.

The gas-masked captors began to unstrap the girl, but she didn't move. Rose felt sorry for her; it must be a terrible thing to have your Gifts removed. By way of parting condolence, she leaned forward, and said to the glass, though she knew no one behind it could hear her: 'You should have tried to block the air vents.'

CHAPTER 8

The train pulled into Earl's Court, and Rose and David got out.

'Don't start any arguments,' he warned her as they passed through the barriers. 'Not on your last day of school.'

'Surely my last day is the one day I *can* start an argument. I can start as many arguments as I want, because I won't be seeing most of them ever again. We'll be going to post-Test schools now, remember? So I can do what I like.'

'Yes, but you don't want them to remember you badly, do you?'

'Dad,' Rose told him as they crossed the street, 'right now, they think of me as the weirdo Gifted girl who's probably only friends with Maria Rodriguez because of bribery or kidnapping or whatever crime they think me capable of. I may as well let them remember me as the weirdo Gifted girl with the astonishing vocabulary who destroyed their arguments both convincingly and wittily.'

He looked at her.

'All right, I won't start any arguments,' Rose said reluctantly. 'But the way I see it, I don't really start arguments. The arguments sort of . . . start themselves.'

'Don't push it, Rose. If you're so willing to fight with them, you shouldn't care what they think of you.'

'Yes, Dad, I know I *shouldn't*. I've spent most of my life trying not to, but apparently it's harder than it looks.'

He grinned. 'Ah, the unsolvable conundrums of adolescence.'

'I hate you so much.'

They approached the Earl's Court Elementary School. There were Year Threes, seven or eight years old – with every colour eyes, as Gifted and Ashkind children weren't separated until after the Test – waiting by the double doors with little glasses of orange juice and champagne.

Rose and David arranged their smiles and slid into the hall. It was very crowded. Rose tried to peer through the forest of students and parents to find Maria, but quickly gave up. There was little point.

'Oh,' said a familiar voice from behind them. 'Hello.'

Rose turned reluctantly. Tristan Greenlow – son of the leader of the Gospel, the anti-Ashkind group who had harassed Rose on the day of the Argent murder – stood behind them, looking as though he had encountered something that came off the bottom of his shoe. Tristan, Rose knew, did not like the Elmsworths. He did not like many things. He was short, blond and irritable, and had been born – so far as Rose was aware – with an unshakeably contemptuous expression on his face, and it was with this that he surveyed her and her father, who had turned with Rose to see who she was looking at.

'Ah,' he said. Rose thought he let the ensuing silence

stretch on slightly longer than necessary. 'You'll be Stephen's youngest, then?'

'Yes,' said Tristan, looking him up and down. 'Are you Rosalyn's father?'

David and Rose exchanged a look. She and Tristan had spent nearly six years in the same class.

'More or less,' said David slowly.

'You don't look much like her,' said Tristan. 'Though,' glancing at Rose again, lip curling, 'I suppose you should probably count yourself lucky. Is your mother very ugly?'

He said it matter-of-factly, and Rose, who was used to this, did not rise, though she could see David beside her calculating the odds of being able to punch a fifteen-year-old boy in a crowded hallway and keep his job. From his expression, they were not good.

'Are you looking for your father, then?' Rose asked Tristan, as politely as she could, before David could do anything stupid.

'Yes, as it happens,' said Tristan, rising onto his tiptoes slightly to look. David, unconsciously she thought, drew himself up to his full height. 'Have you seen him?'

'We haven't had the pleasure, no,' said Rose. She had long since discovered that Tristan didn't understand sarcasm, and so she could make as many jibes at him as she liked in the company of those who did, without fear of retaliation.

Tristan looked at David again. 'He doesn't like you.'

'Oh, good,' said David, before Rose could stop him. 'I must be doing something right.'

'You're some kind of jumped-up policeman, aren't you?'

'Yes, I am. I'm the man in charge of arresting people like your father.'

'*My* father says people like you should be shot.'

'Oh, I'd love him to try.'

'Anyway,' said Rose quickly, before Tristan lost a fight he didn't realise he'd started, 'he's over there, see?'

She pointed to the corner of the hall, thanking the Angels for Tristan's height. He peered around. 'Oh, right,' he said vaguely, and walked off.

David stared after him, narrow-eyed.

'I don't like him,' he said.

'Well, you did a very good job of hiding it.'

'Did I?'

Rose rolled her eyes.

'Have you heard about the Greenlows? The rest of them, I mean?' she asked him, as they weaved their way through the crowd.

'Ah, yes,' he said. He raised his voice slightly, so as to be heard over all of the inane chatter. 'High-level Gifteds. The elder son's quite powerful, very academic. His mother's very proud of him. She wants him to follow her into Government – she's quite high up in the MoD. In fact. . .' They ducked a small fiery bird as it flew danger-ously low over their heads. 'In fact, I've heard that Aaron Greenlow's very popular among girls in general.'

'You are such a gossip,' Rose told him, trying and failing not to go red.

David grinned.

'Well, I've got to pay attention to which respectable young men are going, now that my daughter is of an eligible age. And speaking of eligible young men . . . hello, Nathaniel.'

Nate Terrian drew up to them. He was wearing a second-hand suit and his customary dreadlocks. He was looking very proud of himself.

'I passed!' he said excitedly before either of them could speak. 'What about you, Rose? How did you do? On your Test, I mean,' he added hastily, in case anyone was in any doubt at all about what he meant.

'Yeah, I passed too, Nate!' Rose said, smiling. 'Which school have they assigned you to?'

'West London Higher Training.'

'Great!' Rose said, casting a sideways glance at her father to see how he was taking the news that he and Connor Terrian would be fellow class-parents for at least another year, if not two. His smile seemed slightly more fixed than it would normally have done, but he shook Nathaniel's hand in congratulations all the same. After all, as he said, you couldn't judge people on their parents. Or, he would add slightly more dryly, their children.

'So, what do they teach us in Higher Training School?'

'Well, I think we carry on with mathematics and the sciences,' Rose said, 'and then we get choices of stuff like Artistic Studies, Magical Skills, Craftsmanship, Angelic Studies and so on. Maths, Magical Skills and Combat are compulsory. And maybe War History. I'm not sure about much after that.'

'What do you think you'll be good at?'

'I really don't know any more,' Rose said wearily. She glanced at her father again. 'Is your dad here?'

'No,' Nathaniel said, 'he said he couldn't face it. He's not really good with . . .' He looked around. 'People,' he admitted finally. 'He doesn't like people all that much.'

'He's not the only one,' Rose muttered, glaring at her father. 'Look, Nate, have you seen Maria?'

'No, why?'

'Hi!' David said suddenly to someone over Nate's shoulder. 'How are you? Sorry, Nathaniel, you'll have to excuse me, I've just seen . . .' He paused, considering. 'A friend.'

'I—'

'Wonderful,' David said, and slipped away into the crowd. Rose glared at his retreating back, and saw his shoulders shaking with laughter.

'Someone's looking for you,' said Nate in a low voice, when David was out of earshot.

'Who?'

Wordlessly, he held out a folded piece of paper to her. Her full name was written on the outside of it, and only four words on the inside.

Room Fourteen, it said. *Help. Now.*

CHAPTER 9

'Are you—?'

Rose stopped abruptly in the doorway of Room Fourteen and stared at the silhouette against the whiteboard at the end of the room.

It was not anyone from the Department.

Rose had spent her life there, and she knew the outlines of everyone who worked in the fifth-floor office. This man was not one of them. He was broad-shouldered, tall, and brutally thin. When he stepped into the light, Rose could see his face, hollow and gaunt, his eyes cold and steely, his mouth hard and unsmiling. His hair was white-blond, fair enough to camouflage any grey hairs. He had a seemingly ageless face – Rose would have put him anywhere between twenty and forty – and he wore a small silver locket round his neck. What really caught Rose's attention about him, though, was his weapon. It was a small hand held gun known as an Icarus. Rose knew Icari; they were part of any Department squad team's arsenal. The Icarus was a not a gun designed to kill or maim. It was designed to traumatise. The bullet would not penetrate the skin, but instead attach itself to the victim, and send periodic electric shocks through the body, on signals from the owner of the gun.

The unknown man was pointing his squarely between Rose's eyes.

Rose couldn't feel. Her emotions drained away to nothing: no surprise, no anger, no fear. Her entire being seemed to narrow into the space between her and that gun. She did not know whether this was brave, or clever. In that moment she did not know anything at all.

'Close the door,' the man said. His voice was low and surprisingly mellifluous, not at all hoarse. Rose closed the door and locked it.

'Now,' the man said. Rose noticed his hand was perfectly steady on the gun. Just her luck to be targeted by someone who actually knew how to use lethal weaponry. 'I think you will agree it is in both of our best interests that I do not have to fire this. With that in mind, please sit down on a chair and don't move. We are going to talk.'

The classroom was one of the larger ones: clear of desks but dense with crowded bookshelves, computers thick by the back wall. There were no windows. Rose pulled up a chair and sat down.

'Away from the door,' he said.

Rose moved the chair. She did not say anything.

The man drew up another chair in front of her. He placed the gun in his lap. Rose briefly considered trying to grab it, but then realised she knew exactly what he would do: grab her wrist and probably break it. This would achieve nothing.

'Rosalyn Elmsworth?'

She nodded.

'My name is Loren Arkwood. Your life from here on in would have been a lot easier for not meeting me. And I'm sorry about that.'

Rose put the gun and the unusual name together and began to realise that she was up against a War vet. Many soldiers had changed their names during or after the fighting to avoid any lasting grudges or pre-Veilbreak criminal records. Rose knew her father had. This man pronounced his name oddly: Law-*renn*. It sounded like it should be the name of a small bird, or some kind of forest herb.

'What do you want from me?' she asked, trying for dignity's sake to keep her voice steady. What might it feel like to be electrocuted? Magic was one thing, that soft hum of energy coalescing in your hands, but electricity, hard and sharp and unforgiving and— Painful. Yes. It would be painful. Rose kept her eyes on the Icarus.

Loren Arkwood looked at it ruefully. 'Yes,' he said. 'Not exactly my weapon of choice, but necessary in these circumstances, I'm afraid. Well, I don't want to keep you, so I'll get to the point, then. Rosalyn, I need your help.'

'What kind of help?' Angry, don't sound angry; be afraid, that's what he wants, isn't it?

Arkwood looked at her, tilting his head slightly. 'You are the daughter of David Elmsworth?'

Rose nodded slowly, pinching the inside of her wrist to stop herself trembling.

'You know what he does for a living.'

Rose nodded slowly. The barrel of the gun was very close to her. She could almost feel how cold it was. She was shivering uncontrollably now.

'Then you know about the experimental wards in the Department building.'

'No.'

'I thought not. Well, when a person has done something to really offend the powers that be, they are put in the experimental wards. I was a lucky resident of one for two months. I remember little but the needles. There were a lot of needles.'

Rose was not quite sure where this was going, but she had her suspicions.

'I don't think you really need to know the particulars, but my point is that I am now no longer in the experimental wards, and I was not released on any official authority.'

Rose said nothing. After a while it became apparent that he was waiting for her to speak.

'You escaped,' she said quietly. 'From the Department.'

'Yes, if you want to put it that way.'

'So why . . .?' She couldn't speak properly; the instinct to run was too strong for coherent speech. Her mind – reliable even in her Test – was failing her now. 'Why are you. . .? Why . . .?'

She gave up and pointed to the gun.

Arkwood smiled. His teeth were very white, and sharp. 'The Department does not know that I have escaped. Don't ask me why. You couldn't understand it if you tried. The result is that I now have no access to food, water or shelter, and you're going to help me with that.'

Four beats of silence. Rose was gathering her courage to state the obvious. Fear shivered through her in hard beats of blood.

'I can't help you. I can't work against my father.'

'Rosalyn, I don't want to hurt you.'

'I don't want you to hurt me either.'

Loren Arkwood, quite calmly, picked up the gun, clicked off the safety, and pointed it between Rose's eyes.

That peaceful stillness again. It was almost unsettling. Rose's powers of speech were returning to her.

'Mr Arkwood, I don't think you're going to kill me.'

'Would you bet your life on that?'

'Yes.'

'Would you care to tell me why?'

Rose stopped, waiting for her fear not to show in her face. Then she took a deep, shaky breath.

'You don't know how to use that gun. If you shot me in the head and sent an electric shock through my brain, you would kill me, and you don't need an Icarus to do that. And even if you did want to kill me like that. . .' She shrugged. Adrenalin was destroying her motor controls, and it came out as a spasm. 'You would have done.'

He seemed to be waiting for something.

And then she saw it.

No. Wait, no. Was that—

Was that even *possible*?

It was. It had to be. She spoke before she could stop herself.

'That isn't even a real Icarus.'

He spoke too quickly. 'What makes you think that?'

'There should be a blue light on the side, to say it's charged up, and I can s—'

She stopped at the way he was looking at her. She tried

not to make it obvious how much she wanted to cringe away from him.

There were another few beats of quiet, during which it occurred to her that he didn't need an Icarus to lean forward and snap her neck.

'You're better than I gave you credit for,' he said finally.

She wasn't dead. He hadn't killed her.

Speak, now, he's expecting you to.

'That's what people usually think.'

'Do they?' A smile. It was not kind. 'They must have forgotten whose daughter you are.'

She said nothing to that.

'I knew your father of old.'

Angels, he's not going to kill you; he wants help, not your death, he's going to leave you alive. 'He never mentioned you.'

'No. And has he ever told you what his real name is?'

Pause.

'No.'

'There you go then,' he said. 'I assume you're going to walk away now. Am I right?'

Slowly, not sure what the right answer was: 'Yes.'

'Well, I can think of at least two reasons why you shouldn't do that. The first is this.'

A book plucked itself from the bookshelf and hung suspended in mid-air. At a wave of his hand, it suddenly threw itself through the air faster than Rose's eyes could follow and smashed itself into the door with enough force to snap a cover off and send pages flying everywhere.

Arkwood met Rose's astonished gaze, and she tried

not to flinch from his stare. His eyes were cold and hard and unfeeling; they looked straight through you as if every escape plan, every plot, every twinge of fear was open to his scrutiny. More importantly, however, they were pure yellow-green from the pupil to the edge of the iris, which meant his powers were intact – relatively weak, certainly, what some people would call a Pretender, but still there. Stupid, stupid, stupid. It was written on his bloody *face*. It was the first thing she should have looked for in an adversary. Her father had drummed this into her hundreds of times over the years. Why was she suddenly so *idiotic*?

'And the second,' Arkwood said, 'well, the second. . .'

They stared at each other for a few moments. Arkwood tilted his head to the side, as if thoughtful.

'You know, Rosalyn,' he said softly, 'there's something about you that doesn't seem quite . . . sane.'

A shivering kind of terror thrilled through her, locking her to the spot. Loren Arkwood smiled, and said,

'Do you know about Hybrids, Rosalyn?'

The word stopped her cold. The world seemed to lift and swirl slightly.

'They're a very particular type of Ashkind. That's the Government line, anyway. The official position is that there are no Gifted Hybrids – but I think we both know that's not true.'

He smiled. His teeth glittered.

'They are magic gone wrong. They are errors in the system. They are mistakes, mutations. Monsters. Even Demons are less feared and more respected than Hybrids.

Demons at least are natural; Demons can be predicted, contained, reasoned with, even if they can't be accepted, but Hybrids . . . no. Demons are Rottweilers, but Hybrids are wolves.'

His tone was flat, sardonic, and his smile was mirthless, but he must *know* what this was doing to her; he must be able to see her hands shaking, must understand that the roaring in her ears was the sound of her world collapsing. She was not brave any more. He continued.

'Something went very badly off-course with the magic of Hybrids, and as a result they live on borrowed time for the rest of their lives. Every six weeks their minds fade, or break, and their bodies twist and they become something . . . else. Something very dangerous. And you can never tell who these people are. You never know. It could be anyone, from the lowest convict . . .'

Silence that dragged behind him, slowing time until the breeze might as well have been moving through oil.

'. . . to a major of the Department,' he whispered, and let it hang.

A long, dizzying darkness. Rose couldn't breathe.

'Tell me, Rosalyn, do you know what happens to people who are interrogated by the Department?'

She made herself speak. It was not easy. 'Yes.'

'Good. You've at least seen an interrogation, then?'

'Yes.'

'If I were caught,' said Arkwood, 'and interrogated, I might be forced to tell the police something. Something about a girl and her father. A secret they've been keeping. A very old secret.'

A sick, swooping feeling crashed through Rose, forcing her to close her eyes and swallow.

Calm, she thought furiously. *Keep calm.*

It did not work. She wanted to run, now. She wanted to kill this man in front of her, to shut him up, to kill their secret with him. She could not do either of these things.

'Rosalyn,' said her captor. 'I don't want to have to say anything to anyone. But if I am caught, I will. Am I understood?'

Rose nodded. She couldn't breathe.

'So it is in your best interests to keep me out of the Department's line of sight.'

Rose did not respond. She heard Arkwood get up and push his chair back.

'There is a warehouse on Uxbridge Road,' Loren Arkwood said. 'Do you know it?'

Rose managed a 'yes'.

'Be there in two days with food and water. I will expect you. And, needless to say, if I read anything about myself in the newspapers, someone will get a little note on their desk about the Elmsworths. Am I clear?'

Rose nodded. She looked up at him. As he was about to leave, something inside her threw caution to the winds. Never mind. What did she have to lose now? How else could he hurt her?

'What were you in the Department cells for?'

Then he looked at her almost mockingly with his steely eyes, halfway out the door.

'Oh, please, Rosalyn. You don't really think you need

to commit a crime to end up out of favour with the Department, do you?'

Then he left. The door swung slowly shut behind him. Rose traced his footsteps out of hearing distance. Then she sank to her knees and sat, shaking, curled up against the wall.

CHAPTER 10

The man who committed the greatest crime in human history was never punished for his actions.

Obviously the Government line was that Ichor brought the Angels into the world and as such he should probably be canonised, minimum – and people like Greenlow, who had been made Gifted by his actions, viewed him as nothing less than a messiah – but the fact remained that without Ichor there would have been no War, and without the War millions of people would still be alive and happy and oblivious to the realities of warfare and grief.

Those six years of war, when most people didn't have access to electricity and pandemics blossomed in the wake of the sudden disappearance of basic sanitation, were down to him. Of course, magic was due to him as well, but then – and this was the issue closest to Rose's heart – so were Hybrids, and it was questionable whether the one was worth the other. Rose herself, who had been found halfway through the War, would probably not have been born without Ichor's crime; although, not knowing the identities of her parents or the circumstances of her conception, she had no way of being certain.

Maybe – and this was an idea she rarely contemplated, except when she was angry at David – her parents had been happy and married and well-off, and had the War not happened she would have grown up safe, with a mother, and a father who didn't have to risk his life to save a city every other weekend, and brothers and sisters; she would have gone to school and had friends who she didn't need to keep secrets from.

In the event, the powers that be never got the chance to decide whether to prosecute Ichor: he was never seen after the Veilbreak, nor was his body ever found. His name became an expletive, used to bless or curse in almost equal measure. He disappeared into legend, and though David always said – in private, of course – that he hoped Ichor had died miserable and in pain and alone in a ditch somewhere for what he'd done, his fate had always been the antithesis to Rose's Department upbringing, and she cherished it now.

Just because you did something terrible, didn't mean you had to burn for it.

The sound of glass shattering came to them as they were walking beside the river, and Rose had to stretch up on her tiptoes to watch the shopfront collapse. The alarm went off almost immediately. The police converged; David moved forward. She didn't know what he intended to do – help, maybe – but she put an arm out to stop him.

'This isn't Department,' she said. 'This is civilian police, remember?'

'I still have authority.'

'They don't *need* your authority. I think it's a kid.'

It was indeed a child: maybe eight or nine years old, screaming, with bright, bloodshot green eyes. The mother watched fearfully as the policeman pulled her daughter away from the broken glass. Children that age were old enough to fear the penalties that came with illegal magical use, but not quite old enough to have full control of their powers, so incidents like this were relatively common.

'Legal age?' asked David, from behind her. He meant 'of responsibility': there had been a recent crackdown on magical use in public, and a few weeks ago the Department had dealt with an eleven-year-old given a two-month custodial sentence in a young offender institution for setting a stack of papers on fire to impress his friends. It hadn't been pleasant. The eleven-year-old had been extremely foul-mouthed.

'Nowhere near. Her parents will get a fine, she'll be okay.'

'They should have taught her better.'

'I think they know that now.'

He made another move forward, but she stopped him again. '*Dad*. If you try to help you'll just end up doing their admin.'

He sighed, but rubbed his hands. 'Let's get to work, shall we?'

He moved off into the crowd towards the Department building. Rose paused before following him, letting the stab of guilt twist in her stomach, letting her heart sink.

She had the terrible suspicion she was going to have to get used to it.

Loren Arkwood was a murderer. This was the conclusion she had come to the previous night, and more than that, she knew the identity of his victim. The timing and details matched too well for it to be otherwise. Here was a recently escaped convict; Gifted, clearly dangerous, and appearing not three days after a suspicious magical death.

Loren Arkwood had murdered Thomas Argent.

She didn't know why, but he had, and in order to prevent him from carrying out his threats – the thought of which still stopped her sleeping – she had to prevent the Department from finding out what he had done.

She thought it best to start small.

'James.'

'Yeah?'

James was at his computer. He looked very tired and distracted. The perfect time to tell him.

'I don't think Argent was murdered.'

'Rose, is this really— You *what?*'

He turned to her, and she spoke very quickly and quietly.

'I don't think Argent was murdered. I think it was an accident, if his Leeching maybe went wrong, if it didn't work properly – he had an argument with his partner the night he died, right? So if he got angry, and all the magic just – just *exploded* out of him . . .'

'Rose—' He looked astonished, half-concentrating. 'That might just work, and Ichor knows we don't want there to be a magical killer, but right now—'

'*No.*'

The whole office went very quiet, the stillness spreading outwards like water, and when there was complete silence David was standing at its centre, utterly oblivious to the reactions of the people around him. He was staring in what could only be fear at the small piece of paper in his hand. This was so uncharacteristic that it took Rose a full five seconds to realise that the whisper had come from him.

James, Terrian and Laura were on their feet.

'What is it? Is it an attack?'

Nate was on the other side of the room; he went immediately to Rose's side. She gripped his hand briefly in thanks before running towards her father. James followed her.

'Is it an attack here?' he asked. 'Are they trying to take the Department? Talk to me! David!'

David was frozen. It took Rose, snapping her fingers in front of his face, to bring him back.

'Yes,' he said. It was almost a breath, a release. He did not look at her. 'Yes. Bomb attack. Croydon.' He went to the camera banks. 'CR2 8YA.'

The machine heard his voice – hoarse, dark, breathless as it was – and immediately each of the sixteen screens filled with CCTV footage. Dense, red-brick buildings, grey windows; a glass shop front, through which empty tables could be glimpsed. A restaurant. It looked uninhabited, but the camera angle was too narrow to be sure. James hovered between Rose and David.

'They're not coming here, then?' he asked, urgent. 'It's not an attack on us?'

David shook his head *no*.

'We'll need at least two police cars,' said Terrian, eyes on the screen. 'Let's say three squad teams, for safety—'

'No,' said David, again.

James, Terrian and Laura stared at him. Rose had retreated beyond disbelief, beyond useless confusion: she was watching her father with her eyes narrowed, trying to read him and to understand. She stayed silent.

'What do you mean *no*?'

'No,' said David, almost robotically, still scanning the screens. No, not *scanning* – scanning implied some kind of active involvement, but what David was doing was different. He watched the screens almost fearfully, his breathing fast enough that Rose knew he was running on adrenaline. He watched warily, but not guardedly. His gaze was that of a man who knew pain was coming, but who could not look away. He watched the screens as a slave watched the whip.

'We're not meant to,' he said.

'What do you mean we're not *meant* to? I don't care what they bloody *mean* us to do! We don't *obey* the criminals!' – this from Terrian, defaulting, as he often did with David, to a position of furious incredulity.

'It's too late,' whispered David. He reached up to touch the screens, his hands shaking – another occurrence without precedent. 'They wouldn't have warned me if there were time.'

Laura, wide-eyed: 'Th— What on *earth*! Are there people in there?'

'I don't know,' said David frantically. 'I can't *see*, they haven't said—'

Terrian dived for the phone, and because he did, he missed the explosion. Two screens went bright-white, as

if the black-and-white footage had no means of transla-
tion. It took a while for the picture to come back, and it
did so only on one screen, the other dissolving to static,
its camera destroyed.

The building was in flames, crumbling into the earth
as if the subject of a single, targeted earthquake. David
touched the screen with his fingertips, tracing it.

'What on *earth*—? Give me that!'

Terrian went for the note in David's hand, and David
darted backwards, agility returning to him at exactly the
wrong moment. Nate, though, who was standing behind
him, wrenched the note from his hand.

David almost – almost – attacked; Rose could see the
possibility of violence spark in his green eyes. He and
Nate stared each other down for a long moment, Nate
half-incredulous but secure in his possession of the moral
high ground. A second of stillness. Then Nate walked
away, and handed the note to his father.

Terrian read it out to the silent office.

'Behold the Interregnum.'

They looked at David. He was slumped against the
computer, eyes half-closed. Rose, finally, went to him,
grasped his hands, tried to get him to react.

'Dad,' she said, and the tone of her voice was a plea,
and clear to the whole office: *you can't lie to* me, *surely;
you wouldn't lie to* me. 'How on earth did you get the
bomb attack and the postcode from that?'

He opened his eyes and looked at her, and for one
bizarre moment she thought she might actually get a
response; and then the note in Terrian's hand caught fire.

Terrian yelled and dropped it, and David turned and watched the flames, raising them with his eyes, and the fire was white hot. They twisted into smoke and were gone as soon as the paper was ash, leaving only a black scorch mark on the carpet.

David looked at the office, the fire bright in his eyes.

'Listen,' he said. 'I know what you must think of these people. I know what they've done. But listen – listen. You don't understand what we're dealing with here. We have to just forget about this. We have to pretend that didn't happen. If we try to attack them, if we provoke them—' He stopped. No one understood, and he knew that, Rose could see it. 'You can't imagine the battles you'll start and the ghosts you'll raise if you try to go after them. Just . . . hope they go away. Just forget about it.'

There was silence, and he roared at the office again: '*Forget!*' and no one responded, not a single word.

CHAPTER 11

There was a discreet camera placed in the top right corner of the second, smaller metal room in the basement of 57 Armitage Crescent. Outside of a prison, this room was one of the most secure in the country; its only serious rival for the position was the one next to it. The walls had built-in metal bars and concrete solid enough to discourage a rhino. There were no windows. The one door had been reinforced to within an inch of its life. It fit exactly into its frame, blocking out any light from outside and ensuring that no sound escaped. To ensure this, it was made almost entirely of industrial-strength steel.

The camera could not see all of this, but it could see what the prison was built to hold. The recording for the twenty-first of February showed Rose kissing her father on the cheek, and then settling down in the corner to wait. He wished her good luck – and it would have taken a good lip-reader to know this, as the camera could not record sound – and left. Rose's eyes followed him to the door. She could hear, although the camera could not, the key turning in the lock. She was locked in until morning; her father had the only key, and this would be placed in the small box in the opposite room, the locking mechanism to which could only be disabled by a human handprint. This kind of caution verged on paranoia, and perhaps it was unnecessary, but it couldn't hurt. That was David Elmsworth's mindset, anyway.

The camera was installed before every transformation. This was an old tradition, dating back to Rose's fourth birthday, when David's life was finally stable and safe enough that he could begin trying to research a cure for their condition. The camera had been their first data set. It was almost always destroyed, but it had become something of a reassurance for the Elmsworths to know that it was there.

There were two other battery-powered devices in the room. One was the torch in the ceiling that provided scant, ghostly light; the other rested in a corner of the room. After her father had gone, Rose turned her gaze towards it. It looked like a blood-pressure reader crossed with a defibrillator, and this more or less corresponded to its function.

After a few seconds, Rose got up and walked across to it. She fit the cuff round her left wrist and pressed a couple of buttons. A glint from the screen showed that the device was firing up.

Rose looked at it bleakly for a few seconds, then pressed her forehead against it. She said something to herself, and it was possible to lip-read this one: *Three. Two. One.*

With her eyes closed, Rose pressed the button with both thumbs. Immediately she cried out, her head jerked back and she stumbled; she was breathing hard, her teeth gritted. After a few seconds she seemed to tense slightly;

she clutched her wrist with her right hand and rocked herself tightly, fearing, apparently, that she would have to electrocute herself again.

Rose could not see it herself, but as the camera scrutinised her, her eyeballs turned white, leaking through the dark green irises and obliterating the pupils.

And then something snapped through her and she fell to her knees.

She lifted her hands to her face. These were the first things that showed: a sleek, drifting kind of darkness, like a deep black gas, that seemed to seep slowly from under her bitten fingernails. Then her dark hair, grown past her shoulders, seemed to harden and solidify into a mass that began to separate itself into spikes.

Rose's last words before the ability to speak was lost to her were – grimly – *Here we go*.

Then she collapsed to all fours. Her torso lengthened, so that the sharp black mass of what was her hair retreated into her head; so that her spine poked, darkening, through her skin into spikes protruding from her back. Her clothes smouldered and caught fire, and tore, crumbling, from her skin; this itself was changing, spreading, blackening, splitting into cracks like the landscape of an ash-covered, wasted desert. Her hands were still visible; these were growing, the palms shrinking, the fingers stretching and lengthening to claws, to talons. The last image the camera captured before the massive blast of energy from the newly transformed monster shorted it out permanently was of the creature rising to its feet. As it did so its legs lengthened, but this was nothing compared to the face. There was still a little of the girl left in it; the skin was still slightly paler than the deep-black, smoking wasteland of the rest, but the humanity was leaving it fast. Those white, animal eyes were still there, but the girl's shape remained; something of the fear still haunted her mouth as the teeth expanded and sharpened to fangs. The creature, or the girl, screamed; it was this roar of triumph and terror that smashed the glass of the camera before it shorted out.

CHAPTER 12

Nate was waiting outside West London Higher Training when Rose arrived. Her father would have loved to come – first day of school, and all of that – but he was in the Department, working on the Argent case. Around the office, the name was increasingly being paired with the word 'accident'. Rose had to remind herself repeatedly that this was what she was working towards. This did not stop the phrase paining her whenever she heard it.

Nate was muttering under his breath as Rose approached. Every few seconds, his eyes flashed and a light or a sputter of flame leapt from his fingertips. The words, Rose knew, were meaningless, but they helped to focus the mind.

'It's okay,' Rose told him, half-amused when he jumped. 'You've passed the Test.'

'Not well, though.'

'Irrelevant. *That* you passed is all that matters.'

Nate looked at her sourly. 'Easy for you to say.'

'You don't even know *how* I passed.'

'I don't need to. It's obvious. You're Rose Elmsworth, aren't you? Your dad trained you.'

'Dad trained you, too.'

'Yeah, but he only taught me how to shoot. He's been teaching you how to fight since you could walk. That's what my dad says, anyway.' Nate hissed as the spark on his fingertips skimmed the patches he hadn't numbed beforehand.

'I wish my dad had trained me,' he added grumpily.

'Your dad was a medic,' Rose said, in a voice she hoped was reassuring. 'Mine was a soldier before they promoted him. Your dad probably couldn't have taught you much.'

Nate gave Rose a look that told her quite clearly that she was being insensitive.

'I mean, maybe he could have,' she said hastily. That look again. She gave up.

'Should we rewind this conversation?'

'Maybe,' said Nate, examining his fingers again, this time to hide a slow darkening spreading over his cheeks, 'but I don't reckon we'll get the chance.'

Silence. Rose looked over her shoulder and saw Maria running towards her. Before she threw herself into Rose's arms and hugged her, Rose just had time to register how strained and tired she looked, how dull her eyes were. As if she had spent a few sleepless nights worrying.

Well, she wasn't alone in that respect.

'Rose!' Maria nearly squealed. Out of the corner of her eye, she saw Nate slink away.

Rose half-laughed. 'Breathe, Maria, breathe.'

'I was so worried!' Maria said breathlessly. 'I didn't see you at the reunion, and I was up all night thinking. I didn't know whether you'd passed, you see . . .'

'Well, I did, it's okay. How was it for you?'

Rose didn't really listen whilst Maria talked and the two of them walked up the steps into the building. She had always found Maria's worries difficult to listen to: they never involved anyone's life being on the line, any real danger or secrecy or stakes. In short, they were trivial, and Rose never had time for trivialities.

Not now that her own worries had become so pressing, anyway.

She tried to find Nate among the small crowd, but he was nowhere to be seen. She did, however, spot Tristan and his friend Luke Raleigh talking as they slipped through the doors. Rose tried to crouch lower. Tristan was perhaps the last thing she needed right now.

The hall was crowded with old students as well as new. Some of them Rose remembered by name: Samantha Naismith, Marion Weller. Some faces she recognised. Some she—

Oh, no.

'Rose!' Maria whispered to her. There was a half-giggly aspect to her voice that Rose knew, and feared, all too well. 'Look – it's Aaron!'

It was indeed Aaron Greenlow. Rose generally tried to avoid 'the conundrums of adolescence', as David put it, but even she was prey to the whims of hormones, and as a result she had had a crush on Aaron since she was thirteen. Rose wished it would go away; it was usually her who did the teasing about Maria's many crushes, and having the tables turned on her was a rather uncomfortable feeling, especially as Maria never hesitated to take advantage of it.

'Do you still like him?'

'Keep your voice down.'

'Do you, though?'

Aaron, who was tall, emerald-eyed, dark-haired and very good-looking, caught sight of them and smiled amiably. Rose ducked her head, blushing. Maria giggled rather triumphantly.

'He's only a year older than us, you know,' she said as he turned the corner into the Chemistry corridor. 'You could ask him out. He might—'

'No, Maria. Will you stop trying to set us up, okay?'

Rose may have said it with slightly more vehemence than absolutely necessary, for Maria seemed affronted.

'Well, all right then,' she said huffily. 'You need to let yourself go a bit, Rose.'

'I need to do no such thing,' Rose said through gritted teeth, and slunk away irritably through the crowd towards the opposite side of the hall.

They called people by letter, twenty-six at a time, to talk to their Administrator. When the Es came up, Rose remembered Serena Mitchell, and slipped over to someone who looked vaguely responsible to ask for her. She was directed through a slim door behind the stage to a long corridor with mahogany doors, white name-plates hammered to them. Rose found Mitchell's and knocked tentatively on it.

There was a curt 'Come in'.

Rose opened the door and stepped inside. It looked like an odd kind of classroom, with only two desks and two chairs – one for the teacher and one for the single pupil. One-on-one teaching.

Serena Mitchell was sitting at one of the desks. She smiled thinly as Rose came in.

'I wanted to talk to you about your subject choices,' she said.

Rose had filed them that weekend. This was misleading, because she had *made* them years ago: Maths, Physics, Combat, Healing, Art and Magical Skills offered the well-rounded CV needed for any chance of admission to the Department.

'I am absolutely certain of them,' Rose told her. 'I know what I want to study.'

'Weaponry is a very popular subject. Everyone who takes it speaks of it very well. Are you sure . . .'

'Very sure, Miss Mitchell.'

'Serena, please.'

Rose paused for a second, and then leaned back in her chair. For a split second, the person sitting in front of her had blond hair and cold yellow-green eyes and an Icarus gun in their back pocket. And then it was gone and Rose shook herself, told herself to focus. It did not quite work.

'Serena,' she said, 'I am not joining the army. Nor will I ever. And I already know how to fire a gun. You've seen that yourself.'

'Yes,' Mitchell said, with equal firmness, 'but you have great potential as a soldier, Rose.'

Rose said nothing. She could cope with their trying to 'keep her on the straight and narrow', she could even cope with them monitoring her – insofar as she knew she could evade their surveillance – but this was a choice she would not allow them to make.

Mitchell said nothing more about it, but the set of her mouth made Rose suspect this was not the end.

'Art?' she asked. 'I wouldn't have thought you were the artistic type.'

'Normally, no,' Rose said, 'but I'd like to study how to use magic to make beautiful things. I thought that logically there should be a positive aspect to it.'

Mitchell narrowed her eyes, but let it drop.

'And Physics.'

'Is that a questionable decision?'

Mitchell didn't say anything. Then: 'Rosalyn' – Rose noted the slip back into her full name – 'what do you want to be when you grow older?'

Grow 'older', instead of 'grow up'. They really were trying very hard not to be patronising. They didn't quite pull it off, but Rose appreciated the effort.

'I'm going to be a detective for the Department,' she said.

Serena raised both eyebrows now.

'The Department? You do realise how high their standards are, Rosalyn?'

'I am aware of their standard of acceptance,' Rose said evenly. She was worried about where this conversation was going, so before Mitchell could respond, she asked acidly, 'What did you want to be, when you were my age?'

Mitchell raised her eyebrows. 'When I was your age,' she said, 'there were no Angels.'

Rose resisted the urge to say 'so what?', but Mitchell could see the lack of interest in her face and seemed to snap. 'As it happens,' she said, 'in my early career, I worked for the ACC.'

Rose's blood went very cold. The ACC were the

Anti-Corruption Commission, known to the Department as the Supergrass: their objective was to make sure no Government department considered themselves above the law. Since the Department's operations *relied* on their being above risk of prosecution, the two bureaux were natural and mortal enemies. If Serena had Supergrass history, she should never have been allowed to deal with Rose outside of the Department; that she had been allowed was telling – someone as high-up as the Testing Administrator would only report directly to Parliament – and also meant that those reports would be anything but objective.

Mitchell smiled at the look on Rose's face.

'Your first lesson is in Room Twenty-One,' she said. 'Best of luck.'

Room Twenty-One was in the Combat Area, a huge central building made of whitewashed brick built around a stone courtyard. There were sixteen- and seventeen-year-olds fighting with magic in the courtyard: advanced Combat students training for the army, no doubt. As Rose watched, one of them was thrown six feet backwards into the air, stopped from hitting the stone wall only by her own quick thinking and what seemed to Rose to be a dangerous amount of luck. The stone floor was scored with black scorch marks, some of them inches deep, and ominous red-brown splatters here and there, like irregularly placed floor tiles.

Room Twenty-One itself, however, looked friendlier. The walls were painted a clean, fresh white, and the floor was covered in crash mats. One area of it – a stage, no doubt – was raised slightly. The room was large enough for a class of about twenty to huddle in the corner, and so they did, looking slightly shell-shocked. Tristan and his friend Luke Raleigh were there, to Rose's disappointment, but also Maria, and for some reason, Nate, who seemed more cheerful than he had outside. Perhaps this was because he was chatting to Maria. As Rose watched, she laughed at a joke Nate had told, making him smile so brightly that Rose almost thought his face would split.

She tried to slink away and give them some privacy – this was a situation she had no idea how to navigate – but Maria called, 'Hey, Rose!' before she could get out of their sight. Reluctantly, Rose joined them. Nate grinned at her. He looked almost drunk. Rose had to try very hard to keep a straight face.

'What subjects did you choose?' Maria asked her.

In the ensuing conversation, it turned out that both Nate and Maria had chosen Healing; Rose knew that Maria had only ever wanted to be a doctor, and as for Nate, his father's history as a medic meant that he knew almost as much about the subject as Rose did about Combat. Their choices meant that, because of the compulsories, Rose would probably have five classes with each of them, and four when all three of them would be together. The phrase 'third wheel' kept popping up with unrelenting frequency in Rose's mind. She dismissed it irritably before it could stick.

They were discussing the benefits of Craftsmanship versus Physics – at least Rose and Maria were; Nate spent a lot of the time staring at Maria with a dreamy smile on his face, looking as if the merest of cognitive processes was far beyond him – when someone fired a gun directly behind them. Nate and Rose, being accustomed to this kind of thing due to David's weaponry training, were the only ones who didn't jump or scream.

The man standing in the doorway clicked the safety back on again and strode into the room. For the second time that day, Rose saw, instead of a short, twenty-something man with thick brown hair, a cold-faced soldier with steely eyes and the power to bring her life crashing down around her. And then it was gone.

The teacher pointed to Rose and Nate. 'You two. Come here.'

The two of them looked at each other. Nate was alert now. Together, they walked forward.

'Stand here,' the teacher said. He indicated two spots on crash mats either side of him. Nate and Rose took them.

'Why didn't you react?' he asked them.

Nate opened and closed his mouth like a goldfish. Rose, feeling as if she had to do something, said, 'We've already been trained in how to use a gun, sir, we're . . . used to hearing gunshots.'

'*Sir,*' said the man, tasting the word almost mockingly. 'Yes, you must be.'

There was a silence. The whole class looked between Nate, Rose and the teacher as if watching a three-way tennis match. Out of the corner of her eye, Rose could see Maria looking at her incredulously, mouthing *Used to gunshots?* Ah, well. It had to come out eventually.

'And how have you come to be "used to gunshots?"
Guns are illegal weapons.'

'If you don't have a licence for them, yes,' Rose said.

The teacher stared at her coldly for a few seconds.

'Who trained you?'

Nate reacted first this time, seemingly eager to get a
word in. 'Our fathers work for the Department, sir.'

'The Department?' The teacher looked between them
in surprise. 'Who?'

'My father's Connor Terrian, sir.'

'Never heard of him.' Thank the Angels, the teacher
knew better than to ask what he did. 'And yours, girl?'

Rose considered lying, but decided it was hopeless: it
would be easy for a teacher to find out who she was using
registry databases, so deceit would only get her punished.

'David Elmsworth, sir.'

The teacher stopped. He turned to Rose, giving her his
full attention for the first time. His reaction sent the name
David Elmsworth rippling back through the class. None
of them knew what it meant, of course, but Rose could
feel the name gathering sinister connotations with every
repetition.

She heard Maria whisper, shocked, 'Your dad works
for the *Department*? You never told me that!'

'You're David Elmsworth's daughter?' the teacher
asked. There was something in his voice – wariness, maybe
– that Rose wasn't quite sure she liked.

'Yes, sir.'

'Can you fight?'

'Of course,' said Rose, almost incredulously. And then,

before the teacher could react, she caught herself: 'Sir.'

He gave her a long, dark, searching look. Just when Rose thought she was going to have to tell her father that she'd earned herself a detention on her first day at school, he turned away from her, and pointed to a boy at the front of the crowd. 'You, boy. Swap with . . . what's your first name?'

'Nathaniel, sir.'

'Swap with Nathaniel, then.'

Nate retreated to Maria's side with obvious relief. The boy took his place on the crash mat. Trepidation showed on his face. Rose, who could see what was coming, sized him up mentally. She thought she could probably take him, even though a male of her age or older was never an ideal opponent: only the best combat training could overcome simple gender differences when the opponent was reasonably skilled, and David always said it was arrogant to assume he had given her that. The boy was not too strong, a couple of inches shorter than her, odds-on no hand-to-hand combat training. He was scared, too, which helped.

'You two. Fight. No magic. First with a significant advantage wins.'

The boy's eyes widened in shock. He didn't protest, though. All credit to him for that.

Rose took him out in three moves. This was the first time her fighting skills had ever meant anything outside of the Department, and she couldn't help revelling in it slightly. She tried to achieve a natural-looking balance between 'being impressive' and 'showing off', but she wasn't sure she managed it.

The boy, whose name Rose remembered vaguely as Albert, moved first. Right hook to the head. Rose could have just caught the fist and pulled him into a half-nelson, but she reckoned she should at least give him a chance, so she stepped back, waited until he swung off-balance, then kicked him in the stomach.

The class gasped with him.

Winded, Albert stumbled backwards. Rose moved forward and hooked her foot round his ankles, sweeping his feet out from under him. As he fell, she put an arm to his back and another to his throat, pulling his head back. If she had had a knife, he would have been dead.

The class stared at her. Nate, who had fought against her many times, muttered, half-resentfully, half-amusedly, 'show-off.' Maria's mouth had fallen open.

Rose looked at the teacher, who nodded. She stepped back, releasing Albert.

A pause. Rose felt uncomfortably that she was being examined.

'And your father taught you to do that, did he?' asked the teacher.

'Mostly, yes. I credit myself with some initiative, though.' Another pause, and then, before she could be subjected to his stare again, she turned towards him.

'I'm Rose,' she said. 'To those who don't hate me.'

The teacher looked at her.

'Okay,' he said thoughtfully. 'Rose.'

CHAPTER 13

The Tube to Uxbridge Road was severely delayed, so Rose had to take the bus. At Shepherd's Bush they changed drivers, and Rose, unable to stand the heat and the noise any longer, slipped out there and walked. It wasn't far, anyway, and walking allowed her to think.

After her introduction, the teacher had brought – or dragged, in some cases – other pairs onto the crash mats to fight. Rose had been able to tell from this that she was easily the best fighter in her class, at least non-magically. She was followed closely by Nate, of course, and then, surprisingly, by Tristan Greenlow, who fought with a skill and ease she would not have expected from someone who didn't even know how to fire a gun. Even with her own training, Rose could tell that she would struggle to beat him: he was a boy, taller and stronger than her and he had probably been taught how to fight. But the tables might turn after they were allowed to use magic.

Rose pressed her fingertips to her temples and leaned back against the fence for a moment. Then she forced herself to keep moving. She should probably be glad the Tube was down, anyway; it gave her an excuse for arriving home late.

Today was the day she had to meet Loren Arkwood again.

She didn't think that he would physically hurt her. That would be pointless, after all. But still, she didn't want to spend any more time around him than was absolutely necessary.

The fact was that she was more scared of him than anyone or anything she had ever met. Not the madman who had shot James, not even the thing she became during her transformation. No: Loren Arkwood scared her more than any of them.

And the reason? Well, that was obvious. Loren Arkwood wasn't simply threatening her. He was threatening her father.

The warehouse was tucked away in a corner of the road; a squat, hulking, squalid place that no one on the council had got round to demolishing yet. There was one usable entrance: the back door. It had been left very slightly ajar. Rose pushed it open, spreading a shaft of light along the wall. She closed it behind her, wincing at the encroaching shadows.

The warehouse had been a DIY shop before the Veilbreak, but in the War years it had been coverted into an army stronghold for the Ashkind. It was actually a very good base. The place was laced with shelves, turning it into a maze that you could easily lose an enemy in. In the back corner was a forklift truck, the inside of which had been covered in blankets, and nearly all of the doors were locked and boarded up.

Rose was about to move when she felt something cold and hard pressed to the back of her head. She froze.

'Bag?' he asked. She gave it to him. Behind her, she felt

him rifling through it. For a second, Rose deliberated over whether to attack him while he was distracted, but gave it up. *Rule number one: never start a fight you cannot win.*

She thought for a second, and then stepped away from him. He dropped the aluminium can he had been pressing against her head without looking at her and, after a short pause, threw her bag back at her. He then sat down against the wall and started to eat. Rose noticed a long, white scar along the back of his left hand.

'So,' he said, through a mouthful of chicken leg, 'you made the smart decision.'

Rose waited for him to elaborate. She noticed, again, how abnormally sharp his teeth looked.

'Not to try to kill me,' he explained. She nodded. He looked cleaner, somehow younger than he had two days ago, and almost human with it. 'Unless you've poisoned this.' He gestured to the food.

'No,' she said, 'I haven't.' He looked tired and dirty, almost helpless. Or, at the very least, like someone in need of help. She didn't like that, somehow.

'Where have you come from?'

'School.'

'Your first day?'

'Yes.'

'You're very monosyllabic, aren't you?'

'Wouldn't you be?'

He looked at her oddly, as if he were trying to see past her. 'You weren't the last time.'

Rose said nothing to this. A few seconds' silence.

Friendly as he seemed, that did not change the fact that Rose did not want to be here. She had lied to herself: this place really did scare her.

He looked up at her. 'You can use magic against me, you know.'

'I'm sorry?'

'You have the advantage of magic,' he said, with a grin she didn't like. 'I'm weak. I'm practically Pretender as it is,' no bitterness in his voice at all, 'and even without that limitation, I don't have the energy. Opening a tin would finish me off by this point. You could use magic and I wouldn't see it coming at all.'

There was no response to this. He got to his feet, brushing himself off.

'Come on, you're Elmsworth's kid. What did he teach you about magic?'

She answered warily. It was almost physically painful to tell this man anything valuable.

'Magic is a weakness.'

'Go on.'

An even longer pause. What was this?

'Magic is a double-edged sword. It gives you the ability to use energy from your own blood, your own bones. It's an ability you don't need, and you should never use it in a fight, except as a last resort. If you come to rely on it, you can overuse it, and you can kill yourself just as easily as your enemy. Guns are easier. Guns should be your first port of call.' She watched him apprehensively. 'Is that enough?'

His grin widened. 'So why aren't you using magic against me now? It wouldn't take much to kill me.'

She said nothing.

'Is it because you're not a killer? We both know that's not true.'

She flinched, physically *flinched,* and a hatred stronger than anything she had ever known – a hatred stronger than conscious love – welled up in her, and a window in the corner shattered, exploding outwards into shards. He looked at it, raising his eyebrows. She fought not to bare her teeth at him.

'Can I go now?' she asked softly.

His expression changed, became more sober, as if he realised he'd crossed some sort of line. 'Yes. Come back in two days with more food. And some water.'

'Okay.'

She was about to step out the door when a reckless part of her made her turn back. She said, 'The Department thinks that Thomas Argent's death was accidental.'

'Do they?'

He seemed almost uninterested, and perhaps it would have worked had his muscles not tightened slightly at the mention of Argent's name.

And she wasn't sure whether that made it easier to hate him or harder.

He said nothing else after that. After a few seconds Rose left, closing the door behind her.

And, to her intense relief, that was it.

CHAPTER 14

The next three months passed easily for Rose. School settled into a gentle ebb and flow, and her days acquired the pleasant familiarity that only routine could bring. Artistic Studies became her favourite lesson; she showed no skill with Healing at all, however, and when she slipped off into other worlds – usually the main office of the fifth floor of the Department – she had to rely on Maria to bring her up to date.

Maria, for her part, never seemed to mind. There was no malice in her satisfaction, but nevertheless, Rose knew that she was pleased to have found a subject in which she surpassed Rose at every turn. It didn't really matter, anyway, about how good she was at Healing; Maria was going to be a doctor for her national service, and as for Rose . . .

She saw Serena Mitchell quite often now. Every time she was asked – and Serena asked her a lot – about her future career, she reiterated that she was not, repeat not, going to go into the army; but every time she gave the answer, it seemed to mean less and less. Combat lessons were progressing so well that she was beginning to doubt the matter would be left up to her. If Serena Mitchell decided to take matters into her own hands, and it was beyond doubt that she could, Rose wouldn't be able to stop her. This worried her. It worried David, too.

But there was really nothing she could do now: her Combat teacher, having identified her as top of the class, continually used her for demonstrations. She had never lost a fight, not even – as her skills improved – against Tristan, whose resentment towards her was beginning to show outside of the classroom. He and Luke were often to be found in a corner muttering darkly and throwing nasty looks in Rose's direction.

As for Nate, his nervousness around Maria had settled into something approaching normality. He still stuttered more than normal when talking to her, but despite this, the same dreamy look that entered his eyes when he talked about her had begun to gleam in Maria's when she spoke of him. And she spoke of him a lot. The fact that they were always each other's favourite topic made Rose value her life in the Department even more, as, even when Nate was there, it was the one place where his conversation was guaranteed to be Maria-free.

The shock of Argent's murder had died down now. Nearly everyone in the Department talked about it as an accidental death. Even the coroner admitted that the story was more probable than murder, which Rose took as a personal achievement. Rose began to suspect that her plan had only come off as well as it had by virtue of the fact that no one – not even her father – really wanted to think that there was a brutal Gifted murderer somewhere out there.

She saw Loren Arkwood twice a week now. Their meetings only lasted five minutes or so, however long it took to give him the food and get out. Loren, however, seemed strangely talkative. He had never repeated his threat to tell the Department of her Hybrid status, which was a blessing, although she didn't doubt he'd carry it out if he had to.

It had become difficult to find food for him after a week or so, without letting her father or the school become suspicious, so she had taken to intercepting food packages from the Department military canteen. This warehouse was technically under Government jurisdiction, so she'd 3D-printed the keys off from the office database. The excuse she gave herself for all this was very simple: the Department was the reason she was being targeted in the first place, so she may as well use the advantages that came with it.

She told herself that repeatedly.

After a mere three weeks, she broke her pledge not to let his use of the name Rosalyn annoy her. An unforgivable lapse.

'Why?' he had asked. 'What's wrong with Rosalyn?'

'It's horrible,' she'd told him. 'It sounds like an eighteenth-century countess. Dad's only bad parenting decision.'

And he had laughed. He had a deep, ringing, happy laugh; it was almost infectious. Even Rose had smiled. She thought he might be beginning to like her. He didn't really have much choice in the matter – she was his only company, after all.

Christ.

'I know the feeling,' he had said. 'My prison guards called me '*Laur*en' for the first two weeks I was there. It was almost more humiliating than anything else.'

That week, to try to cut this whole thing off at the knees, she decided to ask him.

When she came with food, he was expecting her. She had got him a book, at his own request: *Firestarter*, a pre-War novel that her dad had always liked. He was immersed in it when she came. She put the plastic bags in a corner and then, hesitantly, stood in front of him, waiting.

After a few seconds he looked up at her in mild surprise. 'Rose. Hello.'

Hearing that name in his voice was almost painful. She should never have told him. He went back to his book – this was the quietest he'd been in weeks – but when she didn't move he looked back up at her, eyebrows raised.

'Yes? Is there anything wrong?'

'No. I wanted to ask you something.'

Now he put the book down; now he was interested. He stood up.

'Why? Usually you run away like I'm going to shoot you.'

'I do always consider that a possibility.'

That laugh again.

'Did I make that bad a first impression?'

'You made a pretty good threat.'

'Then it was a better plan than I gave myself credit for. You said you had a question?'

'I have two.'

He breathed out, raising his eyebrows. 'Blimey. I didn't know you had it in you to be so curious.'

She paused, looking at him.

'Fire away,' he said.

'How do you know my father?'

'Ask him.'

'Oh, come on. That's not an answer.'

'Believe me, you don't want to hear the answer from anyone but him. It doesn't paint either of us in a very flattering light.'

Rose hesitated. There was a sarcastic remark on her lips in the wake of this comment – something about the extremely unflattering light in which his actions had already caused him to be painted – and she came so unnervingly, stupidly close to actually saying it that she moved on quickly.

'Fine. How did you end up in prison?'

'Too long a story.'

'Okay. Did you—'

'No.' Arkwood held up a finger, smiling. 'Two questions, you said.'

'You haven't answered either of them!'

Arkwood raised an eyebrow. Rose deeply resented the way this made her feel like a teacher was threatening her with detention, but did not push it. When nothing else was said, he sat down again and went back to his book. Rose took this as a sign that the conversation was over.

But something rebellious and reckless in her thought: *No. No. I am at least going to get a grip on this situation.*

Halfway to the door, she turned.

'Who did the Department kill?'

Arkwood looked up at her.

137

'What do you mean?'

The reply was too sharp, too quick: verification, and he knew it.

He opened his mouth, and then closed it again. Abruptly he reached round to the back of his neck, fumbled with something, and then threw a silvery gleam in her direction. She caught it, taken aback. It was a locket; not elaborate, but beautiful in its mere simplicity.

'The only thing your Department team didn't take off me,' he said gruffly. Rose didn't like the way he said 'your'; it was sardonic, almost accusatory. 'Open it.'

Rose did. Inside was a tiny picture of two people, sitting on a bench in a park in the beginnings of spring. One was a tall, dark-haired woman in her late twenties or early thirties, with a warm smile and steely grey-black eyes. Sitting on her lap was a little girl, maybe four or five years old, no more. She had hair like her mother's, wavy and cut at the chin, Demon-black eyes, and a look about her pale face that suggested a happy kind of innocence. Rose could see Arkwood in the shape of her eyes and her smile. Rose looked up at him. He was watching her as if not quite sure what to expect.

'Your wife?' she asked.

'My sister. And her daughter. Rayna went abroad after the War; she needed to get away from it all. She was happy there for a few years, but then she fell in love and got pregnant and the father, piece of scum that he was, ran away as soon as he found out. So she came to my flat in London, with no money and a baby on the way. Of course, I took her in. She got a job as a teacher and we raised the child together. I've always been a father to her, always been there for her . . . I suppose David would have taught you the same things.'

'What things?'

'You know,' he said tiredly. 'That blood doesn't matter. That just because he's not technically related to you doesn't mean he's not your fa— Oh, hell.' He looked up at her in horror. 'You do *know* you're adopted, don't you? I haven't just—'

She nearly smiled. 'No, it's all right. I know.'

'How long?'

'Since I was five. But don't try to change the subject – this is your story, not mine.'

He sighed. Rose waited. Somewhere outside, an ambulance sped, wailing, past them.

'Tabitha was like you,' he said, 'a forbidden thing. She was a magical Demon. She was Ashkind, she had the dark eyes and everything – but she had magic.'

'That's impossible,' Rose said automatically, and then fell silent at the look he gave her.

'You're telling me,' he said. 'I used to teach her, at home, as she got older and her powers started to show. Instilled something of a complex in her. Taught her never to do what she could do, not ever . . . I knew if I showed her I was Gifted, did magic in front of her, it would encourage her. The day I broke out of that cell was the first time I'd used magic in five years.'

His voice trembled slightly. It was unnerving.

'That picture,' he said, without looking at her, 'is two or three years out of date, but it's the best one I have.

Five months ago, they stormed our house. Someone must have found out about Tabitha. I don't know how. Your Department attacked us,' he said, and this time there was definite accusation in his tone, 'squad team of six. Outnumbered us three to one. We never stood a chance. I fought; they knocked me out before I could do much damage. They had to go through Rayna to get to Tabitha, though. They shot her in the chest. I was awake to see her die.'

Rose closed her eyes and snapped the locket shut. She'd never been on a search-and-requisition before; she had no idea the Department targeted children. *Naïve*, she thought angrily. *You're a Department kid. You shouldn't be shocked by now. These things have to be done.*

But still a part of her thought, *an eight-year-old girl . . .*

'I don't know where she's kept now,' Arkwood said. 'They'll be trying to get her into psychotherapy, I expect, to find out what she is, how she can do what she can do.'

Rose asked quietly, 'How did you escape?'

For a second she thought he wasn't going to answer.

'After a while in the experimental ward,' he said, 'I had just enough magic to stop my own heart. They thought I was dead, put me in the morgue, and I had enough residual electricity to magically restart my heart. They still haven't realised there's no body, apparently.'

Rose did not bother telling him it was impossible to trick the sensors like that – clearly such mundane obstacles as impossibilities did not factor into this story. Loren seemed to be in the middle of some kind of internal collapse: he said 'She—', as a choke, and then stopped. There was a long moment where the story hung there, like darkness, like a gathering storm, and suddenly he was on his feet.

'How do you live with yourself?'

'What?'

He stepped closer to her, teeth bared, fury showing in his face. 'You in your offices, with your computers and your soldiers, ordering people's deaths! The lot of you. *How do you live with yourself?*'

Rose stood her ground, shaking. 'We do what we have to do.'

'Don't you *dare!*' His rage was palpable; Rose refused to call it frightening. 'Rayna is *dead!*' The words seemed to rip from him, leaving him raw and wounded, but his momentum pulled him onwards. 'Was she for your greater good? Was *she* worth it?'

Rose stepped back.

'The people we fight are worse.'

He looked at her blindly. Then, slowly, he walked away from her and sat down again.

'You disgust me,' he said flatly. She said nothing, and then, in a spurt of idiotic, spiteful courage:

'You were a soldier, weren't you? In the War? You've done worse than I have. At least *we're* not vigilante.'

'That doesn't make you good.'

A pause. He left her in silence, and after a while she walked to the door as calmly as she could.

She broke into a sprint once she was out of sight.

CHAPTER 15

Hypothesis one: The Department were the good guys.

Obviously true. Of course it was true. It had to be. Not everything they did would be considered moral, or any of that, but sometimes you had to fight fire with fire, and the blaze they were up against would burn down the city in an instant if they only stuck to methods that would be unanimously passed by a civilian ethics committee.

Hypothesis two: Loren Arkwood was a bad guy.

That felt wrong, somehow. Sinister and insensitive though he was, and even knowing about Rose what he knew, he was fighting for a loved one. Why should he care what he had to do to Rose to get to his niece?

Hypothesis three: Tabitha Arkwood was a magical Demon.

A different Rose – a pre-Arkwood Rose – would have said it was clearly false: by their very definition, Ashkind, even Demons, could not do magic. But, of course, civilised, intelligent Hybrids were impossible as well, and it was completely beyond the realms of credulity to suggest that one could work for the Department unnoticed for fourteen years.

So it came down to whether she believed Loren or not. And she did. His story made *sense,* in a twisted kind of way. It explained him: his presence, and his actions. It explained why he came after Rose, the daughter of the Head of the Department. It explained Argent's death.

And the anguish in his eyes had not been feigned. He was telling the truth. A terrible truth. An impossible truth.

But truth nonetheless.

Hypothesis four: The Department was secretly requisitioning magical Demons, even *children*, and taking them into indefinite custody.

Tabitha couldn't possibly be the only one. There had to be more. Logically. And so, logically, the Department must be requisitioning them. Obviously they would. Their objective was to keep the peace, and what could be more damaging to the peace than finding out the laws of magic had been suddenly and irrevocably broken? It would be like finding places where gravity suddenly didn't work.

So yes, it would make logical sense for the Department to be taking magical Demons. But there was one thing standing in the way of logic.

If the Department *were* taking children, David would have to have authorised it.

Which was impossible.

CHAPTER 16

That Saturday, Rose's father didn't go into the office. It was the weekend, after all, and he was exhausted. She ignored his regular protestations that he could cope on his own, and that she should get out of the house and go somewhere with Maria 'or something'.

'Dad,' she told him firmly, the fifth or sixth time he did this, 'please, save your breath. I am staying here. I've got maths homework I need to do anyway.'

This was a lie, but the idea that she actually needed to be here, and that he was not the one tying her down, shut him up.

James called in at about eight o'clock. David had wired up their TV to act as an emergency video interface, and they were halfway through the news headlines when James's face flickered onto the screen. He looked desperate. David and Rose immediately sat up, alert.

'David, what's up with you? I emailed you half a dozen times already. We need you in here.'

'Oh, for God's sake,' said David wearily, sitting up. 'It's *Saturday*.'

'Not any more,' James said grimly. 'We've had a breakthrough.'

'What do you mean?'

James was tapping his leg restlessly against the ground; she could tell from the way the camera trembled. 'They were due to burn a load of preserved bodies today,' he said. 'They were being cremated, you know, and protocol dictates you have to tally up the bodies with the list of the dead-in-custody to make sure they match, and today a name came up that shouldn't have.'

'Sylvia Argent was buried, not cremated.'

'It wasn't her.'

Rose looked between them. 'Why would Sylvia Argent come up on a list of the dead-in-custody?'

David put his head in his hands.

'Dad,' Rose said wearily, 'what haven't you told me?'

David looked at her. 'Sylvia Argent died in rewrite therapy three months ago,' he said quietly. 'I'm sorry, Rose.'

'Why? How did she die?'

'Poison,' said James. 'Professional job. She must have had criminal connections.'

'She must have,' David said darkly.

Rose remembered something and turned to her father in horror. 'But she was going to have a *kid*—'

'They got the baby out by Caesarean just after Sylvia stopped breathing. He's been adopted by a foster family, we check up on him regularly.'

Rose put her hands over her face and breathed in. 'And you didn't tell me because . . .'

'She died on the day of your Test,' David said. 'We thought it was probably more than you needed.' He turned back to James. 'Presumably, though, there was another name.'

It hit Rose a fraction of a second before James spoke. 'Yes,' he said. 'Loren Arkwood.'

David stood up suddenly. Rose just managed to keep her face clear of emotion and so her reaction was translated into a wave of sickening, tearing shock that crashed through her body.

'Who's Loren Arkwood?' she asked, trying not to sound too forced.

'I knew him from the War,' David said, still staring at James. 'For a while, I even thought we were friends . . . We took him into custody on criminal grounds.'

Criminal grounds. *What criminal grounds?* Rose thought angrily. *On charges of fighting for his kid, is that it? On being there when you killed his sister?*

She stopped, and had to remind herself irritably whose side she was on.

'I looked at the records,' James continued. 'He showed negative life signs, no heartbeat, flat brainwaves . . . he must have managed to fake his own death somehow. I have no idea how. But he's not on the records of cremation. The body is gone. And a few days after he escaped, we find Argent dead, and it turns out Argent was on the team that took him in. . . You were wrong, Rose. Thomas Argent was murdered. And what's more, he has an accomplice.'

James leaned back in his chair and surveyed them briefly. It occurred to Rose how tired he looked. He took a deep breath.

'Someone in the Department is helping him,' he said. Thank the Angels that Rose had David's shock reactions: she stayed very still, absolutely motionless, until the foundations of her world settled themselves again.

David said, 'No.' No emotion, not yet.

'I'm sorry, but it has to be true. It all fits, all of it. There's been food stolen, keys . . .'

You, Rose told herself, *are the most careless, idiotic, clumsy, selfish moron ever to walk the earth.*

'You've notified Parliament?' David asked, very quietly.

'Terrian did. They've told us to keep it quiet from the press. There's going to have to be check-ups on all of us, David, even you and Rose. And if it turns out there is a mole, under our noses—'

'I will kill them,' said David, and Rose had to pinch the inside of her wrist very hard to keep herself straight-faced and unreactive.

James raised his eyebrows.

'We're coming,' David said, and went to get his shoes.

'No, Dad, please,' Rose said quietly. 'Not on this one. I can't . . . I can't show my face in the office again for a while. I told them Argent's death was accidental, remember. I messed this one up.'

David looked at her searchingly for a few seconds, then nodded. 'Okay. You can look after yourself for an evening, then? I probably won't be back until ten or eleven.'

'Yeah,' Rose said shortly. 'Good luck.'

It was near quarter-to-nine by the time Rose got to Uxbridge Road, and even in the thickening clutches of late spring, it was dark. Rose let herself into the warehouse near-silently. She almost couldn't bear to hold the key, the bloody traitorous idiotic—

I'm sorry, who's being idiotic here?

She hesitated before she whispered into the darkness. 'Loren . . .'

There was an immediate rustle and a bleary, surprised 'Rose?'

'Get your stuff,' she said. 'You're not coming back here. Please, just do what I say, this once. Five minutes, outside.'

She ran before he could ask questions. He was out in two minutes with the bags containing the remaining food, the clothes and the book.

'What is it?'

She ducked into an alleyway. He followed.

'Rose,' he said urgently. 'I need answers here.'

She asked him straight. 'Did you or did you not kill Sylvia Argent?'

'I don't even know who that is.'

'No, please. She was the sister of Thomas Argent. *Did you kill her?*'

'What? No! Come on, Rose, give me some credit. Please, just tell me what's going on!'

Rose took a deep breath. 'They know you're alive. They think you killed Thomas and Sylvia Argent, which is a reasonable assumption, and—'

'How—'

'No, please, let me speak. Loren, I want you to know this wasn't me. I didn't tell them. And they know—' She swallowed. 'They know you're working with someone in the Department. It's . . . I won't say a matter of time, but . . . They're looking for traitors, in the Department, and they'll come to our house and— Anyway. This *was not me.*'

Loren looked at her in amazement. 'I believe you,' he said softly. He swallowed. 'Where are we going?'

'I don't know!' whispered Rose, desperately. 'I didn't see this coming, did I?'

He looked up at the sky suddenly, and Rose saw something dark enter his eyes.

'I know,' he said.

'What?' said Rose warily. She'd been around him too long not to step away.

'I know where we should go,' he said. He wasn't looking at her, but deep into the darkness. Without warning, he slipped backwards, into the shadows.

Rose waited.

He stepped back again, impatient. 'Come on.'

'I'm sorry, who on earth do you think I am? I'm not just going to follow you blindly through London. You tell me what crap you have planned and I decide whether I want to put up with it.'

He stood straighter. 'I don't mean that. If you don't come with me I will *make* you.'

'Oh will you?' She was sick of this. She should have stood up for herself months ago. 'With your fighting and your soldier's training that you haven't used since the end of the War?'

'You think I'm *harmless?*' He was snarling. 'I killed one of your precious Department soldiers. I killed Thomas Argent. I made him *scream* as he died.'

'He was off-guard and he was stupid. You try to get

any closer to me than you are now and I'll use magic to keep you back, and then the alarms will go off and the police will come here, and *then* you'll be in trouble.'

He was sneering. 'You think you're so clever, don't you?'

'You set low standards.'

He moved forward suddenly. Rose didn't know what he was going to do – hit her? Surely not – and she never found out, because his bag jerked forward with his movement and two large, metal, rattling things spilled out onto the pavement.

They stared at them, and Loren looked at Rose.

'They're guns,' he said calmly, as if daring her to not to recognise them, and then: 'I was hoping you could help me—'

'*No.*' She didn't mean to say it, but so strong was her shock and outrage and fury that it burst out without her intention, and after that there was no going back: 'You want me to help you *kill* someone?'

He nodded. 'Someone on Argent's team. One of the people who killed my sister.'

'You . . .' There was no word strong enough. 'You *bastard!*' was the best she could come up with, and he reacted to it in the worst possible way: bringing the sneer back, and saying, 'Well, it's not like you haven't done it before, is it?'

'I *haven't*— how dare you, how dare you think—'

She was shaking, hating him so much she couldn't breathe: around them windows started shattering, and she was trying to stop focusing her magic on him because she wasn't going to hurt him because that would be *confirming his point* and she was not, was *not* going to do that.

'I'm leaving,' she said. Her voice was strangely echoing. 'I'm leaving and I'm not coming back and you can starve for all I care, I don't care what you do to me, just don't come near me, you *bastard*.'

He said nothing. She couldn't even see him through the lowering darkness. She kicked the bag towards him and walked away down the street.

He didn't even call her name, and, against all odds, he didn't shoot.

CHAPTER 17

The first name for Hybrids had been Slovak: *vrah bez vol'by*, 'killer without choice', which, despite not being the catchiest of monikers, was remarkably accurate. The rest of the world had not been so kind.

Hybrids, according to the legend, were monsters: brutal and cold and savage and bloody and murderous. Rose did not delude herself into thinking any of this was inaccurate. Most of them were. Hybrids, in general, were the closest thing to nightmares the world had ever made flesh.

As far as she was aware, there were exactly two exceptions to this rule.

She had never actually met another Hybrid in person. She knew there were others out there, of course, but either they kept it as well-hidden as the Elmsworths – which would require being as clever as David, a criterion that she didn't think anyone met – or they were the monsters who went on killing sprees and whom the Department later had to take down with machine guns. In Rose's lifetime exactly four Hybrids had been discovered this way.

To a man, they had been brutal and cold and savage and bloody and murderous.

So the vast majority of Hybrids were evil. But not all of them were.

Rose and David weren't.

Rose and David weren't, because they didn't kill people. They locked themselves away and kept themselves under control and they never, never hurt anyone.

But no one would believe that. Loren Arkwood didn't believe that – he looked at her and only saw the monster lurking beneath her skin. She wasn't a person, to him; she wasn't anything more than a nightmare. That was fine, of course. That didn't surprise her.

That *shouldn't* surprise her.

And this, this right here, was why it was absolutely crucial – vital – to keep what she was hidden from the Department and her school. Not just because they'd try to kill her. That she could deal with. That she could run from.

What she couldn't deal with was the fact that, if they ever knew, they would believe she was utterly and inherently evil for the rest of their lives, and nothing she said or did would ever convince them otherwise.

On Sunday, her father was in the office again, and so was Rose. Everyone was very tense: the shadow of the Gifted murderer seemed to lurk in darkened corners. Rose kept to the light.

They were in a meeting room. The Department did not do meetings very well.

'What is it?' asked James from a corner. Terrian was sitting at the head of the table, trying to keep the attention of the group. This was not something at which he excelled.

'*Shut up!*' he roared. In the silence and the raised

eyebrows that followed, faint chanting could be heard from below. The Gospel had gathered again, this time protesting about Ashkind being buried in cemeteries usually reserved for Gifted. Apparently their grudge against non-magicals was not limited to the living.

'Can't we do something about them?' Terrian asked in frustration.

'Not unless we have a substantial evidential basis for incitement to violence, no,' said David, who was leaning back in his chair next to Rose with his eyes closed, and had until now appeared to be trying to sleep. 'They don't want to provoke us into actually doing anything. They just want to annoy us.'

'They've gotten bigger.'

'That's nothing. They've got Parliamentary sponsors now.' Everyone looked at him in astonishment; he could not see them, but perhaps he sensed it, because he smiled grimly. 'It's not the official line, so don't break the story, but what do you expect when you fill a Parliament with Angels? They have no love for the Ashkind.'

'Neither do most of us,' muttered Laura, distaste clear in her voice. Rose glanced at her sharply. 'What do you think they're planning, Connor?'

'Nothing more than activism so far,' answered David, before Terrian could speak. 'They're not large enough for a militia yet, if that's what you're thinking.'

The silence fell again, until Nate said warily what everyone was thinking.

'Yet?'

'Anyway,' said Terrian loudly, eyeing the window, 'that's

not what we're here to discuss. As you'll be aware, it has been discovered that not only was Argent *murdered*'– a glance at Rose, which she did her best to ignore – 'but the murderer, Loren Arkwood, has become the first person ever to escape our custody and appears to have an accomplice *here*, within our very ranks. Now, it could be anyone from the tea-lady in a civilian police station to the Minister for Defence, but given the level of security clearance they stole—'

'Stole?' interrupted James, leaning forward. 'How did they *steal* Department security clearance?'

'The defence systems run on a certain unique base code,' said David, tiredly, from his chair. 'If you know that base code you can hack into the central database, and if you're in the central database you can steal identities. I'm guessing the clearances they used were from a range of different areas, different accounts.'

Terrian nodded. 'Ipswich, Croydon, Mayfair, Kensington . . . Westminster.'

'The Department wrote the code,' said James heavily, 'didn't we?'

Terrian hesitated. 'Actually, we have on record exactly who.'

They looked at each other.

'So I guess I'm prime suspect, then, aren't I?' said David, opening his eyes and sitting up.

'You're the first to be inspected, yes.'

Everyone stared at him. He sighed and got up. He was not looking at Rose, thought nothing of her; or of the drawer in his office desk at home with a seventeen-digit number scribbled on the back of an envelope. Third drawer down. Easy to memorise, and, at an abandoned Department computer, whose history could be wiped—

'David?' said Terrian, as he got to the door. 'If it makes any difference, they really don't want it to be you.'

David turned, looked at him, at the room. 'I know they don't,' he said mildly. 'I wrote the base code for this place. I worked out the formulae for the Leeching and Insanity Gases. I have four hundred and sixty-nine convictions secured on Department cases. I've spent three months in hospital because of injuries sustained in the line of duty. I've held every rank going in this place. I led three squad teams. The leadership of the Department military, the special ops captains, they're loyal to me. I just about created this place. Of *course* they don't want it to be me.'

He held the door open for a moment, and in that moment Rose recalled the two metal rooms in their basement, the soundproofed quiet. *He* wasn't supporting Loren Arkwood. *He* wasn't the hacker.

The weight of that guilt rested entirely on her own shoulders.

But he wasn't entirely innocent, either.

The room was in the cellars – cold, white, basic. A table in the centre, and a one-way mirror on the side wall. David sat alert and pale. Rose, on the other side of the glass, watched him. He did not glance in her direction.

A woman with peroxide blonde hair and turquoise eyes sat across from him. She watched him coolly, and turned on the tape. It buzzed.

'This is a staff interrogation,' said the blonde woman, 'of a member of the Department for the Maintenance of Public Order and the Protection of Justice, by the Anti-Corruption Commission. My name is Corporal Evelyn Wood.'

'We're being inspected by the ACC?' James asked Laura hoarsely. 'Why?'

'This is what they're for.'

'But they're *lethal*. I don't want a Supergrass interrogation on my record. I'll never be employed again.'

'This is routine, James. The hacker probably isn't working in this office. They'll clear you.'

Unconvinced, James murmured something obscene into his hands. He held something cold and metal within his fist, and was twisting it incessantly between his fingers. It was a small silver ball webbed with thin green cracks, which glowed as if concealing the remains of a star. Objects began to materialise and vanish at various points around the room: an AK47, a table, a mirror. Once, even the beginnings of someone's face. When James swore, metal began to creep over his hands. It had a thin, almost unnoticeable green haze around it.

'Will you stop that?' snapped Laura, and the illusion dissipated. James put the hologram projector back in his pocket.

'Confirm your name for the tape, please,' said Wood coldly to David.

He nodded. 'This is Major David Jonathan Elmsworth, of the aforementioned Department, reporting for psychological inspection.'

Nate was on Rose's right. She reached for his hand and he took it, and squeezed. His sheer physical presence seemed to settle her anxiety.

'Do you have any loyalties to non-Department members?'

David blinked. 'None that supersede my loyalty to the Department.'

Evelyn Wood was ACC. She would at least have basic contact with Serena Mitchell. Rose should have realised this, and when Wood went for the kill a moment afterwards, she shouldn't have been as shocked as she was.

'Not even that to your daughter?'

David closed his eyes momentarily; Rose hissed quietly, feeling how annoyed he was, how angry at himself he must be. Of course, she was not Department, not officially.

'Of course,' said David, his voice absolutely flat now, 'I am loyal to my daughter.'

'Above all things.'

'Above all things,' he said, his voice growing colder by the syllable.

'You would die for her?'

'Of course, as she for me.'

Something about that statement – its lack of inflection, its certainty – made Rose draw her hand from Nate's grip and wrap her arms around herself. Of course he was right. Of course. She wanted him to know that, know that she would die for him.

Lie for him, kill for him. Hide a murderer for him.

Nevertheless she felt cold.

'You adopted her when she was a baby?'

'Yes.'

He had retreated to single-syllable answers.

'And you have no idea of her biological parentage.'

'None. Is this relevant?'

Everyone behind the one-way glass – Nate, James, Laura, Terrian – was watching Rose now.

'Is there any difference in your relationship because of your lack of biological relation?'

'No,' whispered Rose fervently, behind the glass, the silenced glass, 'no.'

Laura was watching her with narrow eyes.

'No,' said David. His expression was inscrutable. 'None at all.'

'She loves you?'

'Yes.'

Again, the cold in his voice seemed to grow into her bones.

'We IQ-tested her,' said Wood. 'She comes up with a score of one hundred and twenty-six.'

He inclined his head.

'She also displayed many of the characteristics usually seen in criminals.'

Oh, now they were definitely staring at her.

'Why is my daughter relevant to this inspection?' asked David icily.

'Because you raised her,' said Wood, leaning forward. 'Because you brought her up alone, with no other parents or siblings, no peer-group contact for the first five years of her life. Because she is a walking, breathing experiment.

She is evidence of your character, and she is dangerous.'

Rose was breathing very deeply now. Her hands were shaking.

'She's the useful kind of dangerous,' said David angrily to Wood. 'She's the kind of dangerous you *need* in a Department member. *I'm* that kind of dangerous. For God's sake, even Connor bloody Terrian is that kind of dangerous.'

'And since she is that dangerous,' said Evelyn Wood, 'have you ever asked her to lie for you?'

That stopped him. There was a noticeable, cold hesitation before he spoke again.

'No,' he said. 'I've never asked her to lie about anything.'

CHAPTER 18

The next day, Maria asked her why she looked so exhausted. It was near the end of a Healing lesson and Rose, it had to be admitted, had been very near falling asleep.

She had not slept well that night.

'I was reading,' she said.

Maria raised an eyebrow archly. 'Really?'

'Yeah.'

Maria leaned in close. Rose knew this expression by now, and she sighed. 'Maria—'

'How's stuff in the Department?'

Rose had quickly found that she hated this intrusion of the Department into her school life as much as she had hated having to think about schoolwork in the office. At any rate, she certainly did not have it in her to tell Maria what was happening, so she changed tack.

'Why do you never ask Nate this, anyway?'

Maria blushed. Rose pressed her line of attack.

'Oh, that's right – because you *fancy* him, and you're too *shy*.'

Maria rolled her eyes at the jibe, but before she could say anything, the bell rang. Rose got her bag and slipped out as quickly as possible. Outside, however, she heard someone call her name.

'Umm . . . Rose?'

She turned to find the source. To her utter bewilderment, it was Aaron Greenlow. He was standing sheepishly by the Healing classroom, looking at her. Rose walked over to him, trying and failing to stop herself blushing. She was not quite sure why.

'Ro— *oh!*'

Maria came out of the classroom and her mouth fell open in amazement. She backed away, wide-eyed, and covered her mouth to stop herself giggling. Even Aaron, noticing her, turned slightly red.

'Don't mind her,' Rose said, embarrassed. For some reason, her heart seemed to be beating much faster than usual. She wished it wouldn't. Surely someone would notice.

'Umm . . . yeah. Look, Rose'– he paused, and shifted his weight slightly – 'umm, I was thinking . . . you know the cinema on the high road?'

'Yeah,' Rose said, wondering where this was going.

'Well, I was . . . yeah . . .'

He said nothing for a few seconds. He was bright red now. He seemed to be swallowing and blinking a lot. Rose was about to prompt him or ask him – actually, she had no idea what she was going to say – when he said suddenly, 'D'you want to see a film with me tonight?'

Rose blinked, stunned. Something like disbelief was rushing through her, scattering her thoughts into an alignment that did not lend itself to coherent cognitive process.

'Umm . . .' she said, feeling very stupid. 'Umm . . .'

'It's okay if you don't,' he said. 'I mean—'

'No!' Rose said, too loudly. Heads turned. 'I mean, no,' she said, more quietly. 'No – I mean – no, I didn't mean – I just thought . . .'

She had no idea what she was saying now.

'Yes,' she said finally, feeling like an idiot. 'Yeah, I'd love to. Thanks.'

Aaron smiled. It was a sort of embarrassed, happy smile, which later Rose would subject to every method of psychoanalysis she had at her disposal. Now, though, she just felt as if she had descended into a very surreal daydream.

'Great!' he said. 'So . . . meet me there at six, then?'

'Yeah,' Rose said, relieved that this was a question that demanded only a single syllable as an answer.

Aaron grinned, gave a sort of sheepish half-wave, and walked away.

Rose stood there, stunned. The closest comparison to how she was currently feeling, she thought, would be to have been pushed off a skyscraper into a pile of pillows and then punched, hard, in the stomach.

Maybe her day wasn't going so badly after all, then.

They'd met when she was thirteen and he fourteen. He was, just by chance, assigned to be her helper: he was in the year above her, and that year it was part of your coursework to volunteer to help pupils in particular subjects, and Aaron had chosen Magical Studies.

They were learning about levitation: concentrating until objects lifted from the table and hung there, oblivious to gravity. Aaron had been very good at it. He glanced at the coin on her desk and it lifted itself with all the elegance of a many-stringed marionette, swirling and gliding around his head without any apparent effort.

'So,' he'd said. 'What's your name?'

She'd told him, and over the next few lessons he'd prised from her all the information she could give: her father, but not the Department; her adoption, but not the reasons for it; her skill in combat, but not its origins. Secrets, she'd been taught long ago, were like dominoes: spill one and the rest would come tumbling down.

Aaron had treated every piece of information about her with the respect it deserved – knowing, perhaps, how uneasy she felt to give it – and responded with one of his own: his father's occupation as the leader of the Gospel, though Rose already knew about Stephen, of course; his mother Natalie's career in the MoD; his annoying younger brother, Tristan; his fears about his Test next year.

She didn't know why all of this seemed so fascinating to her, at first. She remembered that the first time they'd met she had thought dispassionately that he was what Maria would call 'hot', but weeks passed before she started to *feel* it: his easy smile, the way he pushed his black hair out of his eyes like the action was nothing, the quiet gravity that accompanied his words.

This, she realised slowly, was what 'attractive' meant: the pull towards someone that seemed to happen even when you had your eyes closed and were trying to walk away; the sudden elevation of their every word and action to a treasure, a precious thing, something to be watched and analysed and remembered.

It became certain the day he came over to her in the hall – without consideration or pause, as if she were a natural person to talk to, as if she *mattered*. She was fourteen by then, and it was the day before his Test.

'Listen,' he said, and of course she did, 'do you think I can do this?'

She didn't remember what exactly she said, but it was sincere, and encouraging, and at the end of it he said 'Thank you, Rose. Thank you so much,' and walked away half-distractedly, and she'd fallen in love – or the closest she'd ever known to love – involuntarily, quietly, the pull increasing with his every step.

CHAPTER 19

Rose was at the cinema at five fifty-five that evening. Maria had come round and spent the last two hours finding a dress, doing her hair, and applying make-up that Rose had never even heard of. Rose could only be grateful to her for this, but even so, having your best friend analyse and articulate all of your flaws was a humiliating experience.

David had been as stunned as Maria when Rose had told him, nervously and shifting her weight from foot to foot, that someone had asked her out. He had seemed happy for her – at least when he was able to speak again – but slightly quieter than usual, all the same. Rose suspected he did not especially like the fact that she was dating Stephen Greenlow's son, but he said nothing. He was no hypocrite, and, as he always said, he did not judge children by their parents.

He had told her to be back by nine-thirty, and Rose had agreed, of course. She hated it when she made him sad.

She wondered whether this was what a normal teenage girl's life was like: make-up, dates, cold spring nights in a dress that was uncomfortably short. She'd never done this before. She felt spectacularly unprepared; she had no template for what he might say or do, or what *she* was meant to do, or . . . oh, for Ichor's *sake*.

Why could she look a murderer in the face, but not do this?

Maybe it was instinct. Maybe she'd just *know* what to do, without thinking.

Somewhere in the distance, there was a thud, like construction work. It echoed faintly in the headlight-streaked blackness.

Rose hoped Aaron wouldn't offer her alcohol. Rose had only ever tasted alcohol once, a year ago, at Maria's house. They had shared a glass of wine, giggling and daring each other. The way it had made Rose slightly woozy scared her, and she had resolved to be teetotal ever since. A lifetime of being a Hybrid had made her deeply frightened of being in anything but her right mind.

And oh Angels, there he was.

She could see him standing in the shadow of the entrance. She caught his eye and he smiled and beckoned her over. She measured her walk carefully, not wanting to seem too eager. She still had her pride to defend.

Aaron said, 'Hi.'

She said 'hi' back, slightly breathlessly.

'Look,' he said, somewhat nervously, 'can I speak to you for a moment?'

She nodded and ducked with him into a little alcove by the ticket office. A siren screamed past them on the high road. She was all too aware of how red she was.

After a few seconds' silence, Rose asked, 'So, umm . . . what film did you want to see?'

Aaron seemed to be staring into the middle distance. She had to say it twice before he jerked out of his reverie.

'Oh, yeah,' he said. He looked at her with something strange in his eyes and for a moment Rose's heart was alarmingly still, and she wondered, half-terrified, whether he was going to kiss her.

He said, 'Actually, I just wanted to tell you how much of a bitch I think you are.'

For a second, with her breathlessness and her warm cheeks and the glowing, bustling dreaminess of the night, she did not quite register it. And then, when she did, she waited for a few seconds for him to laugh, for it to be revealed as some sort of a joke, albeit in very bad taste. But his expression was cold and calm and empty.

That was when she realised, far too late, that there was something very wrong about all of this.

'I mean,' he said, still with that inexplicable, shattering coolness, 'I thought this would be the best place to do it. You've never been asked out by a boy before, have you? I'm not surprised. Nobody likes you, you know. You never hang around with anyone but the other Department boy. Did you beg him to take you? I'm not surprised he didn't. I mean, who'd want to be seen with you? You're the ugliest girl in the year.' He laughed. It was a terrible laugh.

More sirens and streaking lights. The cars had stopped. Somewhere a few streets away, people were shouting.

Rose felt herself break. She held herself tall and straight, but there were tears streaming down her face, and she couldn't stop them. There was more dignity in letting them flow than trying.

'Oh, my God,' he said, smiling. 'You would have thought anyone raised by a psychopath would be a bit hardier than that.' Rose jerked slightly at the mention of her father. 'Oh, did I touch a nerve, daddy's girl? Yeah, he's a psycho. Everyone knows it. Or did he not tell you? Has he not shown you a list of the people he's killed? Angels, you're a wimp. No wonder not even your parents wanted you. I bet they wished you'd died.'

Rose's legs wouldn't hold out for much longer. She leaned against the wall. She was genuinely shaking now. She should respond, should say something clever, but her wits had deserted her in her hour of need and all she could do was stand there and take it.

A camera flash went off in her face and she whirled. Of course, of course; she should have known, should have figured this one out. Tristan Greenlow, Aaron's younger brother, stepped out of the shadows, laughing raucously, grinning at whatever it was he had captured on his camera.

Aaron grinned. 'Oh, you're disappointed. Did you really think I wanted to go out with you? Me, with an ugly psycho girl? You've fancied me for years, haven't you? Yeah, I knew. Pathetic. But all I ever wanted to do was slap your stupid face.'

Rose, at last, managed to say something. But it was at Tristan – the orchestrator of this terrible, very clever prank – that she aimed it.

'Nice one,' she told him. Her voice broke. 'Did you think you could beat me this way, since you're too much of a coward to fight a girl in the flesh? Or did you think I would care about your stupid brother. . .'

Her voice trailed off. She couldn't think of anything else to say. Aaron backed away from her to stand beside his brother. Rose's legs gave out at last and she sank to the floor, bringing her knees to her chin. Tristan took another picture. For a few seconds, she thought he was going to kick her in the shins, and was not at all surprised to find that she didn't care.

She could hear them laughing. She sat there and waited until they went away.

No one in the cinema came near her.

When she was sure they weren't going to come back, she let herself cry for five minutes. She timed it by the clock. Rose sobbed her misery out of herself: how she had been tricked, how she had let Tristan attack her, how she hadn't even managed to fight back, how probably even now the pictures of her crying in a dress would be doing the rounds on the email circuits. After the five minutes were up she let the residual unhappiness condense into a cold desire for revenge. Not anger; anger clouded judgement. But she made a mental note that she would make Tristan pay for what he had done to her. She would act like it had never happened, yes, she would do that for now, and as soon they were allowed to use magic in a fight – which the teacher had hinted would be soon – she would destroy him utterly.

That was a good objective. Free of emotion. *Destroy him utterly.*

Then Rose stood up and went outside. The high street was clogged with police cars, following the ambulances to wherever that sound she had failed to recognise as a gunshot had gone off. She could hear the sirens further down the road. They did not change in volume. The ambulances weren't moving.

Rose waited for a few seconds, and when nothing happened, she found the nearest Tube station and caught the train to Westminster.

CHAPTER 20

Rose found her father sitting in his office chair, apathetic, staring into the distance with nothing in his eyes. James was there, too, and he saw that she'd been crying and tried to ask, but she went straight to David.

'What happened?'

He looked at her but he didn't see her. There was a piece of paper clenched in his hand; he did not resist when she took it. In black ink had been scrawled the words *Behold the Interregnum*. Rose closed her eyes for a moment.

'What is this?' she asked him fiercely. 'Who are they? What haven't you told me?'

David's eyes focused at last on his daughter. 'They're going to find out, Rose,' he said heavily. 'They're going to have to find out about us.'

Rose's attention sharpened so quickly it was almost painful. 'No they won't,' was her automatic answer, and then, 'Why do you think they would?'

'Regency,' he murmured. The sound of his voice around that word shocked her into silence for a moment. 'Their leader, Felix Callaway – I think he might have known about me, what I was, years ago.'

'What do you mean? Who are they?'

He fixed his gaze on her. 'I fought for them,' he said,

very quietly. 'Years ago, in the War. I was Regency's secret weapon. This War army, Regency, I was fighting for them, fighting for the Ashkind . . . I had some friends there, that's why . . .' His eyes closed. 'I thought they'd broken up. I thought Regency had been destroyed. But they're alive again, Rose, they've been sending me *notes,* they're alive, and they'll come for me – they'll come for you, they'll use you against me . . .'

'Shush,' she whispered, and gripped his hand. 'Shush. They won't find us. We're safe.'

'You never should have known,' he said. He wasn't listening to her. 'You were never meant to find out about them.'

Rose pressed the heel of her hand to her forehead. 'I can cope. Dad, you know you can tell me anything.'

'No,' he said vehemently. 'No. Oh, Rose, you think I'm good, but the things I've done . . .'

'Shush,' said Rose again, unnerved. She looked around the office for something, anything, to calm him down, to transform this pitiable, broken repentant back into her father. His gun was in his desk drawer. Perhaps he would feel better if he were holding it.

She got to her feet and let go of his hand.

And then—

The whole office heard it: a voice, booming, deafening, coming from every speaker in the room, every earphone and every computer. Without amplification, Rose imagined it might be quite a soothing voice. Now it was hard and clear, and it said, with all the shaking force of that wall of noise: 'We are coming.'

People screamed and fell off their chairs. Terrian froze, and then sped into movement, looking around frantically for the source of the noise. James, behind them, cried out in surprise and anger, and then, hands over his ears, dived for the computer.

'We are coming,' said the voice again, 'and we will find you, you heretics, you Angel-worshippers, and we will destroy you, and we will scatter your ashes into the wind. We are your enemy. We are Ashkind. We are your deaths, you autocratic infidels, and when the Interregnum comes and we rule over this country and every land like it, we will hunt you down, and we will grind you into dust.'

Next to Rose, David was coming awake again. The colour was returning slowly to his face, and his eyes were clearing. Here was his enemy in front of him; here was something he could fight. The voice surged on, promise after promise of destruction rolling over them like thunder, and then David got to his feet, walked forward, and tapped on the speaker.

'Are these microphones on?' he asked mildly. 'Felix? Can you hear me?'

There was a pause. A long pause. Even the silences were loud. Then the voice growled, '*Elmsworth.*'

'Hello,' David said to the speakers. The office was staring at him. 'It's been a while.'

'Don't think I've forgotten about you,' said the voice. The sheer volume of it turned every word into a rattling blow. 'We have been devising your pain for years, and we have no intention of your escaping it, Elmsworth.'

Astonishing how his name could hurt so much in this terrible voice.

'No,' said her father, 'I think you've made that clear.'

'I claim your death as my own.'

'Oh, don't pretend you had that line first,' said David scornfully. 'Listen, Felix. I understand you have some grievances against us.'

'Grieva—?'

'Shush. I understand you have some grievances against us, but there are better ways to say them than this. If you're going to kill me, you are very welcome to try.' Only the office could see the smile that spread across David's face, but it was articulated so clearly in his voice that he might as well have been laughing. 'You want to kill us? You want to grind us into dust? Come and get us. We will destroy you before you come anywhere close.'

'You have no idea how strong we are,' said the voice.

'Oh, I really do. And I'm not scared.'

'You are arrogant to think you can defeat us.'

'And you are delusional to think you can control me. Felix Callaway, I will say this once, and once only. This is your last chance.' He leaned very close to the speakers. 'Go die quietly in a ditch somewhere, and save yourself the pain.'

James, who had been at the keyboards for most of this conversation, pressed the 'Enter' button with something of a flourish, and the voice began to crackle and disappear, which was just as well, as the reply was riddled with profanities. The last audible words were a dark 'we will come for you', and then the voice was gone.

The office was quiet. David looked around at his speech-less audience.

'And that, ladies and gentlemen,' he said, 'was Regency. Expect to hear more from them.' He turned. 'Rose?'

Rose wasn't looking at him. She was looking at something in David's drawer. It was a Government-issued comms tablet, and, though technically she didn't qualify for office supplies, she had been using it as her own for years. There was an email alert in the top-right corner of her in-box. It was from an automated, no-reply address.

The subject line read: *my threat still stands.*

Below that was a house number and postcode.

Rose put her hands to her face and made a small moaning noise through her fingers. Oh, in Ichor's name. Not now. Please, not now.

'Rose?'

David looked concerned. She turned to him blindly. In his face there were a thousand flickering emotions – the exhilaration of a threat curtailed, concern for her, lingering fear of the voice on the speakers, apprehension at anticipated questions. And she wanted to ask those questions. She so dearly wanted to ask them. But first she had to save both their lives. And to do that, she had to leave him.

God, she hated Loren Arkwood for this.

'I need to go home,' she said quietly, and turned away before she could see his face fall.

In the police car on the way over, James kept looking at Rose. She refused to acknowledge it.

'David said you went on a date,' he said finally, and Rose had to nod yes.

There was a pause.

'Do you want me to kill the bastard?'

She had to laugh.

'I'm going to try and do it myself, thanks, but if I need help you'll be the first one I call.'

'That's all I ask.'

They drove the rest of the way in silence.

He dropped her off a few streets away from their house, and from there it was a two-minute walk to the address Arkwood had sent her. She stood there waiting in the cold, arms wrapped around herself. She was still wearing Maria's make-up, still dressed in the clothes she had worn to meet—

How many hours ago?

It felt so close. She didn't want it to. She wanted it to feel like years.

Destroy him.

She hugged herself more tightly against the wind.

'I know how this is going to sound,' came his voice from behind her, 'but I want you to come down this old abandoned tunnel with me, which is near collapsing, and I promise nothing can possibly go wrong.'

She didn't turn.

'Come out here where I can see you.'

A pause. Then footsteps. Warily, he walked round her and into the path of the cold blue starlight. He looked older again – gaunter, dirtier. He raised his eyebrows at what she was wearing.

'If you ask,' she said, 'I will hurt you.'

He closed his mouth.

Slowly, she walked towards him until they were very close. They looked at each other for a moment. Then she slapped him very hard across the face.

He stepped backwards, hand to his cheek.

'But I didn't ask,' he said bemusedly.

'You son of a *bitch*. How dare you— what you said—'

'I know, I know. It was unforgivable.'

'Damn right it was unforgivable. You said— as if I were some kind of *animal,* a monster— as if I was a killer even when I was human, as if I wanted this to happen to me, you bastard, you unfeeling ignorant *bastard*—'

'I know,' he said hastily, stepping away from her again, 'I know.'

For a moment they were quiet. He pulled the skin of his cheek, checked for blood. Rose snorted.

'And yet,' he said quietly, 'you came back.'

'Of *course* I bloody came back!' Now, if possible, she was even angrier. 'You have the power of life and death over me! One word from you and they'd come to our house and they'd drag us away and pump God knows what into us until we died emaciated and screaming! You can do that to us with a *note* to them! A *word!* Of course I came back!'

His eyes widened. They stood speechless for a minute, fast-breathing; the secret hung between them, a knotted rope, heavy and inescapable. He said:

'So that's what they do to you.'

'No. That's what they do to civilian Hybrids. I don't want to think about what they do to ones who have worked for them undetected for fourteen years.'

He was silent. Then, 'I want you to help me rescue Tabitha.'

'Loren, if she's kept down in the cells, not even I could get her out.'

'You said, one word—'

She stepped away from him. 'You would do that?'

His eyes went very cold. 'If that's what I have to do to get her back.'

They looked at each other.

'So will you help?'

She pressed her fingers to her temples. 'Loren . . . I don't know.'

'Rose, don't make me say—'

'Loren.' She glared at him. 'If I do this, you don't want me to be reluctant. I might get you killed.'

He sighed. 'Then what can I do?'

'What, as an exchange?'

'That's the idea, yes. Although you're going to have to think hard – I am currently living in a dank basement and mugging passing strangers for food.' He looked ruefully down at the dark entrance. 'With less-than-lucrative results, I might add.'

Rose leaned against the wall. It was nearing midnight; her father would be home soon. She was exhausted and hungry and her mental faculties were not at their best.

And then the obvious came to her: the voice in the Department, and David's wide smile.

'All right,' she said. 'What can you tell me about my father and Regency?'

CHAPTER 21

'I met David when I was sixteen. It was three months after the Veilbreak and I was roaming London with Rayna, alone: I was just learning how to use my Gifts, and I was arrogant and powerful and clever, and I'm sure things would have gone even more wrong than they did if I hadn't met him. He was our age, or thereabouts, but he looked – *spoke* – older; acted and seemed more adult. There was a heaviness to his words that I didn't recognise then, but I would later – everyone sounds like that after they've killed. He has – or at least he had, then – a hell of a conscience.

Our area of London was taken by the Gifted very quickly. They started rounding up all the Ashkind, and we never saw where they took them, but we'd paid attention in history lessons, we knew it wasn't anywhere good.

They tried to take Rayna, and David and I beat up the bastards pretty well, nearly killed them I think, and after that we knew we had to do something, because who else would? Rayna, of course, was the key factor there. I couldn't see the Ashkind as the enemy if it meant turning against my own sister.

We started evacuating the rest of the Ashkind in the borough. Some of them had Gifted children; they were afraid the Ashkind would take them away. We gathered them into this one warehouse, and guarded it, but of course we had nowhere to take them, nowhere permanent. So we asked for help from the nearest Ashkind army.

That was Regency. They were quite small at the time, only a few hundred of them, but they had guns and ex-soldiers. They didn't have enough that they could afford to waste potential fighters, though, so they took the refugees in. It was good PR for them, anyway. All the Ashkind who could fight were eventually pressured or brainwashed into taking up arms. All the Gifted among us, the adults. . . I don't know whether Regency bullied them into it or they just couldn't take being around so many Ashkind, but eventually they decided it would be best if they left, and they didn't come back.

But not us. Not me and David. Felix – Felix Callaway, he was the leader of Regency – that would have been his voice you heard. He'll be in his mid-forties now, but back then he was young and strong and authoritative and people just accepted him as their leader without him even needing to ask. I doubt he's lost any of that even now, so much the worse for us. And it wasn't undeserved. He was clever, not in David's league but getting there, and he could command crowds with his voice and his words and he knew just how to use people's skills to get what he wanted. He was a Demon, too – he had those black eyes. . . they almost didn't seem human. The Government only really thought Demons were dangerous after they saw him.

That's one of the many things I hate him for. Long

after people forgot his name and Regency's, they hated Demons. Tabitha – people crossed the street to avoid her even when she was an infant; kids used to shout insults at her in the playground, because she was a Demon. . . They were afraid of her because, long ago, they had been afraid of him.

He is a Hybrid, as well, the first legend and the only. People think Hybrids are sadistic killers in part because of him. He came up with the idea of deploying them as weapons on the battlefield. It was the way he killed his enemies: personally, and brutally, and . . . anyway. I didn't know it at the time, and presumably David didn't either. I'm not sure whether even Felix understood what was happening to him, and by the time he did, Hybrids were everyone's nightmares.

So he took us in. David was Head of Security almost immediately. For a start, no one else in the army could do the job, and also he was just . . . *radiantly* brilliant. Felix knew he was clever enough to kill in huge numbers and young enough to be pressured into doing so. Your father did terrible things, Rose, and if he's forgotten that, he deserves to be called a monster; but I won't pretend it was entirely his fault.

He sat in that control room – they'd started to get the electricity back up by then – and pressed the buttons, and it took him months to realise what he was actually doing, the horror of the stuff they'd told him to do in the name of strategy. By the time he knew, it was too late, he didn't feel it any more.

I was worse. I won't say otherwise. I was even worse

than him, because I started off as a foot soldier and I tried, I *tried* to work my way up the ranks. And Felix and Ariadne – she was his right-hand woman – saw what I could do, and they put me in charge of the cameras. I was very, very good at that, Rose. I could read people's slightest intentions, their very *doubts,* through a screen, and I saw the ones who were going to dissent and I ordered their executions because it was the War and these things had to be done.

Rayna knew. She knew what we were doing and becoming and she tried to stop me, but it didn't work, I was too into the ideology and the Interregnum and the cause, the cause, the *cause*.

And David was dissenting. Not actively, and not loudly, but I could see in his face that he wanted out, that he wasn't loyal any more. We were about eighteen at the time, a couple of years into the War, and it was doing something unhealthy to him – and to Rayna, too, though I didn't see it at the time.

I warned Felix about David, told him it would be best if we curbed his privileges, kept him where we could see him. But Felix said no, because David was pretty much essential to the war effort and making him unhappy could lose us several hundred men. He didn't see David's intentions. I'll give David credit for that: he made sure Felix never really knew him.

A couple of months after that, David tried to run. I caught him, and I caught him pretty easily, because I masterminded internal security and at the time he was the biggest threat I knew of. I put him in the cells and I told Felix we should kill him, and we probably *should* have killed him, but Felix said no, again, we needed to keep him alive if we wanted to make any headway against the Gifted armies and the Angels.

So David lived and worked again, and by then he hated me, and he still hates me, for stopping him. I don't blame him.

It took a year for him to act again, and then it was because of you. He disappeared for two days, and when he came back he had a baby in the crook of his arm and he was very pale and very quiet.

I knew what he was, then, Rose. I'd guessed, but I hadn't told Felix. I know your father thinks I told him, but I didn't. That's not to say that no one else guessed, or that Felix never worked it out on his own, but if he did, he never said anything to me.

I knew what your father was because I knew what Felix was – he often boasted about being a Hybrid – and I'd watched them both, and I spotted the patterns. I never said anything because . . . well, that would have been crossing a line even I had never come to. And I'm not saying I was bound by any sense of honour, but I . . .

I knew what Hybrids were supposed to be like. I knew what Felix was like, how he'd embraced it, how he'd become part of the monster. And then I looked at David. He was a terribly old man in those days, Rose, and perhaps he's younger now, but I remember him ancient and dying in the body of a teenager – a skinny, silent kid with too many thoughts. And I imagined, if that was what he was, if that monster was under his skin . . . it must be eating him from the inside, what he does when he's like that.

Eating him from the inside . . .

So I never told Felix.

He came back and he came back with you, a screaming red-faced baby, and that was when I began to guess about you, too. David at nineteen was the least likely parent imaginable, you'd agree with me if you'd known him then, and I thought there's only one reason he would willingly raise a kid himself: if you were like him.

He went into Felix's office, the two of them, with you, alone. I never knew what David told him, but when they came out, Felix was white as a sheet, and he told us not to shoot, just to let David walk away.

I didn't see him again until after the end of the War.

After we lost David, defeat was almost inevitable. We fought hard and we fought valiantly, but remember, we were fighting the Gifted and Angels, and David's innovation and technology had been our only real advantage against their magic. It took us three years, but we lost the War, and they marched us up and made us sign the Great Truce.

We didn't disappear, hard as they tried. By 'they', incidentally, I mean the Department – your father was working for them by then, but he didn't run it yet. Its leader was this woman called Malia Terrian – she's long dead now, but I think her husband and son are still there. The Department picked us off, soldier by soldier. They ground us down until we could almost taste the dust.

We got smaller and smaller. We weren't an army any

more, more of a ragtag militia. Only our hardcore inner circle actually wanted to fight, I think. The rest of us had just been soldiers too long, and didn't know how to be civilians. Felix never accepted defeat, and his slide into full-on, raging insanity – which I admit started years before, but I hadn't really noticed it then, I was too blinded – started to take effect. He didn't trust anyone, not even me. After two years, he decided that I was plotting to kill him, and set his inner guard on me. But of course their hearts weren't really in it – the guards were my men, really, not his – so I fought my way out, hid somewhere in London.

I hid, but I had nowhere to hide *in*. I was twenty-four, then; I'd spent a third of my life in Regency, and I didn't know how not to be a soldier. I had no money, and no one to spend it on. Rayna had gone to America the year before, to help the Ashkind resistance there, but she couldn't get in contact with me for fear of Government interception. I kept subscribing to the BBC reports of the battles, what little they published. I hoped, or feared, that I would read about her.

I almost went to David once, I was so desperate for information about Rayna, and he was Government now, I thought he might know . . . I found your house. I saw you through the window. You were maybe four, five years old, and he was teaching you how to use magic, or how not to use it, or whatever.

I saw you. You were smiling, and you were sending blue flames towards the ceiling higher and higher, and he was encouraging you, and I hated him so much, Rose, for having the person he loved there in front of him and safe, for having a family, having a life.

But I survived. And Rayna returned two years later, pregnant, and then I had my sister back; and even with what Tabitha was, the problems we had to face, I was happy.

Then you came for us. You and your Department.

I'm sorry, it wasn't your fault, but they did. They came. And I saw Rayna die in front of me; Rayna who had been my family and confidante and *sister* for thirty-four years, dying as collateral damage, just because . . . and they took Tabitha, who I had promised to protect always, against anything, and they put her where I couldn't reach her. Can't reach her.

I was in the cells for two months. I counted every day, when I wasn't sedated. They put needles in me and I don't know what they did to me but I felt weak, always weak. They had me on an IV drip and one day I had just enough magic to stop my heart, and I . . . I considered it, Rose, I considered dying, just letting go, but obviously I thought of Tabitha and that stopped me.

I lived and I ran, and then I was alone in London with my family far away, like I had been ten years ago.

And right next to my heart, next to my love for Tabitha, was my hatred for your father. He who led the organisation that had killed my sister; whose cowardice had lost me the War; who kept my niece under guard and away from me.

I needed supplies. I needed leverage. I needed to get revenge on him.

I thought of you.'

CHAPTER 22

'So, I take it the Department is not in fantastic shape these days?'

Loren handed her the cracked mug of coffee over the back of the chair. It was three days since she had returned to him. This flat was on the Department list of witness-protection accommodation; during criminal trials where the defendant was alleged to have violent allies, those giving evidence were hidden here until everything was over.

It was dilapidated, but it had a bed and running water and decent central heating, and he could just about survive here if she carried on bringing him food.

'What do you mean?'

'They can't be happy about Regency.'

Rose closed her eyes. 'It's Regency that's getting to Dad, I think, but what's really annoying them is the inspections. The ACC are all over us because of me.'

She didn't bother keeping the accusation out of her voice, and as such he ignored it.

'Don't the inspectors know how suspiciously your father's been acting? How much knowledge of Regency he suddenly seems to have?'

'God, no. He'd have to kill a colleague for a Department

member to report him to the Supergrass. It would be like you when you were in Regency, ratting someone out to the Angels.'

'You hate each other that much?'

'The ACC think they have authority over us.'

'They do.'

'They *think* they do.'

He left it. 'What are the inspections like?'

Rose shrugged. 'They bring you into their dungeons and they ask you about the weakest person you love. Then they come to your house, and look into your life and go and file it with their bureaucratic Angels, and they never find anything suspicious but sometimes they come back, just to be sure.' She looked at him. 'They enjoy torturing you, even when they know you're innocent.'

He took another sip of coffee. 'I wonder who that sounds like.'

She glared at him. 'We never use enhanced interrogation unless the suspect is guilty.'

'If you know the suspect is guilty, you don't need to use "enhanced interrogation".'

She got up and tossed the remains of the coffee in the sink, angry.

'Rose.'

She turned. He was watching her with detached curiosity.

'Does it not bother you at all? What you are?'

Rose struggled for a moment with her response. 'No,' she said eventually, 'because it's not our fault. We just have to live with it.'

'I see,' he said. 'So having evil forced upon you, and accepting it, is entirely different from choosing evil.'

'*Yes!*' said Rose furiously. 'Because we didn't . . . we weren't normal and just went out *looking* for it, we didn't choose it freely—'

Now when he looked at her, it was with contempt.

'Oh, Rose,' he said. 'You think anyone does?'

She was silent.

'You killed Thomas Argent,' she said, somewhat childishly.

'He killed my sister. I couldn't leave scum like that walking the earth.'

'So revenge is okay, then, in your book?'

He got up and put his cup in the sink. 'That wasn't revenge,' he said. 'That was pest control.'

There was a long pause; she could hear the wind outside.

'Have you thought any more about what I asked you?'

She said nothing.

'I don't need to remind you,' he said, with an edge to his voice, 'what I will do if you don't cooperate.'

Rose put her face in her hands.

'Oh, bloody hell,' she said. 'Fine. I'll help you rescue Tabitha.'

CHAPTER 23

It happened in an Art lesson, when she was distracted, as accidents always did. To be fair, on that day of all days she had plenty to be distracted over. They had put up the posters of Loren on the school walls that Monday: he stared, with those cold, steely yellow-green eyes, from out-of-reach windows as they passed. The Department, as always reluctant to admit mistakes, had at last told the public that a prisoner had managed to escape from their cells. It had only been through David's stubbornness, forceful argument and utter refusal to accept the words 'lost cause' as an accurate description, that the public had been informed at all. The Regency note seemed to have shaken him; he was determined, now, to capture Loren as quickly as possible, and to end all of this.

Rose did not get a lot of sleep these days.

Loren himself, when she had told him, had not seemed particularly anxious about it. She suspected that was only because they both knew it would serve no purpose at all to panic.

So here she was in the middle of an Art lesson with Maria, trying to work with smoke. Miss Edgware had apparently decided that the best way to do this was to fill a room with smoke and let them work with it in oxygen masks and goggles. Right now, they were trying to create models of themselves. Rose was failing.

'Come on, now, Rosalyn!' enthused Miss Edgware from over her shoulder, making Rose jump. She had tried umpteen times to tell her teacher that no one called her that, but somehow she didn't get it. She had eventually given up. 'Try harder!'

Rose resisted the urge to roll her eyes and concentrated. With remarkably little effort, now that she was focused, the figure of a man emerged from the smoke. Rose scrutinised it and found unsurprisingly that the build and contours resembled those of her father. Amazing what the subconscious could do when called on.

I am the form your subconscious takes to talk to you, he had said in her Test.

Yes, she thought irritably, *but do you shut up, though?*

'Well done!' Miss Edgware said. 'Now, I want you to try something. Raise the hand of your statue.'

The figures raised their right hands. The excess smoke was beginning to clear now; Rose could see Maria's outline through the bleary cloud.

'And now, move the hand down again.'

They did.

'Now, can you make your figure sit down?'

They could. Rose, vaguely identifying a chair through the smoke, guided her figure gently onto that.

'And now—'

It happened then. One of the other pupils slipped for a second; the figure exploded with a bang like a gunshot. So like a gunshot that Rose jumped for the first time she could remember, and suddenly the room around her was tiny and metal and her thoughts were disappearing and the pain was rearing, coming for her again—

'*Rose*!'

Her head jerked up. She had bitten her tongue; she tasted blood in her mouth. Across from her, the smoke figure had assumed colour. Its eyes were now a deep, bleak white, and its hands had expanded to claws. It was beginning to sink to the floor and fold onto itself: in a moment it would rear, screaming, its skin would crack and darken, its limbs lengthen to those of an animal, its face—

Rose breathed in, and out, trying to calm herself. Slowly, the figure drifted apart. The eyes were the last to go; they stared at Rose unblinkingly, coldly, until their whiteness was merely the residue of an imprint.

The whole class was staring at her.

'I was . . . experimenting,' Rose said. 'On what I could do with it.'

She was lucky, very lucky, that no one there had ever seen a Hybrid transform, or the game would have been up there and then. They stared at her for a minute more without saying anything. Then someone from the back of the class shouted, 'How did you *do* that?'

The tension broke. A ripple of calm rolled over the class. Even the teacher was watching Rose in astonishment.

'I just . . . concentrated,' she said. 'Look.'

She focused again, and those eyes re-formed from the smoke. She would not have called them back, but it would look suspicious if she was reluctant to recreate what she had unwittingly called into physical form.

Miss Edgware suggested they all try colouring the smoke figures – which, she asserted, was part of the lesson plan anyway – and within a few minutes all the figures were wearing brightly coloured clothes and, thankfully, normal eyes. At the end of the lesson Miss Edgware transmogrified the smoke figures into plastic and placed them in the corner of the room.

After they were dismissed, Rose hurried out of the classroom and leaned against the wall, trying to control her breathing. That had been dangerous – unbelievably, unspeakably dangerous. And it was her fault.

No point worrying about it. Put it behind you, and make sure it doesn't happen again.

She was fine. She was a liar. She could lie about this. She got up and started walking to Combat.

CHAPTER 24

They were waiting outside the Department building again that evening. There were twice as many Gospel members tonight, and their average age had lowered considerably, as well: Rose would have put most of them in their mid-twenties. Presumably someone in the group had realised that nobody was listening to them on the separate-schools front, so they had adopted a new grievance. Not to mention a new chant. This one was very simple, so much so that they hadn't even bothered to make it rhyme.

'Ashkind off our streets!'

Rose recognised Stephen Greenlow's voice. She could find traces of Tristan and Aaron in there as well, if she tried; and then, suddenly, she realised why.

They were there.

They were there, outside the Department – *her* Department – standing smiling on that stage with their father, and chanting stupid bloody slogans and waving stupid bloody banners with that stupid bloody winged door on it, and most of the gathered supporters were Leeched, they couldn't do magic, and the Greenlow brothers stood on the podium, smiling. They hadn't seen her. She had the element of surprise; she could wipe their stupid bloody smiles off their stupid *bastard* faces—

'Is that him?' came a quiet voice from behind her. She turned. James leaned against the wall, eyes on Aaron, hand on the handle of his gun. 'Can I kill him for you?'

'I don't think that will do your career any favours.'

'I don't care about my career. I care about—' He stopped, and swallowed. 'I care about law and order.'

'What do they want this time?'

He shrugged. 'Who cares?' He paused, staring at them, and then suddenly pulled her behind the wall. Something glittered in his eyes. His expression bore a remarkable resemblance to the one David wore just before things went wrong and people died.

'Wouldn't it be terrible,' he whispered, 'if the Gospel should become violent?'

'It would,' Rose agreed, voice equally low, 'but I don't like your chances. They don't want to get arrested.'

'Well, that's where they're going to be out of luck, aren't they?'

'What do you suggest?'

James peered round the corner. 'The kid's using magic.'

'What, Tristan? No he isn't.'

James gave her a my-God-you're-slow-today look. 'He absolutely, definitely is.'

Rose nodded. 'Oh, yes. Loads.'

'Exactly.'

'And I swear Aaron's got a short-action rifle.'

'Yeah, I see it now.'

James looked at her. She could see the beginnings of his smile. He took his walkie-talkie out of his bag and held down the button. 'Laura?'

'Yes?' came the crackly reply.

'We need a squad team out here now, please.'

The response was alarmed. 'Are Greenlow's lot causing trouble?'

'Lots,' said James, and this time his grin showed through in his voice. There was a pause on the other end. Laura knew, Rose could tell she knew; but the Department had no love for the Gospel, and Laura certainly had no reason to want them out of harm's way.

'On their way,' she said finally, and disconnected.

James glanced up at Rose. She smiled at him, pulse racing, and then they stepped out from behind the wall.

'SHUT UP!' James roared. The chanting from the Gospel lowered to murmurs of discontent, and fell silent altogether as they turned to look at him. They'd seen him coming to work often enough, and, despite his age, they knew to be wary of angry Department members. Tristan and Aaron looked between Rose and James, uncomprehending. Stephen Greenlow turned, surprised.

'You're James Andreas, aren't you?' he said, ignoring his sons' expressions of growing anxiety. Their eyes, with those of the rest of the Gospel congregation, were on James's gun.

'Yes.'

'Tomas Andreas's brother?'

James's face darkened; Rose made a mental note not to ask. 'Yes.' They were all staring at him now. 'I'm here to tell you to get lost.'

Stephen's eyebrows rose so high it was almost comical. 'And why is that? We're doing nothing wrong.'

'You're using magic illegally,' said James. 'You're under arrest. All of you.'

'You're going to arrest *all* of us? Just on your own? You'll have a lot of work on your hands, my boy.'

'There's a Department squad team on its way.'

'Well then,' as mutterings began to rise and Aaron and Tristan looked genuinely alarmed, 'today will mark another lost battle in the fight for free speech.'

'And a victory in the fight against bigotry,' said Rose before she could stop herself. The Greenlows switched their attention to her. She met their gazes unblinkingly.

'You call us bigots?' yelled Tristan. He didn't have the advantage of Stephen's microphone or the worried silence that accompanied James's and Rose's speech, and his voice was thin on the May breeze.

'I'm sorry, did you not hear me the first time?'

The mutterings among the Gospel crowd were growing; they looked angry now, and Rose was abruptly aware of the fact that there were only two of her and James. He seemed to have had the same realisation, and brought out his walkie-talkie again.

'Laura, what's their ETA?'

A silence. Then, suddenly, a very different voice came onto the intercom.

'What in *hell* do you think you are doing?'

Rose and James glanced at each other in alarm.

'They have weapons, sir,' James said hesitantly, but he did not sound at all convinced now. 'They're a danger to public order.'

'The hell they are,' said Terrian angrily. 'What is this?

Revenge? A prank? What in Ichor's name makes you think you have the right to use Department troops for your own purposes?'

James was defensive now. 'Nothing, Connor, we just—'

'*We?*'

James glanced at Rose, biting his lip. There was another, longer pause. Everyone in the Gospel had heard the reply. Greenlow looked amused. Tristan and Aaron, on their stupid bloody podium, started laughing.

'So,' said Stephen, 'free speech survives another day, then, does it?'

The laughter grew steadily, monstrously, until the crowd were howling. It was like the most absurd nightmare in history; Tristan and Aaron were pointing at her, screaming with the hilarity of it.

Nobody likes you.

She walked away as quickly as she could, tears withheld but blushing, leaving James in front of the gathered Gospel.

CHAPTER 25

There were posters on the school walls the next day. Not of Loren – those had been ripped or vandalised to the point of illegibility within a week. The face that now stared down from the walls was very different: younger, stronger, dark-haired and bright-eyed. Even Rose couldn't stop herself sympathising with the family when the word 'MISSING' was written in stark black letters under his photo.

It was Aaron Greenlow.

Tristan had been crying. Of course, Rose couldn't blame him for that, whatever else she wanted to blame him for. What worried her, though, was that Tristan broken-hearted, brotherless and unhappy was likely to be far more malicious than Tristan content. And he had been bad enough then.

Aaron Greenlow. Missing.

He had vanished the previous night, after Rose's confrontation with him and his father's mob. But it couldn't have anything to do with that. No.

Aaron Greenlow. Missing.

Presumed dead, Rose knew. Because Aaron was the son of an MoD official, the Department had bumped him up their list. They had him on file as a suicide victim – David had told her heavily that the case of the Mysterious Disappearing Teenage Boy was one they had encountered many, many times before – but they weren't telling his mother that.

Aaron Greenlow. Missing, presumed dead.

And Rose wasn't quite sure how she felt about that. She hadn't got used to the idea of him as a bully in thrall to his younger brother. In her mind, he was still the handsome boy she had not been able to stop thinking about for two years.

And now he was gone. And she felt nothing. Nothing overwhelming, at least. There was some sadness, of course, but that couldn't be helped.

The thing was – and she gave credence to this thought with great reluctance – Aaron didn't act like a suicide victim. He had never acted like a suicide victim. He was doing well in school, and he was popular, and he was Gifted.

And she'd seen him just yesterday. He'd looked fine.

There was no note. No previous behavioural indicators.

So what had happened to Aaron?

For the first time in weeks, Rose found herself thinking of poor, dead Sylvia Argent. Killed by Regency, for whatever reason. Poisoned whilst pregnant. Cold, now, and rotting with her brother in the earth. She had found Tom again, in the end, Rose thought with a dull smile. Perhaps she was happy there, with him.

But she was still dead. And no one knew exactly why.

Rose was not sufficiently lost in these musings, however, to ignore the expression on her teacher's face when he walked into the Combat classroom that afternoon. He was grinning slightly too widely to be just generally happy. No: this was his sadistic face. It meant a fight.

And Rose knew whom it would be between.

'All right, settle down!'

The class settled down. They always kept remarkably quiet in front of the teacher when, as now, he had a gun in his hand. Amazing what the presence of lethal weaponry could do for you.

'You've been practising magical combat techniques for the past three weeks,' he told them. They knew. Six burns, four cuts and a broken jawbone marked their progress. 'Some of you aren't even atrocious any more. So you know what happens. I'll pair you up. You come up to the front of the classroom and fight it out. First break in the shield wins.'

Rose stayed in a corner and watched the fights before hers. She was too deep in thought to pay attention to any of them; they played out before her in an uneven blur of thuds and grunts. When it came to Nate and Maria's, she blinked herself alert. This, she thought, would be a straightforward victory for Nate, but she had underestimated them both: Maria, who couldn't fight anyway, didn't even try to beat Nate. He stabbed at her shield, which she blocked, and then he blasted her into the concrete wall, trusting to her magical defences to keep her from feeling any pain, and then twisted her shield apart.

It was Maria's grateful smile that gave it away. The teacher noticed it immediately: Rose, who had been watching him narrowly throughout the fight, knew that everything had been too expertly choreographed for the deception to pass unnoticed. He held up a hand to stop proceedings.

'Well done,' he said. He clapped slowly. The sounds fell like blows over the class, who stayed utterly silent. Knowing their teacher, they knew nothing good would be coming next.

'You.' He nodded to Nate. 'Stand beside me.'

Nate did. If he was afraid, he didn't show it.

'Rose, come stand across from Maria.'

Turning as one as if by a strong wind, the class swivelled round to look at her. They cleared a path for her as she walked through them; she did her best to ignore their whispers, their wide eyes. She took her place about ten feet away from Maria in a combat stance. She thought she might know what the teacher was doing. If she was right, he was both cleverer and more utterly vicious than Rose had thought.

The teacher addressed the class now. 'This is what will happen if you voluntarily lose a fight. Rose will now proceed to fight Maria. Every blow Maria takes will also be felt by Nathaniel.'

He was very perceptive; not many teachers would be able to sense an unspoken relationship between two pupils, let alone find a way to use it against them.

She wondered whether he could feel the palpable hatred radiating from all three of them towards him.

'Adopt combat stance.'

Maria did. She looked scared but determined.

'Begin.'

Maria struck faster than Rose had expected her to: a spike-strike straight to the stomach. Spike-strikes were ideal for taking people off-guard, because they were almost impossible to detect and didn't use much energy. Rose, however, had guessed that this was what Maria would use and had a block ready. She responded with a hard, rushing block of energy that pressed Maria to the floor.

Somewhere to her left, she heard Nate grunt in pain.

Rose, not wanting to draw this out by any means, slammed Maria one more time and then, at the flash of light that indicated a break in her shield, stepped back and nodded. She turned to the teacher, who seemed displeased.

'You didn't try,' he said.

'I won in two blows. How is that not trying?'

Nate got to his feet, wincing. He met Maria's eyes and nodded in thanks. The teacher's gaze flashed between them and back to Rose.

'Fight again,' he said.

Maria's mouth dropped open in outrage. Nate made a small noise between a groan and a sigh.

'No,' Rose said.

Absolute silence. The class was riveted now.

'I said,' the teacher repeated dangerously, '*fight again*.'

'And I,' Rose told him calmly, 'said no.'

The teacher stared at her, and it was like trying to stare Loren down in Room Fourteen all those months ago, except the teacher didn't know what Loren had known and so this situation was nowhere near as frightening.

There was a very long pause. After about ten seconds, the class's whispers rose to the level where the teacher's control was being disputed and he told them, sharply, to shut up.

'Nathaniel and Maria,' he said slowly, 'go stand with the class again.'

They did, albeit hesitantly. Nate's eyes did not leave Rose's. She didn't need David's skills to know what he was thinking: *Be careful.*

'Next fight,' the teacher said in a louder voice, returning to his clipboard, 'Tristan Greenlow versus Rosalyn Elmsworth.'

The class openly gasped now. Rose had just used up a substantial amount of energy fighting Maria: it had been assumed that she had done her fighting for the day. Rose narrowed her eyes. She would have to fight Tristan outgunned and under-strength. Now he was really testing her.

As Tristan walked up, grinning despite the tear tracks still etched onto his face, the teacher whispered something in his ear. Rose stiffened. Okay, now *that* was unfair. He was making this fight impossible to win.

'Combat stances.'

Rose closed her eyes and breathed in. She felt her shield billow into life around her.

'Ready.'

She breathed out and opened her eyes.

'Begin!'

And the world went dark.

Utter and complete darkness, so dark she couldn't see her hand in front of her face. Only the sound of her own breathing, and murmurs.

Rearing panic.

Don't be afraid of the dark. A stupid saying.

'What the *hell?*' she whispered.

Something hard hit her in the back of the head and she dropped, dazed. Distantly, the class murmured in confusion. The darkness was closing in on her; she was beginning to hyperventilate; she couldn't fight she couldn't fight she couldn't *fight*—

The next blow came to her ribs and she gasped in pain, rocking back. *Keep your shield intact,* said a calm voice in her head, and she poured energy into it, curling into the foetal position. *Hold yourself together. Wait*—

Another kick, this time to her spine. She cried out. Surely this was breaking the rules, surely he was only allowed to use magical attacks – but of course the teacher wouldn't stop him, the teacher had given him every advantage, he wanted Tristan to win this fight—

The teacher had *told* him to do this.

The *bastard*.

Someone in the crowd, defiant, yelled desperately, 'Come on, Rose!'

Well, you wouldn't do it any better, Rose thought savagely, *if you couldn't see your opponent.*

A kick to her leg. Rose poured the pain into keeping the shield together.

But they can *see him*.

It was true. The class wasn't panicking; they weren't screaming at the sudden dark, and if Rose had lost her composure then *they* sure as hell should have done—

Oh, come on, this is obvious. Stupid, stupid!

This was an attack on her eyes. He was blinding her with magic. He was blocking her sight, they'd learnt it in Healing, oh come on why on earth hadn't she thought of that before—

He was attacking her *eyes*.

He'd started before her shield went up. He'd gotten within her defences.

And that was a mistake.

Rose pulled all her strength into herself and then directed it all into pushing her shield out from herself in a wall of energy that spread across the entire room – and, more importantly, caught Tristan. She heard it smash him into the concrete, not distracting him enough to break his shield, but certainly enough for his mental attack to waver, which was all Rose needed.

Vision returned to her abruptly, in a flickering wave of light. She blinked, and was in the classroom again, her heart thundering.

And Tristan was down.

His shield had protected him; he was getting to his feet, his face twisted into something that was almost a snarl.

He's a boy. He's taller and stronger than you. You cannot let this become a physical fight.

Well, not again, anyway.

She pushed a spike-strike towards his head, but he

blocked it and responded with a punch to her head, which she dodged, throwing him off-balance. He was angry now. And that gave her an advantage like nothing else had.

Destroy him.

There was blood running down her face. She hit him from the side with a hard block of power and he stumbled. She swept her feet under his ankles, but he was strong and it didn't move him. She had lost her opportunity to press her attack.

I just wanted to tell you how much of a bitch I think you are.

He ran at her. She waited until the last moment and hit him at short range with a blast to the stomach followed by a punch. That made him double up. She didn't lose a second this time, but kicked him hard in the head. He staggered sideways and she dodged nimbly on limbs with injuries she didn't feel yet, stepped behind him, grabbed his windpipe and squeezed.

Nobody likes you, you know . . . you're the ugliest girl in the year.

Aaron's voice. Tristan's words.

The Gospel, laughing.

Destroy him.

He couldn't move, but gasped for air. She didn't need to tell him anything; he knew the ultimatum.

Maybe if she squeezed a little harder, he would die.

Why would I want to be seen with you?

He dropped to his knees. She moved with him, keeping her grip strong.

The teacher said sharply, 'Rose.'

She did not let go. Tristan was going blue.

'*Rose!*'

The flash of light came at last and Rose released Tristan, letting him drop. His breaths were wheezy, his blond hair bloodstained.

Rose turned to the teacher, pushing her hair back and wiping some of the blood out of her eyes.

'Did I pass, then?' she said coolly.

He met her gaze narrowly. She noticed his pen was lying on the floor now.

'Yes,' he said finally. 'Yes, you did.'

There was silence in the class now, but for the sound of Tristan trying to breathe.

'Sir,' said someone in the class nervously, 'I think . . . I think he might need an ambulance.'

It was Maria. Rose looked at her in surprise. She wasn't meeting Rose's eyes. She was staring at Tristan with an expression of something close to fear. Was she still afraid of him? He wouldn't harm them for a long time now. She didn't need to be.

Destroy him.

'Yes,' said the teacher, 'yes, he might. Go get the nurse.'

Maria ran, casting a frightened glance back at Rose as she left. Nate followed her. There was a new wariness in his gaze.

They weren't afraid of Tristan. They were afraid of *her.*

For the first time, Rose began to wonder whether she might have gone too far.

The class was looking at her like Nate had done, like

people sometimes looked at her father: almost afraid, guarded, suspicious. Rose watched them file out, and was about to follow them when the teacher's hand on her shoulder held her back. She stood with him as the nurse came and took Tristan away. There were sirens outside.

After the sirens faded, there was silence for a few seconds.

Then the teacher said quietly, 'Rose, exactly what did your father teach you?'

'To stand up for myself.'

He raised an eyebrow. He looked almost shaken.

'Rose. That wasn't standing up for yourself. You almost *killed* that boy.'

'I know.'

'Rose, did your father ever teach you when to *stop?*'

He *was* shaken.

'No. If someone is trying to kill me, I kill them first. That's the way it works.'

He turned sharply to look at her in astonishment.

'Rose, do you realise what you're saying?'

Yes. I chose to harm him. I chose it freely.

Oh, bloody hell.

'Of course I understand, sir.'

'No. No, you don't. Rose, have you ever killed someone?'

'No.'

'No, you haven't. *Could* you kill someone?'

There was another long silence.

'I think I just proved that, sir,' Rose said quietly.

The teacher put his face in his hands. After a while, he

took out a pen and a notepad and scribbled something down and gave it to Rose.

'Go to Serena Mitchell,' he said tiredly. 'Tell her it's time.'

CHAPTER 26

Serena's office was empty when Rose arrived. The sign on the door said that she would be back in five minutes, so Rose sat in a chair and waited, feeling the blood dry on her face and the wounds in her leg and chest begin to throb. She had not realised that she was badly hurt: now she thought maybe she had cracked a rib. The teacher had not offered to heal her, and Rose doubted that she herself could.

She thought of Natalie Greenlow. They would have called her by now, told her that her son was in hospital, and she would be happy at first, happy because she would think it was Aaron, and they had found him, and he was safe, if injured, and not dead. And then they would tell her that it was Tristan who had been hospitalised. And then her heart would lurch and she would be terrified, terrified that her remaining safe child had been nearly killed – nearly killed by someone in his own class, no less. She would see danger everywhere, and Rose's father would be under suspicion again, and Rose—

The creak of the door announced Serena's arrival. Her expression flickered only slightly when she saw Rose's bruised, bloody state. Rose turned slowly to look at her. Every movement sent a throb of pain through her head.

'I see. Did you decide to come, or did they finally run out of patience?'

Rose said nothing. When she continued to say nothing, Serena closed the door behind her and sat down.

Rose said emotionlessly, 'He said it was time.'

Serena considered her carefully. 'Whom did you fight?'

'Does it matter?'

'What sort of state are they in now?'

Rose didn't think it worth answering.

'There were ambulances outside the school ten minutes ago. Was that you?'

Rose nodded.

'I see,' Serena said again.

There was a pause.

'So your Combat teacher sent you, did he?'

Rose nodded again, and winced. The wound in the back of her head was still bleeding; she could feel the warm, slow run of blood in her hair.

'Did he tell you why?'

'No.'

Serena nodded, seemingly to herself. 'All right then.'

Another pause.

'Rose, are you aware that you are the most skilled fighter of your age that we have ever taught?'

Rose did not reply. Well, of course she was. She had been raised a fighter. Most of the others were just starting out.

'So you will understand that – given your reluctance – we have been obliged, in your case, to speed up the required processes somewhat.'

Rose tilted her head slightly. 'What exactly do you mean?'

Serena seemed to breathe in slightly more deeply than normal.

She said, 'Rosalyn, on behalf of the Angelic Parliament of Great Britain and Ireland, I hereby inform you that you have been chosen to perform your civic duty as a member of the armed forces of this country in the post of private of the Third Royal Battalion.'

Rose stared at her for a few seconds. Then she started laughing. She laughed so hard that her voice cracked and split and for a few seconds she thought that she was going to cry. She could feel Serena's bewildered eyes on her.

'And tell me,' she said, when she had finished and regained her voice, 'who was the last to vacate this position as a private of the Third Royal Battalion?'

'I believe,' Serena said, 'it was one Thomas Argent.'

Rose's face twisted into a smile that she did not at all feel.

'You can't do this to me,' she said, still smiling. 'I'm underage. I'm not even sixteen yet. You can't put me into the army.'

'You do not have a choice,' Serena said stonily. 'Perhaps, if you had been a little more receptive to the idea of being a soldier, later in life . . .'

'So you're conscripting me.'

'*I* am not conscripting anyone.'

'Oh, listen to yourself,' Rose said, grinning. 'This was your idea, wasn't it? To put a child into the army and send her off to die, just because she happened to be better at hurting people than the rest of them? Why couldn't you at least have waited until I was of age?'

'Circumstances . . . change,' Serena said. 'London needs new soldiers.'

Rose's focus sharpened. 'You're saying the city is under attack?'

'Not from without, no.'

'But from within – Ashkind insurgent groups, you mean? Old War armies?'

Regency.

'You will see,' Serena said, standing up. 'Your ceremony will take place tomorrow. I doubt you will see your home or your family again for a long time after that, so I would do your best to say goodbye now.'

She left, closing the door behind her. Rose gave it thirty seconds before following her out. She found her way to the nearest bathroom, ran the taps and dipped her head in the water, washing the blood from her face and wounds. When she was perfectly clean again, she stared at herself in the mirror.

What did she look like?

An objective observer might conclude that *she* had been beaten up. Fifteen-year-olds were not the most common aggressors, after all, and fifteen-year-old girls least of all. The water in the sink was a pinkish-red and she was pale and cold and her hair was near-black with water and blood.

She didn't look like a monster.

She didn't look like someone who had chosen to be evil.

She didn't look like someone who *did* these kinds of things.

She walked out of the bathroom and out of the school, towards the nearest train station. She waited for the District line, found an empty carriage, sat down and started to cry. She cried for a very, very long time. She cried until the train reached the end of the line and started to go back again. No one came into the carriage. No one asked her what was wrong. She did not know what she would have replied if they had.

'Hello, Dad,' she said quietly. Her voice was still hoarse. The Department was bustling with staff in their usual state of near-panic, and no one glanced at her twice except him. He was sitting in front of his computer, and she had walked up behind him with all the stealth and silence that her worn-out state would allow.

'Rose! Why are you here? Shouldn't you be at school?'

Rose studied his face carefully. The exact layout of the slight lines on his face, the shape and depth of colour of his eyes, the way he smiled, the tiny grey hair just behind his right temple. She seared it into the wall of her mind and promised herself never, ever to forget.

Then she told him.

He sat there for a very long time.

'No,' he said.

'Dad—'

'No.'

'Dad, be reasonable.'

'I'm going to—'

'You can't.'

'I'll find—'

'No. Dad. That won't help me. It's too late.'

He didn't say anything after that, and when he did move it was to get up and walk towards Terrian.

'I won't be coming back for a few days,' he said. His heart was breaking in his voice.

She went over to James and told him and said goodbye and smiled before he could say anything. Then she went back over to her father. He walked away with her to the door. James was up on his feet by now, and he ran over to them and he took her hand and he looked at her, and he said, 'Rose, I—'

And then he fell silent. Rose couldn't see anything in his eyes. After a pause, he hugged her awkwardly.

'I'll miss you,' he said. 'Please – don't die out there. And email me. You'll be allowed to do that, won't you?'

She smiled. 'Yes, James. I'll miss you too.'

He pulled back, and looked at her as if he wanted to say something else, but then he stopped himself and simply gave a little wave.

'Stay in touch,' he said, weakly.

Rose nodded. And then she walked away.

When evening fell, David and Rose were sitting together at the table. The cuts on her face were healing, with the help of magic. She was resting her head on his shoulder. They were planning.

'I won't let them do this. I am not going to let them do this. They can't take you away from me.'

Rose didn't say anything. David had been repeating this like a mantra for the past hour. His voice was growing slowly more anguished.

'Promise me,' he said, 'that you won't let yourself be hurt.'

'I won't really have any control over that, Dad. And anyway, maybe it would be good if I got injured. I can be like James. You can draft me into the Department.'

His face twisted. 'I don't care. I want you to stay safe, do you hear me? And I want you – I *need* you to stay hidden, do you understand? I don't think I could live with myself if—'

'No,' she said angrily. 'I won't be found out. This is the army, for Ichor's sake. They have secret places. Soundproofed rooms. I can do this. I'll find a way.' She knew he couldn't quite believe her, so in lieu of a stronger argument, she said it again. 'I won't be found out, Dad.'

He swallowed. Rose waited, feeling the slow rise and fall of his chest.

'I'll be okay, Dad,' she said gently. 'I'm nearly sixteen. I'll be an adult in a few months. I can look after myself. We have the Internet, don't we?'

'Yes, but that's monitored. I won't be able to tell you about anything important. We have to . . .' His voice trailed off and then came back with a vengeance. 'Can't we do *anything?*'

'I don't technically work for you. You can't override them. If they have the DoE's approval, and they do, they're within their rights to do this.' She smiled. It hurt. 'I'm sure you'll cope. Nate can be the sleeper while I'm gone. It should be his turn by now, after all.'

David turned his head to look at her.

'Aren't you going to say goodbye to him? And Maria?'

Rose shook her head.

'Why not? They're your friends. They'll miss you.'

'They'll cope. They don't need me.'

'Oh, no, Rose, don't think that!' He hugged her to him, rocking her back and forth like he had when she was a toddler. 'No, Rose.' His voice grew soft and pained. 'Don't you ever, ever think that.'

There was a long, long silence.

'Dad?'

'Yes, Rose?'

'I love you.'

'I know. I love you too, Rose.'

She waited until he was asleep and then left the house, taking the Tube to Loren's flat. When she arrived there, he was gone. Maybe he had just packed up and left. Maybe he had had to relocate, and there was a note hidden somewhere among the decrepit furniture and the remains of the plastic bags she had brought the food in.

He would be fine.

She had bigger problems than him now.

Rose stood and stared around at the abandoned flat, and then she headed back home.

Loren, she thought, sitting on her bed. *I didn't choose to do this. I don't want to do this. Please don't hurt my*

father. You'll understand what happened, won't you?
   I swear to God this isn't my fault.
   But if I didn't choose it, why do I have to do it?
   What in the hell is the use of not choosing to do evil things if they make you do evil anyway?

CHAPTER 27

She woke up early the next morning. For a few wonderful seconds she forgot what had happened, and then it slid slowly back to her and she rolled over, staring at the ceiling of her room. She would not see it again for a very long time.

Or she would never see it again.

Don't think that.

Rose got up, put on her clothes and went to her father's comms tablet to check her emails. They had sent her an automatic message. Rose skim-read most of it. The gist was that she had to be at the Military Induction Centre at ten o'clock.

Her father was up early too. Neither of them ate. For a while, they simply sat on the sofa together, trying to find something to say. David held Rose's hand, and for the first time in weeks, she felt safe.

It lasted a brief, fleeting moment, and then it was gone.

When nine-fifteen came, they put on their coats and set off for the induction centre. They did not speak. The world around Rose seemed slightly blurred. She was going to be a soldier. She would not come home for a very long time.

If she ever came home at all.

There were no other candidates to be inducted that day. Later, when she examined her memories, she found that there were seven people in the yawning, cavernous, echoing room where she was inducted. Herself, her father, Serena, the Induction Administrator, two guards, and an official she could not name who watched her inscrutably throughout. It seemed very empty, and very frightening.

When she arrived at the centre, they gave her a uniform and showed her to the changing rooms. Rose hugged her father one last time. She did not need to say she loved him. She did not need to say that she already missed him. She did not need to describe how terrible she felt, or how afraid she was. He knew.

She kissed him on the cheek and walked away. When she looked back, he was still standing there, watching her.

She changed into the uniform. Khaki trousers and shirt, boots, thick socks, belt and holster, ammunition pouch, gun. It was a good gun, warm and steady in her hands. It would help her.

She leaned against the wall and took five deep breaths.

Rose walked out of the changing room into the hall. There was very little natural light here. The Induction Administrator gave her a single bullet and walked away. Rose loaded it into her gun. She did not wonder what she would need it for.

That, in retrospect, was a mistake.

She climbed the stairs into the wide open hall. It felt almost like a wedding, if not for the distinctly funerary expressions of the spectators: the long walk down to the official on the platform, six pairs of sharp eyes locked onto her. Music started playing, tinny through the speakers in the corners of the room. She didn't listen to it; she took strength from ignoring the trinkets and frills they added to the act of sending her off to die.

She reached the end of the aisle without stumbling, and the music cut off. The Induction Administrator himself was there. He recited the vows to her in the disorienting silence, and she repeated them seamlessly.

'I, Rosalyn Daniela Elmsworth, gladly give myself to the service of the Angels and to their Government. I rejoice in my choosing and repent of all my sins. I give my life, should it need to be taken, to the service of all that is good and just. If this be untrue let me face the wrath of the Angels.'

He nodded. Rose could feel her father's eyes on the back of her head, but she did not dare look to him.

'Do you swear your loyalty to the will of the Angels?'

'I do.'

'Do you promise to obey them gladly and willingly?'

'I do.'

'Will you always enact the orders of the Government, whatever the cost?'

'I will.'

'Then I command you to prove your loyalty with a steady hand in the execution of justice.'

There was no cue. Rose heard the rumbling and creaking of wheels behind her, a crack and a small cry of pain. She did not look round.

'I bring before you a convict, condemned for providing service to the enemy. As proof of your obedience, you must be the harbinger of order in the deliverance of his death.'

Oh, she could have guessed. She could have guessed: the shiver down her spine, the flicker in the Administrator's smile, the very small intake of breath from the space where she knew her father to be standing. She took the gun out of her holster and turned to face the man she had to kill, and her hand was halfway to the safety catch when she saw his face. He had been beaten up badly: his nose had been broken, one eye was black and he moved gingerly, as if with a cracked rib.

It was Loren Arkwood.

She registered it subconsciously first, and by the time it fully hit her she was sufficiently in control of her wits and motor functions not to drop the gun. She clicked the safety off and aimed squarely between his eyes.

He saw her face, too, and managed just in time to control the shock in his expression. He had been hurt badly: they had had to tie him to a metal pole on wheels, and the glances he shot at the guards were full of a fear she had never seen in his eyes before. His face was drawn and grey. He looked tired, starved.

How long had they had him? It had only been four days since she had seen him. And she had been to his flat only last night, and there had been . . . a broken vase on the floor, a tear in the sofa, something too dark to be water staining the tiles. They had taken him two, maybe three days ago. And she had been too unobservant to notice.

His mouth formed her name. He hung his head.

'Do it quickly.'

His voice was hoarse and broken and painfully familiar. It echoed through the hall. David flinched at the sound of it.

David would have known they had him. David had not told her.

Rose's hands were steady on the gun. Five seconds had passed since she had seen Loren's face. The pause of any fifteen-year-old set the task of killing someone.

One bullet in her gun.

Rose breathed in, and then out again.

Herself. Her father. The Induction Administrator. Serena, watching her victim with unrevealing eyes. Two guards standing around Loren. The quiet official, who had, unconsciously it seemed, started fiddling with her watch, twisting the frame around and around. It made a small clicking noise in the silence. Her face seemed slightly familiar.

One bullet in her gun.

Please forgive me.

One bullet.

Rose allowed the count to reach ten seconds, and then twisted and fired at the chain link holding Loren to the post. She had counted on at least two seconds of confusion before someone realised that Loren was not dead. She got three. She reached out with her magic, and the guns of Loren's guards jammed and the bullets started to explode in their chambers, making the guards yelp and drop them on the floor. Loren stumbled forward, hissed in pain, realised he was free, and then the next thing Rose felt was his hands on her wrist, wrestling the gun from her.

He was weakened, too weak to be able to use magic, but still stronger than her: he took the gun from her, got her in a half-nelson, and pressed the gun to her temple. He didn't know the gun was useless now. Luckily, neither did anyone else bar the Induction Administrator, and he seemed to have temporarily lost the power of speech.

'Drop your weapons,' he said, 'or she dies.'

In any other room, there would have been no response. This one, however, happened to contain three of the one-in-a-thousand people in London with firearm licences. David, the Induction Administrator and the quiet official all dropped their guns down and kicked them towards Loren.

David's gun spun slowly across the floor, and then suddenly snapped up into the air, the handle shooting towards Loren's temple. Loren ducked, and David's gun flew past him and slammed into the wall behind him. David narrowed his eyes, white-faced with anger, and the tiles around Loren's feet began to break into small, sharp pieces, which lifted into the air and opened up cuts on Loren's arms.

Loren pressed the barrel harder into Rose's temple. 'I mean it,' he said loudly. 'I'll kill her.' The tiles hovered in the air for a moment, but perhaps the blood running down his arms gave the statement more weight. Slowly, they began to drop and shatter against the floor.

David was giving Loren a glare of such utter murderous hatred as would make most people – including Rose – run very fast in the opposite direction, but Loren simply looked back at him with cold, calm yellow eyes.

'You know I will,' he said softly.

Rose was shaking. She closed her eyes as David and Loren stared each other down, trying to visualise what the people around her – currently wearing expressions of equal parts fear and bewilderment – would think they had seen. It would look like Rose's hand had slipped, and that she had hit the chain link by a mere stroke of good fortune. Or bad fortune, depending on your perspective.

Not David, though.

Not David, who knew that her aim was nearly as good as his own. Not David, who knew that her hands never, ever shook. Not David, who even now would be calculating the amount of excess energy left in Loren's body and coming to the conclusion that it was nowhere near enough to put two guns out of action.

Not David.

Slowly, agonisingly, Rose began to feel the pieces start to come together in his mind.

'I'm going to walk out of here,' Loren said, very slowly and clearly, 'and if I hear anything even vaguely resembling footsteps behind me, the girl gets a bullet through her brain. Am I understood?'

He was.

Loren started walking, half-dragging Rose with him. Rose could tell that he was making an effort not to show how badly injured he was. He still walked with a slight limp, his nose was bloody and at an angle, and there was definitely something wrong with his ribs. Belatedly, Rose realised that she should look a lot more terrified than she currently did. She attempted to haul a fearful expression onto her face, and failed.

Never mind. Too late now.

They walked through the deserted lobby and down the steps outside the building. As soon as they were sure no one could see them, Loren sank to his knees. Rose, all too aware of the ever-present CCTV, half-helped, half-pulled him round to the back of the building, where he sat, coughing, against the wall. Rose leaned against the brick, felt for the thrumming buzz of the wires within it, and then sent a shot of electricity into it that should – with luck – short out the entire camera system. It would have been far more efficient just to take out the cameras watching them, but that would be as obvious a giveaway as lighting a fire.

Rose pulled back and looked down at Loren. He was trying to say something, and failing. After a few seconds of this, he simply reached for her hand, which she gave him uncertainly. His grip was disproportionately strong.

There was an odd pulling sensation, as if something was draining slowly out of her. She looked at Loren. His bruises were fading, the light returning to his eyes. There was a series of cracks as his nose and ribs healed and a few things that were dislocated located themselves again. When Rose felt they were into the danger zone, she pulled her hand away. She ignored the sudden, dull beat of weariness, and put her ear to the wall again. Faintly, she could hear angry, terrified shouting. Her father, of course.

Rose closed her eyes and pressed her forehead to the cold brick.

Other voices joined his. Quieter and more soothing. Trying to calm him down, prevent him from running into whatever trap Loren had laid. Good luck with that.

She could hear the words now.

'That bastard has my daughter! Don't you dare— don't you *dare* try and stop me—'

That one wasn't going to work. Okay, Dad, play the Department card.

'I am an officer of the Angelic Empire—'

There you go.

Loren was trying to speak again. This time, he managed it.

'Okay,' he said hoarsely, 'so why aren't we running?'

'—my daughter! Don't you understand what that means, you bunch of heartless—'

'Because not running,' Rose said, finally pulling herself away from the wall, 'is perhaps the most stupid thing we could do in this situation.'

Loren got to his feet, wincing. 'And I suppose there's logic behind this?'

'Yes. Because Dad knows how I think. And he probably knows how you think. And this kind of decision is not, logically, one either of us would make.'

Loren nodded. 'All right. So we have, how long exactly?'

'Only Dad is going to make a move. None of them will alert the police, because in this case, the Department is the police, and Dad is the Department. So Dad's the only one we have to worry about.'

The pain cracked through her composure on the last three words and her voice broke. There were tears in her eyes. She stood there calmly until the broken pieces of her settled back into place and her face was dry.

Loren looked at her.

'Why didn't you kill me?'

She sighed

'I chose not to,' she said, and her tone was sincere but also sardonic, because they both knew that killing him would have meant the end of a secret and made her life that much easier. He nodded, and looked away.

'What do you think our chances are?'

'Of escaping Dad?' She ran a hand through her hair. 'Slightly under zero. Of escaping? Fairly high.'

Loren's head turned so fast he nearly cricked his neck. 'You want to negotiate with him?'

'It is possible, you know,' Rose said, in a voice that was edging towards breaking again. She swallowed. 'He's not a thug.'

'No, not that,' Loren said softly. He pursed his lips. 'You're going to tell him?'

Rose closed her eyes. Inside her head, she saw her father's face. Oh, God. Hadn't she had to break his heart once already in the last twenty-four hours? Wasn't that enough?

'You told me once that if I did that, there would be a little note on a Department desk.'

'Rose, if you still thought I would do that I would be in that building right now with a bullet through my head.'

There was a long, empty silence.

And another few seconds before Rose realised what that silence meant.

She leaned back against the wall and pressed her ear to the brick. Faintly, she could hear murmuring. They'd either subdued him or let him go. Or he'd forced them to let him go. Either way, their situation remained the same.

'Loren,' she said softly, in a voice of forced calm, 'get back against the wall.'

He did so just in time. David came running down the steps, looking wild and almost crazed, with several guns in his belt, none of which were his. Rose closed her eyes.

Come on, Dad, she prayed silently, *run the other way, please, give me some time – you've got to give me a chance in this one, come on, please . . .*

David's voice. An anguished yell. '*Rose!*'

The echo came back loudest from a deserted alleyway across the other side of the empty street. Rose supposed it looked plausible, or at any rate David did, because he crossed the street without bothering to check for cars and sprinted down the alleyway. Rose did not breathe until his footsteps were out of earshot.

Neither did Loren.

He asked again, his voice tighter. 'How long do you think we have until he works it out?'

Rose backed away from the wall slowly, checking that no one else was going to emerge from the building.

'Oh, he's worked it out,' she said. 'He just doesn't want to accept it yet.'

'What do we do if he finds us?' He paused, and

corrected himself. 'What will he do *when* he finds us? Come on, Rose, you of all people should know this.'

Rose sank to her knees and pressed her eyes shut. He was right. She should know this. But nothing occurred to her.

Come on . . . what would you do if Loren had Dad?

This answer came quickly. *I'd try to take Loren out without hurting Dad. But he'd be expecting that, so I'd try to put him off guard. I'd have to make him think that I—*

There was something weird about Dad just now.

Wasn't there?

Around him, it was like he was almost. . .

Glowing.

Oh Angels.

Glowing green.

Her eyes flew open. Loren looked at her, and then his eyes widened, staring at something over her shoulder.

Slowly, very slowly, she stood up. She was shaking.

'Dad,' she said to the empty air in front of her, 'please listen to me—'

'Turn round slowly and raise your hands to shoulder height,' said the voice coldly from behind her.

Rose did. So did Loren. Her father was standing with his gun aimed squarely between Loren's eyes. His face was blank and stony. He was beyond anger. He was beyond hurt, or distress. His eyes were dead, and Rose could see the monster flickering behind them. She wanted to run, but she knew, with cold certainty, that it would be terribly dangerous to move.

'So,' Loren said calmly, 'you're good at optical illusions, I'll give you that. Exactly how long have you been standing there?'

'I followed you out,' David said. His voice was steady, but his left hand was clenched by his side. He opened it and flexed it and Rose saw that the third and fourth fingers of his hand were shaking. Inside his hand was a small metal ball, lined with thin green light: James's hologram projector.

Yes, she really, really should have seen that one coming.

'So now I want you to tell me,' David said in a voice quieter and more dangerous than Rose had ever heard it, 'What. Have. You. Done. To. My. *Daughter*?'

He said the last word so savagely that even his right hand shook with the force of it and the gun went off. The shot hit the wall behind Loren. He did not flinch at that, either.

'I haven't done anything to Rose,' Loren said, in a voice of quiet calm.

She could see that his casual use of Rose's name threw David. Only people who knew her called her by that name, and that would mean prolonged familiarity over a long space of time. Which clashed with his current theory: that Loren was, against all the laws of magic and biology, controlling Rose's will.

Anything but the truth.

Okay. So they were making progress.

'Dad,' Rose said, fighting to keep her voice low and steady, 'put down the gun, please.'

That was a mistake. As if David Elmsworth would ever

233

put down a gun. Instead, he switched his focus onto Rose, aimed at her, his eyes flickering back to Loren.

Loren almost growled.

'I would have thought that was beyond even you,' he said softly. 'Your own daught—'

David snapped towards him and fired as soon as he started speaking, but Loren dived as soon as his hand moved and with a jerk of his head the gun flew out of David's hand. Rose caught it reflexively, reloaded and fired into the air.

David and Loren stared at her.

'Thank you,' Rose said, with the closest thing to calm that she could summon, which was probably numb shock. 'Can we be civil and stop trying to kill each other now?'

Loren glanced at David tightly. 'Rose, what are you doing? The *Department* will have heard that. They'll be coming.'

'Yes, they will,' Rose said, clicking the safety back on, 'which gives us about five minutes to get this straight. Dad, you are not going to kill this man. You are not going to kill him because to do that you're going to have to kill me first, and you know you would never do that.'

David was staring at her.

'Oh, Rose,' he whispered, 'what has he done to you?'

Rose opened her mouth to speak, to try, somehow, to explain – and all of her words left her suddenly and she stood there, helpless under her father's gaze, floundering.

'Dad, I . . .'

Loren took over before Rose could say something terrible. She could only be grateful.

'I cornered your daughter nearly four months ago at her school, shortly after I escaped from your cells,' he said curtly. Rose followed his eyes. He was tracking David's every movement, waiting to see how he would react, whether David would try to kill him again. So far, nothing. 'I presented her with an ultimatum. Either she would help me, or I would tell the rest of the Department – anonymously, of course – that the both of you have been concealing your Hybrid status from the authorities for going on fifteen years. She agreed. Specifically, if my powers of understanding have not left me yet, she agreed in order to protect you.'

Rose had seen this before. She could see the Loren Arkwood of Room Fourteen emerging in his manner again: polite, menacing, eloquent, ruthless. This was the Arkwood who had terrified her.

She could only assume that his re-emergence was not a good sign.

David's voice was terrifying in its emptiness. 'We knew you had an accomplice.'

'Yes. That was Rose.'

David did not so much as glance at her.

'Four months . . .' he said quietly. 'She was meeting you for *four months*?'

Loren nodded. David, to their astonishment, started to laugh. It was a very bitter laugh. Rose had no idea what mode *he* was defaulting to.

'Well, I suppose it was me who taught her how to lie,' he said. 'And she didn't try to kill you? Not even once?'

In any other set of circumstances, Rose would have

resented being talked about as if she wasn't standing three feet away from him. As it was, she merely felt that she was being spared.

'I don't doubt that she wanted to,' said Loren calmly. 'But killing is hard on a first-timer.'

David was staring into the air now, but his gaze was not at all vacant: it was sharp and focused, and his eyes moved quickly as if he were looking at an intricate painting. Fitting all the pieces together. The stuff of nightmares.

'So she knew . . . what, all the way from Argent?'

Loren shook his head. 'The first Regency bomb attack.'

David went motionless. 'You told her about Regency.'

'Of course I did. She deserves to know.'

'How much?'

'Almost everything.'

Now his rage was blistering. 'It wasn't *your* history to teach her, Arkwood—'

'You had no right to withhold that kind of information from her. They're coming for you, David, Felix is coming back for you and if he's targeting you he'll target her.'

'Don't you dare lecture me on how to raise my child.'

'Oh, I think I have every right to talk to you on parenting technique,' said Loren, in the coldest voice Rose had ever heard, 'seeing as you saw fit to advance my niece's upbringing by depriving her of her mother.'

David switched his gaze back to Rose with alarming suddenness. There was something new in his eyes: a wariness, almost, a hostility.

'So you've been lying to me all this time?' he asked.

Definitely hostility.

'I lied to protect you!' Rose cried desperately. 'I couldn't face— they'd kill you, I knew that— you would have lied to me, you *have* lied to me, I know—'

She swallowed. His expression had not changed, but now she could identify something else in his face. Not hostility, not quite. Astonishment. Utter shock. And, could that be . . . pride?

'You complete bastard,' he said with no change in tone at all. Rose had to double-check that he was speaking to Loren. 'You would blackmail a child?'

Loren's expression hardened.

'My sister is dead on your orders,' he said. 'My niece has been held in your cells for nearly half a year, and you spent two months torturing me. Don't you dare talk to me about morality.'

There was a silence again. Rose wished someone would speak, and immediately regretted it when they did.

'Rose,' David said softly, silence trailing behind his words like water, 'why, *why* didn't you tell me?'

'Because you would have arrested him,' Rose said, her voice breaking, 'and if he was caught he would talk. Dad, you know I couldn't let him talk, you *know* that!'

She had not meant to shout: the words echoed through the alleyway with piercing volume. In the distance, Rose could hear sirens approaching.

'And we have his kid,' she continued, now painfully aware that she was fighting a losing battle. 'So I couldn't abandon him. I couldn't let him *die*, Dad. I can't kill someone in cold blood.'

There was a long silence. The sirens were closer now.

'Okay, Elmsworth,' said Loren tightly. 'If you want to kill me I would be grateful if you would hurry up with it. If not, now would be a good time to let us go.'

'*Us?*'

'Yes. For Rose's sake, not for mine. If I appear to let her go now it will look suspicious. If she stays with me, it will still look like I have her hostage.'

'You've forced my daughter to work against me for *four months*, and now you want to take her from me.'

'If I don't,' said Loren, his voice corrupting into fire, 'she will end up in one of your cells.'

The sirens had stopped moving now. David fixed his gaze on Loren, who met it unflinchingly.

'If you let anything happen to her,' David told him, 'I will never rest until I find you and, I promise you, your death will be long and slow and very painful.'

Loren considered this. 'Fair enough,' he said. 'You have my word that she won't be hurt.'

'I don't care about your word, Arkwood. I want your self-preservation to hold you to this one.'

Loren smiled grimly, and nodded. David looked at Rose. The shadow of the monster had not quite left his eyes.

'Rose,' he said flatly, 'stay safe.'

'I will. I love you.'

He looked at her for a moment, and turned. Over his shoulder, he yelled, 'They're not here! Look down the alleyways!' Then, slowly, he looked back at Loren and Rose.

'Run,' he told them.

Rose did not move. 'Dad—'

'*Run,*' he growled. 'Arkwood?'

Loren turned, eyebrows raised.

'I didn't give the order for Rayna to die,' David said. 'I would never have allowed it to happen if I had known.'

Loren searched his face for some sign of a lie, found none, and nodded.

'Now run,' David said. 'I'll buy you as much time as I can.'

He gave Rose one last searching look, turned, and walked away. Rose watched him go. Loren tugged at her arm.

'Rose,' he said. 'We need to run. Now.'

She did not reply. For a moment, she considered not replying to anything ever again.

'Yes,' she murmured, finally. 'Yes, I suppose we do.'

CHAPTER 28

They ran for half an hour without looking back, taking random turns every few minutes to try and get the Department off their scent. Then they kept moving on and off until nightfall, when they were physically unable to continue. The running hurt, but Rose was glad of that. It meant she did not have time to think about how much she had just lost.

In the end, Loren collapsed against a wall in a dank side-street, and Rose sat down in a corner with her face in her hands, trying to breathe. She had no idea where they were going to go; it seemed that they had no hiding places left. Luckily, Loren seemed to have planned for an eventuality roughly akin to this one. He had stationed small packages of non-perishable food and makeshift sleeping bags in inconspicuous hiding places within a five-mile radius of the flat. There were two sleeping bags. Rose eyed the second suspiciously.

'You knew I would be with you,' she said.

He nodded, gasping for breath.

'How?'

Loren worked a water flask free of the fabric and took a gulp from it.

'I doubted you would be able to hide me indefinitely,'

he said. 'And when you were found out, you'd have to run. You may not have noticed it yet, but I am dangerous company.'

Rose did not waste her breath replying.

There was a silence. Loren's face looked very gaunt in the unflattering, ghostly illumination of the streetlights. Night was falling. Her father would be in the Department, pretending to try to find her. Nate would still be reeling from the news that she had been conscripted. And James— Rose cut herself off there. No point. No point to any of this.

She watched Loren as he sank down onto the ground. They were in an arch below the Tube line, a few minutes' walk from the Thames. Rose could hear the soft, gentle swash of the river behind the squeals of cars, which echoed eerily under the bridge.

'So what are we going to do now? Just wait for the Department to find us?'

He was silent for a while before he answered.

'We'll sleep here tonight,' he said, 'and tomorrow we'll try to come up with a plan. You go to sleep, you need it.'

She said, 'No, I . . . I can't.' She swallowed. 'I'll stay awake.'

Despite the hours of running, she was not at all tired. And then there was the problem of seeing her father's face every time she closed her eyes.

You're strong enough for this, she told herself. *You can take this.*

She didn't believe herself for a moment.

'I have questions,' she said.

'I may not have answers.'

She hesitated. 'How can your niece do magic?'

'We don't know.' Something unreadable passed over his face. 'I don't know.'

'But if she's a Demon—'

'If you say it's impossible, Rose, I will actually kill you.'

'It's supposed to be.'

'I am fully aware that it's *supposed* to be. But some Demons, some really powerful Demons, can do magic. I don't know why, I don't know how, but they do.'

'But the laws of magic they taught us at school—'

'Are wrong,' he said flatly. 'You know full well how uncomfortable the Government is with unwanted truths. And we are the collateral damage of that discomfort. Next question.'

Quiet.

'I've been thinking,' she said slowly.

'Oh, not again. You know how bad that is for you.'

She glared at him. 'I've been thinking – Dad always told me people became Hybrids because of an error when their souls fused, but . . . he said something, during his inspection, about how he never let me take a blood test, and I thought . . . is it in the blood? Is being a Hybrid something to do with my blood? I mean . . .'

She trailed off, but he looked astonished.

'Well, yes,' he said blankly. 'Obviously.'

'What do you mean *obviously?*'

He had something of David's stillness about him for a moment, the utter motionless brought on by indecision. Then he turned to her. He looked very serious, and the sunset was slowly darkening the edges of his face.

'How far do you trust me, Rose?'

'As far as your own self-preservation will take you, and no further.' As he started to look hurt, she backtracked. 'All right, sorry. Are you going to tell me my father has lied to me again?'

'Does it really surprise you by now?'

'You're asking me to trust you over him.'

'No, I'm asking you to trust the weight of the evidence over him.'

She leaned back against the brick. She had betrayed her father, and that was painful, but more painful still – if untainted by the burden of guilt – was the idea that he had betrayed and lied to her. And she could believe that. She could. Those years of his life at Regency he had never confided in her; the way those notes had broken him, the frightened, savage animal they had awoken in him; and, worst of all, the furious, indignant way he had reacted on finding out how much she knew. As if he had a *right* to control what she knew about him, when he knew her so completely.

She sighed. Immediately, Loren took the opportunity.

'How do you think he knew where the bomb attack in Croydon was going to be?'

She closed her eyes. 'You're about to tell me he planned the attacks, aren't you?'

'Yep. Fifteen years ago, all those buildings were Gifted army bases. Felix asked him to work out a schedule of attacks that would cripple the enemy's supply routes, but David left before it could be used. Someone must have found it and used it. That's why it hurt him so much. They're using his own plans against him.'

'Please stop, Loren.'

'But it's all true.'

She buried her face in her hands.

'All right,' she said. 'Hit me about the Hybrids.'

He gave her the ghost of a smile. 'I don't know what he's told you, but being a Hybrid is in the blood. It changes DNA. If you get attacked by a Hybrid and you survive, the venom gets into your bloodstream, and it changes you. You *become* one. That's how it spreads.'

Rose went cold. '*Spreads?*'

'Oh, yes. The paranoia about Hybrids today – you know, the "they walk among us" kind of thing – was caused by a point about eighteen months into the War where there had been so many Hybrid attacks that almost every street had one living on it. It was an epidemic. Obviously if you were a Hybrid you couldn't stay around your family and friends, so you joined an army, and that was around the time that we started developing weapons like the Leeching Gas.'

'Leeching Gas stops Hybrid transformations?'

'Of course it does. It's designed to destroy magic.'

Rose looked at him. 'But before my Test, I asked Dad whether if I was Leeched, I would still be a – a Hybrid.'

The word still felt difficult to say; the underlying concept sharply painful.

I am a Hybrid.

She had said it, and still there was no hatred in his face. When had that stopped being miraculous?

'And what did he tell you then?' he asked.

She had thought he had said yes – yes, you will still be a Hybrid, it will make no difference. But what he had actually said was, '*suffice it to say that it wouldn't be beneficial to anyone if you failed*'.

'I don't know what he said. He didn't really answer.'

Loren shrugged. 'The Leeching Gas was designed as a weapon. It doesn't just take magic from you. It does something to your second soul, your Gifted one. It damages it. I can understand why he wouldn't want that happening to you.'

'So are you saying I was attacked when I was a baby?'

He hesitated. Rose could see something else – another truth? – flicker across his eyes. 'Most likely, yes. It's astonishing you survived without any significant scarring, but we had magical healing even back then, so it's possible.'

Rose looked up at the underside of the bridge.

'I don't understand,' she said slowly. 'Who would have healed me? Who would have wasted magic saving my life, and then left me out in the rain to die?'

'I don't know,' Loren said. 'Perhaps you have a guardian Angel out there somewhere.'

She looked at him. He appeared not to be joking.

'Good for me,' she said darkly.

Loren smiled.

'You need to get some sleep, now. For all we know this is the last time we'll get to sleep at all.'

'Ten more minutes.'

He looked at her, half-amused, half-annoyed.

'All right, then.'

Silence for a few seconds.

'Loren?'

'Yes?'

'What does war do to people?' He looked at her again. 'I mean, I know what it does to them from the outside. I know what soldiers look like. But what does it . . . what does it *do* to you, to make you like that? What changes?'

He leaned back against the wall, considering.

'You know how they say that if the whole of the history of the universe was a mountain, say, as tall as Everest, then a single human life would be the width of a snowflake?'

'Yeah?'

'War makes you understand that,' he said. 'If you've seen the way human life . . . vanishes . . . and how little it seems to matter, how the world keeps going, keeps moving . . . You always think the sky must go black and the wind fall silent and everyone in the world lay down their arms and break with grief, but they never do. You understand, slowly, that they never will. And you can't forget that knowledge. After you're a soldier, you are afraid, constantly, in the back of your mind. And you *have* to be. You can't live without fear, because without fear there can be no courage, and courage, after war, is all you have. So you have to keep finding new fear to overcome. If you have none, you must create it.'

He looked at her.

'So that's what war does to you.'

Quiet again.

'Go to sleep now, Rose,' said Loren, wearily.

She doubted then that she'd ever sleep again, but she got into the sleeping bag just the same, if only to try. The ground was hard and cold but strangely comforting. Her dreams caught up with her within a few minutes. As she slipped into darkness, her last thought was of Sylvia Argent, and the calm, peaceful way she had slept, and how it would feel to never wake up again.

Things got a little better after that.

CHAPTER 29

She woke restless. She had no watch, but the dawn was lighting the little she could see of the archway, and the roar of the road was louder than it had been when she had fallen asleep. Loren, it seemed, had not slept. He had packed up everything except her sleeping bag, and had been waiting for her to wake. He had lit a fire against the wall with some of the pages of *Firestarter* and a cigarette lighter, and was now drinking some lukewarm coffee. Rose got up, poured herself some hot water from the pan, and settled beside him. For a while, they merely sat in silence.

Rose said abruptly, 'I think we should break Tabitha out today.'

Loren did not move for a few seconds. Then he said, with no inflection at all, 'Do you?'

'Yes.'

'And exactly when and why did this idea enter your mind?'

Rose sat up, pulling her legs in. 'Well, I just think . . . if we were going to do it, we may as well do it now. They won't be expecting it. And if we try . . . well, we've got nothing left to lose, do we?'

He tilted his head in agreement. 'That's true.'

'And anyway,' Rose said, gathering confidence, 'I might be able to break in if I gave myself up, pretended that you'd released me – or better, that you were dead . . .'

'Rose,' said Loren, 'do you want me to point out all the flaws in this plan, or should I just let you ramble on for another few minutes?'

She looked at him, then sat back, slightly deflated.

'Go on.'

Loren held his left hand up, counting them off. The white scar on the back of his hand caught Rose's eye again, and this time she could make out a hard, circular nexus at its centre: the mark of a bullet, perhaps. 'One, that's suicidal. Two, they'll work it out straight away. Three, they won't give you any leeway if they think you're cooperating with me. Four' – his voice hardened – 'it'll just get Tabitha killed. Five—'

Rose opened her hand and showed him what lay there, the tiny piece of metal her idea relied on. Loren raised an eyebrow. Rose told him the rest of the plan. He raised the other eyebrow, and fell silent. Rose let him consider it for a moment.

'All right,' he said, 'that just might work. When did you come up with this? In your sleep?'

The honest answer was *no, I'm just making this up as I go along, Loren, because right now if I sit still and have to think for more than about thirty seconds I will break down and probably never get up again.*

'Yep,' she said.

'Okay,' he said. 'Okay.'

He pressed the heels of his hands into his eyes. Rose

could tell that he was thinking very hard, so she shut up.

'Okay,' he said again. 'So exactly how hard would it be to break Tabitha out?'

'Extremely.'

'And what would our chances of success be?'

'Very, very low.'

'And would they ever believe that you weren't working with me again?'

Rose swallowed. She said, 'No.'

He looked at her. 'And remind me,' he said, heavily, 'what exactly are our other options?'

She let her silence answer that one.

Loren looked up at her, and grinned. 'All right,' he said. 'So let's get going, shall we?'

CHAPTER 30

Department records show that Loren Sebastian Arkwood, convicted *in absentia* of three charges of first-degree murder and one of resisting arrest, gave himself up outside the Department's Westminster branch at 09.34 hours on the morning of 22 April. The first anyone in the Department knew of it was when James – who had been standing at the camera banks through the night, desperately searching the city for any sign of Rose – took a break to stare out of the windows and caught a flash of blond hair outside the doors.

'What the *hell?*' he whispered. He did not dare to turn, lest it turn out to be a trick of the light or a mirage that would vanish if he looked away. 'David!'

David came to the window. There was something odd about him tonight. His boundless energy had been replaced by a kind of shell shock that limited him to sitting in a chair and muttering to himself. James had caught Rose's name several times.

He would find her. He *would* find her.

'I have to admit,' said David, 'I did not see this coming.'

Arkwood was standing, straight-backed, staring into the reflective glass.

David fumbled for the walkie-talkie, dropped it, and

bent to pick it up again. James looked at him incredulously.

David held the button down. 'Are you seeing what I'm seeing?' he said.

The voice came back, tinny. 'Yep. We're sending out a team to neutralise him. I'll assume you want to take this one, David.'

David did not bother to reply, but disconnected. He went to pick his coat off the back of a chair, but James was already storming past him, pulling on his coat, halfway to the door. It was only after he had clicked off the safety of his revolver – fumbling angrily with shaking hands – that he heard David's voice.

'James . . .'

James turned back towards him. David seemed to have forgotten his bomber jacket, which he held on two fingers, as if he had been partway through the process of putting it on. His eyebrows were raised and he was looking at the pistol in James's hands.

'What exactly are you planning to do with that?'

James looked down at it. His eyes wouldn't focus properly.

'We don't kill key witnesses,' said David gently. 'That's protocol. More, actually; that's logic. But you're thinking perfectly rationally, aren't you, Private Andreas? You're not letting emotion get in the way of a case. You wouldn't do that.'

James shook his head wordlessly, trying to put the safety back on again.

'But then,' David continued, pulling on the bomber

jacket at last, 'you wouldn't have any reason to do that. This is the Department, after all. Friends and valued colleagues get lost all the time.'

He walked towards the door and stopped just in front of James. They looked at each other.

'A friend,' David repeated softly, 'and a valued colleague.'

Despite everything, there was a glint in his eye and the hint of a smile in his quiet voice. James stared at him. He knew. God damn him to hell.

'Umm . . .' he said, stupidly. 'You . . .'

'James,' David said tiredly, 'I'm a professional detective. Please do not insult my competence.'

James wasn't quite sure what the appropriate facial expression was for this.

'Umm . . .' he said again. He was sure he had been able to manage something more eloquent than this, once. 'Umm . . . what?'

David almost looked like he was going to roll his eyes. 'Subtlety is not your forte, James. You never look anywhere else when she's in the room, and good God, you *never* stop talking about her. I was thinking of keeping her out of here for the sake of office productivity. But don't worry, I'm not the type of man who would shoot your head off for this. Not at the moment, anyway. I have better heads to shoot off.' He nodded out of the window, to where Arkwood was currently being handcuffed and forced to his knees. 'Now, do you want to help me, or not?'

James, slightly stunned, pulled a gun from his drawer and accompanied David down the stairs to the reception. David paid no attention to the dozen guards surrounding

Arkwood, who backed away as soon as they saw him coming. David, ever the marksman, fired two shots either side of Arkwood's ears. Arkwood flinched twice, but did not otherwise react.

David flipped the gun on his thumb, caught it, and pressed it to Arkwood's head.

He said, very, very quietly, 'Where is my daughter?'

Arkwood grinned. The guards had been rough with him: James could see blood staining his teeth. He said, 'I'll take it to my grave.'

David kicked him, hard, in the stomach. The sudden motion startled even James. Arkwood cried out, doubling up. David turned and walked away. 'Take him to the experimental wards. I'll deal with him there.'

The guards pulled Arkwood to his feet and dragged him across the floor towards the entrance. David strode away towards the wards. James, however, hurried towards the lifts. He wanted no part in what went on in the experimental wards, no matter what Arkwood had done.

But if he had done something to Rose—

Rose, who had never even looked twice at James.

Rose, completely out of his league, even if she was almost two years younger than him.

Rose, strong and brave and clever and beautiful in the way that mysterious people were when they smiled.

No. David could handle this. James was not a torturer.

Not even for Rose.

He went back into the Department and got up the visual readings for cell E46, Arkwood's old one, just in time to catch Arkwood being hauled onto the white slab.

They attached the sensors to his heart and temples and strapped him down. David walked in after the guards. He was smiling as they retreated.

James heard him say, 'Hello, Loren. Long time, no see.'

Arkwood said hoarsely, 'I wouldn't say that.'

David did not pull his gun. He didn't need to.

'So, first things first,' he said casually. 'Why did you give yourself up?'

Arkwood grinned, and then he said something that came through the speakers too crackly for James to hear.

David stiffened. His voice was quiet. 'Where – is – my – daughter?'

Arkwood glanced at the camera.

'Do you really never learn from your mistakes, David?' he said softly.

David looked at him, and then he went still.

'What?' James whispered to the computer screen. 'What is it? Where is she?'

David said, 'All right.'

He stood up, and said something into the walkie-talkie that James couldn't hear. The reply was equally unintelligible. David did not take his eyes off Arkwood's face.

There was a minute's silence, and then the soldiers brought Tabitha Arkwood into the cell. She looked very serene. She was maybe seven years old, dark-haired; the last few months had worn out of her the inclination to smile. She resembled her mother, but it was easy to see in her the fall of Arkwood's hair, the curve of his chin, the steadiness of his eyes – but of course, hers were deep, deep black, so dark it was almost impossible to distinguish the iris from the pupil. With those eyes she could destroy the laws of magic: with those eyes she could bring the Parliament of Angels tumbling down. If the world found out that Demons had the potential to be just as powerful as Gifted, then society could come tumbling down around them.

If the world knew about this girl.

The Department had an unofficial motto, and it was one that James lived by now: some secrets are better kept.

He settled back in his chair and watched David and the girl.

'I know you don't respond well to physical pain, Arkwood,' David said slowly, 'after all, I trained you not to, didn't I? But maybe this will change your mind. You have five minutes to tell the cameras where my daughter is and to say your goodbyes. I'll give you two some privacy.' The words were loaded with menace. 'Five minutes, Arkwood.'

They stared at each other for a moment, and then David walked away. The soldiers followed him.

Arkwood breathed out with the close of the door, and relaxed. He let his head fall back onto the slab.

'Dad. . .' Tabitha whispered.

Arkwood said, 'It's all right, Tabitha. It's okay.' He looked directly into the camera. 'James, please, for this five minutes, the cameras aren't working. Please.'

James leaned in, stunned. How could Loren Arkwood know who was on the cameras? Arkwood had never met him. And why would he think—

Unless. . .

Oh.

Oh.

Arkwood's face was in shadow, but his features were still visible. A soft illumination showed the hollows of his skin.

But the lights of the cell weren't doing that.

The lights of the cell weren't *green*.

'Dad. . .' whispered Tabitha.

'Tabitha. I need you to give me . . .' he struggled to check the palm of his hand. 'Seventeen seconds, and then I'm going to get you out of here.'

Tabitha looked frightened. 'But you can't do that, Dad. David told me, you need security clearance or something, they have us trapped here—'

'That's true,' Arkwood said. 'And Loren Arkwood doesn't have security clearance.' He grinned. 'But *I* do.'

James caught a glimpse of something rolling out of his sleeve; it was small and silver, and rang clearly when it hit the floor. Arkwood began to glow a deeper green, and the flesh of his face retreated into the light, dissipating, hazing, revealing another, deeper flesh beneath it.

Tabitha shrieked, '*Dad!*'

And, as quickly as it started, the glow vanished; and Rose Elmsworth sat up, slid her hands out of the cuffs that were too big for her, and pulled the sensors off her chest and throat. 'Ah.' She shook herself. Her long hair slid out of its bun, down her back. 'God, that was *weird*.'

Tabitha backed away to the wall. Rose slid off the slab, stretching. James caught the glint of the dying green light from the ball that lay on the floor.

The hologram projector. David had gone to Rose's Induction with it.

David had not come back with it.

Had Rose *stolen* from her father?

'It's all right, Tabitha. It's okay. Your dad's waiting outside to meet us. He's missed you very much.'

Tabitha's eyes were wide.

'Ah, right. I'm Rose. David's daughter. I'm helping Loren.' She paused, and stared down at the girl. 'Hang on. You knew his name. You knew my father's name. How did you know that?'

James stared at Rose onscreen. *I'm helping your dad.* What?

What the hell had Arkwood done to her?

Rose went to the wall and started pulling down tranquilliser darts – more usually used on captives – and loading them into her gun. 'All right kid, we need to move *now*. Dad gave us five minutes. I'd say we've got about three-and-a-half left.'

'Have you come to rescue me?' Tabitha asked in a small voice.

Rose smiled. 'Yes,' she said. 'I have.'

James leaned back slowly. *Oh, Angels,* he thought. *She's working with him. She's working with Arkwood. How long has she been working with Arkwood?*

As if she could hear him, Rose raised her head to look at the camera again.

'Okay, James,' she said. 'Please, you have to trust me. I know I look like a traitor, but . . . we killed his sister, and we took the little girl, and . . . he threatened Dad.

What could I do? He's innocent, James. And we're guilty, on this one. Please, James. Trust me.'

James sat back and watched her. So what were his choices? He couldn't harm Rose, no matter what she'd done. No matter whom she'd betrayed. Even him.

He loved her.

Even if she never even looked at him.

'Thanks,' Rose said softly.

Then she went to the keypad by the side of the door and pressed in her name and security clearance. It scanned her, and then opened the door. Rose bent down, took Tabitha's hand, and ran out of James's sight.

James waited a minute, and then deleted the entire five-minute-long camera reel from the records.

Stay safe, Rose. Please.

For me.

Rose ran with Tabitha down the corridor of the cells. She couldn't possibly be ignorant of their circumstances, but the little girl seemed happy. She had a smile like her uncle's – at once serious and mischievous. Every few seconds, she looked up at Rose, as if to check that this was really happening.

Rose, for her part, wanted to let go of her hand, and run away without her; every lesson and instinct she had ever learnt was shrieking at her to do it. The girl's black eyes were demonic – violent, evil, dangerous.

No. No. This was Loren's niece, almost his daughter – swallow your qualms, you idiot, who are you to talk of avoiding monsters?

They had two minutes at most. Rose took random turns, hoping to get to the stairs. She knew where the lifts were, but lifts could be hijacked and stopped. Left, left, right, left, left – and there. Another door, another keypad. Rose pressed in the code and pushed the door open. This whole place was watched. Any second now someone would pick them up on the camera banks. Just thirty more seconds—

Up the stairs: five flights. Tabitha was beginning to tire now. Three flights, and Rose saw the red light on a camera blink and turn to follow them round the corner. Four, and she could hear shouting from below. Five, and they burst through the doors into an empty lobby and Rose ran with Tabitha out of the automatic doors and Loren burst round a corner and a bullet whizzed past Rose's ear. Rose caught the gun Loren threw to her, stolen from an unsuspecting guard. She ducked behind a pillar and started firing tranquiliser darts indiscriminately at the soldiers who burst up around the building. With a sinking heart, Rose realised they were surrounded.

Tabitha started to cry. Loren knelt beside her, whispering, 'Shh, shh, I'm here, sweetheart, it'll be all right. Shh, shh . . . count of three, Rose . . . shh, there, there, one . . . okay, calm now, two . . . all right – *three*!'

They burst out from behind the pillar and ran. Rose poured her power into the physical shield Loren had set up around them. Physical shields used up a lot of power; they had ten seconds at most, considering how tired they were. They ran down the steps and into the high street and down a deserted alleyway and Rose heard someone yell her name, and there were footsteps following them; footsteps, far too close.

'Rose,' Loren said, gasping for breath, 'get Tabitha out of here.'

Rose shook her head. 'I'm not leaving you like this.'

Tabitha looked between the two of them, terrified. Loren turned.

'I said, *get*—'

The bullet didn't *hit* Rose, not exactly. She saw Tabitha gasp in horror before she felt the pain; it was a shining, white-hot line across her cheek, which dulled in the stream of warm blood. Her first reaction was confusion. She had been shot before; surely she should feel some kind of solid impact. Then she realised the bullet had only skimmed her.

She let out a deep, shaking breath.

Tabitha, though, did not share Rose's relief. She became angry slowly, absorbing it as if from the air, her face pale and furious in a way that was very rarely frightening in a seven-year-old.

'No,' she said, and Loren tried to say something to calm her down but she ignored him. '*No!*'

She turned towards the soldiers and reached out a trembling hand. Rose was only half paying attention to her; she put a hand to the wound on her face, stupidly astonished when it came away bloody, and tried to summon enough strength and concentration to heal it.

'*Don't hurt her!*' screamed Tabitha at the soldiers, and the buildings next to them began to rumble.

Loren, to his credit, clocked what was going on almost

immediately, and tried to pull her away. The soldiers did not. They stared at the furious little girl bemusedly, not sufficiently afraid to fire on her again, and not until bricks started to crumble from the walls on either side of them did they start to understand what was happening, and of course by then it was too late.

Loren started whispering to Tabitha, glancing nervously at the walls. Something he said must have got through to her, because she started to go with him, stumble through the collapsing alleyway with Rose following them.

They got clear of the passage before it fell, and stared as the buildings collapsed onto each other. They could not see the soldiers from where they stood. For all they knew, the men could have run before the walls fell, and survived without a scratch on them. It must have been this that Loren whispered to the little Demon girl, softly, soothingly, as his eyes flickered wildly over the rubble. Tabitha's small body was trembling violently. She stared at what she had done and hugged herself, trying to listen to what Loren was telling her.

None of them heard anything over the echoes for a very long time.

CHAPTER 31

'First-aid-kit. First-aid kit.'

They sat in a different, darker alleyway, several miles away, and Loren was rummaging through his emergency pack. Rose knew he wasn't going to find anything in there. Tabitha was asleep against the wall, and the blood on her face was starting to congeal.

'There isn't a first-aid kit in there,' she told him tiredly.

'How do you know?'

'Because I put that emergency pack together for you,' she said, 'and at that point, if you'd been wounded, I would have tried to finish you off, not heal you.'

'Ah.' He sat back. 'Well, that backfired on you a bit, didn't it?'

'Thank you for rubbing it in.'

'Can you heal yourself?'

Rose bit her lip. 'I don't know,' she admitted. 'I'm terrible at Healing, and I'm not sure I have the strength.'

They looked at each other, and she could tell they were both thinking of the same thing.

'Hospital's out of the question,' he said. 'I suppose . . .'

'No. You're not healing me.'

'I would rather heal you of a flesh wound than an infection, Rose.'

'I don't care. I would rather die of gangrene.'

'You're too proud.' He saw her expression and sighed. 'I promise I won't tell anyone.'

'You bet you won't. I would *never* live this down.'

'Why are you so against being healed?'

'I'm not. I'm against being healed by *you*.'

'Oh, for goodness' sake.' He opened the pack and shook it absent-mindedly, but nothing came out. Then he frowned, and turned it upside down, and tried again. One forlorn-looking plaster drifted down onto the pavement. 'You've done more than enough for me.'

'I know! That's the point! I've done *everything*! Saved your life, rescued your niece, given you food and shelter . . . I had the high ground. Completely. If you heal me, I'll lose all my leverage.'

He half-smiled. 'You have your water?'

She took it out of her jacket pocket and pointedly poured some of it over her own face, washing off most of the blood. She sat up as he came over.

'Please don't touch me.'

'I'll try not to.'

He held his hand over the wound, and she felt the edges of the skin begin to prickle and pull together. She tried not to shiver. It was like having someone else brush your hair, but significantly more painful.

Tabitha stirred in her sleep and turned over. Rose glanced at her. The Demons of her childhood were burly, angry men with guns and murderous intentions. They had never been seven-year-old girls.

'Did you know she was this powerful?'

He did not glance at her. 'I knew she could be, in theory. I didn't know she *was*.'

'She chose to use her magic. She knew how dangerous it was, but she chose to use it anyway. And she chose to do good, too.'

'Don't throw my own words back at me, Rosalyn Elmsworth,' he said, and the edges of her wound began to knit together. It was an odd, crawling sensation. 'I know what she did, and why she did it. But she's *seven*.'

'Yes, and?'

'She's too young to know what her power means. She doesn't know what she's chosen.'

'She's perfectly old enough. You don't know what she's been through down there.'

There was pain in his eyes now, enough to make her want to take back what she'd said.

'No,' he said, 'I don't.'

He was beginning to look tired. He had not slept in a long time, and his Gifts were not strong enough to maintain this for long. She pulled away. 'It's okay. I can take this from here.'

'Are you sure?'

'Yes.' He had closed most of the wound; it was simply a matter of strengthening the connections now. 'Get some sleep. I'll keep watch.'

'You're absolutely sure?'

'Yeah.'

He nodded, and went over to Tabitha. He stood over her for a moment, and the look in his eyes was so full of love and concern and joy and grief that Rose looked away.

Then he lay down beside her, curled like a she-wolf protecting a cub, and Rose, behind him, was angry at herself for thinking she had known the extent of what he was fighting for.

He fell asleep almost immediately. Rose heard only distant police cars that night.

'This is a bad idea.'

'I'm hungry.'

'I don't care. There are easier ways to do this.'

'Yes, and are any of them legal?'

'They're *less* illegal than this.'

Loren gave her a sceptical look. 'Cannibalism is not less illegal than shoplifting.'

'I wasn't thinking of cannibalism. I was thinking of breaking and entering. A house, I mean.'

'We don't know they'd have food.'

'Oh, come on,' said Rose irritably. 'What kind of house doesn't have food?'

'An uninhabited house.'

'We'll choose an inhabited one, then.'

'And if we have to hold someone up to do it? Will you condone that?'

She hesitated.

'At least there won't be CCTV cameras in the house.'

'We don't know that.'

Rose rolled her eyes. 'Please don't make me have to stop you.'

'Like you could. Rose,' as she raised her eyebrows, 'we're going to have to steal food from somewhere, and

Tesco has Pringles. *Pringles,* Rose. I haven't had crisps in five months.'

'And it's probably been very good for your health.'

Tabitha turned over, murmuring in her sleep. It was the very edge of dawn; Rose's cut showed only the barest of scars, and the supermarkets near their alleyway were beginning to open.

'I want to get this done before she wakes up. I don't want her seeing me doing anything illegal.'

'Loren, we are on the run from the *police.*'

'Well, that can't be helped.'

'It doesn't mean we don't have anything left to lose.' He started forward, but she grabbed his arm. 'I swear, if you get yourself caught, I'll kill you.'

'I'll be in and out before anyone sees me. Trust me, Rose.'

She sighed, but let him go. If he was going to do it, the earlier the better; maybe there wouldn't even be any witnesses. They deserved some luck by this point. She had spent most of the night staring blankly at the church clock in the yellow illumination of the streetlights: midnight, one o'clock, two o'clock, and now six o'clock in the morning, the dawn cold and grey and thick with the smell of wood and rain.

This was the third day of her life as a fugitive.

A landmark.

She didn't know what David and James would be doing now. Trying to find them, doubtless, but what else were they doing? What were they thinking? Had they reconciled the events of the last few months with

what they now knew about her? Would they have
worked out who had hacked the Department database,
who had stolen food from the military canteens, why
she had told them that Thomas Argent had not been
murdered?

She hoped not, but she knew she hoped in vain.

Could there be forgiveness for something like this?
Certainly there was no precedent; the history of the
Department bore no marks of such a betrayal as hers. *It
is very, very bad practice to have a civilian know as much
about our operations as you do,* Serena had said, and,
galling though it was, Rose had proved her right.

Was it possible there could be redemption for this? Or
had her crimes been too grave?

'Why are you helping us?'

Rose gasped as she turned, although there was no
obvious threat in the unexpected question. Tabitha sat
up in her sleeping-bag, watching Rose with alert, curious
dark eyes. She smiled, and touched her face where Rose's
wound had been.

'You're better,' she said, and there was genuine happiness in her voice.

'Yes,' Rose said, because it was all she really could say,
faced as she was with this black-eyed girl, easily as
powerful as an Angel, the depth of her apparent innocence
belying the fathomlessness of her power.

Those eyes. . . was it possible to ignore them?

Oh, get lost. Loren puts up with you, and you are far
more dangerous than this kid. Do not judge her. Speak
to her as if she were a normal human being.

She's not evil. Right there – that is not an inherently belligerent political dissident. She's a *child*.

'Where's Dad?'

'Gone to get food.'

'From where?'

Rose gave up. 'Tesco.'

'Does he have money?'

'No.'

Tabitha considered this. 'Is he stealing?'

'Look, kid, you want to eat or not?'

'Yes,' said Tabitha, but she seemed unhappy about this. 'Isn't that wrong, though?'

'It's better than letting you starve.' When she still looked discontented, Rose added, 'Or letting *him* starve.'

Tabitha nodded. 'Mum said sometimes you had to do a little bad thing to do a big good thing.'

'That's one way of putting it.'

'Mum's dead,' said Tabitha – tearlessly, and five months after the event. Rose felt the painful inadequacy of her own, 'I'm sorry.'

'You're David's daughter.'

Rose sat down next to her. 'Yes. How do you know about him?'

'He came to visit me sometimes in my cell. To talk to me. Try and get me to do magic. But Mum and Dad always said I never should. So I didn't. He said they might hurt me. He said he would try to stop them hurting me. They never hurt me. They just talked.' Tabitha looked up at Rose. 'Did he say anything to you about me?'

'No. Never.'

'Did he lie to you a lot?'

Rose put her face in her hands. 'It would seem so.'

Tabitha seemed to understand how much this meant to her; she waited until Rose was sufficiently in control of herself to look at her again.

'I'm sorry. About what my father did.'

'It's not your fault,' said Tabitha, so gently that it almost seemed as if the younger girl were comforting *her*. 'Is that why you're helping us?'

'No.'

'Why, then?'

'It's a long story.' Rose glanced back at the alleyway entrance. 'Your uncle persuaded me.'

'Did you *want* to help us?'

Rose hated perceptive children. 'No, not at first. But I do now.'

'Why did you help, then?'

'Because your father knew a secret of mine, and he used it against me so he wouldn't be captured.'

Tabitha went very quiet, absorbing this. 'I don't know if that's good or not.'

'Well, from his point of view, I suppose it was.'

'What was your secret?'

Rose looked at the child for a long time, and considered lying.

'I'm a Hybrid. You know what those are?'

Tabitha shook her head.

'We look human for most of the time, but every six weeks, or when we feel that our lives are in danger, we turn into monsters.'

Rose didn't dare look at her after saying this. She had never in her life told anyone what she was before, not in such terms. It felt obscene. When she did look at Tabitha – tentatively, apprehensively – the girl's eyes were filled with pity. It still made Rose want to hit something, but it was better than fear.

What did it say about you when not scaring a seven-year-old was an achievement?

'That can't be very nice,' said Tabitha softly.

'No, well, it isn't.' And then, hating the plaintiveness in her own voice: 'I don't like having to hurt people.'

'You never *have* to hurt people.'

Rose looked at her, and did her best not to sound contemptuous. 'You don't believe that.'

They sat in silence for a while.

'What are we going to do now?'

Rose shrugged. 'I'm assuming Loren has a plan that will go wrong, and after that, who knows?'

The girl smiled, and took her hand. 'Thank you,' she said, with unexpected sincerity, and Rose, feeling desperately out of her depth, was saved from having to respond by the return of Loren: dishevelled, grinning, and carrying five whole tubs of Pringles.

Tabitha slept again that afternoon. Exhaustion had followed close behind them all since the prison, but Rose knew she stood no chance of sleep. Loren glanced at his niece every few seconds, as if she were merely a hologram who would vanish if he stopped concentrating on her.

'You need to get out of the country,' Rose told him.

His gaze flickered distractedly towards her. 'What?'

'Loren. Look at me. The two of you need to get out of England. As soon as possible. It's the only way you'll outrun the Department.'

'We can't.'

'Of course you can. We're on the bloody Thames, for God's sake. Get a ferry to the Netherlands, or France, or Portugal. Their Departments are barely functional, and they don't talk to London. They'll never find you there.'

Now he was paying attention. 'We don't have any money there.'

'Get a job. Learn Dutch. You'll be fine.'

'What about Tabitha?'

'Oh, you can tutor her for the school she's missed. She's clever enough. Even if she weren't, Loren, you can't stay here.'

He was quiet for a moment. 'What about you?'

She took a deep breath. 'I'll go back to the Department and hope.'

'*Rose*. Don't be an idiot.'

'I'm not being an idiot. With any luck James deleted the footage of our escape, so only the Department know I'm not your hostage, and I can deal with what they think of me.'

'No, you can't.' He leaned forward. 'Rose, you're not *safe* with that man.'

'That man is my father.'

Loren said nothing for a while. 'You're going to be sixteen in seven months. What are you going to do with your life when you're an adult?'

She wanted to say 'work for the Department', but she realised with a hollow heartbeat that that wasn't going to happen any more. 'I don't know. I can't really . . . I can't really do anything until he's safe.'

'Or until he's dead.'

'Don't say that. Don't ever say that again.'

He hesitated. 'Sorry.'

On the fourth day, they ran out of supplies. The bread and cheese Loren had brought with the Pringles went bad very quickly without refrigeration, and they woke in the morning cold and hungry. They were a good few miles from Tesco by then, and sending Loren to shoplift twice in two days would be asking for more luck than they were ever going to get.

Tabitha wanted to go, and of course initially Loren was extremely reluctant to let her, but she was far less likely to be recognised – the Department could hardly set up a public manhunt for a child – and, it had to be said, was the most capable of all of them at defending herself. After a while, and with Rose's backing, Loren relented, and let her go.

After that, everything went to pieces very quickly.

The first Rose heard of the explosion was the distant, ominous *boom*. Her first instinct was to recognise it as thunder, and then she remembered the glorious blue sky and the distinct lack of clouds. Then she heard the screaming, and decided it probably wasn't thunder.

Loren was white and motionless where he sat, staring at the rising smoke from the high road. Rose, familiar with the symptoms of shock, considered hitting him, evaluated the likelihood of him hitting her back, and shouted at him instead.

'Loren!' She could barely hear him over the rising screams. 'Loren, *what is it?*'

He said something in a soft, terrified voice that she couldn't make out. She threw caution to the wind and hit him, and then he was on his feet. She ran after him, shouting things along the lines of how imperative it was for him to get back, and what an idiot he was to run out undisguised, until she thought of her father, and the fraught, anguished look he wore when she was in danger.

After that she just ran with him.

They stopped dead on Shepherd's Bush Road and stared. They were not the only ones. Westfield shopping centre was gone: it sat, a shattered wreck, beside the Tube station, a great hulk of smoke and fire and broken glass that littered the streets.

The sky was no longer blue.

Loren yelled furiously, desperately, 'TABITHA!'

Rose saw her first. She was huddled, ash-covered, under the awning of a grocer's. Rose shook Loren's arm, pointed, and Tabitha looked up and saw them and her black eyes brightened through the blood on her face.

Loren started to run.

The Department car came, screaming with sirens, round the corner, and there was a screeching of wheels and a skidding and Loren was down. Tabitha and Rose both cried out. Loren was lying in the road clutching his ribs. The Department squad team got out of the car, and a medic ran towards him and then the squad team realised who he was and pulled her back. They dragged him roughly to his feet. Rose saw the glint of handcuffs.

She backed away, horrified, and ran.

She managed three steps before there was a strong hand across her mouth and arms round her waist and they dragged her backwards. She bit down hard into her captor's palm, tasted blood, and someone cried out. Then there was metal across her wrists, and fabric instead of flesh against her mouth. Someone slammed her into the car.

She glanced, terrified, to either side and saw Loren and Tabitha similarly bound and gagged beside her. Loren was unconscious, but whether that was from the pain from his ribs or because they had pre-emptively sedated him Rose didn't know. Tabitha was still struggling, wide-eyed and screaming through her gag.

A Department officer stood in front of the three of them and started to read out their arrest warrants. Rose thought with anger that any law-enforcement officer worth their salt should have been rescuing the wounded from the destroyed shopping centre.

'Loren Sebastian Arkwood, Rosalyn Daniela Elmsworth and Tabitha Rayna Arkwood, you are hereby arrested . . .'

Rose looked at Loren in frustration. He lay against the car, stubbornly unconscious. Damn him.

Damn all of this.

Damn it all to hell.

She crumpled against the car and watched the black smoke drift slowly across the sun.

CHAPTER 32

In spite of the officer's warnings, Rose did not remain silent. She managed to work off her gag when they shoved her into the police van, and during the ride her captors were treated to every obscenity the Department's fifth-floor office had to offer, which was quite a substantial vocabulary. When they got to Westminster, they shoved her into a cell away from the other two. Rose swore at the cameras for a while, and then, when her voice became hoarse, she sat against the wall and thought furiously.

So, this is it, huh?

All that worry. All that lack of sleep, the planning, the fear.

For nothing. For *nothing*.

Loren and Tabitha had been captured after all.

The sense of utter failure and disappointment was not one she was used to, and she let it swamp her, pressing her eyes to her kneecaps for a moment and staring bleakly into the dark, before gaining control again.

This was the Department. She had home advantage here: she and David had long ago taken note of the security system used to keep prisoners in custody, just in case it was ever turned against them, and she thought that if she tried, if she really tried, she might be able to escape.

Escape, and run . . . where?

This *was* her home: she had nowhere to go but back to her captors.

That was depressing.

In practical terms, any escape plan would probably also involve magic, and that was far too risky. Any food they would give her would be deliberately low-calorie, just enough to keep her alive, but not enough to leave her with any excess energy to use in magic.

Enough to fume, though.

Four days. You lasted four days *out in the open.*

What on earth is the actual bloody point *of you?*

Apart from her own imprisonment, there was the matter of Loren and Tabitha to consider. After all she'd done to keep them safe, Rose didn't want to leave them in Department cells, especially not with Loren injured.

And then there was David. Rose had no doubt he would have planned for their capture; he would have some kind of control over their situation, would come for Rose eventually.

She was not sure whether that was good or bad.

Hope came in her morning porridge on the third day of her arrest.

Thankfully, she saw it before she tasted it: something glinting at the bottom of the plastic tray, beneath the grey sludge. She reached in and pulled it out, dousing it with her water to clean it.

Smooth. Round. Silver.

Oh Angels, it was Loren's locket.

He had taken it off the chain, but it was there: the photograph of Rayna and Tabitha inside it was undamaged, the figures still smiling. Rose didn't know how he'd gotten it into her food. He must have needed help, but whether it was willing or coerced, and *who* – a guard? James? Even, dare she hope, David?–, she didn't know.

Still, to give it to her, he must be awake, and coherent, and planning, and – crucially – *not dead*.

She sat in the blind spot in her cell and smiled.

The wait this time was longer. The suspense of not knowing what was happening nearly broke her resolve. But she knew David would want her to stay where she was, safe, at least for the moment, so she resisted the temptation to try to escape.

Six days after she was arrested, there were crushed pieces of paper underneath her plastic plate. Rose sat in the blind spot to read them with trembling hands.

The first was a fragment of what looked like a speech. It had been ripped out of the original document; the edges were yellowed slightly, torn, but the paper itself was white, recently printed on.

—dies and gentlemen of the jury, I speak not from the heart but from the head when I say that Private Elmsworth and Tabitha Arkwood have committed no crime. They are victims of circumstance, no more; and it is circumstance, not principle, that should guide the hand that decides their fate. We live now in a time where pragmatism must be foremost in the minds of men and Angels. There will be time for justi—

David, in a courtroom. They were trying Tabitha. That was odd: she wasn't even at the legal age of responsibility. The circumstances, as David had said, must be very dire.

Just how dire became apparent in the second scrap of paper. It had been ripped from a printed-out BBC News article, from the Breaking News section. That in itself was odd: it had been months since an article had been published there without redaction. The corner of the paper had a fragment of a photo – black smoke against glass and sky.

—ield shopping centre was destroyed last week in a blast that claimed seventy-four lives. Regency, an Ashkind militia, claimed responsibility for the attack on Wednesday. There is no news yet on the exact identity or location of the bombers, but the Department last night issued a communiqué stating their intention to bring them to justice as quic—

The last scrap of paper contained five words, scribbled in biro in her father's handwriting.

You know I love you.

Rose pressed the paper to her face, breathing it.

Such certainty.

You know I love you.

On the eighth day of her imprisonment, David came. He was not alone – Rose could hear other voices, other footsteps, loud and angry through her cell door – but he sounded like himself again: not Dad, not quite, but David, in the middle of a case and arguing in that way he did when only courtesy stopped him from telling his opponent in no uncertain terms how thick they were being.

Love and anguish and fear and guilt twisted inside her like warring snakes, and she crushed them and tried to stay emotionless. Of course it didn't work.

Rose was on her feet when the cell door opened, and he was the first thing she saw. He was tired-looking and drawn, but he was smiling, smiling at *her*. Behind him was such a congregation as Rose had never seen before down in the Department's underground wing. She saw Terrian there, disapproving as always; Nate, refusing to meet her gaze; Laura, sympathetic but stern; James, red hair as bright as ever, outshone only by his smile; and Loren and Tabitha, looking pale and shaken, but safe.

Rose did not have time to wonder what was going on before her father spoke.

'Private Rosalyn Daniela Elmsworth, your appeal has been successful. You have been cleared by the High Court of murder and attempted murder. You do still have' – David glanced at the others – 'a *very* suspended sentence for resisting arrest but, what the hell, who needs the law when you've got bureaucracy on your side?'

The others remained silent. Rose wasn't quite sure whether she was still going with the formal military procedure, but decided she probably should, just to be safe.

She glanced at the Arkwoods.

'And as for the legal status of my fellow defendants?' she asked stiffly.

'Drop it, Rose,' Loren said. His voice seemed hoarse,

but he looked otherwise undamaged. 'We're free. All three of us.'

'What?' Her mind had gone blank. 'Where's the catch?'

'None,' said David brightly. 'Well, *he's* still technically in protective custody—'

'I'm *what*?'

'. . . but otherwise, yes, you're fine.'

Loren stepped forward; the motion made him wince, and he put a hand to his newly mended ribs. 'What did you say about me?'

'You're still in protective custody. James told you, surely?'

An awkward silence, during which everyone's heads turned to look at James, who looked very sheepish. 'The Demon girl looked so happy—'

'My name is Tabitha,' she said, quietly, from beside Loren.

A longer silence. Terrian pushed forward so that he stood directly in front of Loren. This was, in retrospect, a bad strategic decision; Loren was noticeably taller than Terrian, and though he was pale and gaunt and considerably weaker magically, he did not back down. He raised his eyebrows. Only Rose noticed him gently pull Tabitha behind him.

'You have something to say?' he asked.

'Yes,' growled Terrian. 'Listen to me, you son of a bitch. You're not forgiven. You're not just unconditionally released. We spent months – *months* – trying to track you down, and if *someone*' – a glance at Rose filled with such concentrated resentment that she flinched backwards and David stiffened

– 'hadn't gotten in our way, you and your kid would be locked up way down there behind feet of steel with no chance – *none at all* – of seeing the light of day for the rest of your pathetic lives. And that will happen, make no mistake, if you so much as think of stepping over the line, or running away. You will end up there, and you won't get so much as a dream of freedom ever again. You are only out here because we need what you know. Do you understand?'

Loren looked at him. The contempt in his eyes was unmistakeable.

'You've made yourself clear,' he said softly.

Terrian nodded. He seemed somewhat at a loose end; perhaps he had expected – hoped? – that it would come to blows. After a pause, during which he seemed to become aware of the astonished eyes of everyone else on him, he turned suddenly to Rose.

'And you,' he said, furiously, but his vocabulary seemed to have run out here, and he merely repeated *'you'*, menacingly; and then he turned sharply towards the stairs and stomped up towards the light. Loren glared after him; his breath seemed to be returning to him now. If Tabitha was unsettled, she did not show it.

A silence. Terrian's shadow seemed to hang in the air.

'Anyway,' said David brightly to Loren, 'you're still arrested, technically. Tomorrow a hearing will be held concerning your bail, which will be granted, while you await trial. This will be postponed until such time as we gather enough evidence to clear your name.'

'He's a murderer,' said Nate abruptly, glaring at Loren. 'That evidence doesn't exist.'

'Not yet.'

It was James who said it, as if in an attempt to redeem himself; they glanced at him again.

'Diplomatically put,' said David dryly.

'So . . . I'm back in the Department?' asked Rose incredulously. It was as if a ten-tonne weight had been lifted from her shoulders; she was free, she was *free*, Loren was not dead, and David—

'Yes,' David said. 'We applied for your conscription to be shifted here.' At her blank look, he explained, 'You work for the Department now. You're officially on the payroll.'

This would have been good news at the best of times, but coming after two weeks of being on the run, being shot, arrested, and waiting eight days to find out whether she'd be locked up for the rest of her life, David's words were the best to ever reach Rose's ears. Paradise came to her after weeks in hell, and she felt lightheaded with happiness.

She ran over to him and hugged him in front of almost the entire Department. He hugged her back.

'Welcome back,' he whispered to her.

She pulled back a little and said hesitantly, 'I'm . . . forgiven, then?'

'Absolutely not. You are grounded for a very long time, Private Elmsworth.'

There was something off in his voice; trust in their world, she knew, was hard-won, and easily lost. She did her best to block off the hurt. It was completely understandable: any parent would react like this at such a large-scale betrayal

283

on the part of their child. She would simply keep her head down from now on, then, obey orders without question and so on.

If that was the price she had to pay, then she would do so gladly.

A small, selfish voice in her head complained about his own myriad betrayals, but she shut it down angrily. What had that to do with anything? These secrets were his; keeping them had not hurt her in any way. Helping Loren Arkwood behind his back? Now that had been hurtful. David owed her nothing; she owed him her life so many times over that it hurt to remember.

He released her. She saw him glance at Tabitha, who met his gaze with something like happiness, and the eyes of everyone in the group flickered between the two of them.

A *very* awkward silence for a long five seconds.

Rose turned to Nate and James. 'I'm sorry. About everything. I really am.'

'Just . . . don't do that to me again,' said James. His smile looked painful.

'I won't, I promise.'

Nate ignored her. He wasn't looking at Rose; he was staring fixedly at the wall. Rose took it she was not forgiven – which was obviously to be expected, but nevertheless it felt like being stabbed. After it became clear that he was the reason for her silence, he turned, and started up the stairs towards the ground floor. The rest followed him.

David lagged behind with Rose and the Arkwoods.

After a while, despite everything, a smile was beginning to grow on Rose's face.

'So,' Loren said after a moment, 'who was that?'

'Colonel Connor Terrian,' David told him darkly. 'My . . . senior. Word of warning, he doesn't like you much.'

'Why ever not?'

'Argent. Connor is in charge of clearing up after suspicious incidents. He nearly lost his job over that.'

'Ah.' Loren unconsciously pulled the sleeves of his shirt further towards his wrists. 'Can't blame him for that, then.'

Rose noticed Tabitha watching Loren.

'Who is Argent?' she asked.

David, Loren and Rose looked at each other.

'He killed your mother,' Loren said shortly.

'So you killed him?'

'Yes.'

Tabitha paused and considered this. They watched her.

'That's very bad, Daddy.'

Rose raised her eyebrows at Loren.

'I know,' he said. 'I . . . won't do it again.'

David nearly snorted. The Department tended to leave its employees with a very well-developed sense of gallows humour.

'So we're free?' Loren asked.

'Yes,' David said. 'Sorry about the long wait, we had to conduct a very arduous face-saving operation – which I did my very best to avoid,' he added at Rose's glare. 'Terrian, mostly. We had to convict you first, so we didn't look like idiots for chasing Arkwood – fine, Loren – around for six months. Then we had to get the conviction overturned, so we could set you free and blame it on the courts for their bad judgement.'

'And exactly how many times did you have to pull rank to get the Department to agree to setting Loren Arkwood free?' Rose asked.

'Not once,' said David cheerfully. 'As long as you comply with your conditions of release, you're a free man, everyone agrees.'

Silence.

'*Conditions of release?*' asked Loren, icily.

David looked at them, and took a breath.

'Ah,' he said.

When their argument had grown into shouting, Connor Terrian met her again at the top of the stairs. Nate stood behind him, arms folded.

'Don't,' said Terrian, 'even think about holding onto a shadow of a hope that this is over.'

Rose said nothing. He considered her for a moment, disgust clear in his expression.

'How could you,' he said quietly, not a question, and walked slowly away. Rose stared after him. After a moment, Nate came forward and hugged her. Rose leaned into him, breathing him in. She tried to remember him as a laughing child. She tried to remember him lovestruck beside Maria. But he leaned back and looked at her, and all she could see was a grave young man with hurt in his eyes.

He left her sitting there in David's chair. Rose looked around at the office, at the white walls and the grey carpet, more familiar to her than her home, so nearly lost to her for ever, and something inside her twitched.

She frowned.

For a moment there it had felt like she wanted to cry.

CHAPTER 33

Rose spent her first few hours as an official member of the Department watching it implode.

Everyone who even vaguely mattered, which apparently now included Rose and Nate, had gathered in the meeting room. Terrian's laptop, which sat in front of him, was hooked up to the hologram projector. James had brought in the tea. That was when Rose first knew that the news would not be good.

David had his feet up on the table, eating a biscuit and calmly watching Loren rail against the inevitable. He had gone through anger, righteous indignation and reasoned argument, and had now resorted to monosyllabicity.

'No,' he was saying. 'No. I won't do it.'

'Well, you're welcome to go back to jail,' said Terrian. 'And what will happen to the girl then?'

'Dad,' said Tabitha quietly. Loren had as yet refused to let her out of his sight, and as such she had spent most of the conversation sitting silently beside the window, watching the argument with wide, frightened black eyes. 'I don't want to go back there.'

Loren was silenced for a moment. Then: 'You can't *make* me do this! This is illegal!'

David took his feet off the desk and leaned closer to

Loren. 'Come on, let's be frank here. We're a law-enforcement agency. *Everything* we do is illegal, or ethically dubious at best. But I'm afraid the buck doesn't go much higher than this, partly because we'll shoot it down if it tries. So it's take it or leave it, I'm afraid: you work for us, or you and Tabitha go back to jail.'

'You killed my sister!'

'One of our squad teams killed Rayna. It was never officially sanctioned.'

Loren's face darkened with fury. He stood up very quickly, and for a moment it almost seemed as if he was about to hit David. Six hands went to their guns. Loren looked around them, and let Tabitha pull him down to his seat.

'But why can't you use someone else? Why do you need me?'

Silence round the table. People exchanged glances that ranged in significance from amused to grim to exasperated.

David nodded at Terrian.

'Mr Sulu,' he said, 'you have the con.'

Terrian glared at him, and clicked something on his computer. The hologram flickered into place. It showed the broken, smoking hulk of Westfield shopping centre.

'At eleven forty-six a.m. on the twelfth of May,' David said, 'this happened, as I'm sure you all know. Seventy-four dead; three hundred and fifty-three wounded; and one hell of a slap in the face for us. I don't need to tell you how much pressure we are currently under to get the cause pinpointed and destroyed as quickly as possible.'

'Could it have been a gas explosion?' Laura ventured tentatively.

'Unfortunately for us, no,' David said, 'not a chance. Nail bomb. Very messy, but ideal if you want to do as much damage as possible in a building that incorporates a lot of glass into its structure.'

'So this was definitely a terrorist attack,' James said. 'Do we know who did it?'

'As a matter of fact, we do. DNA was found on some of the nails and on the remains of the bomb's container. More to the point, we have CCTV footage of what happened. Can we get the film up, Connor?'

The hologram flickered and was replaced by a picture of a carry-on suitcase on wheels. The handle was just visible: the hand of its carrier was tight and white.

'And with the X-ray overlay?'

The hologram flickered again, and the contents of the suitcase were shown stark and white as the bones of the carrier's hand. It was unmistakably a bomb.

'Who is this?' Loren asked. 'What kind of idiot walks into the range of X-ray equipped cameras with a bomb in a suitcase?'

'It's quite a good bet, actually,' David said. 'The cameras in Westfield are notoriously dodgy. The shopping centre was renovated after the War, and ever since then their electrics have been appalling. The cameras go on and off every few hours pretty much randomly. If you had to carry a bomb past any security system, Westfield's would be it. And look who did. You're going to love this, Rose.'

An image appeared beside the X-ray projection: a

throng of distracted shoppers on the first floor, frozen in mid-step by the pause function. Terrian zoomed in on it, further and further, until the face of the bomber filled the screen.

Nate and Rose both made identical half-gasp, half-groan noises.

It was Aaron Greenlow.

Loren raised his eyebrows at Rose. 'Explain?'

Rose looked at David, who gestured for her to do so. Rose had been to many Department meetings before, but she was unused to having people listen to her during them.

'His name is Aaron,' she said. 'He's seventeen, at most. He's Stephen Greenlow's son. He disappeared about a week ago. Possible suicide victim, but no body was ever found. Come on, he was on the Department records. Does nobody here remember him?'

Laura and Terrian nodded. James's jaw had dropped.

'You're joking,' he said. 'Stephen Greenlow's son, the Westfield bomber? Do you think his father ordered him to do it? Oh, that would be *brilliant*! And tragic, of course,' he added hastily, at the look everyone gave him.

Terrian cleared his throat awkwardly.

'Did you know him?' he asked, looking between Nate and Rose.

Rose laughed bitterly. 'Oh, yes.'

'And is he the type of person who could blow up a crowded shopping centre, do you think?'

Rose nodded to the picture. 'Well,' she said hoarsely,

fighting back memories of a softly smiling fourteen-year-old boy, 'there's little doubt over that now.'

David said, 'Surely he—' and then stopped, leaned forward, and scanned the picture sharply.

'Connor,' he said, 'zoom in on his eyes for me, will you?'

Terrian, bewildered but knowing enough not to stop David when he was on to something, did so. As the camera zoomed in closer, the picture became grainier, and then Loren was on his feet wearing an identical *eureka* expression.

He and David looked at each other.

'Oh,' they said simultaneously.

'What?' asked Terrian, looking between the two of them. 'What, what is it?'

David said nothing, but stared at the picture. The beginnings of a smile crept onto his face.

'*What?*' said Terrian and James together exasperatedly.

'Rose,' David said, 'can you confirm this?'

'Confirm what?'

'Look at the edge of his iris,' he said. 'He's high-level Gifted, correct?'

'Yes.'

'Look very closely.'

Rose did. At the very edge of Aaron's bright green eyes was a sliver of dark.

She looked at him.

'No,' she said.

'Yes,' said Loren. 'He's right. It's painful to admit it, but Elmsworth is right.'

'Right about *what*?' shouted Terrian.

David looked at him and smiled.

'The little black line at the corner of his eye?'

'Yes,' said Terrian impatiently. 'What about it?'

'The eyeball,' David said, 'is a convex shape. No shadow from the outer edge can reach the centre.'

Terrian looked at the picture, looked at David, and looked back at the picture again. James was on his feet, his mouth open.

'You're saying,' Terrian said slowly, 'that the son of the leader of the Gospel is a Demon disguised as a Gifted.'

'That is exactly what I'm saying.'

Rose shuddered at the thought of Greenlow's reaction. Stephen was high-level Gifted – more powerful than David and Rose, but still far off being an Angel. Knowing him, he would have been disappointed if Aaron had been a Pretender, and deeply, deeply wounded if he had been Ashkind. But a *Demon* – second only to Hybrids as societal enemies; dangerous to the Government, to everyone else in the world . . .

Stephen would have hated him for it. Never mind that Aaron was his son, his blood. Stephen would have hated him.

'But that's impossible,' Terrian said. 'He can't be a Demon. He can do magic. He passed his Test.'

Everyone in the room looked pointedly from him to Tabitha and back to the picture of Aaron.

'Right,' he said. 'All right. But his eyes—'

'Who invented the hologram projectors?'

All eyes on James now.

'No one invented them,' he said hesitantly. 'They're War inventions, the MoD just updated them. They've been using them for ages—'

'Yes,' said David, almost breathlessly. 'The MoD has been using them for *ages*. How much area could they cover before, James?'

'Not much,' said James. 'They could only disguise about ten square centimetres.'

'That's about the size of two eyes,' said David. 'And who do we know who would have had access to them? Who works in the MoD?'

'Natalie,' said Laura, quietly. 'Greenlow's mother. Oh my God.'

They all looked around the table at each other.

'That's two magical Demons discovered in a year,' Laura said. 'And born nearly ten years apart . . . how does it happen? What's different about these two?'

They looked at Loren, who shrugged his shoulders.

'Trust me,' he said, 'if Rayna and I had known, we'd have done something about it long before now.'

'All right,' Terrian said. Rose could see him trying to think of a logical conclusion and failing. He sat down. 'Okay. David, do we have any idea as to his motivation?'

'Oh, yes,' said James darkly. 'We do.'

Terrian looked at him. 'What do you mean?'

James pulled over the computer. 'We got this on the night of the attack.'

He punched in the commands and the picture of Aaron's eye vanished, replaced by another hologram of the destroyed shopping centre. It had been taken with a grainy camera, and across it in black Arial were the words *Behold the Interregnum*.

David gave a shuddering kind of sigh when he saw it. It sounded like a surrender. For a moment, all the fight seemed to have gone out of him.

'Regency,' he whispered. It was the first time Rose had ever heard him say it as if he had some control over the word, and watching him she finally understood what it meant to him: a collection of old, wild ghosts.

'Fine,' he said, without anyone asking. 'The truth. Anyone here remember Felix Callaway?'

Rose and Loren nodded, but no one else did.

'Seriously?' David said incredulously. 'No one? Is he not on our records?'

No answer.

'Oh, come on. Give me that.'

He strode round the table to Terrian's laptop and punched in a couple of commands. The picture of the attack vanished, replaced by a rotating hologram of a tall, broad-shouldered man in his early forties with dark hair and the blackest eyes Rose had ever seen. The darkness of them shrieked *Demon* so loudly that she stepped back, uneasy even at the sight of them.

David was staring at Felix. Rose noticed a certain, sudden stiffness in his posture, a wariness in his frame, and looked again at the black-eyed man in the hologram. She tried to match the voice to the face. *I claim your death. . .*

She shuddered.

'I don't know if anyone remembers,' David said, scratching the back of his neck, 'but there was a clause in the Great Truce that forbade the Government from prosecuting any army leaders for War crimes. If we had, this man would have been the Department's first target.'

'Well, that was poor negotiation on your part, wasn't it?' said Loren lightly.

'Yes, well,' said David darkly, 'he isn't the only one who would have been hunted down without that particular piece of legislation.'

Loren glared at him.

'Is there a point to this?' James asked impatiently. 'People have died.'

David looked up at him, and sighed.

'Felix Callaway ran Regency, the largest and most powerful Ashkind army during the War. They were defeated in the Battle of Vancouver, but the army never quite managed to destroy them completely. In recent years, they've become more of a terrorist group than a military organisation. Destroying a packed shopping centre is trademark Felix.'

Loren had not taken his eyes off the hologram of Felix since David had stopped insulting him. 'Yes,' he said. 'Remember Ariadne?'

'I never forgot,' said David darkly. 'I believe that was the point.'

Nate looked between the two of them. 'Can someone please explain—'

Without looking away from Felix, Loren said, 'Ariadne Stronach was third-in-command of Felix's army. She was also his girlfriend. It was difficult to get anything done when they were in a room together, believe you me. They were inseparable for years, and then one day . . .' He sighed. 'One day, after a particularly destructive battle, Felix had all the Gifted survivors rounded up and shot. In the morning, Ariadne was gone.'

'That was when he first started to distrust me,' David said. 'I was Head of Security. I was supposed to stop people deserting. He thought I'd helped her.'

'And did you?' Rose asked.

He looked at her wearily. 'What would you have done?'

A silence. James was watching David narrowly.

'Anyway,' Loren continued, 'he spent months looking for her. Had patrols out day and night. I thought it was because he loved her. Until we found her body.'

Tabitha gasped, horrified. Loren looked down at her as if remembering she was there.

'Felix transformed to kill Ariadne,' he said softly. Rose closed her eyes. Loren did not look at her, or at David. He kept his eyes on his niece.

'How was a man like that allowed to run an army?' Laura said, appalled.

'Oh, come on,' David said, looking between her and Terrian. 'You two were both in armies, you understand. Psychopaths make the best leaders. Felix was the most brilliant strategist I've ever met. The Ashkind almost won the war because of him. He was the one who weaponised the use of Hybrids.' Rose could see the stiffness in his muscles as he spoke; she had to stop as well, force herself to relax. 'He'd gather hundreds of them, as many as would come out of hiding, stagger their six-week cycles so there were always some ready to transform. He'd trigger them and release them onto the battlefield. Hybrids can't discriminate between friend and foe, of course, so he had to get all of his soldiers away from the action first. That was when you knew it was coming. The retreat.'

David glanced at Rose to see how she was taking this – the sudden escape of so many old secrets – and alarm flickered into his eyes. Rose looked down at herself and saw that she was gripping the table so hard that her knuckles had turned white. She let go with some effort.

'Some of his enemies thought they'd won, started getting closer. That made it worse. Nothing stands a chance against a Hybrid. Fathers and sons, sisters, brothers, mothers and daughters, husbands and wives – almost everyone had lost a loved one to them. There were no unscathed hearts in those days. That's why Hybrids are so feared. Because of Felix.'

The hatred in his voice now was old, bitter, snarling.

'Of course, Hybrid transformations don't last for ever. They were – were killed, tortured and killed, as soon as they were human again, and vulnerable behind enemy lines, so more were created even as the old ones died.' He was losing control. 'They were dying in their hundreds and in their thousands, and still more with that venom in their veins, still more with that blood on their hands, and still. . .'

David had to take a long breath, clutching the chair, before he could speak again. His voice closed and he looked up at them.

'They all died,' he said evenly.

The hologram floated there obliviously. They looked at it in silence. *Never let anyone tell you someone is evil,* David had told her once. *There are evil people, and there are normal people doing evil things, and if you have to ask yourself which one someone is, it's the latter. When you meet an evil person – when you look into their face – you will know what they are instantly. True evil is impossible to hide.*

Rose sat forward in her chair and looked for the true evil in Felix Callaway's eyes.

'I've been watching Regency for years. I thought Vancouver had destroyed them. I thought Felix's paranoia had driven everyone away. I thought Regency as an organisation had curled up and wasted away. And yet.' He gave a hoarse, shuddering sigh. 'And yet. They didn't die. They're getting stronger, damn them all to hell. And they want me back. Me and Arkwood. Without us they don't stand a chance. They won't tell themselves that, of course – if we don't come back to them soon they'll just try to kill us and have done with it – but for the moment they're trying to re-recruit us.' David glanced up at them, saw their astonished looks. 'Of course they won't actually get us,' he said impatiently. Then he looked at Arkwood. 'I speak only for myself, of course.'

'How little you think of me,' said Loren coldly.

'How much reason I have to do so.'

'So you think Felix Callaway recruited this boy to blow up Westfield?' Terrian asked.

'I'm almost sure of it,' David said. 'From the sound of

it, Aaron Greenlow is prime material for Regency. Young, strong, malicious; had to hide that he was a Demon all his life; wanted a chance to prove himself.'

'Also, he's seventeen,' said Laura. 'Joining Regency would be a way of rebelling against his parents. Especially Stephen. The Gospel hates Ashkind – he wouldn't like having one for a son, especially a Demon, but joining an Ashkind army . . . that's something else.'

'Did he survive?' asked James.

In answer, James closed the image of Felix and brought up CCTV footage from 11:44 a.m., two minutes before the bomb went off. It showed Aaron leaving the building hurriedly. His eyes were full black now. Rose winced.

Terrian put his face in his hands.

'All right,' he said wearily. 'I'll send faxes out to the media reporting it as a terrorist attack, shall I?'

Loren smiled grimly.

'Oh no,' he said, 'this wasn't a terrorist attack. This was a declaration of war.'

CHAPTER 34

Rose was allowed to go home with David that night. They took the District line from Westminster in wary, uncertain silence. Each had been through so much in the past two weeks that they were no longer sure how the other would react. The rattling of the Tube echoed strangely in Rose's ears.

They got home safely. Rose was almost surprised. David locked the door and collapsed onto the sofa. Rose resisted the temptation to go straight to her room to think, and to check it was still there, if only because she knew it would offend her father.

'So.'

Rose looked at him.

'I assume you have questions,' he said. 'The girl. I'm sorry about that.'

Rose stared at him.

'A couple of Angel Parliamentarians contacted me six months ago,' he said. 'Promised me a pay rise if I acted as psychotherapist to Tabitha Arkwood. Of course, I knew who she was. I hoped the name was just a coincidence at first, but no . . . They told me she was a magical Demon. An impossible case. They come more often than you'd think.'

His eyes were closed, and he spoke as if from memory. He was not watching her.

'So I did it, of course. I felt I owed it to Rayna. They told me they needed the most trustworthy person they had to keep this secret — it is always so amusing when that happens. They asked me to keep it from you. I agreed.'

His voice was flat; it was clear that, whatever qualms he had had about that before, they were gone now.

'After six weeks, the girl still wasn't talking, and they wanted to use ECT on her — I don't know what they hoped to achieve, perhaps shock the magic out of her. I stood in the way. Tabitha trusted me by then, and they knew that if they took me away that would set them back months. So they kept me on. When they realised she wasn't dangerous, they lost interest. They stopped running the tests on her, and just kept her there, in custody. I was waiting for an opportunity to quietly release the two of them, but of course, then Arkwood escaped, started killing people . . . came after you . . .'

He sounded almost cold now.

'I won't pretend I didn't suspect something. Not anything as large-scale as what you were up to, but still, I knew something was wrong. I thought it was just normal teenage problems. Hormones, et cetera.' He opened his eyes. They were fixed on her. 'And I thought myself a detective.'

Rose couldn't speak for a moment; when speech returned to her, it was very small.

'Are you angry with me?'

He took a moment to consider.

'No.' His eyes flickered to the door of the cupboard under the stairs. 'After all, there are worse secrets to keep, aren't there?'

She hesitated.

'Why didn't you tell me about Regency?'

He sighed. Then he moved to her sofa and sat down beside her.

'Rose,' he said. 'I lived through the War, and surviving that meant I had to do terrible things. Regret has a tipping point like anything else. If you let it build up, it will crush you, so you have to start running eventually.'

She looked into his eyes, and found no trace of a lie within them.

'I'm running from a lot of things, Rose, and I can't tell you about all of them, but you have to trust me that I mean the best for you.'

She opened her mouth, but now he cut her off.

'*No*. Rose, no. Please. Not now. I promise you, on everything, that after this is over I'll tell you and I'll answer all your questions. But not now. Let me have my secrets until the bastards are gone, and then I will tell you everything.'

She waited uncertainly for a moment. The tremor in his left hand was back again: Rose could see him gripping it with unnecessary force with his right.

'You probably need some sleep,' he said. 'In your own bed for a change. Go on. I'll see you in the morning.'

They both smiled grimly at the suggestion of getting a sound night's sleep. Still, Rose stood and began to make her way up the stairs. He was right: it would be good to sleep in her own bed, in her own room, with no one coming after her, and no soft murmurs of passers-by jerking her into terrified wakefulness every few hours.

'Oh, and Rose?'

She looked back at him.

'I love you, you know.'

'I love you too, Dad.'

They found her in the road beside the back entrance of the Department the next morning.

David stopped dead in the street and put out a hand to hold Rose back. She ignored him and dodged round before he could stop her, but when she saw the corpse she took several steps backwards very quickly.

It was Laura.

Oh, Angels.

Laura – who had looked after Rose when she was a baby, witness to her first steps; who had been kind and sympathetic to even the most heinous of criminals; brilliant, ingenious, sweet, strict, forgiving Laura, who had not said a word about Rose's betrayal, who had smiled at her nonetheless. . .

She was unquestionably dead.

David was white-faced. 'Rose, get Connor and James.'

Rose ran past Emily, ignoring her protestations, and took the stairs two at a time. She burst into the Department office. All heads turned to look at her. Terrian's was not among them, but James's was. He saw her expression and was on his feet immediately.

'What is it? What's happened?'

She could not speak, but gestured for him to follow her. They were halfway down the first flight of stairs when a scream, a girl's scream, reached them from outside. They broke into a run, and found David, Nate and Maria in the street, staring at the body. Maria had her hands over her mouth.

The two girls looked at each other. Maria's jaw dropped even further. Nate looked between them uneasily. 'Okay,' he said. 'I can explain—'

'What are you doing here?' Rose said, aghast. She looked at Nate accusingly. 'Just because she's your girl-friend doesn't mean you can come round here showing a law-enforcement agency off like it's your house.'

'It's not like that!' Nate said heatedly. 'I just thought . . . it would be nice . . .'

'Shut up, both of you,' David said harshly. They fell silent immediately. 'We don't have time for this. Nathaniel, where's your father?'

'Flu. He's at home.'

'Not any more he's not. James, get him on video contact. Tell him Regency have . . .' he swallowed, 'struck again. Maria, this is no time or place for a non-staff member to be. Go home.'

Maria managed to lower her hands from her mouth as James ran inside. She looked between the body, the slashes, tears, and missing parts that marked it unmistakably as a Hybrid killing, and Rose's face, as if she could not believe what she was seeing.

'Rose,' she said in a hushed voice. 'I thought you were dead.'

It took a moment for Rose to answer. She, too, was staring at the body. She had not seen a Hybrid kill for a long time, and her instincts marked it out as her own expertise. She remembered how it felt to carve those wounds in metal. She remembered the desire to carve them in flesh.

She checked her rising horror, and forced herself to be human again.

'So did I, for a while. Look, I'm sorry, there'll be time for explanations later. Right now I need to get you home. Nate, please. . .'

'No,' he said. He flushed. 'We— we bunked off school, Okay? We can't go back now.'

'Go inside, at the very least,' said David, not taking his eyes off the corpse, as if he feared it would run away. 'Rose, you too. This is no sight for a fifteen-year-old.'

'Dad, I'm a member of staff—'

She did not mean *member of staff*. She meant *Hybrid*, and for the first time in her life she was angry that he seemed to have forgotten this – as if this internal, conflicting, grim monsterhood were a club to which only he and Felix belonged.

'*Go inside*,' he repeated. His tone brooked no argument.

Rose took one last, repulsed look at Laura's body and turned away. She helped Nate guide Maria through the lobby and into the lift, despite Emily's reproaches. Nate pressed the button for the roof.

It was the longest and most awkward silence of Rose's life.

The lift ground to a halt and the doors slid open. It was a sunny day; the roof gave an excellent view of the Houses of Parliament and the Thames. Rose helped Maria to a chair, sat down opposite her and tried to force the images of the mutilated body out of her mind, with little success.

'Okay,' she said. 'Fire away.'

Maria seemed unable to speak for several minutes. Rose doubted that this was due to any actual inhibition of speech, and more to do with an inability to decide which question to ask first. She waited.

'Who was that woman?' Maria whispered finally.

'Her name was Laura,' Nate said. He was standing by the railing, staring unseeingly out over London. 'She was . . . the closest thing we had to a medic. Now she's dead.' He turned to Rose. 'Do you have any idea who killed her?'

Rose nodded grimly.

'Who?'

'*What* is the better question.'

He looked at her blankly. She shook her head.

'Not now,' she said quietly.

Maria looked from Rose to Nate and back to Rose in obvious confusion.

'What . . . what *happened* to you?'

Rose laughed. It felt very unnatural.

'If I could explain it to you in a sentence, Maria, I would.'

'But you work for the Department now?'

'Yes.'

'How?'

'I was conscripted. I'm sorry, Maria, but I won't be coming back to school. I don't think Nate will, either.'

Nate blinked. 'Me? Why not me?'

'I think they'll want as many people on staff as possible now that we're one down.'

Maria said tearfully, 'But what am I going to—?' and stopped, swallowed, and said more evenly, 'Don't you get a choice about whether to finish school?'

'Nope,' Rose said. 'I'm afraid that's kind of what conscription is.'

The grinding of metal on metal announced the lift doors opening. All three of them turned to see Loren step out, blinking in the sudden sunlight. Maria screamed and stumbled backwards.

'Oh my God!' she shrieked, pointing at him. 'It's Loren Arkwood!'

Loren raised his eyebrows.

'Quite the budding Sherlock Holmes, aren't you?' he said. 'Who's this, Rose?'

Maria stared between Loren and Rose as if unsure who to be more afraid of.

'Her name's Maria,' Rose told him wearily. 'She's— never mind. Where's Tabitha? Have you seen . . .'

His expression told her well enough.

'Did you know her?'

'We both did,' Nate replied. Rose regarded him curiously. She had never seen him react to a murder before. A sort of galvanising, determined fury had gripped him: neither the lethargic, broken helplessness of his father after Malia's death all those years ago, nor David's cold, reasoned calm. Perhaps he would make a better detective than Rose had given him credit for. 'Do you have any idea who killed her?'

'Well, I would have thought it was obvious,' Loren said. 'That's a Hybrid murder.'

'What, you mean the Regency leader? Felix? But why would he want to kill Laura?'

'I don't think he did,' Loren said grimly. 'Come on. There's a meeting on the fifth floor. Umm . . . girl: Maria. You're going to need to calm down. I'm not going to kill anyone, Okay?'

Maria looked between the three of them as if watching a gripping three-way tennis match. Eventually, she appeared to regain her power of speech enough to say, in a tone of such horror you would have thought she had just caught Rose killing someone herself, 'You *know* him?'

'Do you remember how I told you that what happened to me was a long story?' Rose said. 'He was heavily involved. And before you say it, yes, I do know him; yes, he is a murderer; yes, I know that means he's killed people. Come on. I don't want to miss this meeting, and you may as well get the full tour now that you're here.'

They had to nearly drag Maria down to the fifth floor. Rose noticed, as they ran through the corridors, that David had managed to persuade Emergency Response not to sound the alarms. Good. They didn't want a panic.

The rest of the Department and Tabitha were gathered round the table. Terrian had arrived: he looked frail and shivery, which Rose doubted had much to do with flu.

Everyone was avoiding Laura's conspicuously empty chair.

Terrian looked between Nate and Maria. 'Nate, who's this? You know non-staff members aren't allowed into meetings.'

'*I'm* a non-staff member,' Nate pointed out.

Terrian started to tell him off, but David said wearily, 'Just let her in, Connor. It will be more hassle to take her home. Maria: this is technically all classified, so I'd keep your mouth shut about it. Starting now,' he added, as she opened her mouth to assent. She closed it again, looking affronted.

'All right,' Terrian said. 'I'm sure you all know what's happened. Umm . . .' He swallowed, apparently unable to think of anything that encapsulated the situation better than what he had just said, or else simply overwhelmed. 'Uh, Elmsworth, Arkwood, you'll probably know more about this than I do.'

David and Rose raised their eyebrows at each other. This was the first time they had ever heard Terrian make this kind of admission.

'We probably would, yes,' said Loren, getting to his feet. 'Laura was killed by a Hybrid. I could list all the evidence, but . . . I don't think anyone needs to hear it. How good is your surveillance range?'

'Not good enough to catch it on film,' Terrian said. His voice was not entirely steady: he had been here since his wife was Head of the Department, and would have known Laura longer than almost any of them. He kept his grief quiet, though. 'Why?'

'We know there was a Hybrid murder, but we don't

know which Hybrid,' Loren said. 'Contextual evidence like Ariadne Stronach's murder would suggest this was Felix's own work, but it would be good to know whether Felix has any other Hybrids under his command.'

'One would suspect not,' David said, 'given the circumstances.'

James looked at him in astonishment, as if infuriated by how unemotional David seemed. 'How can you take this so calmly? Laura's *dead*! If this Felix killed her, then what are we waiting for? Let's go shoot the bastard out of existence!'

'I am all in favour, and have been for a number of years, of *shooting the bastard out of existence*,' David said evenly, 'and God knows I'm sorry about Laura, but don't you understand? Felix only personally killed people, if you can apply that description to his methods, if there was a good chance that the target might survive other assassination attempts. Laura is—' He stopped for a moment. 'Laura was,' he said slowly, 'a medic. She was a Pretender, as well, so she didn't have a lot of magic. She was someone who could easily have been taken out with sniper fire from a rooftop.'

'So what are you saying?' James said impatiently.

'I am *saying*,' snapped David, his composure finally breaking, 'that Laura was not Felix's intended victim. Hybrids have no control over who they kill. If he wanted to kill someone in that form, the most he could have done to ensure their death would be to have triggered his transformation a couple of streets away and trust that the right person would wander into his sights. And this time they didn't.'

'Then who do you think *was* the intended target?'
David sighed.

'Me, presumably,' he said. 'Or Loren, if Regency has been paying attention, which from past experience is unlikely. Either way, he's given us a lot of information about himself in trying: that he knows it's us who are trying to find and destroy the perpetrators of the Westfield attack; that he knows . . .' A hesitation. 'He knows that Loren and I aren't coming back, and so he is trying to kill off the two people who are most dangerous to him. Clearly he considers it likely that the pair of us could survive a non-magical attack. That's a lot of useful evidence that he's willing to give away, just to kill us.'

'That's all very interesting,' said James impatiently, 'but we still don't know how to kill him, or what his weak points are, or how many soldiers we'll need to take him out, or even where he is.'

David ran a hand over his face. 'I know. There are about twenty buildings he could be using as his base at the moment, and I reinforced and booby-trapped all of them. We can't march the whole army through the city to twenty different locations.'

'You don't have to.'

They turned to look at Maria. She was on her feet, looking pale but determined. They stared at her.

'What do you mean?' Nate said.

'I know where he is,' Maria said. She took a deep, shaky breath. 'But if I tell you, you'll have to promise me something.'

'We don't accept conditions,' Terrian snapped.

'Yes, we do,' David said. 'Maria. Say that again. You know the location of Regency's headquarters? How?'

'My sister,' she said. Rose stared at her. She knew Amelia Rodriguez, of course; she and Aaron Greenlow had been inseparable until their Test year, when Amelia, who was Ashkind, had been sent to a non-magical school. Rose hadn't seen her since. 'She disappeared on my Test day. She left a note, saying she was okay, she didn't want to leave us, but she didn't have a choice. She said she was fighting for freedom for . . . her own kind.'

Pause. Maria swallowed. Rose was recalling in astonishment the way she had looked on their first day of school: exhausted, red-eyed, anxious. Rose had attributed it to stress at the time. She had not thought – not even considered the possibility – that it might be something more than that.

Rose had never had time for trivialities.

'Yeah, I know,' Maria said hastily, as if forestalling criticisms that they were all too stunned to make, 'they're her beliefs, not mine, okay? But, anyway, she sends me emails every now and again, to let me know that she's safe, and doing well, and not dead. I was thinking maybe if you traced the emails, you could find where they were sent from. But I'll only show you them if you agree to something.'

Terrian attempted to interject again, but all six of them stopped him this time. Even Tabitha, who up until this point had been sitting in a corner, reading a book and paying no attention to the conversation whatsoever, was watching Maria now.

'What are your conditions?' said Loren.

Maria swallowed, and seemed to lose her resolve under their scrutiny. 'You say Amelia's army blew up that shopping centre? Killed all those people?'

'Yes,' David said. 'And carried out another bomb attack besides.'

'And her commander killed that woman?'

'Yes.'

Maria took another deep breath. 'Okay. I'll show you the emails and let you trace this . . . Regency, if you promise that when you find them, you keep my sister safe. You don't hurt her, you don't arrest her or put her in prison or anything, you just let her go. Don't wipe her memory, either – I know you have ways to do that. I want you to sign to it. On a piece of paper, so you can't delete it or anything. And then I'll give you the emails. Okay?'

David, Loren, Terrian and James all looked at each other.

'Deal,' they said together.

'James,' David said, 'go draw up that contract. Maria, go with him. I'll sign it too if you want. We all will.'

Maria, who had been clutching the table so hard it looked like she would soon lose the ability to ever let go of it again, headed out of the room with James. Rose caught her at the doorway and hugged her. Maria smiled bemusedly before James near-dragged her out the door. Rose knew how eager he would be to get to the computers on something this big.

She turned to the remaining people in the meeting room. David, Loren, Nate and Terrian, all still looking slightly stunned, were staring at the doorway after James and Maria.

'Well,' Rose said into the sudden silence, 'I have to say I did not see that one coming.'

CHAPTER 35

It took James six hours to track Regency down. After Maria had given the Department access to the emails, there was nothing more she could do to be of use to the operation; thus, along with Nate and Rose, she was assigned to what Rose assured her was the high-ranking and well-respected post of Tea Fetcher. In those six hours, the three of them fetched thirty-four cups of tea, twenty-eight mugs of coffee, and three biscuit trays – most of it for the consumption of Terrian, Loren and David, who were in the meeting room, pacing back and forth by the windows and looking very tense.

At about four o'clock, the morgue staff came and took Laura's body away. After this, David assumed a sort of comatose state, sitting in front of an untouched cup of tea with his head in his hands, unmoving. Rose knew better than to try to stir him.

'Is there anything we could have done?' asked Nate quietly, a few hours after that. He was staring out of the window at the marks of Laura's blood on the pavement. His voice was hollow. 'Anything at all?'

'No,' said David grimly. 'Nothing.' He moved a hand slowly over his face, his movements stiff; he had not stirred for a long time. 'There is no defence against Hybrids.'

For a moment Rose worried that someone might take note of the clear, heavy weight of knowledge in his voice, but no one seemed to; the silence picked up from there and stretched long and light ahead of them.

Maria fell silent after a few minutes and spent the rest of the time sitting in a corner, looking pale and frightened. Rose could see her determination crumbling, her unvoiced fears playing out across her face. Rose could not begrudge her worrying about her sister, having not known Laura herself, but as the anxiety on Maria's face deepened, Rose looked away. She couldn't bear the weight of someone else's loss as well as her own.

After a while, Nate, who had been pacing up and down by the window, sat down next to Maria and put his arm round her shoulder. She leaned against him. Terrian stared at them for a second, opened his mouth, closed it again, and looked at David, who gave him a half-amused *What can you do?* kind of look, and then made an odd little nodding gesture between Rose and the door that led to the computer office, which Rose had no idea how to interpret.

Rose herself sat in the opposite corner, thinking. Mostly, she thought about Laura; the years she had spent in the suggestion therapy wards, looking after distressed relatives; the games she had played with Rose when she was little and David was on a case; her husband and grown-up son, who would have been informed by now of her death; the way Rose had had to take a second look at her bloodied corpse before her face became recognisable . . .

No, not Laura. Please not Laura.

What had Laura ever done, to deserve this?

She had had nothing to do with Hybrids, had borne no particular grudge against them; in fact she had been Rose's only hope if their secret ever came out – the one person whose forgiveness and acceptance she could have been fairly sure of . . .

Oh, stop being so selfish, for the love of the Angels. Laura is gone.

Laura was gone.

She pressed the heels of her hands to her eyes and groaned.

Finally, just as the sunlight began to fade from the sky, James's cry rang from the computer office. Everyone was on their feet immediately. Rose was nearly crushed in the doorway and in the stampede down the corridors. They burst into the office and gathered around James's computer. He looked exhausted, but his eyes were bright.

'Got him,' he said, triumphantly, sitting back in his chair. 'He's got good people on computer security, I'll give him that.'

Loren's finger found the pulsing green dot on James's screen. His eyes widened and he leaned back.

'Oh, no.' He half-laughed in disbelief. 'The clever bastard.'

'Where?' asked Nate impatiently. 'Where is he?'

'The War Rooms,' Loren said blankly. 'He's in the Cabinet War Rooms.'

'But the Gifted armies bombed that.' David leaned in to squint at the screen. 'Felix abandoned it years ago.'

'Apparently not,' said James. 'I've hacked into the camera database and found the thermal registers. There are life signs for about seven hundred people there, easily.' He looked up at David. 'This is bigger than we thought. Much bigger.'

Nate held up a hand. 'Hang on. Explain. What are the War Rooms?'

'They were built during the Second World War – one of the human wars, before the Veilbreak – as a sort of bomb shelter-cum-government base,' Loren said. 'The leader of Parliament ran the country from there when needed. The Ashkind took it as a base during the War of Angels and expanded it. But the Gifted armies bombed the entrance. Apparently they didn't destroy as much of it as they thought.'

'It looks like they didn't destroy *anything*,' David said, examining the diagrams more closely, 'just the entrance. It would have been fairly easy to build another, though. Angels.' He leaned back in amazement. 'He's been using the whole thing as an underground base for years. And we never noticed.' He tapped the floor. 'Right under our feet.'

There was a silence for a few seconds.

'Right,' Terrian said, after a while. His voice had a new strength to it. 'Let's go bomb the bastard, shall we?'

David looked at him sharply. 'No! Weren't you listening? That's exactly what we *shouldn't* do!'

'What on earth do you mean?'

David sighed in exasperation and pulled down a map of London from a shelf. He found Westminster and circled the War Rooms with a pencil.

'This is where Felix is hiding,' he said. 'He would have had to dig further to create enough space to contain seven hundred people. He can't dig sideways, because it's surrounded by buildings with basements. He could dig into St. James's Park, but there's a high risk someone would notice the tremors from the work, and eventually he'd end up digging into the middle of the lake. So he has to dig *down*. If you tried to bomb it, you'd only skim the surface and drive them further underground. And there are only going to be a couple of entrances, which will be very well defended. It'd be suicide, Connor.'

'So what exactly do you suggest we do, leave them alone? After they blew up Westfield and killed Laura?'

David put his head in his hands. He looked very tired. 'No. I suggest we try subtler methods.'

Terrian laughed harshly. 'Look at this! David Elmsworth, suggesting subtlety.'

David looked up at him sharply. Everyone was staring between the two men now. Rose and Nate glanced at each other nervously.

Slowly, very slowly, David straightened up and stepped towards Terrian. To his credit, Terrian did not step back.

'I suggest,' David said, very softly, 'that if you dislike my methods, you should stop listening to me. Fire me if you must. After that I give you six months, maximum, before this whole Department collapses and your career is consigned to the Governmental dustheap. This whole operation is useless without me and you know it.'

Fury blazed in Terrian's eyes. James's gaze flickered between them uncertainly. Loren was watching David, his fists clenched. Nate leaned back against a filing cupboard and folded his arms.

There was a pause of about six seconds, wherein Rose could see Terrian struggling for a dignified response and failing to come up with one.

The ensuing dialogue could only be described as a detailed explanation of what Terrian thought about David's advice, its quality, and its giver, followed by a suggestion as to where David could shove it.

James and Loren were on their feet immediately, but Rose was faster. Anger blurred her vision, and with a bang Terrian was thrown backwards onto the desk. She focused, and before he could strike back the desk was swept from under him. By the time he hit the ground, Rose's gun was out and pointed between Terrian's eyes.

'Take that back,' she said, her voice shaking with fury.

'*Rose!*' David said sharply. 'Rose, get away from him.'

She felt Nate's hand on her arm, pulling her away, and she wrenched herself out of his grip. He went for the gun, but Rose dodged and stepped back, clicking the safety off and aiming it again at Terrian's head.

'I said,' Rose repeated, '*take it back.*'

She had honestly never seen anyone look so furious in her life. His eyes were fixed on the gun. It did not quite register with her yet, but the fact that he didn't try to get up meant that he considered it a genuine possibility that she might fire.

'Rose,' said James hoarsely. 'Jesus Christ, put the gun down.'

'Not until he takes it back.'

'*Rose.*'

She looked at him. He was standing two feet away from her, his computer screen forgotten, hands raised uncertainly to shoulder height. Even Loren, behind him, looked slightly wary. David looked shocked and angry in equal measure. Beside him, Maria was just managing to stop Nate, who looked angrier than Rose had ever seen him, from running at her.

So having evil forced upon you, and accepting it, is entirely different from choosing evil.

Loren's words, a far-distant memory.

Put the gun down, said a weary voice in her head. *Aren't you one of the good guys?*

But good guys had guns. Without guns, they would never get anything done.

Put it down.

No.

Put it down, you monster.

Slowly, Rose lowered the gun and stepped away from Terrian.

Maria let go of Nate, who promptly walked up to Rose and hit her. Rose did not react. It stung, but she did not react.

'If you ever,' he said, 'do that again . . .'

'I very much doubt I will have cause to,' Rose said quietly.

Nate turned away and stormed out of the office. Maria followed him hurriedly. Everyone stared at each other.

After a few seconds of silence, Terrian picked himself up out of the scattered papers and crushed wood, brushing himself off. He was almost spluttering with anger. From an uninvolved perspective, it would have been almost funny.

Terrian straightened up and moved towards Rose. She did not move, but David hastily stepped between them. Loren took a step closer, hand on his gun, watching the three of them closely.

'Connor,' David began, 'whatever my daughter has done—'

'Shut up,' Terrian hissed. 'Get out of my way.'

'No,' David said calmly.

'I said,' Terrian repeated, '*get out of my way.*'

'No,' David said again.

Terrian glared furiously at Rose. She hated hiding behind her father, but she knew from the look in Terrian's eyes that to do anything else would be stupid. Then he looked back at David. Rose could see him reasoning it out: to back down now would make him look weak, but if Rose could knock him to the ground, starting a fight with David would be next to suicide.

'All right,' he said. He took a deep breath. 'All right, then, Major Elmsworth. You think you can just defy a senior officer, in a time of crisis? All right then.' Another breath. 'This department is going to bomb the War Rooms tomorrow and go in with two hundred army troops, and you' – here he jabbed a finger into David's chest – 'you' – pointing at Loren, who raised his eyebrows – 'you' – at Rose – 'and *you*' – at James – 'can lead them. I'll sit here in Westminster and watch you make fools of your-selves. *Then* see how eager you are to defy me.'

He gave the four of them one last, triumphant glower, and stormed out after his son.

For a long time, no one moved.

'Okay,' Rose said quietly, 'I'll admit that wasn't my best move.'

'No,' replied Loren curtly, 'it was not. Well done, Rose.'

Another long silence. James got to his feet, pushing his hair out of his eyes.

'Well, he never really liked me anyway,' he said cheerfully. 'If we're leading a suicide mission tomorrow, I may as well get some sleep beforehand. Goodnight, everyone.'

And with that he picked up his bag and left.

Another silence, this time broken by the sound of the door creaking open and Tabitha poking her head nervously into the room.

'I heard . . . noises,' she said. 'Is everything okay, Daddy?'

Loren leaned back against a filing cabinet, closed his eyes, and swore.

CHAPTER 36

They arrived at Westminster the next morning to find fifty people gathered around the War Room entrance, all wearing the grey uniform of the Department squad teams. David stared at them in confusion.

'We were supposed to have the army,' he muttered. 'Why is this not the army?'

'Are squad teams not better than the army?' Rose asked.

'Not here,' he said. 'Squad teams are just soldiers with extra training, and in any other situation they'd be great, but we're not going to win this battle using skill, we're going to win with sheer force of numbers. Fifty is not going to cut it. They'll outnumber us fourteen to one. Excuse me?' He ducked under the *Do Not Cross* tape and looked around. 'Has anyone got Connor Terrian on communications?'

Someone had. They handed him a walkie-talkie, saluted respectfully, realised David wasn't paying them the slightest bit of attention, and walked away. David held the button down and spoke, staring at the bricked-up entrance to the War Rooms. Rose had to admit it looked, at first sight, fairly innocuous.

'Hello, Ground Control,' he said. 'We appear to be somewhat lacking in arms.'

'Yes, I know,' came Terrian's voice, crackly over the intercom. 'I put in the application for two hundred troops last night, and . . .'

'Yes?'

'It didn't go through,' Terrian said. 'Apparently the Department needs to prove its competence against Regency before the government will commit two hundred troops.'

'Did they?' David asked innocently. 'Did they really say "the Department", Connor?'

Silence.

'Ground Control, are you still there?'

'No,' snapped Terrian. 'No, they didn't. They said me. Is that enough?'

'Oh, yes,' David said, grinning. 'Yes it is.'

And he disconnected before Terrian could start swearing at him.

James and Loren approached from behind the War Rooms. James was doing a quick headcount of the troops, and the look of confusion on his face was quickly descending into one of anger.

'All right,' he said, as he and Loren accepted walkie-talkies from the soldiers, 'how's he messed up this time?'

'It's not so much how he's messed up as his likelihood of doing so again,' David said. 'Where's Tabitha?'

'At home,' Loren replied. 'I thought she could look after herself for a day. Anyway, my only other options were leaving her with Terrian or taking her into this. What's our situation?'

David ran a hand over his face and sighed.

'Well, as I see it,' he said, 'less than ideal. We've got fifty troops, lots of explosives, a target that extends about twenty feet underground, and no visible entrance to bomb.'

'But that's ridiculous,' James said in disbelief. 'They don't seriously expect us to take Regency out with this, do they?'

'Apparently they do,' David said.

There was a grim silence.

'You're being very quiet, Rose,' Loren said. 'Any ideas?'

'None,' Rose said. 'Just a thought. And not a very nice one.'

'Well, fire away,' David said. 'We haven't got anything.'

'It's not even a plan,' Rose said in frustration. 'It's just . . . we may as well go ahead with whatever Terrian thinks, mightn't we? We've got nothing to lose.'

David grimaced in acceptance, but James looked at her as if she had gone mad. His hair was still wet. It had darkened to a gold-brown in the light of the morning clouds.

'Nothing to lose?' he repeated incredulously. 'We have *everything* to lose, Rose.'

'Not like that,' Rose said. 'I just mean . . . our chances of actually succeeding with this aren't good, so we may as well follow Terrian's plan, because it's his fault all of this is happening, isn't it? If he can be seen to mess this up, they'll take away his control, and we can use – what was it you said yesterday, Dad? – *subtler methods* without him sticking his nose in.'

A pause while they absorbed this.

'Actually,' David said slowly, 'that's true. I spoke to Terrian just now, and the reason we've only got fifty troops is because the army don't trust him enough to give us the two hundred he asked for. Specifically *him*. He messed up the Argent case, remember?' Rose noticed Loren shift slightly where he stood. 'And Laura— Anyway, this is backfiring on him. He thought that sending us on a suicide mission was a win-win situation, because if we fail, he can blame us, but if we succeed, he can take the credit. But the government is allocating troops based on *his* reliability. As far as they're concerned, ultimate responsibility rests with him.'

James considered this for a second, and then grinned. 'You're a genius, Rose,' he said. David rolled his eyes exasperatedly. Rose looked between the two of them in mild confusion.

Loren, who had been staring darkly back at the War Rooms throughout most of the conversation, blinked and returned his attention to David. 'Sorry,' he said. 'What are we doing?'

David sighed, and brought the walkie-talkie to his mouth. 'Ground Control, request orders as to proceedings of attack.'

'I thought you'd never ask,' said Terrian. 'Blow the entrance wide open and drop in explosives from there. When they come out, shoot them.'

David put a hand to his face and grimaced at Rose, whose jaw had dropped open in shock and anger. Had Terrian seriously just given them orders to kill seven hundred people on sight?

James appeared to feel the same way about this, and seemed to be on the verge of grabbing the walkie-talkie from David's grasp. David put up a hand to stop him.

'Ground Control—'

'Stop calling me that!'

'*Ground Control*,' David repeated, making sure to properly enunciate every syllable, 'permission to speak freely.'

Terrian sighed. It came over the intercom as a wave of static. 'Permission granted.'

'With all *due* respect,' David said, 'we don't know the layout of their base. We could be dropping explosives two feet down. We'd blow up the street.'

'Then send troops down to check the depth.'

'Send fifty troops,' David said quietly, and only then did Rose begin to realise just how angry he was, 'down into darkness with explosives where seven hundred enemy soldiers are *known* to be hiding?'

James had his walkie-talkie out and seemed to be trying to locate Terrian's frequency. Loren was watching David narrowly.

'Do you have any better ideas?' Terrian asked tightly.

'Not only do I have better ideas,' David said, 'I am fairly sure you do. I doubt any of them involve fifty troops attacking an embedded and well-defended enemy base with explosives, alone and outnumbered fourteen to one.'

Silence.

'Connor, please listen to me. This is suicide. Pull out. Give the order. Or the blood of God knows how many people will be on your hands, and your hands alone.'

More silence.

Terrian said, 'I will await the attack progress report,' and disconnected.

All four of them groaned.

Someone stamped to attention behind Rose. She whirled. It was the squad member who had handed out the walkie-talkies.

'Awaiting orders, sir.'

'Orders received from Connor Terrian of the Department,' David said. 'Detonate devices by the entrance and send soldiers down to check depth before detonating lower. Shoot on sight.'

The soldier seemed slightly surprised by this, but saluted and turned anyway. At the last moment, Rose remembered.

'Wait!'

He turned, surprised.

'Yes, ma'am?'

'There's a girl,' she said. 'Seventeen or eighteen years old, blonde hair, grey eyes. Her name's Amelia Rodriguez. Don't shoot her.'

The soldier saluted again. 'Yes, ma'am.'

She turned back to the others. David was already talking.

'All right, everyone, since we're all fairly good shots, we may as well get on the roof and help with the sniper fire. Loren and I will cover the back entrance. Rose, James, you cover the front.'

Loren raised his eyebrows at David. 'You're asking for trouble there,' he muttered.

David made a shushing gesture at him. Rose stared at him, bemused.

Loren and David walked away towards the fire escape stairs of the nearest building. James and Rose headed towards a large office block just to the right of the War Rooms. They looked up at the wall. There were no stairs here.

'All right,' said Rose uncertainly, 'do we have a plan for this?'

'Can you levitate?'

She looked at him. 'Umm. . . yes. Where is this going?'

'Up, I hope. Come on.'

And with that he closed his eyes and began to float upwards. Rose blinked.

The trick to moving yourself upwards was to imagine that you were remaining perfectly still and the world was moving downwards. Rose realised she was already ten feet off the ground, and tried to push the image of falling nine stories onto tarmac from her mind. It refused to budge.

James landed on the roof before she did. She moved herself a few feet forward, so there was no chance of her slipping off the edge, and dropped. Something unexpected cracked in her ankle and she gasped, stumbling in pain. James caught her.

'Are you all right?' he asked anxiously.

Rose gritted her teeth and flexed her ankle. She was fine: it wasn't broken, just twisted. 'Yeah,' she said. 'Thanks. It's all right, I can fire lying down anyway. Come on, they're setting the bombs.'

They knelt at the edge of the roof and took out their guns. The squad teams had moved back now, away from the explosives that leaned against the bricked-up entrance to the War Rooms. Sparks of light on the pavement tiles indicated that the fuses had been lit.

'Good luck,' James said to her quietly. She looked at him.

And then the bombs went off and everything descended into chaos.

There was a great, heavy, rumbling *boom*. The entrance to the War Rooms crumbled into smoke. When it cleared, the great dark hole in the ground was empty of enemy troops. There was not a single form, living or dead, to be seen through the mist.

But there should have been, Rose realised, in slowly rising panic. There *should* have been. Where were Regency's soldiers?

'This isn't right,' James muttered under his breath. 'This isn't right at—'

Shouting from below, and the troops emerged from the building beneath them. Twenty soldiers, all carrying bombs, vanished into the hole to find any surviving enemy. Rose looked over the rooftops at her father and Loren. From what she could make out, they had not yet relaxed.

And then Regency's bombs went off.

There was a deeper, louder *boom,* and then twenty successive, deafening *booms,* that shook the building James and Rose were kneeling on. The possibility of death roared in Rose's ears. She listened to it numbly, immobile.

When the ground was still again, she looked over the edge of the building, coughing. She could hear screams. James had gone white.

'Oh God,' he said. 'That wasn't— That wasn't us . . .'

The soldiers would never have detonated their explosives at such proximity. This was Regency's counterstrike. In the chain of fire and crumbling earth, in the unimaginable noise, in the rubble of the square lurking behind the grey smoke, Rose could feel them. Aaron's cold laugh echoed wildly in her head.

James was whispering.

'No, no, this can't be— this can't—'

The soldiers were screaming and running. Some were running towards the hole, yelling the names of comrades who Rose knew would not yell back. Some were running away.

And that was when the second lot of Regency bombs went off.

CHAPTER 37

'All right, so whose bloody fault was this?'

Nine o'clock the following morning. In the twenty-two hours since the failed attack on Regency, the names and faces of the lost troops had been broadcast by every channel in the country, adorned stickers and protest boards, made the headlines in five national newspapers, and featured on what seemed like every single major news bulletin in the world. The reasons for their deaths had not yet been pinned on the Department. Many were calling this an attack by a group of lone terrorists. Which was not, of course, a million miles from the truth.

The data had been collected and the reports had been written up. The details were too painful to recount, but the gist was this: the Department had sent in twenty troops with a very large bomb, which had triggered Regency's own bombs, buried under the square in the form of twenty packages of Semtex. This had, in turn, triggered several smaller bombs in the hands of the Department soldiers, which had reduced their bodies to clumps of red-stained earth. Taken together, the explosions had collapsed the square, taking thirty-eight Department squad members with it. Rose had their names memorised. So, apparently, did the British press's leader-writers.

The ACC had sent in Evelyn Wood, the woman who had once interrogated David, to interview the Department in order to isolate the cause of what was, by general consensus, an unmitigated disaster. By the looks of it, she had no more love for the Department now than she had last time. In part because of this, Loren had left Tabitha at home. Numerical reinforcement came in the form of the Department's newest member: Nate had received his conscription orders yesterday, and was now officially on staff. He still wasn't talking to Rose, though. Or indeed looking at her.

'Answer me,' Wood repeated, staring round at the six of them, seated at the meeting-room table. 'Someone has to be responsible.'

David, Loren, Rose and James stared pointedly at Terrian, who cleared his throat. Rose tried and failed to ignore the way Nate was glaring at her.

Wood watched Terrian as he straightened up.

'I sanctioned the attack, yes,' he said. 'However, the troops were under Major Elmsworth's control at the time.'

James and Rose both jumped to their feet in outrage. Wood gestured impatiently for them to sit down.

'Elmsworth,' she said. 'Can you answer to this accusation?'

'I can,' David said calmly. 'The day before the attack, Colonel Terrian and I had a . . . professional dispute, regarding our preferred methods for taking down Regency. The Colonel wished to – what were his words? – "bomb the bastard". I suggested we take a more discreet course of action.'

'And he overrode you?'

'*Overrode* doesn't really cut it,' David said icily. '*Overrode* affords it a veneer of civility. *Colonel* Terrian felt he had the authority to dismiss the opinion of a Major, despite that Major's experience and track record within the Department – which, might I add, is considerably better than his own.'

Wood glanced between him and Terrian, who looked furious. Nate was glowering at David and James. Rose, however, kept her eyes fixed on Wood. She noticed that Loren did the same.

'But you had control over the troops at the time,' Wood said to David.

'Colonel Terrian was giving me orders from the Department building. Given his adverse opinion of my calibre as a strategist, he had severely limited my freedom to interpret those orders. I had fifty troops – nowhere near enough to take down Regency – and a lot of explosives, and I was under the impression that I would be forced to remain at the site of the attack should I attempt to leave.'

Loren raised his eyebrows at Rose. David had her tendency towards polysyllabicity when under pressure.

'And do you confirm this account?' Wood asked Terrian.

'Absolutely not!' he said, nearly spluttering with rage. 'He's making it up. He has no proof of this— this *professional dispute.*'

Even Nate looked slightly dubious at this blatant lie. For the first time, David looked angry.

'Apart from the words of everyone around this table,' he said coldly, 'no, I cannot prove it.'

'He can, actually,' James said. They looked at him. 'The office is under constant video surveillance. If you'll let me, Ms Wood . . .'

She nodded. He took his laptop out from his bag. There followed a few very tense seconds as he accessed the Department security database and brought up the footage. Then he spun the screen round so the rest of them could see it. It showed David standing between Terrian and Rose, with Loren and James standing warily to the side. James turned up the volume so they could all hear what Terrian was saying.

'All right, then, Major Elmsworth. You think you can just defy a senior officer, in a time of crisis? All right then. This department is going to bomb the War Rooms tomorrow and go in with two hundred army troops, and you, you, you and you can lead them. I'll sit here in Westminster and watch you make fools of yourselves. Then see how eager you are to defy me.'

There was a long, very pregnant silence. Wood turned slowly to face Terrian. Nate had his face in his hands.

'Well, Colonel Terrian,' she said calmly, 'do you have anything to say?'

He opened and closed his mouth helplessly like a fish drowning in air. Then, finally, he said: 'Yes. Rewind the footage thirty seconds back.'

He jabbed a finger at James. Wood raised her eyebrows. Rose's heart sank. She, James, David and Loren all glanced at each other nervously.

'All right,' Wood said calmly, 'rewind the footage then, Private Andreas.'

Reluctantly, James did so. He made sure to rewind it far enough back to get in Terrian's insult to David. Nothing, however, could draw attention away from Rose's violent reaction. Her stomach writhed in embarrassment as she watched herself blast Terrian back into the desk, then sweep it out from under him and point her gun at his head.

Now it was her turn to be scrutinised by Wood.

'You can't say I wasn't provoked,' she said defensively. 'Nate would have done the same if Dad had said that to Ter— the Colonel. I'm sorry about it, and I wouldn't do it again, but given the Colonel's retaliation. . . Well, would you call sending us on a suicide mission in revenge reasonable? Especially given what happened.'

Wood nodded.

'Ms Wood,' Terrian protested, 'you can't seriously—'

'Shut up,' she told him sharply. 'Your incompetence has caused thirty-eight deaths. Your career is in enough trouble as it is. Don't make it worse.'

She stood. Rose looked around the table. James looked satisfied, Nate furious. David and Loren were watching Wood narrowly.

'All right,' she said. 'Luckily – and unfortunately in my view – I can't fire any of you, given the particularly low staff numbers at the moment due to . . .' She coughed. 'Recent events.'

How quickly had the news of Laura's death reached the ACC? Rose exchanged a worried look with David. It would benefit neither of them if the Supergrass panicked and started asking Parliament to brief the public on how to spot suspected Hybrids.

'But after seeing how badly you lot messed this up, the ACC – with the full backing of the Ministry of Defence – has decided to go ahead with our own plans, whether you lot welcome them or not. No,' as David started to protest, 'not even you, Elmsworth. Though you'll be glad to know that our plan should meet your criteria for *subtler methods.*'

They waited, tense. Wood leaned forward and put her hands on the table, looking round at all of them.

'We're sending in a spy,' she said. 'One that fits the template you described for Regency recruits. Young, preferably teenage; good fighter; high IQ; previous contact links with law enforcement agencies—'

David realised about a second before Rose did. He was on his feet immediately, and real fury darkened his face for the first time. 'No,' he said. 'Absolutely not.'

Loren looked from Wood to David to Rose and then it hit him as well, and he stood up so fast his chair toppled over. 'Send Rose to Regency?' he said, outraged. 'Are you mad?'

'What?' said James in horror. 'No. No way.'

Even Nate got to his feet, feud apparently forgotten.

'Why does it have to be Rose?' he said angrily. 'James and I both fit that description, we can go—'

'No you cannot,' Wood said. She was watching Rose carefully. Rose met her gaze with all the calm she could summon. 'It has to be Rosalyn.'

'*Why?*' James asked furiously.

Why seemed perfectly clear to Rose; and, by the looks they were giving Wood, it was obvious to David and Loren as well. While the fault for the War Room disaster lay undoubtedly with Terrian, the government still did not quite trust David, and they certainly didn't trust Loren. Having Rose in constant jeopardy – dependent entirely on the mercy of the army to rescue her if anything went wrong – would keep the Department in check nicely.

Rose tried to breathe evenly and keep her eyes fixed on Wood.

'I will not let you,' David said in a very soft, very dangerous voice. 'If you lay a hand on my daughter I swear I will make you regret it. I will make you wish you were never born.'

Wood switched her gaze from Rose to David. 'Oh, but you will let us take her,' she said. 'Unless you want your circumstances to change drastically.'

David laughed harshly, mirthlessly. 'You think I'd give up my daughter for the sake of my own career?'

'Oh no,' Wood said. 'But I do think you'd give up your daughter for the sake of your own life.'

That stopped David cold. The look he gave Wood was one of icy hatred. He was very pale, but hatred radiated from him so strongly it was almost palpable. Rose burned with shock and anger; she had never seen David threatened like this, never seen it affect him this way, but of course Wood was right. The Government would never let him go. He was too dangerous to set free, knowing all that he knew, especially if he left with a grudge against his old employers.

Wood looked at James.

'The same goes for you, Private Andreas,' she said. 'We

wouldn't want anything bad to happen to your brothers, would we? And as for you'– here she turned to Loren, who appeared just as furious as David, and looked him up and down scornfully – 'I'm sure we can find some incentive for you. We had your niece in custody once already, didn't we?'

The temperature in the room appeared to drop ten degrees. If Loren had had a gun with him then, Rose was sure that Wood would not have survived another moment.

Terrian was still sitting, open-mouthed, at the table, staring around at them all.

'I warn you,' David said in that same dangerous voice, 'we are not good enemies to make.'

'Oh,' Wood said, smiling, 'that's what we're counting on.'

She brushed past him, walking towards Rose, who kept her eyes locked on Wood's. Out of the corner of her eye, she saw David and James reach for their guns. Rose gave a tiny but unmistakable shake of the head, and their hands stopped inches from their weapons. She could, and would, handle this on her own. The liberties, and indeed the lives, of everyone else in the room were in dire enough straits already.

'You have until tomorrow morning to say your good-byes,' said Wood. 'Don't worry. You'll be perfectly safe.'

'Oh, I have no doubt,' Rose said.

Wood stared at her for another few seconds, and then turned on her heel and left. The rest of them remained utterly motionless until they heard the door snap shut behind her.

James was the first to move: he collapsed into his chair, like a puppet whose strings had been suddenly cut.

'The *bastards*,' he said, in a tone that seemed more astonished and outraged than angry. 'The absolute *bastards*.'

'Insulting them won't change what they're doing, James.'

'They're not doing anything,' he said, with more firmness in his voice. 'I won't let them. I will not let them.'

Terrian stood up very suddenly.

'Come on, Nate,' he said. 'We're going home.'

'What?' said Nate, outraged. 'No! They're taking Rose, Dad! I can't leave now!'

'Yes you bloody well can,' said Terrian grimly, looking around at the others, all of whom met his gaze with dark looks of their own. 'If I know those two'– he gestured to David and Loren – 'they're going to come up with some plot to get her out of it, and when the Government finds out and it all hits the fan I want nothing to do with it.'

Nate stared at his father.

'No,' he said.

Terrian seemed to inflate with anger.

'You,' he said, 'are coming with me. Do not argue.'

'No,' Nate said again. 'You can't make me. Rose is my best friend. I'm staying here.'

Terrian's eyes bulged, apparently speechless with rage, and then he appeared to bow to the inevitable and stormed out of the room. Loren sat down in his chair in relief.

'That's got rid of him,' he said. 'Does anyone have a plan?'

No one answered.

'David?' said Nate.

'Yes?'

'You know how we're supposed to be professional detectives, and observant, and things like that?'

'I think it was somewhere in my employment contract, yes.'

'Rose is gone.'

CHAPTER 38

It took her twenty minutes to get home; accounting for how fast she had run and Tube delays, she reckoned she had maybe five minutes before David arrived home behind her. Her hands were shaking as she turned the key in the lock.

She wasn't going to put up with this any more.

She was so intent on getting to the basement that the fear that usually accompanied her trips down there could not touch her. She pushed open the door and stood there, breathing hard.

Hybrids are wolves

Don't you dare talk to me about morality

Having evil forced upon you and accepting it is not the same

She tried to push it away, but couldn't. She pressed her forehead to the cold metal.

Just one spilled secret, and none of this would matter. They wouldn't try to do any of this to her.

They would be too afraid.

I am not human. I shouldn't have to deal with this.

She sent a pulse of flame into the wall. It blossomed into gold against the grey metal, blackened with scratches from inhuman hands, and curled smokelessly into the air.

'You should treat your possessions with more care,' he said from the doorway. She jerked backwards in automatic self-defence, and he raised his eyebrows. 'I spent years saving up for these rooms.'

'I thought I had longer,' was all she could say.

'Yes,' said David mildly. 'You did.'

He stepped forward and pressed his hands to the wall, examining the soot that came away on his palm.

'I think this may be my last chance to say in so many words that I don't judge you for what you did concerning Arkwood, Rose.' He looked up at her. 'I am many things, but I am no hypocrite. Not where it counts, anyway.'

She swallowed. 'That . . . that matters a lot. Thank you.'

'If I didn't think it would, I wouldn't say it.'

They didn't say anything for a moment. They stood on opposite sides of a room with dark silver walls, carved deeply with claws that were both hers and not hers.

'Dad, I don't think I can do this.'

'Of course you can. You can and you will, or they'll come for the both of us and we know exactly how wrong *that* will go.'

'Then what do I do?'

'You survive like the rest of us.'

She stared at him, angry and hurt, and then she saw the gleam in his eyes and she knew.

'You have a plan, don't you?'

He took something from his pocket and threw it to her. It was the Department's handbook on various types of criminal, designed by David when she was very small in order to help Department members spot various types of suspicious characters. When she was younger, Rose had had it read to her many times as a bedtime story.

She caught it, and at a nod from him the pages fluttered open to the section on murderers. Rose stared at it.

There was a drawing there, as there was on every page. The drawings were David's own creations. On this page was the Department's standard portrait of a killer.

She looked at the lines David had traced, so many years ago, in faded pencil: the physique, the smile, the hair, the shaded eyes.

Felix Callaway.

David grinned.

'Oh, Rose. Of course I do.'

CHAPTER 39

The door slammed closed before Rose worked her blind-fold off. For a second, she thought she had failed to do so – the air around her was so thick with oily darkness that it was almost impossible to distinguish it from the inside of her eyes. She crawled forward towards the door and ran her hands over it. There was a line where the smooth metal of the door became the cement of the wall, but the seam let in no light.

Rose groaned, and pressed her head to the door.

'My name is Lily Daniels, and I want to join your army.' That had been the easy part. The soldiers had grabbed her from behind, blindfolded her almost before she had started speaking, spun her round and shoved her against the wall.

'How'd you get down here?'

It had been easy, she'd explained, with all the patience she could muster: the square around the War Rooms was almost completely destroyed, and it was easy to jump down into the cavity beneath.

'What do you want?'

'I want to join you. I want to fight with you.'

James, Angels bless him, had fitted her with a hologram

347

projector – under the skin, this time, so it couldn't fall out or slip away from her. Thanks to that, her hair was a deeper black, the set of her cheekbones slightly sharper, and, most importantly, her eyes were deep grey.

'Who did you say you were?'

That was when the voice started to sound familiar, and the depth of her bad luck became clear. Her captor was female, and young, and – clearly – a new enough recruit to be sent to patrol the upper floors immediately after an attack. Cannon fodder.

'Lily Daniels,' Rose had told her, but she was beginning to make the connections, and finally she got a name. Amelia. Amelia Rodriguez.

Oh, for Ichor's *sake*.

Maria's sister. Why on earth did the first Regency soldier she encountered have to be Maria's sister? *Why?*

'Do you know her?' another voice had asked. This one was even younger than Amelia, young enough to be a child: a boy in early adolescence, perhaps twelve or thirteen. What were Regency doing with child guards?

'I don't think so,' said Amelia, but she sounded uncertain.

'Come on. If she wants to join we'll have to put her in the Darkroom.'

Amelia's voice turned nasty. 'I know procedure, Angelboy. Don't talk down to your senior officer.'

'Angelboy', or 'Angelgirl', was a pejorative term used by Ashkind children to describe any Gifted child, even the weakest Pretender, with the telltale green eyes: not knowing the actual definition, or power, of a true Angel, they automatically assumed that every Gifted was at the extreme end of the spectrum. It was a matter of fear more than anything else.

But wait, that would mean—

Angelboy?

The boy was Gifted? But this was an Ashkind army. Gifted were the *enemy*. Unless this boy was as invaluable and dedicated as David and Loren had been, Rose couldn't understand why he would possibly be tolerated here.

They'd shoved her hands roughly behind her back and pulled her along unseen corridors. Rose had been constantly scraped along stone, and at least once she had felt blood trickle down her cheek. For some reason, the thought of leaving her blood on the walls of Regency's compound put her strangely on edge.

Suddenly, ahead of them, there was a terrible rumbling sound, amplified – or at least that was how it seemed to the blindfolded Rose – a thousand times by the fact that it came from above as well as below them, as if the sky had decided to join in with an earthquake.

'Don't worry,' said Amelia, sounding bored, 'it's just drilling work from the next street,' but not before Rose had stumbled backwards into the wall in an instinctive attempt to get away from the shaking. The next thing she knew, she was on the ground, aching and *definitely* bleeding.

There was a click in her ear.

'Don't move,' said the Angelboy, in a voice that, in fairness, he probably thought was menacing.

Amelia sounded more shocked than Rose. '*Oscar!* You son of a bitch!'

'Don't call me that. If I tell my dad—'

'I don't care what you tell your *daddy,* you're underage. You can't have weapons.'

'Don't tell me what I can't do.'

'Help,' said Rose weakly, from beneath them, partly because her head was aching, and partly because she owed it to Maria not to let her sister get attacked by a hormonal Gifted teenager. There was a silence, and then someone – Amelia, she thought – pulled her to her feet, the world spinning, and pushed her forward.

'Come on,' she said, and Rose could tell by her voice that she was glaring at Oscar. 'Let's get you to the Darkroom.'

After a while in the dark, she came to her senses enough to try and get to her feet. She used the door to steady herself, and then manoeuvred herself into a crouching position, hands pressing against the cold, smooth floor.

Slowly and carefully, she stood up and turned in a full circle.

The doors let in no light. There was a word for that, wasn't there . . . God, she was tired . . . come on, think. Yes, there was a word for that: *airtight*. And if the doors were airtight, and there certainly weren't any windows, there would have to be some kind of ventilator to prevent Rose suffocating.

Rose bent her head and listened.

Yes – *yes* – there was something to her right, quite far

away, but distinctly the *whoosh*ing hum of some kind of fan. Was it a fan? Yes, it would definitely have to be, wouldn't it: they were underground. The air would still get stale, though. That was a point: where did Regency get its air?

Rose put her face in her hands. All right. If she wasn't getting out, she was at least going to find out more about the place she was trapped *in*. Length of the room would be good: it would allow her to estimate the angles she was being filmed from, assuming the cameras were in the corners. Come to think of it, how *would* the cameras be filming her? Regency had to have some way of monitoring their new recruits. Maybe they employed infrared technology. That would make sense. But where on earth would an underground terrorist group get infrared cameras from? Where would they get money from at all?

Behold the Interregnum. Loren had told her what it meant to them: the Interregnum was how they referred to their war efforts. A time between kings, a brief interlude before the installation of a new absolute leader. And that leader would be Felix, of course. To Regency, *Behold the Interregnum* was a warning.

Perhaps that would explain why they repeated it so often.

But they weren't winning, of course. They couldn't possibly. Not in a million years.

Unless.

Unless they were as deeply entrenched in the Ashkind community as the Gospel were among Gifted and Angels.

Unless they were getting some kind of *donation*. From Ashkind civilians. It would only take a little from each of them, and they could have thousands in weeks, if they had enough Gifted-hating Ashkind willing to—

If, if, if. . .

Yes. Fine. That's all well and good. Now work out what you're going to do about the *immediate* situation. Trapped, remember? In an airtight room?

Thank you. Oh, *now* you're concentrating.

She took a couple of steps backwards so her back was flat to the metal door, and walked forwards with her hands outstretched through the darkness, making sure that the heel of each foot touched the toes of the last one.

Before she reached a wall, however, she walked into something waist-height and metal. She stumbled back, winded, and took a moment to recover her balance. Then she crouched down, and ran her hands slowly over the unknown obstacle. It had ridges every few inches, and the metal was dented and thick. A barrel, maybe? She slid her hand up to the rim and reached over it. Her hand found cold liquid, water most likely, and lots of it – maybe ten gallons. Rose didn't know much about poisons, but natural paranoia told her not to drink it, so she edged around the barrel and kept moving forwards.

She found the wall eventually. It was smooth and high, and she could find no edges or ridges in it. She followed it around the whole room, which turned out to be very large – forty paces by sixty. There was no light, no food, nothing but her and the barrel of water.

She sat herself down in a corner and waited.

She waited for a long, long time.

Time passed with terrible slowness. Rose sat in her space by the wall, occasionally taking a walk round the room to ease the pain in her legs. The pain in her stomach, however, she could do nothing about. After a while, she had given in and drunk from the barrel, figuring that if Regency wanted to kill her, she would already be dead; but no amount of water would soothe her, and there was no point in wasting the little she had.

God, she was hungry.

There was no way of telling the time, but Rose estimated that she had been here about two days. She was not blind, at least she knew that: she could see little dancing spots of light whenever she closed her eyes.

After a while, she stopped walking because it hurt to move.

She slept a lot.

When she was awake, she hummed. Humming was good, because if she arranged the beat of a tune so that there were two seconds to a bar she could tell how much time was passing. So she hummed every song she knew. Working through those took her another day or so.

Then she went to sleep again.

She woke slowly. Far too slowly.

Alarm bells were ringing inside her head. She didn't know why, not yet; it took her a long time to realise that she should care, and by that time it was too late.

The air she was breathing seemed very dense.

That was what was wrong, the density of the air. And

there was something else, too, something – not *wrong*, not exactly, but not right, either. Her conscious mind was numb and sleepy, but her instincts were still running, and they were telling her one fact, over and over again:

The air was too dense.

The air was too bloody *dense*.

'Here's what you should be thinking about,' said her father, from beside her. 'You should be worrying about your Test.'

She tried to turn her head, but it was too much effort.

'Insanity Gas,' she said blearily. She wasn't sure whether she said it aloud. 'I'm breathing Insanity Gas. It's a hallucinogen. You're not actually here.'

'Yes, well, obviously, but that's beside the point. The point is me. Why am I here?'

'You're my subconscious.'

'I was in your Test, yes, but that was a long time ago.'

She groaned. 'Please go away.'

'No,' said another, familiar voice from the other side of the room. She looked up at Loren, looking as old and dishevelled as he had the first time she had met him, the deadened Icarus in his hand. There were broken-down computers flickering around him. 'He won't. You've failed him. You've failed all of us.'

She groaned. She was too tired for this. 'Not you, too.'

'I'm not here. You're just hallucinating me.'

'I *know* that.'

'I told you that you could be good if you chose to be good,' he said. 'I was wrong. You can't. I was too late.' He sounded terribly sad. 'I was too late for you.'

'What the hell is that supposed to mean?'

'You're too evil. You were evil from the moment you became a Hybrid. You were beyond redemption before I ever met you.'

'Shut the hell up. That's not true.'

'It is. Or maybe you're right. Maybe you're not *evil* just because you're a Hybrid. But you've done terrible things, whether you meant to or not, and that definitely makes you evil. Irretrievably, irrevocably, unspeakably evil.'

Every word was heavy.

'Shut up. Stop talking.'

'No. It's true.'

'Leave me alone. Let me sleep.'

'No,' said Loren. 'Not for a million years. Not for eternity. We are your ghosts. We will never leave you.'

'You don't speak like that.'

'No, because I'm not Loren Arkwood. I'm *you*.'

'I hate you.'

'That's unfortunate,' said the woman at the other end of the darkness. Her eyes were bloodshot and her hands were folded protectively over her swollen belly. 'Do you hate me?'

In the computer room above, the monitors had started flashing. The soldier on duty brought up the infrared feed from the Darkroom.

'Look, guys,' he said. 'She's started talking.'

Rose knew she was speaking aloud because it felt like her throat was being torn up.

'No,' she said. 'Please not you.'

'You understand what's happening, don't you?' said Sylvia Argent. 'They're giving you the Insanity Gas to try to drive you mad. Make you talk. Tell secrets while the cameras are watching. You're so weak already, it's easy.'

'So they're not . . .'

'No. No one's controlling this hallucination. This isn't your Test. They give it to you straight, without nano-robots, because it's cheaper, and because they know that you can come up with nightmares more potent than they could dream of making.' She smiled. It was not, by any stretch of the imagination, Sylvia's smile. 'And aren't they right?'

'Please,' was all Rose could say, hoarsely. David and Loren were also staring at Sylvia now: blank-eyed, dead-eyed.

'Why?' said Sylvia, smiling wider. 'Because you put me to sleep and put me and my child in your Department's care? Because I died there?'

'You're very clever, Rose,' said Loren, without inflection, tilting his head slightly. 'And that's going to kill you in the end, isn't it?'

Rose tried to curl up, block it out, but she couldn't move.

'I'm not going to die,' she said, defiantly. 'I'm going to survive this.'

'That's what they all think,' said her father beside her. 'Don't you think all the people I killed were clever? Clever doesn't matter. Not against bullets.'

'Shut up. I'm imagining this.'

'You're very repetitive,' said Nate, from behind her. She looked down at her elbow, and found that her scar was opening, leaking blood. The bullet was cold grey beneath the skin. 'You always bored me like that.'

'And me,' said Maria, beside him. Her eyes were bleak. 'I was the one who you lied to the most, didn't you? And it's as well you did. If I'd have known you were a monster, I would have called the police, would have made you run miles, you and your father—'

Her features were changing, dripping, melting; Laura's features began to emerge from the mess. Her face was open, bleeding from the wounds that had killed her.

'—you and your bastard father,' she hissed. 'You're monsters.'

'Don't say that,' Rose told her, voice breaking. 'We're not—'

There were three security guards gathered around the screens now. The girl was crying white, night-vision tears. She was whispering to the darkness, breathing too fast.

'She's close,' said the first guard, darkly.

'You always thought you were better than us,' said Nate. 'That was who you were, weren't you? Our superior. You were *wiser* than other kids. You were *stronger* than them. Better than them.' He smiled Loren's sharp-toothed smile. 'And you never put that to the test, did you? Because you wouldn't have liked the truth. You never like the truth, Rose. You're a coward.'

I can't do this, she thought desperately.

'Then what's the point of you?' whispered Tabitha. 'What is the *point* of you?'

'You're a monster,' said Loren again, dispassionately. He looked at her with scalding objectivity.

I'm not.

'Oh, but Rose, you forget,' said Laura, smiling. It did horrible things to her wounded mouth. 'We're not real. We don't have to convince you that you're evil. You already know.'

The girl's vital readings were skyrocketing. Her heartbeat was too fast. After a week in the Darkroom most recruits were on an IV drip. The guard on the controls knew all of this, and it still took him thirty minutes after the gas canisters had been opened in the ventilator shaft to glance at his colleagues, acknowledge their nods, and ask the operator to patch him through to High Command.

'Boss?'

The voice that came back was deep, rich, dark. The guards raised eyebrows at each other. The Commander himself was watching. This *was* unusual.

'Can you see her?' asked Felix Callaway.

'Yes, sir,' said the guard, 'and I was wondering whether we should get her out.'

'Leave her in there for a bit longer,' came the reply. 'This is interesting.'

Another worried glance.

'But sir,' said the guard, hesitantly, 'with all due respect, she's stopped talking.'

There was a very long, thoughtful pause, punctuated with hikes in static, and the sound of the girl's breathing.

'Exactly,' said Felix.

I have control over this.

The darkness around her was beginning to blur. Clouds of whiteness were coalescing around her hallucination: they solidified and dissolved, so fast it was almost a flickering, into guns, faces, small balls of green-and-silver metal, a silver locket, a blue notebook with writing on the cover—

'You're panicking,' said Nate, matter-of-factly.

'You can't use magic,' said Laura. 'It would kill you, by this point. The hologram projector they implanted in your wrist? The one that's disguising your eyes? It'll be running on battery now. What are you going to do? You're drugged, Rose. They'll discover you, and you'll die.'

It sounded almost kind.

She focused, as hard as her exhausted mind was able, and the clouds latched on to her loved ones and started crawling over them, solidifying, encasing them. They watched without emotion as it crept up their limbs, freezing their legs and then their torsos into immobility; and then Loren reached out and touched the mist and it began to retreat from around them, releasing them.

'You can't fight your own imagination,' said David quietly, still sitting next to her. 'Anything you can think of, you can do to yourself. See, at the moment, you're worried about this.'

The hallucinations stepped forward as one. Their hands

were outstretched, their faces dead, expressionless.

'But nothing's going to happen,' he said. 'If you want, if you stop thinking about it, we'll fade away. Look.'

The hallucinations started dissolving with the mist, separating into empty air. They did not fight. Rose and the figure of David watched them fade into the darkness, until they were alone, sitting together.

Rose was very cold.

Thank you, she thought.

'Don't thank me,' he said. 'I'm not real. I'll go too, if you want.'

No—

'You've forgotten something,' he said. 'We're only as clever as you are, and there's something that's slipped your mind.'

I'm too tired for this.

'I know you are,' he said. 'But I tell you the truth even when you don't want to hear it. And this is the truth, Rose, pure as Gospel.'

He smiled white.

'All of this?' he said. 'The Insanity Gas is meant to make you imagine horrible things. It traps you in nightmares and lets you do the rest of the work. But you're strong, Rose, stronger than you know, and it hasn't managed to touch your subconscious yet. Not really. I'm just your instincts. I'm the voice inside your head that stays calm when you're panicking.'

Please—

'No,' he said. 'I tell you the truth. Your pure, unfettered subconscious? The Insanity Gas hasn't managed to touch that yet. You're too strong, like I said. But now you're broken. Now we're at the edge, Rose. You're worn out. You're tired.'

I can't—

His smile was cruel now.

'This is obvious, Rose,' he said. 'Really, truly obvious. But you've lied to other people for so long, you've stopped questioning it when you lie to yourself.'

I can't do this.

'I'm not your subconscious, Rose,' he said. 'Let me introduce you to your subconscious.'

Metal started to spread over the walls, thicken, close in on her until the room was no more than five foot by seven. The hallucination of her father had faded away; she could feel his going, though she could not see it. It was late at night, and she was at home.

She knew this, but she did not know how.

Silence in the empty room for a moment.

Then, suddenly, a girl stood in front of her in the thin, cold light. It took Rose a moment to recognise her own face.

You're the ugliest girl in the year. . .

The hallucination was grim-faced, but there was no life in its eyes. It wore green khaki: a soldier's uniform. It walked forward to the metal door and tried it. It did not open.

The door would not open.

And suddenly Rose knew what was going to happen.

'No,' she said suddenly. 'No, please—'

The hallucination-Rose's eyes widened. Its hand went

361

to its throat. It couldn't breathe. Rose saw its eyes drain to that animal white. She tried to start forward, to do anything, to *run*, but she couldn't move.

'No,' she said again, weakly.

The hand at the hallucination's throat was turning grey. Rose could see the smoke leaking through the cracks in its skin. It dropped to its knees.

'Don't,' she said, plaintively.

She could hear the cracks of changing bone, the cold roar of darkening blood. Then the screaming. Rose heard her own voice screaming. She pressed her face to the metal wall and groaned.

No, no, no, no—

And she looked back, and too late, because there, in the faint dark, against the grey metal, was the monster.

The operator was tetchier the second time the guard asked her for High Command.

'Are you sure?' she asked. 'You know how he is—'

He cut her off. 'This is urgent.'

An affronted silence, then a click. The reply took a moment to come through. The other security guards were watching the screen with wary resignation: the girl was white, gaunt, flat against the wall, screaming without end at something the gas was showing her.

'Private Farrow?' came the soft voice at the other end.

'Yes, sir.' A hesitation, and the reckless decision to state the obvious: 'We've broken her, sir.'

'Yes, I believe we have,' said the Commander. He sounded almost disappointed. 'Call the medical bay, th—'

To say he *gasped* would have been somewhat insolent; all the guards heard was an intake of breath, sharp, on the other end of the line. They glanced at each other.

'Sir?' said one of them tentatively, but even the static had gone: he had disconnected.

'What do you think it was?' asked Farrow. No one seemed to have an answer. The girl's screaming had risen to an irritating pitch, so he reached for the volume control. His colleague went for the intercom again, and had just managed to get the operator back when he looked back at Farrow, who was staring blankly, open-mouthed, at the screen.

'What is it?' asked the third guard.

'Get the Commander back online,' said Farrow urgently. 'I don't care what the operator says, do it now.'

'Ryan—?'

'*Do it.*'

Bemused, the second guard went for the intercom, only to find that the operator was gone.

'Are you seeing this?' asked the Commander, from behind them. They gasped, and turned. He was in his full military uniform, and he was staring past them, at where the girl screamed onscreen.

'Yes, sir,' whispered Farrow. He swallowed. 'Sir, what's happening to her *eyes?*'

The monster reared, shrieking, and Rose watched it, mouth open, eyes wide.

It was fully seven feet tall, but that, of course, mattered little; it could have been half that size and still wreaked the same amount of damage on the human psyche. It was grey-skinned, corpse-skinned, seeping shadows, clawed, white-eyed. Its face and its features were Rose's, her eyes, her mouth; and she was screaming, because it was coming for her, coming for her, just like she'd always known it would one day and then she wouldn't be human any more she would be monster for ever and that would be the end of her and—

The air was thinner again. She could feel it as she screamed: it was thin, clean, cold. The Insanity Gas was being pumped out of the cellar. The monster's screams began to fade, re-root themselves inside her head, so that it didn't sound so real to her own ears, but—

But—

She hadn't eaten for days. She should not have the energy for her hands to tremble. She should not feel strong. Her skin should look gaunter than this, even in the dar—

Even in the—

The dark.

How could she see in the dark?

The air was clean again, the world around her returned, but her heart was in her mouth and her fear had not left her.

How could she see in the dark?

The girl had begun to scream again. She should not be seeing anything unusual now, not unless the Insanity Gas had broken her irrevocably. The grey in her eyes had faded slightly – for a brief moment they looked almost *green*, olive-green, and suddenly the colour vanished from them completely. Farrow leaned in closer. Those cameras were always acting up. Annoying that they should do so now, just when the Commander was here. Because of course her eyes could not possibly have gone *white*.

The Commander was at the computers, staring at the girl.

'She's a monster,' he whispered. He said it wonderingly, like a naturalist discovering a new species of butterfly. 'Isn't she beautiful?'

They glanced at each other. They all knew about the Commander's highly individual status; if the girl was like him that made her very dangerous, and very valuable. They might have just stumbled upon a promotion.

'Is she—?'

'Yes,' whispered Felix. 'Yes.'

The girl was holding her hands in front of her blood-less face, her white eyes. They had begun to turn grey, seep a deeper darkness, a smoke-filled kind of shadow, into the air. The girl looked terrified.

'What did she say her name was?' asked Felix, eyes still fixed on her.

'Slythe's boy brought her in, ask him.' A terrible pause. 'Sir. I mean, I would— I would recommend that, as a course of action, sir. Commander.'

It didn't matter. The Commander wasn't listening. The girl's screams were separating, into something human – high, reedy, fading – and something distinctly *not*. The guards were trying to look away. The girl's face wasn't human either.

Felix stood up.

'A Hybrid,' he whispered, as the girl on the screens lost all traces of humanity. The guards' eyes were wide; they looked between the creature onscreen and their Commander with horror. *Monster. Monster.* They knew, of course, but they had never seen exactly what it meant before.

Felix Callaway turned and regarded them. He could clearly see the fear on their faces, but he did not react; he was staring beyond them, watching something else behind his eyes. Then, slowly, he walked to the doorway. The monster onscreen screamed at them.

'Go,' said the Commander to the guards, gesturing to the corridor outside. 'You are relieved.'

They glanced at each other. Then, hesitantly, they walked out, filing past the Commander and trying not to cringe as they passed him. Inwardly, Farrow had already half-forgotten about the girl; with the afternoon off, perhaps he could go to his wife and son, out in the civilian world. He had a few hours' leave owed him.

'Wait,' said Felix suddenly, behind them. They turned. The Commander scrutinised them for a moment, opened his mouth to say something, but seemed to think better of it. Instead, he took out his revolver and shot all three of them in the head. Then he walked back into the control room.

He sat down at the screens and looked over the buttons. There was only one he was looking for, and there it was – big and blue, and with its function helpfully emblazoned next to it. He pressed it, and onscreen he saw the doors to the Darkroom open.

THE CATALYST

The monster roared, and lunged forward to freedom. 'Oh, my beautiful,' whispered the Commander. He sat back in his chair and smiled. 'Go on. Go on.'

CHAPTER 40

'Angels.'

No one who heard Loren could doubt that he said it as an expletive. In fairness, the list on the screen merited the obscenity; it stretched across three A4 pages, in tiny print. Each entry was an address. Each had been recorded in the last two weeks.

'*Angels,*' he said again, hoarsely, running his finger down the list. 'How many have there been?'

'Eighty-five in the last three days, and at least forty before that,' said James. 'They're all Regency, and they're everywhere. Bomb attacks, most of them, but shootings and ambushes as well.'

'Concentrated in specific areas of the world though, am I right?'

James glanced at David. 'Yeah. Shanghai, Aleppo, Seattle, Moscow, Belfast – all the cities that took the longest to settle after the War. Regency were still alive and kicking there.'

'And they haven't died yet,' murmured Loren. 'Oh, Ichor's name . . . They're really stepping up their offensive, aren't they?'

'They have worldwide support. More than we ever realised.'

'Destroy them,' said Nate, from the corner, as if it were obvious. Maria, looking tired and drawn, stared at him in shock, but he carried on regardless. 'Destroy them as quickly as possible and get Rose out of there before they can hurt her.'

'I'm with the boy,' said David, sitting down on a chair and staring up at the list. 'Get their leadership and leave them disorganised and helpless. Then hunt them down.'

He appeared to relish this last idea.

'What happened to *subtler methods*?' asked Loren incredulously.

'Screw that. They have my daughter.'

'And she wouldn't thank you for losing the ability to think clearly the moment she leaves. You do know what you mean by "get the leadership", right? These are people we *knew*, people we worked with, people whose lives we saved—'

'You don't seriously still have any loyalties to them, do you?' asked James in heated disbelief. Loren glanced up at him as if he had forgotten he was standing there. He stepped away from David.

'No,' he said at last. 'No, of course I don't.'

Maria came forward. 'I agree with Loren. We shouldn't just kill them.'

Loren sighed. 'Thank you for your input. David. We can't do this. Rose is in there, and I hate that almost as much as you do, but it means we have an opportunity to take them down from the inside.'

'And Rose can do that on her own, can she?'

Loren began to grow angry. 'No, of course she can't.

But you're saying we should kill Felix, and if we do that—'

'Regency will collapse.'

'I don't care about its *collapse*. I care about what it takes with it. It might go down, yes, but it'll go down fighting, and there'll be bomb attacks and street fights and they will destroy law and order.'

'Not if we destroy their commanders first,' David said. His eyes were bright. 'When their leaders are killed they'll be too weak to act. We'll have a crackdown, take them from the streets—'

'And if you get innocents? If there are too many of them to arrest? David, you *know* this man. Don't pretend you don't. You know what he inspires in people. If he dies, you will make him a martyr. Don't you remember what we used to think of him? If Felix Callaway is anything, he is a catalyst – he starts revolutions and then stands back while they happen. He isn't changed by wars or wounds or even peacetime. He just *is*: he is a figurehead and an icon, and if you kill him you will start a war in his name.'

'A war against whom? Us?' David stood. 'A war of the people against Government? Gifted against Ashkind? Peaceniks against revolutionaries?'

'Everyone – anyone and everyone. You know what that kind of hell looks like, David, you've seen it before.' Loren stepped forward so he was in David's face, staring him down. 'You want to be the one to start it again?'

David started to say something, and then closed his mouth. He stepped away and went to the screen.

'One hundred and twenty-five attacks,' he said softly.

He stood there for a moment, considering. Then he turned to Loren.

'Felix Callaway is going to die,' he said coldly. 'If I have it my way, he will die, screaming and in pain. If not, it might be quick, which is more than he deserves. Either way, he will die, Arkwood, no matter what you say about it.'

'You think I can't stop you?'

'I don't think you have a hope in hell of even trying. I might have held back for the girl's sake, but you, you, Arkwood—' The look in his eyes could not honestly be said to be one of disdain, not even at the most positive of stretches: it was icy, murderous hatred, and Loren bore it resignedly. 'I would not hesitate to kill you if you tried to stand against me.'

Loren gave the tiniest of nods towards Nate and Maria, who were looking terrified. David turned and looked at them, the terrible light still there in his eyes, and then strode over to his chair and pulled on his coat.

'Don't try,' he told Loren, and then he left.

Afterwards there was a silence.

'There is something really, really wrong with him,' said Maria, quietly.

Loren laughed, long and low and dark.

'Oh,' he said, looking around at them all, 'oh, you do not know the half of it.'

CHAPTER 41

Amelia Rodriguez was in the training room when it happened. The guns Regency used were mostly second-hand, and the targets had been shot to pieces years ago. They used plastic training bullets, as ammunition was precious.

Amelia emptied her gun at the target, mostly missing it, and walked over to Aaron. His aim was near-perfect: he fired again and again at the centre of the target until it collapsed. He threw his gun to the ground in frustration and kicked it. It spun over the smooth wooden floor until it came to rest at the foot of the downed target.

'Your brother?' she asked.

He nodded. 'Liam said he was in the park yesterday. I'm not allowed out to see him, after Westfield.'

'You're under punishment orders?'

'They caught me on CCTV.'

Amelia winced. 'You're going to be down here for a long time for that.'

'I know.' He turned to her, pushing his hair out of his eyes. 'How's Maria?'

'No idea,' she said, slightly too quickly. 'No one's allowed outside contact now. People are saying that's your fault, that the Department tracked you here.'

'People?' He smiled, putting an arm round her waist. 'Who cares about people when I've got you?'

He kissed her. She let him for a few seconds, and then disentangled herself.

'Sorry,' she said, picking up her gun and fitting it into her holster. 'Duty calls. I should have been on patrol ten minutes ago.'

'Don't be long,' he said. 'I'll see you later.'

'I know you will.'

She grinned at him and turned to the door. It wouldn't open. She pulled at the handle as hard as she could, but it refused to give.

'Aaron,' she said, 'what's wrong with the door?'

There were quite a few things wrong with the door. The first thing was that it was soundproofed to prevent the noise of firearms deafening anyone who walked past. Unfortunately, this meant that Aaron and Amelia had not been able to hear the screaming of the dying guards mere feet from the door.

And the second was that its lock had been smashed in.

Aaron tried the door handle. His brows contracted, and after a few seconds he picked up his gun again.

'Do you have to do that?' Amelia said. 'They'll kill us.'

Aaron didn't reply, but destroyed the door in three concentrated bursts of fire. When it was reduced to splinters he kicked down what remained and stepped over the rubble into the corridor.

He froze.

'What is it?' Amelia asked.

He did not answer.

'What's wrong, Aaron?'

When he still said nothing, she pushed past him impatiently into the corridor.

There was a two-second burst of total silence, and then she started screaming. Aaron clamped his hand over her mouth.

'Shut up,' he said harshly. 'You're a soldier. Get used to it.'

Amelia did not get used to it, but stared at the bodies in horror.

'Who did this?' she whispered.

'No idea,' Aaron said. 'Come on. We need to get to Command, now.'

Getting to Command was rather a tricky proposition, given the suddenly large number of obstacles littering the corridor. There were at least five or six bodies in here alone. They decided against taking the stairs, but reconsidered when they saw what was in the lift.

Command was on the bottom floor of the Regency complex, so it was a long stair journey. A steady stream of shocked new recruits and grim-looking veterans streamed through the stairwell. No one was panicking. A dark-skinned boy with a tattoo on his arm and buzz-cut hair, wearing the uniform of a Lieutenant, fell into step beside Aaron.

'Liam,' Aaron said in relief. 'What's happening?'

Liam looked solemn. 'We have a body count,' he said. 'Twenty-six dead.'

'Did anyone survive being attacked?'

He shook his head. 'They think it's most likely a

Department attack,' he said, 'but after the explosions . . .
Well, just look at how open we are. It could have been
anyone.'

They were almost crushed in the push to get through
the doors into the central Command room. This was big
enough to fit two thousand people, far enough underground that not even Government sensors could see it,
and, through the corridors leading off it, connected
indirectly to every room in the complex.

The army was lining up as it had done in drills, assem-
bling into their respective divisions. Aaron and Amelia
were in Fourth Division and Liam in Sixth, so they divided
and stood with their cohorts in neat lines in front of the
speaker's podium. Gaps were forming in the lines, those
who were meant to fill them lying dead in the corridors
around the complex. Amelia shivered.

The Commander stood on the stage, flanked by his
two senior advisors: Head of Security Anthony Slythe,
father of Oscar, and Isabel Vinyara, head of the sharp-
shooters. The captains stood, stony-faced, at the heads
of their divisions. The Commander's expression was calm,
almost placid.

This boded ill.

'Comrades,' he said quietly, into the microphone, and
the hall fell instantly silent. The last stragglers shifted
into place as quietly as they could. 'We have been dealt
a heavy blow tonight.'

There were people outside in the hall. The sound of
shuffling. They were removing the bodies.

Amelia shuddered.

'We have lost brothers,' said Felix. He did not need to raise his voice. 'Brothers in blood, for some of us; for the rest, brothers in spirit, brothers-in-arms.'

A pause.

'Regency has been struck to its very heart,' said the Commander. 'It is our duty as soldiers, as loved ones, as keepers of the revolution, to find and destroy those who harm us. In this case, we do not have far to look.'

A low, angry, sustained murmuring had begun near the stage; it was spreading slowly, growing in strength as the Commander continued. He did not try to stop it.

'The Department,' he said, and it surged, spilled over into outbursts of furious shouting, loud enough to almost drown him out. He spoke over it. 'The Department has attacked us tonight, attacked us with monsters – sent one of their operatives down here, alone, one of their Gifted' – he spat the word as one might an obscenity – 'soldiers, and sent them after our beloved brothers and sisters. What are we to do about this, my friends?'

The response that came was loud, but staggered and incoherent. He made it easier for them.

'Shall we allow this murder of our comrades to go unpunished?'

Much clearer this time. '*No!*'

Vinyara, beside him, looked upon the clamouring soldiers with distaste; but, as Amelia knew, that was the way Vinyara looked at most things. Slythe's greasy, pallid face was twisted into an expression of determined blood-thirstiness. It was common knowledge that he hated the Department more than most, even when that 'most' was

Regency; rumour had it that Felix still held it against him that he did not have the genius of his predecessor Elmsworth. No matter how brilliant Elmsworth had been, it was still quite a feat to be considered worse than a traitorous green-eyed bastard like that.

The Commander was still talking.

'Shall we let our fallen die unavenged?'

'NO!'

He was shouting now. 'Shall we *take our revenge* on those who harm us?'

'YES!'

He stepped back, satisfied, and let the shout disintegrate into a chant as the rumbling outside grew louder. Slowly, and with an infectious solemnity, the medical staff – there were five of them now; Dr Yates had been killed last year in a kidnapping attempt on a Government official – began to roll in the trolleys. The shouting faded, collapsed into muttering, and then silence. The bodies kept coming. They were covered in what looked like green tarpaulin. Bare white hands and feet hung, swinging gently, from off the trolleys. Sometimes threads of red would stretch and drop from their fingertips. And still they came.

Twenty-six dead.

Softly, collectively, Regency stopped breathing.

They had not suffered losses like this since the days of the War. They'd lose one officer, maybe, in an attack, two or three if they were especially unlucky, but the recent flood of recruits prompted by the growth of the Gospel had more than made up for that. Never twenty-six. Not in an army of seven hundred.

Twenty-six lives to the Department.

'No.'

Everyone looked up to see where it had come from. Slythe, on the stage, was staring at a forearm that hung from the last trolley. He said it with no expression, nothing but blank disbelief. He said it again.

'Not you.'

And then he said, in that spiralling moment before grief, in the last dim instant of hope, and almost in the plaintive hope of a reply:

'Oscar?'

CHAPTER 42

'Lily?'

There was something hard and cold under the skin of her arm.

Hologram projector.

It had survived.

Huh.

'Lily?'

She had been wounded, too. Someone had tried and failed to shoot her. It left a burning gap like a picked scab on the skin of her neck; not dangerous, with any luck, but irritating.

Maybe that would end when she worked out where she was.

Why she had been sleeping.

Why there was a needle in her arm.

Whose the voice was.

So many bloody *questions*.

'Lily?'

The voice – persistent, gentle, deep, rich – aroused a certain, instinctive kind of fear in her. That was annoying, because she had wanted to ask it what was going on.

Who was Lily?

Who was—?

What was—?

Where—?

Oh.

Oh.

Regency. She was in Regency. With the hallucinations, and Amelia, and the—

She had transformed.

She'd transformed in self-defence. She'd never done that before.

It had been just as unpleasant as she'd thought.

No, shut up. Don't think about that. Had everyone been safe?

Panic began to rise. Had people been hurt?

Had she been able to fight her way out on her own?

No. No. She couldn't think that. She couldn't even consider that for a moment – the implications were so apocalyptically terrible as to be unbearable.

No. Everyone must have been safe.

She must have been shot at some other way.

Where *was* she?

'Lily?'

That voice. She'd heard it before. It had boomed over the Department office. *I claim your death as my own.*

She opened her eyes.

She lay in a hospital bed, in a darkened, artificially lit room. It had all the warmth and atmosphere of a prison cell. The man who sat on the end of her bed was smiling at her with black eyes. She knew him: he had been in a hologram, back in the Department, and in a notebook from years ago, crafted from her father's memories.

This Demon made her want to run. His very proximity, his *smile* made her want to flee, as fast as she could, fly if she had to, back to safety.

Wherever that was.

She needed his name. Come on. Stupid bloody malfunctioning traitorous brain.

Felix, that was it.

Felix Callaway.

He could see she was awake. His smile broadened. It made her cringe.

'Hello, Lily.'

The name she had given Amelia was Lily. Lily Daniels.

'How are you feeling?'

She would need to speak. She opened her mouth, and found her throat cracked and hoarse.

'Well, thank you.'

She was posing as a Regency soldier. She must have passed whatever test the Darkroom had been, because, if she had failed, they would have killed her by now.

Therefore, he was her commanding officer.

'Well, thank you, *sir*.'

He nodded. 'Very good. You've seen me before, then?'

Oh, bloody hell.

'I've heard you described, sir.' A pause. No, that wasn't convincing at all. 'You're hard to mistake, sir.'

It was beginning to dawn on her now. Slowly, and with the impact of a bullet: she had transformed, and been taken here, and all of that must have been done by *someone,* and all of the possible someones who could have done it reported to this man.

So he knew.

He knew her secret.

She was going to panic, wasn't she?

'You're a very unusual girl, aren't you, Lily?' There was no obvious response to this but to clench her hands under the bedclothes to stop them shaking. 'How old are you, then?'

Aim upwards. 'Sixteen, sir.'

Ah, but she was forgetting – he didn't know who she was. He knew Lily Daniels's secret. He didn't know Rose Elmsworth's. He would make no links with David. Her family would be safe.

She missed David so much.

Please tell me what to do I'm out of my depth here I can't What did I do?

I don't remember anything what did I do?

'And why,' asked Felix Callaway, deep black Demon eyes still fixed on her, 'do you want to join us, Lily?'

She swallowed. Use the truth. 'My condition, sir.'

'Your *condition?*' It was almost a whisper. 'Who taught you it was a condition? What we are, Lily, what we are is a *blessing.*'

He had not once taken those black eyes off her, not once, his deep black eyes, and suddenly Rose realised: this was why the Government was afraid of Hybrids and Demons: this man, here, was what they feared, this man who had killed his ex-girlfriend *while he wasn't human* and who had tried to kill David and Loren and who talked of monsterhood in an almost reverential tone. This was what the Parliament of Angels existed to fight.

This was what the Department existed to fight.

David must have hated him.

Felix rose from her bed. Rose caught herself releasing a deep, shaky breath.

'What did your family think of your . . . condition?'

The way he said it indicated that he considered the answer self-evident, so she played along. 'They thought me a monster, sir.'

'A monster,' he breathed.

Silence.

'Are you strong enough to hold a weapon, Private Daniels?'

Her new title made her smile slightly. David would be proud. 'Yes, sir.'

IV drips were calorie-filled; she should easily be strong enough, in theory. She pulled the needle out of the back of her hand as gently as she could, and ripped off the tape. It brought on astonishing pain.

Three short breaths and she pulled herself out of the bed. She had to hold on to the stand until the world stopped spinning.

'Do you know why you transformed, Lily?' asked Felix.

She had to focus to answer. 'No, sir.'

'Really?' He raised his eyebrows. 'There are two ways of triggering a transformation like ours, Lily.'

His use of the first person plural made her want to hit him.

'The first is every six weeks, when we hit the deadline.'

She knew that, obviously.

She was breathing too fast.

'The second is if we feel our lives are in danger. It's a last resort. A built-in defence mechanism.' He turned away from her. 'Why did you think you were going to die, Lily?'

It took her a second to respond: she had just realised that someone had re-dressed her, in a T-shirt and jeans, while she was asleep. They'd undressed her. The nausea and disgust prompted by the thought rendered her silent for a moment.

'I saw . . .' She swallowed. 'I saw horrible things.'

Lily Daniels was not Gifted. Lily Daniels had not taken the Test. Lily Daniels would not know what Insanity Gas was.

Felix nodded. 'There's something interesting about your story, Lily. How did you become a Hybrid? Do you know?'

Rose thought of Loren. She thought of her father.

'I . . . don't know, sir.'

'Curious,' he said. 'Were you attacked, as a baby? That's one of the ways you can get it. Infection changes your DNA. Those who survive Hybrid attacks are always Hybrids themselves.' He paused. 'Not many survive, though.'

He didn't sound sad about it.

'I don't know. My parents never told me I was. They just said. . .' She swallowed, trying to stand straight and get her breath back. 'Keep quiet.'

'Keep quiet,' repeated Felix. It washed over her again how intensely physical this man was, how his very presence made you reconsider your spatial awareness, work out how far there was to run from him.

'What do you think of the Department, Lily?'

A moment of fleeting panic. No, he couldn't possibly know.

But how to answer *that* question.

'I don't think they should be underestimated, sir.'

He smiled. Run— run from those eyes.

'You know of David Elmsworth?'

She considered.

'Vaguely, sir.'

'You should fear him,' Felix told Rose. 'He is our most dangerous enemy, Lily Daniels. Do not forget that. Turn your back on him for a moment and he will betray you; he will weave deathtraps for you from air.'

Damn right he will, you bastard.

'And yet,' said Felix softly, 'he can be outwitted.'

Not by you.

'We can breach his defences. A few months ago one of our food suppliers was taken into custody by his soldiers: a woman called Sylvia Argent. One of our soldiers broke through into that very building – his *lair*, Lily – and silenced her before she could reveal anything. We left a warning, though – we frightened him. He can be *frightened*.'

He spoke as though he considered this a miracle. Rose, for her part, could not speak for the lump in her throat. Sylvia, poor Sylvia. . . Her hatred of the man before her, if possible, intensified.

He walked forward. She did not run.

He pressed something into her hand. She resisted the urge to flinch, and found that it was a gun handle.

'Welcome to the fold, Private Daniels,' he said. He was uncomfortably close to her. 'I have a feeling you're going to be very valuable to us.'

A terrible moment where she thought she might break – was she strong enough to kill him? No, not with magic, not yet, but this gun, he'd given her a gun, was it loaded? – and he stepped away.

'There's going to be an event tonight,' he said, 'quite an important event, actually, which I thought you might want to take part in. Your first blood.' He smiled again. His smile was like Loren's: all shark-teeth, no mirth or mercy.

'I'd be honoured, sir.'

'Good,' he said.

He let her out slowly, allowing her to slip into the corridor like some kind of noxious gas. He looked at her, the door between them.

'Privates and medics are on the deepest floor,' he said. 'Find yourself a bedroom and get ready.'

Then the door closed. He never stopped looking at her.

Slowly, when he was gone, Rose sank to her knees. She hugged herself and pressed her head to her legs. Everything about her seemed to be shaking.

CHAPTER 43

She found herself a bedroom on the bottom floor of the complex. The loneliness of it was almost comforting: four white walls, a creaky bed set against the far wall. A wardrobe with a mirror.

Enough to survive, no more.

There was a communal toilet at the end of the corridor. There were about twenty other bedrooms, most of them unoccupied; while Regency was large for a militia, there were still nowhere near enough of them. This corridor – one of about four on this level – was for the newest recruits. Anyone with any kind of potential would have been promoted by now.

Rose looked up and down the corridor and went back inside the bedroom.

She put the gun Felix had given her on the back of the door. It was an SA80. Basic. Not as good as her Department one.

She stood there, looking at it.

Then she went back into the corridor.

She looked up at the ceiling. It was curved, painted a messy white. If she reached up, stretching her body and her arms and standing on her toes, she could just about touch it. Above that ceiling would be the Corporals' floor, and then the Lieutenants', and then the Sergeants', and then the Majors'; and above that the second floor, with the assembly hall and the canteen; and then the actual War Rooms, the old War Rooms, where Felix lived, and where the Darkroom was; and above that earth, and finally the open air.

Sunlight and wind and open air.

After she realised that, she started to get very bored, and very angry.

'So why did you join?'

Rose's neighbours were kids. Older than Rose, true, but that had never counted for much. They looked to be about eighteen or nineteen; a dark-haired, leather-jacketed girl with an earnest face, and her boyfriend, who had about five piercings in one ear and an expression of unshakeable disinterest. Needless to say, they were both Ashkind.

'I don't know,' said the girl. Her name was Katya. 'I couldn't get a job, because of my eyes, you know?' They were dust-white-grey, the Ashkind equivalent of a Pretender. Darker-eyed Ashkind looked down on the almost-human.

'The Angels got my brother,' said the boy. 'Those Department bastards came and got him for armed robbery.'

'You're saying he was innocent?'

The boy sat up from where he lay on the bed, glaring at Rose fiercely. 'It didn't matter! They only got him 'cause he was a Demon!'

Rose said nothing.

'Calm down, Jordan,' said the girl, alarmed. She turned to Rose. 'You know they're saying the Department attacked us today?'

Rose blinked. 'No.'

Katya nodded earnestly. 'They killed *twenty-six* people. How could they do that?'

Rose looked down at herself, and the floor quietly fell away.

Oh no.

Oh, God, no.

She hadn't. No. No. She couldn't possibly have. She couldn't possibly have killed—

No, no, please, Angels, please, no. No.

All those years trying not to— all those—

No, but the Darkroom—

No.

She looked at her hands. They were shaking. There was no blood on them.

How could there be no blood on them?

'Lily?' Katya's hand on her shoulder, her anxious voice. 'Are you all right?'

A stronger thread of thought broke through the horror – *speak, don't give yourself away.* 'Yes,' she heard herself say, 'just . . . I need a minute.'

No. No. No. She was breathing very hard. No, no, *twenty-six*, no, all those lives, it couldn't possibly be, no, Jesus Christ, no—

She pressed her hands to her face.

Try and remember. The metal room, seeing the metal room in front of her, and the girl, and—

The monster rears above her and the fear—

Yes, yes. We know that bit. Move on.

The pain breaks through her, breaks her, and the human girl falls away, like ill-fitting clothes, and the creature beneath—

Yes. And after that?

The room, the dark room, and the creature roaring at it, waves of magic crashing against the walls, and the door slides open, and the light, the people outside, the way they—

The way they bleed. . .

No. Stop. Stop remembering. No, no, please—

Not this, not—

Oh, hang on.

How did the door open?

. . . the door slides open . . .

Beneath the shaking, shivering, looming horror of what she had done, redemption could be glimpsed, like a silver coin in a compost heap.

Regency had opened the door.

It started to come together. Felix, or someone else in High Command, had opened the door and let her kill his soldiers. Then he called it a Department attack, which meant the thing tonight, which he had called *first blood* . . .

Rose looked up at Katya and Jordan again. With great effort, she envisioned, as clearly as she could, the twenty-six people whose lives she had taken – no matter that it was with another creature's body and mind, and with someone else's intent – and she shouldered for a moment the full, crushing horror and guilt of the blame she bore.

When it grew too much to bear, she put it quietly away, to weigh on a different part of her mind. She would deal with the guilt. But not right now.

Now – revenge.

Katya was still speaking. 'How could they do that?'

'I don't know,' said Rose calmly. She looked at the boy, who was turning his gun over and over in his hands. 'You like being soldiers, then?'

They glanced at each other. 'Actually, we've never been in an attack before.'

'Ah,' said Rose. 'You think you can survive it?'

They stared at her. 'What do you mean?' asked Katya, tremulously.

'You do know we're attacking the Government, right?'

'Yeah,' said the boy. 'I'll get my brother back.'

'That's if we win.'

Another glance.

'What are you saying?' asked Jordan suspiciously.

'Well,' said Rose, shifting in her seat at the end of the bed, 'it's not the only way, is it? I think the Government would be willing to negotiate. I mean' – at their looks – 'I'm not saying we should. But the bomb attacks have been pissing them off, and we could carry on with those. We have professionals for that kind of thing. Just not a full-scale attack, you know what I mean?'

They looked suspicious. 'We should hit them where it hurts,' said Jordan.

'Yeah, but we don't know it *will* hurt. I mean, look at us. There are fewer than seven hundred of us, right? And the army, the civilian police, the Department – just counting the ones in London – will be four thousand, at least.'

Their expressions were blank. Rose started to get annoyed.

'We'll be *slaughtered*,' she said, emphatically.

Katya and Jordan looked at each other.

'Slaughtered?' whispered Katya.

CHAPTER 44

There were six of them by that afternoon: Rose, Katya and Jordan, a girl from further down their corridor called Marlene, and two Corporals by the names of Dunstan and Amory. The Corporals had been a stroke of luck: they'd heard Katya and Marlene's whispered conversation and, instead of immediately reporting them to the High Command, had actually sympathised.

They, at least, had military training. Apart from these two, Rose's comrades were all young, inexperienced, almost-human, and low-ranking. She had not been lying to them: they really would be the cannon fodder.

'All right,' said Amory, low-voiced. 'Do we go up together, or on our own?'

They stood in front of the lift. Katya and Jordan, who only now seemed to be realising what they were doing, were staring at it in trepidation.

'Together,' said Rose in a whisper. She had no idea where the cameras were, but with the amount of arms they were carrying, she could only assume that the lack of soldiers swarming them right now meant they hadn't been seen. 'You, me and Dunstan stand in front, in case they ambush us.'

Dunstan, for her part, looked wary.

'How come you get to be in charge?' she asked Rose. 'How old are you, sixteen?'

'It was my idea,' Rose told her. 'I'm the one who started this. If they come for us, do you want to take the credit?'

The doors of the lift opened. Katya, Marlene and Jordan shuffled in. Rose and the Corporals followed, cocking their guns.

'Why are you doing this?' asked Dunstan.

'I don't want other people to die,' said Rose. 'I'm one of the good guys.'

The doors closed and they started moving upwards.

'Our Commander,' she added, 'is not.'

When the doors opened on the first floor, there were two guards standing outside the lift. They took one look at the six of them and did the stupid thing: ran at them, instead of firing their weapons, or sounding the alarm. Then again, Dunstan and Amory didn't fire either – no wasted lives, as Rose had ordered – but waited until the guards were right up against them before putting them down with two vicious kicks. They stepped out of the lift, and the others – Marlene and Jordan stony-faced, Katya terrified – followed.

'Marlene?' asked Rose. The girl nodded, and took out her knife. The cameras were positioned visibly above the door; they cut them down, sawing at the wire with the serrated blades, and when they finally fell to the floor Marlene and Rose crushed them to glass under their boots.

They were taking no chances with being seen.

While they did this, Jordan, Dunstan and Amory worked on the door to Felix's office. Amory pushed against it, grunting.

'I don't know,' he said. 'We might have to shoot it down.'

'We can't,' said Rose automatically. 'Absolutely not. He'll hear us.'

'Kat,' said Jordan, staring intently at the lock, 'you got a hairpin?'

Katya pulled one uncertainly from her hair and handed it to him. Jordan straightened it and slid it into the lock. Within a few seconds there was a *click,* and the door swung open.

Jordan looked around at the others.

'What?' he said, trying to put the disinterested expression back into place again, 'I've got skills,' and then he realised what they were all staring at.

The office was empty.

'Dammit,' whispered Dunstan. 'What are we going—'

'Excuse me,' came a voice from around the corner, 'what on earth do you think you are doing?'

Felix Callaway walked round the corner, astonished, edging towards furious, and Rose did not hesitate.

Her power exploded from her hands and smashed him back into the wall. Blood smeared the path of his head as he slumped to the floor. The others, who had not been watching Rose at the time, looked around in terror for the source of this attack.

'Oh no!' said Rose in mock surprise, then stepped forward to kick Felix in the head. He was too strong to be knocked out by that, though, and stared up at her. There was actual hurt in his eyes.

'That was for Laura Gaskell,' she told him.

'Lily?' he whispered. He looked bemused. This only infuriated her further.

'No, actually,' she told him. 'My name is Rose.'

She pulled the syringe of thick, white memory serum out of her back pocket, and turned to the others. She held up the liquid.

'Don't worry,' she said to them, and held out her hands so they could see the fire that sparked from nothing on her fingertips. 'Don't be afraid. In a minute or so, you won't remember any of this.'

'I mean, it's not like we think Gifted are inhuman. We know that.'

Katya sat with Jordan on her bed in their room on the bottom floor. They both looked slightly dazed, their gazes shifting into blankness and voices trailing off at random intervals.

'We just want equality,' she said earnestly to Rose. 'Some of the rest of these people' – she waved a vague hand at the complex in general, which Rose took to mean 'Regency' – 'want, like, Gifted to be second-class citizens, like we are now, but I think . . .'

She stared into the distance for a little while.

'I don't remember,' she said softly.

'Bomb the bastards,' said Jordan, vehemently. 'I don't care about equality. Just kill them, and take away their bloody Gifts, and we can have an Ashkind Parliament, and there won't be magic, just us . . .'

'Yeah,' said Katya. 'Yeah. I mean, there's nothing wrong with magic in general, is there? But when, like, luck gives it to some people, and not to others, then you get, like, inequality, and it's not fair on us . . .'

'Bomb the bastards,' said Jordan, again.

Rose nodded, and tried to make her smile reassuring. Katya reached up to scratch her ear. A drop of blood had dried around the injection point on her wrist.

'Yeah,' said Rose. 'Definitely. Bomb the bastards.'

CHAPTER 45

'Are you ready to take the fight to them?'

They stood in the Command Hall, roaring to Felix's rhetoric, armed to the teeth and already shooting up on adrenalin. Rose watched him carefully. He looked pale, but he was still smiling that shark-tooth, merciless smile, and he did not look at her. The attack had been wiped from his memory. He did not suspect anything at all.

'Are you ready to raze the institutions of magic to the ground? Are you ready to eliminate Gifts, and all who possess them? Are you ready to take back this society for those who deserve it?'

Another roar. Felix, it seemed, was definitely on the 'bomb the bastards' side of things. He saw no way to negotiate with the Parliament of Angels, or indeed with the Gifted in general; so he had decided to destroy them.

'Private Daniels?'

It took her a second to realise the voice was addressing her, and then she turned. A dark-haired Ashkind stood beside her, clearly not part of the rank and file. He looked somewhat frightened. Rose immediately christened him 'the Minion'.

'Private Daniels,' said the Minion. 'The Commander would like you beside him for the attack.'

Her first reaction was a terrible shockwave of fear: had he found out what she'd done to him, was he intending to kill her, had the plan failed? Then she came to her senses. Of course not. If he had worked it out, he wouldn't have bothered with asking her to do anything. She would be dead by now, by proxy or sniper fire.

The thought was oddly reassuring.

She slipped with the Minion through the ranks of soldiers, resisting the urge to cover her ears against the screams of bloodthirsty rage, and eventually came to the bottom of the stage.

'You're Daniels, then?' asked the Minion. He was watching her with an expression of contemptuous disdain. He didn't look afraid any more.

'Yes,' she told him. 'And you?'

Clearly this was insolent, because his sneer only deepened. 'Anthony Slythe,' he said, 'Head of Security.' She noticed his eyes seemed rather red. He turned on his heel and strode up the stage.

She followed him, bewildered.

Felix's speech was coming to its conclusion. She stayed just below the sightline of the audience, having no desire to draw the attention of an army. Felix looked as bulky and intimidating as ever, but his eyes, too, had that slippery quality, sliding quickly off anything they focused on.

'We're ready, Lily,' he said intently to her, as the army started muttering and heading for the exits. 'We're going to take everything back.'

She could only nod.

'We won't have to hide,' he said, still with that bright,

almost childlike earnestness. 'We won't be monsters. We'll be gods.'

She was a spy. She was a spy for the Department, and hitting him would not do anyone any good, no matter how much she wanted to.

Asking questions would, though.

'Where are we going to start, sir?'

He smiled, and there were the shark teeth again.

'We're going to attack the Parliament of Angels,' he said.

CHAPTER 46

Rose's first impression upon reaching the Houses of Parliament was that Regency was even bigger than the Department had realised, and that Felix had enough troops to send some ahead, to cover Parliament.

This was not the case.

Rose was marching ahead of the troops with the High Command. Felix did not speak to Rose, but she caught him watching her, as if her very presence were a comfort to him. It occurred to her that he had not met anyone else like him in a long, long time.

Flanking Felix were Slythe, whose face looked constantly contorted in some emotion that looked oddly like grief, and the woman – Vinyara, Slythe had called her. She was tall, in her mid-fifties, blonde, and sharp-faced. It was she who realised first.

'Sir,' she said, when she saw the troops. 'Sir. That's the Gospel.'

Far back in the ranks, Amelia Rodriguez realised something: the space beside her was empty.

She turned, searching the blank faces behind her. 'Aaron?' she asked of nobody in particular.

No answer. She started to panic.

'Aaron?'

A slight, dark-haired figure broke from the ranks of Regency, which were currently lurking in the shadows of the darkened alleyways, and burst from between the shops of Westminster High Street towards the mob of Gospel. Rose, up front with the High Command, was the first to see him.

She recognised the figure immediately, and her heart lurched.

Of course it would be him. Of course.

Oh, for the love of the Angels.

He's seventeen, Laura – poor Laura – had said, when they'd found that Aaron had defected to Regency. *It's teenage rebellion.*

Rose had now underestimated Aaron *twice*.

She'd hated him, so she'd been perfectly willing to believe he was merely being idiotic, albeit murderously so. But even knowing him better than anyone else in the room, even knowing that he was Stephen Greenlow's son, she hadn't considered the *actual bleeding obvious*.

If Rose could be a double agent for the Department, why couldn't Aaron be one for the Gospel?

Stephen Greenlow was not one to miss an opportunity. The moment he had discovered that his Demonic son could do magic, he must have realised that he had hit upon a strategic goldmine. Much as he hated all Ashkind, much as he must have hated having a Demon for a child, here was the perfect chance to infiltrate the ranks of his enemies. And when Regency had resurfaced, he had seized that chance.

A Demon spying for an anti-Ashkind activist group. Who would have thought it?

No one. It was a masterstroke.

Poor Aaron, Rose thought dispassionately. Never able to abandon your loved ones, even if they hate you; never able to fit in with your own kind, even if they accept you. Bound by love and blood and magic and terrible bad luck. A magical Demon. An impossible thing. Never fitting anywhere. Never able to tell the whole truth.

I wonder what that feels like?

'Don't fire,' said Vinyara immediately to the sharp-shooters behind them. Felix nodded, and Rose, though she was aching to shoot Aaron herself, understood why: lurking in the twilit darkness between the buildings might give them cover if the Gospel didn't know they were there, but they couldn't shoot Aaron without inevitably firing on the Gospel, and no prizes for guessing who would win that fight. The Gospel outnumbered them at least three to one.

'We have waited too long,' came a thin, reedy voice, floating on the early summer breeze, and Rose recognised it and sighed involuntarily. Stephen Greenlow stood on his makeshift platform, shouting to the gathered crowd, and everyone there, Gifted and Leeched, was utterly quiet, almost breathless, spellbound by this man's voice.

'Wait,' said Felix softly, and the command rippled backwards through the Regency ranks. 'I want to see this.'

'We asked for our rights,' said Stephen, and he didn't

need to raise his voice at all. 'We asked for our true-born privileges as the kin of Angels, the possessors of souls Gifted, or once Gifted, with magic. We asked for these, and we asked for them patiently, but we have waited too long, and now we must act.'

There were canisters next to him: great, hulking, silver blocks of metal. They were attached to thick cables that stretched over the top of the wall and down beyond, and Rose could not begin to guess what they contained, but her thoughts kept returning to one fact: Stephen Greenlow's wife Natalie worked for the Ministry of Defence.

What kind of weapons did she have access to?

Tristan stood beside his father, still bruised but looking annoyingly alive, and Aaron, shaking, clambered up on stage to stand beside his father and brother. Tristan gave him a congratulatory pat on the back and said something to him; the words were incoherent, but the tone was unmistakeably relieved. Stephen did not glance at either of his sons.

Rose's mind was clicking further onwards, watching Aaron. Stephen must have valued him as a spy within Regency; it must have been one of his greatest assets. And now Aaron had blown his cover, and for what? What had it gained?

Rose's eyes flickered between the three Greenlows. They were together. That was what had been gained. Aaron was with his brother and father now, and out of harm's way, but why? Why had his safety suddenly become more important than strategy?

Rose's trepidation increased.

What exactly did Stephen think was going to happen to Regency?

'I address *you* now,' said Stephen, 'my kindred whom they call Leeched, from whom they took half your *soul*. They hurt you because they were afraid of you. They thought you were unworthy of keeping the powers you were given, and they did not once seek to look inwards – to see how unworthy they themselves are of being Angels, for siding against us, their own kind, for tolerating and *promoting* the Ashkind in our society.' He was snarling his words now. 'They thought you were dangerous? They thought you were beasts?'

Aaron had something metal in his hand. It was attached by a wire to one of the canisters.

'Well,' said Stephen, 'let us give them *reason*.'

Rose realised what he was going to do an instant before it happened, and stepped forward as Aaron pressed the button. Felix and his advisers switched their gazes to her, astonished.

'Leeching Gas,' Rose said, ignoring them. There was a hissing sound growing swiftly audible above the rising voices, and it made her shudder, because she knew what it meant. 'That's Leeching Gas. They're going to Leech the Angels.'

A shocked silence swept back through the crowd – *Leech the Angels? That's impossible* – followed slowly by cheering, soft but growing louder. Rose could hear them: *Victory! Victory!*

Rose stood there shaking. This was the destruction of the

state, pure and simple, more apocalyptic than any worst-case scenario the Department had ever dreamt up. The Angels Leeched, their powers destroyed; this was anarchy, the end of the world. This would start a Second War of Angels.

No, no, no.

The Department had sent her to Regency; but it was the Gospel whom they should have been watching.

And if Rose herself had only seen—

Slythe stepped forward and addressed Felix. 'What do we do now, sir? Who do we attack?'

Rose was pulling herself out of her shock and doing some quick calculations. If Regency attacked anywhere, the Department would have to deal with it, and the further away the attack was, the fewer troops and equipment they could send, and the more people would die. There was, logically, only one place where the Department could deal with an attack using all the might and intelligence and resources at their disposal.

She stepped up to Felix. She did not drop her gaze, but met it, as if they were equals. His gaze still slid off hers like water, and his eyes stopped just short of properly focusing.

She smiled.

'Sir,' she said. 'I think we should attack the Department building.'

He nodded. 'Yes,' he whispered, staring at her as if trying to see through her. 'Yes. I think we should.'

The Angels were being Leeched behind them even as they spoke; even as Regency trudged, with a very dangerous combination of bewilderment and murderous intent, through the streets of London; even as the roads before them began to fill, slowly, with low murmurings, drifting through the windows, growing louder and louder by the minute. Word spread quickly through the darkness. The city awoke.

No one quite knew the whole truth, of course. The story fractured and grew as it raced ahead of them, by email and videochat and word of mouth, changing to accommodate several different versions of events. Demons had overrun the Houses of Parliament. Some kind of terrorist attack had destroyed the Gospel and the Angels together. A Hybrid rampaging through Westminster had infected the entire Government, turning them all into monsters . . .

Whatever strange and terrible atrocity was fixed in people's minds, however, everyone knew the essence of the truth: the Angels in Westminster were gone. Their authority was destroyed.

Anarchy. Anarchy. Anarchy.

Or close.

The curfew broke first: slowly, and then all at once. People began to filter from their homes, out into the streets, whooping and yelling. Then magic – fires and lights and explosions, *in public*. Shop windows shattered and gunshots riddled the air. When Regency came through the streets, it was greeted with cheers and welcomes from the Ashkind around them, and attacks – sometimes verbal, sometimes violent – from the Gifted. Soldiers on the edge of their lines began to fall. Never mind. Never mind. They walked on.

Felix was smiling; Slythe and Vinyara looked wary; Rose felt utterly bewildered. Whatever world she had been trained for, it was not this one. In her world the Department was always there, the police were always there, and any breaks in law and order were small and containable. This was neither. This, she imagined, was what war must look like. And here she was, marching with the enemy, not back where she belonged, with her father and James and Nate and Laura . . .

Rose looked at Felix's smile. Laura . . .

'Sir?'

A Regency soldier, breathless. The High Command looked at him without breaking stride.

'The Gospel are coming after us, sir. They're right on our tail.'

'Then we move fast,' said Felix, with complete certainty. 'We destroy the Department before Greenlow can attack us.'

Rose didn't run, no, not at all. She didn't scream or flee or cry for help, like she wanted to. Nor, for that matter, did she say anything at all, not even the obvious: what did he think this was, a coincidence? She did not say that Stephen, through Aaron, had known that Regency was going to make its move tonight, and that if he got to Parliament first Felix would have to go somewhere else and the Gospel would therefore get two attacks for the price of one. She didn't say that by attacking anywhere, now, they would be playing into Greenlow's hands at best and destroying themselves against the Department at worst. She did not say any of this, because she did not know what good it would do.

She just kept moving, like he said, and stayed quiet.

And it was most likely credit to Felix's control over his army that Regency *did* get to the Department first. Had everything gone to plan, that could possibly have been a key move, a turning point in this sudden conflict. But it was not to be.

It seemed, in that moment, that Regency was destroyed by the single sentence Felix uttered when the army found themselves, guns out and bristling for action, in the court-yard in front of the building: 'It's empty.'

CHAPTER 47

'Sir. Communication for you.'

Loren stood with all twelve squad teams in the alleys on the other side of the river from the Gospel. They had received the alert of an attack on Parliament and had immediately evacuated all non-military personnel before rushing to the scene of the incident, as was typical. The military staff were currently here, skulking in the shadows and trying to work out what was going on.

The sinister hissing sound had yet to reach them.

The rest of the Department – official and non-official – seemed to have vanished. James, Nate and Maria were gone, God knew where – home to safety, or what remained of safety, if they had any sense in them. Rose was in Regency. Laura was dead. Terrian was refusing to have anything to do with them. Loren, obviously, had balked at the idea of bringing Tabitha into this and had left her at home, so when the officer handed him the walkie-talkie, he knew it could only be David.

It occurred to Loren that it was a sign of how drastically his circumstances had changed that he was actually *glad* to hear that bastard's voice.

'David! Why aren't you here? Where are you?'

The voice that came over the line did not sound like

Elmsworth's. It was thin, hoarse, and weak. It trembled when he spoke.

'I think this might be it,' he said. Static crumbled the smaller words to dust. 'I— I think it's happening. You're not going to see me for a long time.'

He didn't sound like he was talking to Loren at all. 'What on earth are you talking about? This is Arkwood, Loren Arkwood, you remember—'

'Of course I do,' came the voice, sounding marginally stronger now that it was annoyed. 'Listen to me. This is important. You forgot your basic chemistry.'

'What? Elmsworth, I don't have time for—'

'You called Felix Callaway a catalyst because he sets off conflicts and revolutions without ever being damaged by them, but you forgot the definition of a catalyst. They don't *start* reactions. They just speed them up.'

'Sir,' came a voice from behind Loren, 'what's that noise?'

There *was* a noise: a low, constant, strengthening *hiss*, distinctly originating from the Gospel crowd. This was when Loren saw the gas canisters, and two and two came together violently in his head. He swore.

'This reaction,' said David softly, 'was always going to happen.'

Loren didn't notice when he disconnected. He was there, speaking, and then abruptly when Loren checked next he was gone. In fairness, Loren got distracted.

The first reason was the Gospel and what they were doing.

The second was the rising mutters from behind him.

He turned, irritated, to give his orders, and saw the source: James, striding angrily towards him, brandishing a copy of the Department's handbook for spotting criminals. Behind him, Nate and Maria, looking astonished and terrified.

'Arkwood,' said James. He looked more solemn and furious than Loren had ever seen him. 'I have to tell you something about David.'

CHAPTER 48

It took Regency half an hour to decide on the best course of action. Felix knew whose command the Department operated under, and was extremely wary of their base even when empty. He had decided to attack the building in the end, but, given the risk involved, not to commit all of his troops to this attack. Six hundred were on their way back to base, and safety, with Slythe and Vinyara.

Halfway up the first staircase they realised that the fifth floor was in lockdown. Felix gave the order for twenty soldiers to stay behind and guard the stairwell entrance.

When they got to the second floor, another twenty were sent to guard that entrance, just to be sure. The remaining sixty were sent up to the third floor and beyond.

Amelia was in the second twenty. Guarding the stairwell was dull, and her thoughts were on Aaron. They stood there awkwardly, a confused huddle of half-trained Ashkind. They barely knew how to use guns. They shouldn't be here, she thought.

They should never have been here.

'Look!'

One of her comrades was at the window, staring, astonished, at the scene before them. 'London's burning,' he said.

It was: tiny fires were erupting like sparks over the skyscrapers. Glass could be heard shattering across the city. Amelia's division glanced at each other. What was this? It was not what they had wanted – power to the Ashkind, and peace with it. This destruction was the Gospel's doing. Regency could not claim credit for this.

'Wait,' said Amelia's leader suddenly. She was staring out north, towards the houses. 'Listen to that. Can you hear it?'

No, nothing at first. Then: gunfire. Sudden bursts. They overlapped like birdcalls, and they spread across the city, slowly, dying out quickly to leave silence in its wake. The fires started to dim and go out.

Someone was trying to restore order. Someone with an army at their disposal. Was it the Department, wherever they were, or the Gospel?

Amelia looked up at the ceiling and half-prayed for High Command to be quick.

By the time Regency reached the fifth floor, there were only twenty of them, plus Felix and Rose. As per lockdown protocol, the door of the office had been entirely reinforced with imposing grey steel.

Rose's hatred of Regency had peaked at around the first staircase. This was her *home*. These were the corridors she had grown up in. These were the walls that housed her memories. This place was private and intimate and Felix Callaway's very presence here made her want to kill him.

The fact that his presence here was *her fault* made her want to do so even more.

Look, she wanted to snap at him. *This is where Laura Gaskell worked. These are the corridors she walked. These are the lives she saved and the marks she left. And you killed her. For nothing. And you made me kill all those people, too, and what good did it ever do? Any of it?*

He came up to the metal door and looked it up and down. His solution was fantastically stupid, but efficient.

'Well,' he said, 'I suppose they'll know we're here anyway,' and he stepped back, pulling out his gun. The twenty and Rose hastily scrambled round the corner, keen to avoid ricochets. The resulting noise sounded like a thunderstorm confined to an echo chamber, and it was followed by a huge, wrenching crash, which Rose could only assume was the tragic demise of the door.

They moved forward. Beyond the door was a yawning darkness, which Rose knew to be the office. Guns were cocked.

'Should we secure it, Commander?' asked one lieutenant.

Felix's eyes had started focusing properly again, and they had acquired a sudden, determined glint.

'No,' he said, with abrupt certainty. 'No. I'll go in on my own. Wait behind until it is over.'

'Sir, are you sure—?'

Felix turned to him, and the soldier recoiled: the monster was clear and bright in his eyes, and his expression was a snarl, and Rose knew without doubt why David feared this man.

'I will go alone,' said Felix softly, and the soldier said nothing more. 'This is *mine.*'

He looked around at the cowering twenty, and then walked into the darkness, with a shuddering calm.

The twenty and Rose stared blindly after him for about a minute: hesitant, nervous, expectant. Then there was a thud and a cry and the lights came on, and David Elmsworth stood beside the computers, his legend stripped away, staring at the assembled fighters in astonishment and almost childlike fear.

In that moment, he did not look like Rose's father in the least.

The one thing she remembered thinking afterwards – in the thundering moments before her brain properly kicked into gear – was that he didn't deserve what happened; he didn't deserve it at all.

Rose saw the recoil; that was it. The lieutenant's hand jerked back with the force of the shot, and of course by the time she saw that, there was nothing that could be done. The woman's reflexes were admirably quick, it had to be admitted.

Nevertheless, her aim was terrible. The first bullet hit David in the stomach. The blood came immediately, spreading through his thin shirt like discoloured shadow – deep red, crimson, browning maroon.

The effect was also immediate. Something about him seemed to fade: the irises of his eyes seemed to leak out of his eyeballs, leaving them white and empty. The skin of his hands began to blacken and smoke, and when he opened his mouth to cry out, his teeth were wolf-sharp.

That was as far as it was ever allowed to get, however,

because the rest of the soldiers fired then, an unstoppable hurricane of bullets. Nearly all of them hit their mark, whatever that was. He jerked with countless impacts, a canvas of blossoming wounds, until he was more blood than skin.

He died, of course. At no point did he have time to speak.

CHAPTER 49

The Department fighters arrived ten minutes later, just too late for it to matter. They worked their way up the building slowly, arresting the Regency soldiers floor by floor, in slow, manageable clumps. Callaway had made it easy for them, really. Those they couldn't arrest, they knocked out, or killed. The killing was relatively infrequent. Arkwood had said he wanted them alive.

They reached the fifth floor in time to subdue the final twenty, who fought back viciously but in vain; they were, of course, vastly outnumbered. One of the more junior soldiers was sobbing hysterically, terrified, and they asked her – once they had her on the ground with her hands behind her head – where her Commander was. She told them he had been lying unconscious in a corner of the office. They looked towards the space she indicated. There was nothing there. Callaway had gone.

And then there was the girl, who stood unblinkingly still as her comrades were dragged away. The Department didn't arrest her – Arkwood arrived at the fifth floor just in time to stop them – but they doubted it would have mattered to her, anyway.

She stepped towards her father's bullet-riddled, half-monster body with a blank look on her face.

She knelt down beside him slowly, shaking with every movement, and stared at him, and touched his hand, and when it came away bloody she stared at that, too. She said 'Dad?' as if it signified nothing; as if she couldn't understand what the word meant. The shaking of her body was uncontrollable, and she started crying dryly, for all the world as if she didn't know what she was doing.

Arkwood looked bleakly at Elmsworth's body. He thought about closing the eyes. Then he went to the window and looked out over London. The night was quietening now; the gunshots were fading from the sky. The army and the police were sweeping through the streets, restoring order under cover of darkness. No one knew what world they would find in the morning.

The Gospel were still just visible, clumps of white catching the streaks of illumination the streetlights provided. They swirled together like whirlpools, and then slowly diminished, folding in on themselves.

Going underground.

CHAPTER 50

'Sir?'

Three in the morning. He didn't know where Rose was. The soldier stood before him expectantly.

'We have the body down in the morgue, sir.'

The morgue beneath the cells. Ah, yes. He remembered that place.

'Do you want to . . .?'

Did he want to take a look? He looked over at the space where Elmsworth's body had lain, the blood that soaked the carpet. He thought of Tabitha, on the third floor now, trying to heal the soldiers with her magic, wincing whenever they flinched away from her eyes. He thought of Felix Callaway, wherever he had escaped to. He thought of the cells, overcrowded with Regency soldiers.

No, of course he didn't want to take a look.

He stood. 'Show me.'

They guided him down the stairs, deeper into the darkness. He trailed a hand along the walls. Greenlow and his sons might be deep in the earth as well by now, in some trailing, uncharted catacomb. It didn't matter. He would find them. Whatever anarchy ensued tomorrow, when London's criminal underworld digested the full truth of what had happened, it was ultimately the fault of the Greenlows, and they would be brought to justice.

'Here, sir.'

Loren opened the door of the morgue and nodded to the surgeons. They were gathered around the body, cold on its slab. He looked away, disgusted by their expressions. They weren't hard to read: this investigation was clearly forbidden, but Hybrids were such fascinating creatures, and it would surely be a waste of such a specimen not to take a look. . . That was the line the surgeons took, anyway, and he let them, because he highly doubted David would care.

But anyway: the Greenlows. Yes, he would find them – he would make sure they rotted in their own, specially created hells. Especially the older boy; he owed that to Rose, he thought darkly, at l—

Wait, no.

No, hang on. This wasn't right.

This wasn't right at all.

The wounds on the body were wrong. Their positions were distorted. The skin had somehow lightened, and there was a newly healed scar on his wrist, and—

'Um,' said one of the surgeons.

The body was not David Elmsworth.

It was Felix Callaway.

CHAPTER 51

'You have a plan, don't you?'

'Oh, Rose. Of course. Of course I do.'

'This can be programmed, you see?' James, wonderful James, explaining to her how the hologram projector worked:

'We sew it into your skin and it's programmed to change your hair and your eyes, even when you're asleep, so you don't have to think about it all the time.' He smiles, half-proud, half-sheepish. 'I helped invent it,' he admits, and then he cuts open her wrist. It hurts like hell.

She finds a pile of them in a box in the corner. While her wound is healing, she sits beside it, trying to look innocent, and surreptitiously slips one into her pocket. Small green and silver spheres. They look like children's toys. They look tiny. They don't look like they should be able to harm anyone at all.

Her last night in the Department before leaving for Regency, and this is what she sees: her father sitting at the computer, typing furiously, and the stolen hologram projector in the small metal slot below the screens, absorbing its commands.

Then, when he's done, he gives it to her, along with several syringes full of memory serum. Each will allow her to destroy about a quarter of an hour's worth of recollections. When she acts, she must be fast.

'Keep them safe,' he says.

'Yes.'

'I'm sorry I can't tell you everything that's going to happen. Just do what I've told you, all right? I have it under control.'

'I know.'

'You know where to meet me, when it's over?'

'Of course I do.'

He kisses her on the forehead. There is nothing more to say, so she leaves.

Felix Callaway lies unconscious in the corridor. Rose's little band of counter-revolutionaries – Katya, Jordan, Marlene, and the corporals – lie very still, too, bloodied on the floor. She is fairly certain all of them are alive.

Clearly, they have not fought Gifted one-on-one before.

She takes out the syringes from her back pocket. She kneels beside each member of her team and injects just enough of Laura's memory serum to wipe the memory of the attack completely from their minds, and cast uncertainty over the hours before it.

She is very careful. Her hands do not shake.

She drags Felix's body into his office again. There is a collection of knives on the wall – she tries desperately not to think about why – and she chooses the smallest and most delicate.

She wakes him with magic, firelight on her fingertips flickering open his eyes. She wants to kill him now, in revenge for those twenty-six deaths and all those that came before them, but David was clear not to do that: she would never escape Regency alive, and he cares above all things for her life.

The suggestion she gives him is very simple. She has watched Laura do this hundreds of times to bereaved relatives in memory rewrite therapy – 'stay calm, it's all right, it was a heart attack, he's buried at the cemetery near your flat, I can take you there . . .'

but never like this. Never under these circumstances. Never with a trembling voice and wavering resolve. Never without Laura here. Never like this.

'When you have the Department office under your control,' she says quietly to the monster on her table, 'you must go in alone.'

He goes to sleep again. She takes the programmed hologram controller from her pocket, and cuts through his wrist. The silver ball glows green as it slides beneath his skin, and she passes her hand over it, concentrating until the cut heals. Now there is no mark; all that is left is a slight bulge, and Felix will not notice that.

She trusts David's programming. At the right time, in the right place, the hologram will be ready.

'James?' Nate pauses. 'Maria?'

The Department are evacuating, but David Elmsworth

is nowhere to be seen. On his desk is a copy of the Department's handbook on how to spot a criminal. James rushes over.

'What is it? Is it Rose?'

'No,' Nate says slowly. 'Look.'

Elmsworth has left the book open at the page on Hybrids. He has bookmarked it, oddly, with a printout of his yearly appraisal. Circled in red pen is a section that James himself had to write. The sentence Elmsworth has highlighted reads:

The appraisee is occasionally prone to minor episodes of ill-health; these occur on a fairly regular basis but have never as yet disrupted his work to any significant degree.

'What on earth . . .?' murmurs Nate, and he looks up at James, but James seems not to be able to hear him: he has frozen, gripping the table so hard his hands have gone white, and the colour is slowly draining from his face.

Nate follows James's gaze. He is staring at the page in the handbook. Under the passage 'Characteristics of the Criminal', Elmsworth has underlined a section in green ink:

The Hybrid finds sanctuary in the complacency of others. He hides in homes, offices, open streets; he could be a friend, a colleague, even a family member. Such is the nature of the Hybrid that one cannot discover him simply by looking; in human form he might seem friendly, even harmless. However, as his transformation approaches or recedes, he may seem pale—

Nate's blood goes cold.

—he may seem pale, sick or stressed. This happens at

such regular intervals that, if you do suspect, it is not difficult to determine a pattern.

At the very bottom of the page, in biro, Elmsworth has written five words – five words alone, and yet it is enough to stop both their hearts.

And you called yourselves detectives.

At the shattered door to the office, with the utter darkness looming inside, Felix's eyes suddenly acquire a determined glint.

'I will go in alone,' he says. 'This is *mine*.'

In the office, Felix is blind, and he knows his troops are waiting behind him but he does not say anything. He knows without doubt, with an almost otherworldly certainty, that he must be alone.

There is a soft *click* from the corner, and he turns towards it. The screen of one of the computers has come on. It tells him, in soft green letters:

`Activating hologram.`

Something in his right wrist starts to burn. It is very quick, and excruciating, and then it is over.

A faint green glow issues from the darkness, out of sight of the doorway. He squints, and sees the window, and then his faint reflection.

Except it is not his reflection.

It is David Elmsworth's.

He looks down at himself and his body is David Elmsworth's.

He makes the connection too late and scratches his

wrist, finds something hard and metal there, in his wrist, *David Elmsworth's wrist,* and draws blood but he is still Elmsworth, he still looks like Elmsworth—

He cries out in frustration and pain and fear – what magic is this? – and from behind him comes a *thud* of someone hitting a desk. The impact of wood on skin sounds like a punch to the skull. He whirls, and sees, through the darkness, the silhouette of Elmsworth, the *real* David Elmsworth, and from what Felix can see, he is smiling.

Elmsworth's wrist jerks reflexively, and suddenly his silhouette flickers. He glows green and the hologram settles, and suddenly Felix is staring at himself across the darkened office – Elmsworth disguised as him, Elmsworth with his eyes and his face and his body – and before Felix can do anything, he lies down as if unconscious.

A cry. A thud. A man who looks like Felix unconscious.

He begins to realise too late what this must look like, but by the time he does, the lights have come on and he is staring at his own soldiers.

They see David Elmsworth before them, and, of course, they shoot to kill.

CHAPTER 52

'Rose!'

Loren ran out into the courtyard in front of the Department building. He looked furiously excited. He stared around wildly.

'Rose! Where is he? Where on earth is he? He's not dead! *He's not dead!*'

CHAPTER 53

'You know where to meet me, when it's over?'

Rose stood in front of their old house in the darkness.

The door was just as it had always been: blue and wooden and solid. She put her hand on it and hitched the duffel bag with their money and passports over her shoulder. She looked up at their house.

She grinned broadly, and pushed open the door.

CHAPTER 54

Somewhere on the other side of London, a girl guarded
a body in the dark.

It was the body of her Commander. He was not dead,
only sleeping: she had dragged him out of the wreckage
and chaos when the green-eyed soldiers attacked. Now he
lay flushed and cold on the paving stones beside the road.
He looked very serene when he slept. The girl could not
quite imagine this to be the same man who had screamed
with them into blazing fury only that evening in the
Command Hall; had led them into gunfire in countless
battles; had called them brothers, sisters, comrades . . .

There was a swelling in his wrist. It had not coloured
like his other bruises; the skin was pale and white. The
girl wondered who had caused that wound.

She looked back up at his face, and saw his eyes open
and staring at her.

She gasped and edged away; surely being this close was
impertinent. 'I am sorry, Commander . . .'

'Commander?' Felix Callaway laughed hoarsely. 'No
one has called me that in a long time.'

He blinked, pulling himself up on his elbows.

'Do you have a knife?'

The girl gave it to him silently. The Commander pulled

back the sleeve of his left arm, so that the swelling in his wrist was clearly visible. He paused, took off his jacket, twisted the sleeve into a hard knot of leather and bit down on it. Then he opened up his wrist with the knife. The blood came quickly, in slow, pulsing beats.

The girl stared in fascination as the Commander closed his eyes and prised something round and silver from his wrist. It was small and bloody, but it could still be seen to glow softly green in the darkness. The Commander took the jacket out of his mouth, opened his hand, and let the silver ball drop onto the pavement.

The moment it left his skin, he changed. There was a snap, as if of static electricity, and a flash of green light, and abruptly the Commander was gone. Another man – younger, taller, green-eyed, brown-haired – watched her warily, kneeling on the concrete.

The girl shrieked and pulled away, but David Elmsworth lunged forward and seized her arm with his injured hand. His grip was almost painfully tight. She stared at him in horror.

'I saw you die,' she whispered. 'You died, in front of me . . .'

'I know.' His eyes darted around the street, checking for lights clicking on in the windows. 'Where are we?'

She was too terrified to answer for a moment. His eyes hardened. 'Where are we?'

'Dartford station. By the river. Nearly out of the city.'

'Good,' he whispered. He looked back towards the end of the road, where the blackness thickened to impenetrability. 'Were there any casualties?'

'What?'

'Tonight, in the Department. Who else did you see die?'

She shook her head and swallowed. 'No one. They were all arrested. I dragged you into a cupboard until no one was looking.'

'No Government soldiers died? None of your own? No . . . no girls with dark hair?'

'No. We didn't even have a chance to fight.'

He nodded, slowly. She cringed away from him again and he rose to a crouch, still holding her wrist.

'You're dead,' she said again, wishing desperately that it were true.

He was looking behind him again, at the darkness at the end of the road. His blood had seeped into the palm of her hand. He turned back to her. 'It's all right. What's your name?'

'Katya.'

'I'm not going to hurt you, Katya. You'll be fine.'

He waited until she had stopped shivering with fear, then leaned forward and reached for her throat. A sharp blow to the jugular vein and she dropped before she could fight back. He got up, pulling the green bomber jacket back on.

He pressed his right hand to the wound in his wrist and it sealed up. Then he walked down to the end of the road. He could hear the low murmuring of the river ahead of him. The darkness was almost complete, and he had to feel for the road, listen for oncoming cars. There were none. He crossed to the riverbank.

To his left were the lights of London. Streetlights and

shouting and police cars. And somewhere in the midst of it all, his daughter, waiting for him.

Goodbye to all that.

He knelt beside the river alongside the grass-lined road and let the water run over his hands, cleaning them of his own blood. He looked down at the tarmac path, leading into the darkness, the wide starless hills and silence. He stood for a moment and listened to the shifting of the rippling black waters beside him. Then he walked away.

ACKNOWLEDGEMENTS

The long, wonderful, unlikely process of writing this book has taken almost two years. Throughout all of it, I have received constant support, friendship and encouragement from various people who had far better things to do with their time, and for this I am inexpressibly grateful.

Firstly, my wonderful editor, Kate Howard at Hodder. Kate, it was you who took the time to read this manuscript, you who pitched it to the board, you who have given up so many months and so much effort towards it, and you who introduced me to butternut squash cake. To this day I am not quite sure why you did any of these things, but I am lucky – incredibly, astronomically lucky – that you did. I have you to thank for so much of my happiness these days.

Also at Hodder, Emily Kitchin's insight and thoughtfulness vastly improved the book from its original drafts; Zelda Turner's keen eyes and infinite patience made it far easier to read; and at John Murray, the generosity and kindness of Georgina Laycock was the beginning of all of this. My eternal thanks also to Becca Mundy, whose championing of the book did so much to get it out into the world, and to get people reading it. I am so grateful for her hard work, her patience and her faith in the book and in me, which remained steady, even when my own confidence was distinctly underwhelming. Her ability to make someone feel as if they can do anything – for just long enough to get them through the task at hand – has been especially invaluable, and I owe her a lot.

To my friends: if I am in any way deserving of the encouragement, sanity and support you have given me, you already know how grateful I am to all of you. If not . . . well. Thank you so much for everything. I would not be here without you.

Tika, Lara, Carlotta, Hannah, Frannie, Francesca and Grace – you all read various drafts and contributed immensely to it with your wise and thoroughly rational advice, of which I hope the final book is worthy. I thank you for that, and the hours – it must be hours by now – you have spent listening to me hark on about this. I will continue to siphon off your wit and wisdom for as long as you let me hang around you. Now, please, for the love of God, wipe those drafts from your hard drives and never tell anyone how terrible they were.

Some of my teachers have had to put up with almost as much of my talking about this as my friends, and all of them have added hugely to my knowledge and well-being. Lest I run out of space, I won't try to catalogue everything I have to thank them for, but suffice it to say that without them this book would most certainly not exist. So, trolls: you know who to blame.

And, of course, my family. All of them, especially my grandparents, have been fantastically excited and supportive about the prospect of publication. I hope this book is worthy of that support, and that it lives up to your expectations. With that in mind, I hope your expectations are very, very low.

My parents, being journalists, know that everything you read in print is invariably true. So, with that in mind, I would like to state for the record that my mother is the cleverest and kindest woman in the world, and my father the bravest and wittiest man, and neither of them can correct me now because I'm ending the paragraph ha ha.

And then there is Catherine. Catherine – you are the sweetest, sanest, happiest, smartest, wisest and most violent younger sister anyone ever had. This book is dedicated to you – yours, for ever – firstly to as a tribute to that, but also by way of an apology, for all the time I spent writing it when I should have been with you. I hope you enjoy reading it, but while you do, always remember:

I love you more than any of this.

An extract from

The Reaction

The thrilling sequel to

The Catalyst

The knock on the door came at half-past five in the morning. Rose, who had long since trained herself to be ultra-sensitive to any kind of suspicious noise, woke immediately. She stared for a few long moments at the glowing clock on her radio, and turned on the light. Angels knew she did not need this now.

She sighed, wrapped herself in a dressing gown, and got up. Her co-ordination was not at its best this early, but she tried to keep her footsteps light as she passed Tabitha's bedroom. The girl got precious little sleep as it was.

Loren was waiting at the bottom of the stairs, messy-haired and disgruntled. 'If these are journalists again,' he whispered, 'do I have your permission to kill them?'

'Do you need it?'

'No, but it would be nice to know you wouldn't hold it against me.'

'I wouldn't do anything of the sort. I'd help.'

'It might be messy.'

The knock came again. Loren considered, and nodded. 'It will be messy,' he said, and went to the door. Rose made to follow him, but he put up a hand to stop her. She ducked behind the doorframe of the living room.

'Who is it?' she heard Loren call hoarsely.

'It's me,' came a familiar, muffled voice. Rose froze. There was a noticeable pause before Loren pulled the door open. His voice was abruptly curt.

'I don't know what you think you're doing here,' he said, 'but I'm going to give you one chance to leave.'

A hesitation. 'I need to talk to Rose.'

'No you don't.'

'She needs to explain—'

'Like hell she needs to explain anything to you, you traitor.'

'Please, Loren. You don't understand—'

Rose stepped out from behind the doorframe and waited as James' voice trailed off. He stood in the doorway, dressed in khaki, pale and shivering. There was snow and streetlight glow in his red hair. He stared at her. Loren looked between them, and sighed.

'Come in,' he told James, 'but one wrong word—'

'I understand,' said James immediately. 'I won't— I'll behave myself.'

'And if you say—'

'I *understand*,' said James vehemently, almost angrily, and Loren stopped. James glanced at him, and stepped over the threshold.

'Why are you here?' asked Rose in a low voice. 'It's been—'

'Six months,' he said. 'I know.' He looked at Loren. 'Any chance of a coffee?'

'No,' said Loren, and walked past him. James sighed, and gestured to the living room. Rose nodded, and sat down on her armchair. He took the opposite sofa. He'd been working in the army, apparently, over the past half-year, as a strategist. He was up for promotion. Suitable, really, for the man who revealed her father's secret to the world.

Big break for a seventeen-year-old.

Of course it would have been embarrassing, working with David Elmsworth and his daughter for eighteen months and not suspecting a thing, but then Elmsworth had taken everyone in. And true, the story almost certainly would have broken without him. But it had been he who had filed the report, he who informed the authorities. He whose career had benefited most from her father's downfall.

Rose watched him settle himself uncomfortably on the sofa. He looked up at her.

'I need to talk to you,' he said, somewhat lamely.

'Clearly,' was her reply. From the kitchen, she heard Loren chuckle.

James bit his lip.

'They say your father's not cooperating with his lawyer,' he said, softly enough that Loren would not be able to hear him. 'They say he's refusing to confirm his name and address.'

'Is that why you're here, James?'

He hesitated. 'No.'

'Then get to the point,' she said. 'What do you want?'

He paused again. 'I needed to ask you some questions.'

'Then ask them.'

'Why didn't you tell anyone what he was?'

'Because I love him,' she said. 'Next question.'

He persisted. 'But *why*? Surely it would have been better—'

'To hand him over,' she said. 'To tell people what he was.'

'Yes.'

She leant back into the armchair, studying him, trying to keep her voice flat. 'James, you think he murdered those people, don't you? Rayna Arkwood and Thomas Argent and God knows how many others?'

All sound of movement from the kitchen stopped abruptly at the mention of Loren's sister's name.

'That's not what I'm here about.'

'Oh yes it is. You think he's evil, and you want to get me to admit it.'

He lowered his voice. 'Rose, he's a monster. You don't know what he's capable of.'

Something inside her burned and broke. She got to her feet.

'I do,' she said. 'I know exactly what he's capable of. James, you worked with him. You *trusted* him. You don't really think he's evil. The man you knew was not a monster, not in any voluntary sense.'

'I didn't know – I wasn't paying attention. He could have—'

At her look, he faltered; she was giving him a glare of such utter contempt that anger flashed across his face for a moment.

'Get out,' she said. 'You don't deserve answers.'

'Rose, I need to know—'

'No, you don't,' she said. 'You haven't come here for information. You've come here to try and convince me that he's a killer. And that's not going to happen.'

'No! Rose, I just— I want to know— do you care more about justice, about what's right, that you do about him?'

'Of course not, you bastard. He's my *father*.'

'I know it looks like that to you, but – the circumstances in which he found you – the fact that your birth parents never came forward – it looks suspicious, you must see that –' He stopped. Loren was standing in the kitchen doorway, watching him in the half-curious way a hunter might watch a deer he had just shot. After a second's hesitation, James burst out, 'He's brainwashed you, Rose, can't you *see* that?'

'Get out,' said Loren quietly, 'or I swear to God I will kill you.'

James got up, half-furious now, pulling on his coat. 'Rose, please see sense, I'm trying to help you—'

'Get out of my house,' said Loren again, with no change in tone. 'Now.'

James edged his way out of the living room, backing towards the door. 'Rose, we used to be friends.'

Loren pulled out his gun and cocked it. Rose glanced at him, worried. He was stony-faced.